GENOA BAY

GENOA BAY

A novel

BETTE NORDBERG

MONARCH
BOOKS

Oxford, UK, & Grand Rapids, Michigan, USA

First published in the UK in 2009 by Monarch Books
(a publishing imprint of Lion Hudson plc),
Wilkinson House, Jordan Hill Road, Oxford OX2 8DR.
Tel: +44 (0)1865 302750 Fax: +44 (0)1865 302757
Email: monarch@lionhudson.com
www.lionhudson.com

Published in conjunction with MacGregor Literary.

ISBN: 978-1-85424-892-3 (UK)
ISBN: 978-0-8254-6296-2 (USA)

Distributed by:
UK: Marston Book Services Ltd, PO Box 269, Abingdon, Oxon OX14 4YN;
USA: Kregel Publications, PO Box 2607, Grand Rapids, Michigan 49501

This book has been printed on paper and board independently certified as having come from sustainable forests.

British Library Cataloguing Data
A catalogue record for this book is available from the British Library.

Printed and bound in England by MPG Books Ltd.

For Ron and Sandy,

who introduced us to Genoa Bay.

And for Char,

who prayed.

While Genoa Bay is a real location, the persons and events in this story are fictitious. Any resemblance to an actual person or event is purely coincidental; thus no similarity to actual persons, living or dead, should be inferred.

ACKNOWLEDGMENTS

I first encountered Genoa Bay on a boating trip to the Gulf Islands. We had breakfast in the most unusual Bed and Breakfast there, and before we cast off the next morning, I knew I'd found the location for my next novel.

Michael Card insists that all art springs from community. In this case, at least, he is correct. A great many friends helped me to discover the story for *Genoa Bay*. I'd like to thank them here: Mark Howard and Karl Zeiger of Puyallup, and Carol Brown of British Columbia, all attorneys, helped with the legal details. I'd like to thank Clyde Praye, Ron Loper and Dennis Polari for the development of additional story details. Ron and Sandy Loper made several return trips to Genoa Bay, so that my husband and I could take pictures and complete interviews there. Thank you, Kim, for the great collection of photographs. Carol Messier, owner of Maple Bay Marina, drove me through and entire afternoon of research. Fire investigator Richard Carmen, of Carmen Investigations, provided critical guidance in the book's fire scenes. Writer Andy Snaden assisted in finding my Canadian contacts. Carmen Timmermans, the unlikely guide at Providence Farm, spent hours guiding me through the property, answering my questions and telling me about the many outreach programs there. In truth, bad guys don't come out of their ministries! Bob and Beulah Whitlow contributed lists of stories from their own "inn keeping" days.

Of course, once a story is born, it must be shaped and perfected, and finally sold. As always, I thank Chip MacGregor, agent and friend, for finding *Genoa Bay* the perfect publishing home. And for shaping the novel, and seeing the potential in the junkyard, I give my most sincere thanks to editor Jeannie St. John Taylor, and to Tony Collins, of Lion Hudson. The pleasure, my friends, has been all mine. Thank you for helping me to live my dream.

PROLOGUE

March 8, 2004

GOD TALKS TO ME.

Now, hear me out. Before you put me in the same category as the loony folks who hear voices just before they go on a shooting rampage at the local shopping mall, remember: In general, I don't have visions. I don't hear voices, either—at least not audible ones.

Still, sometimes, even in the most mundane of moments, I hear the voice of God.

Most recently, it happened down at Waterfront Park at Navy Point, right here in Pensacola. I'd taken Gabby, my seven-year-old, and Liz, our golden doodle, for a walk. Gabby rode her new bike, a fluorescent pink Speed Demon complete with training wheels, and Liz trotted along on a leash. By the time we began the final loop toward the car, my daughter had begun a serious meltdown.

"I don't want to ride anymore," she said, climbing off the silver seat. "It's too hard. The wheels get stuck."

She had me there. It seemed her bike's only demon resided in the five-inch-diameter wheels that wobbled and froze in every quarter-sized pothole along the trail. Her short legs had powered their way through nearly two miles of these freeze-ups; she'd had enough. Who could blame her?

If Timothy were still alive, he'd have figured out a way to fix the wheels. Me? I'm no tool man. Instead of fixing the bike, I hoped that Gabby would outgrow the need for wheels. Didn't most kids, eventually?

"We're almost to the van," I said. "You can make it that far, can't you?"

Gabby shook her head as tears began to roll down her cheeks. Crossing arms across her chest, she said, "Go get the car!"

Wanting to avoid yet another battle, I resigned myself to pushing the bike back to the parking lot. I wrapped the dog's leash around my wrist, threw my purse strap across my back, and bent over to push the bike. Glancing over my shoulder, I discovered that Gabby and the dog had chosen not to follow. Instead, Gabby—with both arms around the dog's neck—was enjoying a face wash, compliments of Liz's sloppy dog kisses.

"Come on, you two," I called. "We don't have all day."

By the time we reached the van, my back ached, and sweat rolled down the space between my shoulder-blades. Florida humidity does that to me, I've discovered. I unlocked the car and started the engine, turning up the air conditioning before I did anything else. After settling Gabby in her safety seat, I loaded the little bike into the passenger compartment. Finally, I opened the back hatch and spoke to the dog. "Come on, Liz," I called. "Jump!" I gave a little tug on the leash.

The dog circled around behind me, as if to gain speed for the leap into the cargo space. But, just as her front paws touched the bumper, she balked, backed up, and sat down, whining.

"Come on," I pleaded. "Just get in the dumb car. We're already late!"

Once again the dog circled. This time, instead of leaping for the cargo area, she stopped dead and circled back the other way. Apparently changing your mind is not a prerogative saved entirely for women. "Please, just get inside," I begged, losing what little patience I had.

After two more false starts, I began to exert my position as leader of the pack. This time, as Liz approached the car, I used the leash to drag her forward. Why wouldn't the stupid dog just get into the car? How hard could it be to simply leap?

That's when I heard God speak.

"Don't be so critical," his voice said clearly. "Lately, you're not all that different from the dog."

The problem with hearing from God, I've discovered, is that sometimes, he gives you an answer before you even ask the question.

Such was the case that day at Waterfront Park. From the day Liz refused to enter the van, until I clearly understood God's meaning, nearly four months passed. And until I put the pieces together, I felt as clueless as a blind man at the bottom of a deep well.

One

April 28, 2004

Eᴠᴇ ᴀʀʀɪᴠᴇᴅ ʟᴀᴛᴇ, ᴀs ᴀʟᴡᴀʏs, and I found her standing on my front porch with one hand full of brochures, a diaper bag slung over her shoulder, and Olivia, her youngest, hanging like a bag of potting soil—very heavy soil, I might add—over her opposite hip. "Sorry," she said simply, edging past me as I held open the front door. "Phone call."

In the instant she spotted me, Olivia grinned and held out her dimpled hands. "Here, let me take her," I said.

Eve offered me the diaper bag, which I ignored, reaching instead for the smiling, drooling baby. "There, now," I said, holding her in front of me. "You need to be held by someone who appreciates your sweet face." Olivia laughed, her feet swimming in the air.

Eve frowned, and tossed me a diaper. "She's teething. Protect yourself."

Waving my friend's concern away, I took Olivia to the kitchen and fished a graham cracker from the pantry.

Eve poured herself coffee, her long lean body moving gracefully through my kitchen. "Don't say I didn't warn you. I'm in my third shirt this morning. The drool alone could fill an Olympic swimming pool." Her Southern accent made even complaining sound positively cosmopolitan.

Laughing, I settled the baby on my hip, and reached for my own glass of sweet tea. "I have notes from last time on the kitchen table. This morning, I've been wondering. Don't you think we're going to need more help? More parent helpers?" I spread a blanket on the family-room floor, and put Olivia down, dropping a few toys beside her. With her free hand, she began banging a teething ring onto a baby doll's back.

"It's just Field Day, Brandy, not the World Cup."

"I know. But a whole elementary school! We're responsible for almost five hundred kids!" I dropped into a chair at the table and pulled my hair into a ponytail.

"We're not responsible, silly." She shrugged. "We're just volunteers suckered into planning the day. It's no problem. The kids'll be playing. Running. Competing. We'll do it like we planned. Two parents per game." She pulled out a chair and sat, dropping the brochures over my notes. Sipping her coffee, she nodded at the paper. "Take a look at those."

I rolled my eyes. If Eve were in school, I swear her teacher would suggest medication for attention deficit. "What about Track and Field Day?"

"In a minute," she said, smiling, her eyes full of mischief. "First, brochures."

I picked up the brochures. Each pamphlet came from a different cruise line. The glossy covers pictured slim women sunning themselves on elegant teak deck-chairs. "Caribbean?"

Eve nodded. "All of them."

"They look great. When are you going?"

"We haven't booked yet." She reached over to take a brochure, turning it to the chart featuring rooms and booking fees. "It's so reasonable. A bargain really, when you figure that food and rooms and travel are included."

She paused and her sudden silence caught my attention. I looked up from the room diagram of *Carnival Fantasy*, one of the many ships headed to the islands. Confused, I asked, "What? What is it?"

She leaned forward. "We want you to come. All of us. We talked about it and we think you should come."

I knew exactly what she meant by "we." Timothy and I had shared our lives with four couples from his squadron. Since our earliest years in Florida, we'd done nearly everything together. Church. Camping. Hiking. Kids. Even a few vacations. Though the Navy had separated us for various training assignments and sea duties, we'd stuck together through it all. "Are you kidding?"

"Dead serious."

"Eve. I can't go. I don't have anyone to watch Gabby. Besides, I can't afford it." I closed the brochure, leaving my hand palm down on the cover. I didn't dare look up. I couldn't let Eve see the truth in my eyes.

She wasn't fooled. "It's not about the money, is it?"

"Of course it is. You know money is tight these days."

"Don't use that old insurance excuse. I'm not taking that any more."

For the hundredth time, I pushed down resentment. It wasn't an excuse. It was real life. My life. A battle I seemed destined to fight until my dying day. "It's not an excuse," I said. "Really. Since Timothy died, even with my salary, I'm having trouble making it."

"So, you can go. Our treat."

"I couldn't." I shook my head.

"Because you don't fit any more."

"I didn't say that."

"You don't have to. I can see it. You never hang out with us any more. We don't shop, or run errands. You avoid any place where there might be a group of pilots' wives talking squadron talk."

"I'm not part of the squadron any more."

She reached out and squeezed my hand. "You never were, Brandy. Timothy was. He's gone. But you and me, we're still here. You're still part of us. The girls. Our families. And that can't change. It won't ever change."

Truthfully, I've grown tired of this same conversation. We repeat it over and over. No matter how many times I try to explain, Eve just doesn't get it. Dear sweet Eve. She just won't give up. From the first day I met her, when her husband arrived for flight training, she's been a bold and vital part of my life. No sisters could love one another more. "I just can't go," I said.

"You don't know that. Look, we don't even know when we're going. You could have Timothy's parents keep Gabby."

"Would you like more coffee?"

"Don't change the subject."

The phone rang, and I sighed. Sometimes, relief comes directly from heaven. As I stood up and went to the kitchen, Olivia started to cry. Eve went to her daughter and settled down in my recliner to nurse. I watched, feeling a little jealous as I picked up the receiver.

Still focused on Eve and Olivia, I listened to the words that would change my life. Still shaking, I hung up and headed for the couch across from Eve.

"You look like someone just died," she said. "What's happened?"

I must have looked as shell-shocked as I felt. "It's Maggie," I said. My voice sounded wooden, even in my own ears. "She's had another stroke. I have to fly to Canada."

❀

I'd hardly settled Gabby in her seat and buckled her belt, before the older man beside me took it upon himself to invoke the wonder of his native country. Raising his voice over the thunder of jet engines, he said, "You'll love Canada. Vancouver Island is so remote. We have a summer place up-island, near Nanaimo, right on the water. The people there are so friendly."

"Actually, I grew up near Duncan," I said, smiling. "I know the island quite well."

I watched as he tried to process this new information. "But you're not Canadian," he said.

"No," I answered, as agreeably as I could. I didn't want to spend the entire flight explaining my past to this stranger. How could I? I hardly understood it myself.

"Mommy," Gabby said, pulling at the sleeve of my sweater, "I want my Daddy Book." She pointed to my carry-on, already stashed on the floor.

"I'll get it after we're in the air." I patted her on the knee. "You can wait that long, can't you?" I turned to the stranger beside me. "She does love that book," I explained. An understatement, clearly.

At the ripe old age of seven, Gabby loves her Daddy Book more than any other possession; we never leave the house without it. The custom-made photo book, designed by Eve and given to Gabby by some of the squadron wives soon after her daddy died, with its worn cover, bears fresh fingerprints, always. In the three years since

Timothy passed away, I've learned to love the little book almost as much as Gabby does. Where it once reminded me of loss, now it keeps his memory alive.

Though Gabby reads exceptionally well for her age, this book, written all about her father, has a vocabulary far too complicated for a second grader. Still, my daughter has memorized every word, and recites it with the enthusiasm of a theatrical audition. She managed to read the book twice before we reached cruising altitude. The man sitting next to me settled into a newspaper as Gabby's questions began, as they always do, at the beginning.

"When did you meet Daddy?"

"At school. We went to college together."

"Was he handsome?"

"The handsome-est. His eyes were exactly the same blue as yours."

"Did you love him?"

"Almost as much as I love you."

"Did he think I was beautiful?"

"The most beautiful baby in the world." At this point in our Daddy Book routine, Gabby expects me to re-tell the story of her birth, of our midnight drive to the Pearl Harbor Hospital, of the smell of plumeria wafting in the air as I waited for Gabby to arrive, of Daddy bringing Bird of Paradise to the Hospital on the day she was born. Before the beverage carts started down the aisle, I obliged the tradition.

"I miss Daddy," she said, sighing.

"I miss him too." I tucked Gabby's book into my carry-on. Though I have adjusted in the three years since my husband died, I have not recovered. It is not possible, I believe, even in a world where God often speaks, to fully recover from such an injury—no more than it is possible to recover from the amputation of a limb. Part of me worried that Gabby did not truly remember her father, no matter how many times we reviewed the Daddy Book. A man like Timothy deserved to be remembered.

"Will Maggie be at the airport when we get there?" Gabby asked.

"No, honey, she's too ill to drive. Besides, we have another plane to catch before we can go visit Grandma Maggie." I reached over to pull down her service tray. "We'll fly to Vancouver Island and rent a car. Then, we'll drive to Maggie's hospital and visit."

"Can I get you anything?" the cabin attendant asked my daughter.

"I'd like orange juice," Gabby answered.

"Please," I added.

"Please," she said, nodding to the woman. "And, my mom would like a Diet Coke, please." My daughter spends far too much time with adults.

We drank our drinks in relative silence for only a moment. "I'm named for Maggie," Gabby said. "Right?"

We'd had this conversation before. "Why don't you call me Maggie? I like Maggie better than Gabby."

"It's all your daddy's fault," I said. "The first time he went to sea, you were almost two; you could walk and talk and you loved to name everything you saw. But as soon as he left, you just stopped talking. I think you missed your daddy so much, you just didn't have another thing to say."

Gabby smiled at me, her smile so exuberant that her eyes completely disappeared. Even now, that smile, so exactly like her father's, takes me by surprise.

"But I got over it," she said, confident about the end of the story.

"When Daddy got home, you started talking again. A lot. It was like you were making up for lost time. And he nicknamed you Gabby. Because you talked so much."

"And I haven't stopped, ever since."

"That's exactly right."

"Does Grandma Maggie talk a lot?"

I shook my head, unable, for the moment, to speak. Maggie wasn't much of a talker. Instead, she was a woman of action—a woman who lived out every conviction she ever possessed. I found myself thinking about Maggie, about the last time I'd seen her, and against my will, a procession of pictures paraded themselves across my mind's eye. *How could anyone explain Maggie?* I wondered. Though Gabby had met her namesake only twice, she would not remember.

How would I ever let Gabby know how much there was to love about that wonderful old woman?

I drank my soda, and wondered how I would answer Gabby when the real questions about Maggie inevitably began.

Two

BY THE TIME WE LANDED in Sydney, Gabby's infatuation with international travel had faded to complete collapse. Slumped in her seat-belt, she slept through the entire flight into Sydney, through most of the car rental procedure and all of the drive into Victoria. Having schlepped her through the airport and all the way to the car, I don't think my arms will ever be the same.

As I navigated evening traffic, my windshield wipers kept up with a heavy rain, and I thought about the conversation I'd had with the social worker from Brentwood Gardens. "Mrs. Blackburn listed you as the person to call in case of emergency," she said. Though I knew Maggie had no nearby relatives, this was news to me; I assumed that I lived too far away to notify in case of emergency.

"I'm sorry to tell you by telephone, but Maggie has had a stroke. She was taken to the hospital in Victoria, and is in the ICU there. I've given the hospital your contact information. You should be hearing from them soon."

I did not hear from the hospital, though I hadn't given them much time. Leaving Eve to plan Field Day by herself, I had Maggie's nurse on the line moments after Eve and Olivia left the house. Sandra told me that Maggie had not yet regained consciousness, and the odds on her recovery were not good. "Her heart isn't as strong as we'd like, and she has fluid building in her lungs. The CAT scan shows massive damage to the right side of her brain. If you can come, I think it would be a good idea. At this point, no one can be sure how this will turn out."

Keeping one eye on traffic and the other on my printed directions, I found myself praying for Maggie, praying that in spite of the stroke, we might have one last moment together, that I would have one more opportunity to thank her for all she'd done. As car horns honked, crowds of umbrellas streamed down Victoria's sidewalks and Gabby stirred in her seat, I found myself remembering the first time I'd seen the woman who had changed my life.

I was sixteen when I first met Maggie, barely sixteen, because I'd lied about my age to get a job as a deck-hand and kitchen assistant on the sixty-five-foot schooner *Odyssea*, sailing from Juneau to Hawaii. As are most life-changing moments, on the surface at least, my meeting with Maggie seemed quite accidental.

On that hot, sunny morning, she found me crouched over the cockpit of the sailboat, replacing the traveler line on our main sail—or at least that was what I was supposed to be doing. But the knots were too tight to open with my fingers, and everywhere I looked I found more signs of rust and neglect. The line itself was so frayed that I couldn't believe it had held together all the way from Alaska.

Already I'd discovered extensive damage to the mainsail. Most of the reefing eyelets were coming apart. The sail, such as it was, had been patched together with wide, uneven hand-stitching, the thread as decayed as the traveler lines. In places friction had worn the sail material so thin that I could nearly see through it. As eager as I was to escape the desolation of my home, I'd managed to overlook the dubious condition of the vessel when I signed on.

On the day I met Maggie, the rest of the crew had taken the marina van into Duncan for supplies, leaving me to work on the boat. I worried as I worked the traveler, wondering what might happen should this particular sail encounter anything more rugged than a stiff breeze. Frustrated, I'd begun cutting the line with a dull box-knife I'd found in the captain's tool-box, and running it back through the pockmarked pulleys as carefully as I could.

Between the added difficulty of the task, and my own increasing anxiety about safety, I was sweating heavily, my face already starting in on its usual burn-and-peel routine. With each knot, I grew more frustrated, more resentful of the whole situation.

"It's a mistake," I muttered to myself. "I don't belong on this boat. At least now, I've got a whole ocean between me and that guy. I should jump ship here and get on with my life."

My thoughts raced as I worked. There was no telling what else didn't work on board this old, dilapidated ship. If I didn't get out now, I might lose the very life I'd managed to reclaim. Most people think that the young have little belief in their own mortality. But as I worked in the heat, I clearly remember shuddering as I thought of drowning somewhere in the wide South Pacific.

At sixteen, my short life seemed to be represented by a series of rejections and abandonments. Though I didn't have the contemporary vocabulary to name such disappointments, I felt them all the same. I understood my loss more by comparison than by definition. Most of my friends had two parents, at least one of whom cheered from the stands of the stadium, or gymnasium, or dance studio whenever students gathered for performance or competition. In my case, there was no cheering, no loving embraces after disappointments, no family dinners, no loving boundaries.

And there were other, deeper losses as well.

Still, as lonely as my early life had been, I didn't relish giving my life away to the foolish whim of an inexperienced captain and this rusting hole in the ocean. Feeling angry and betrayed, I tried to convince myself that I'd find another job.

Perhaps I could pump gas for the marina, or make a living as a boat detailer, polishing the miles of fiberglass exterior surrounding modern powerboats. Though I knew how to clean and polish fiberglass, clean chrome, and do small repairs, I didn't own the equipment for such a venture. While detailing might be my best option, I could tell in one glance that the marina at Genoa Bay was too small to find enough boats to support myself. Even if I found a larger marina, with more potential customers, who would trust a strange American kid with a valuable yacht?

Caught between fear and despair, I sweated and swore at myself, muttering as I moved to dismantle the last section of line. Throwing the frayed pieces onto the dock, I'd managed to make a nice pile of useless bits of rope. As I pitched the last piece, I heard a strange voice say, "Nice toss."

I glanced up, noticing that a bit of line had landed across the toe of a pair of Keds sneakers, the old-fashioned kind, white and stained, with a single hole exposing most of a coral-pink toenail.

From those peculiar shoes, I looked up to sockless ankles and navy-blue knit pants hanging below a fuzzy, pilled sweater. The sweater reminded me of something my stepfather's mother would wear, a once-white button-up, whose color had evolved to that of weak tea in places around the armpits. Above this remarkable costume reigned an old woman's soft, fleshy face.

Though her dark brown eyes had not faded, the eyebrows above them looked as if they had been drawn on with a child's crayon. Thin, dark hair swirled around her head in the breeze, like dust on a gravel roadway. The hair color and the lined face didn't go together, and I knew immediately that this woman was a coupon shopper at the local Clairol counter.

She lifted a pie tin into the air, a perfect lattice-topped apple pie with cinnamon sugar oozing through the crust. "Do you know where I can find 28 C?" My stomach grumbled, and I remembered that I'd planned to serve nothing more than canned soup to the ship's crew for lunch.

I stood up, shading my face from the glaring sun. "We're in slip 19. So, I guess it's further out." I pointed toward the bay. "Probably on the other side."

She smiled, and in that expression, I somehow forgot about her worn clothes and odd hair color. By smiling, her lined face seemed to warm me up from the inside out. "Replacing line, are you?"

I frowned, reminded of my task and the condition of the boat. I put my hands on my hips, nodded, and looked up at the mast. "It's a disaster," I said. "The whole thing. Should be taken out in the bay and sunk."

She laughed. "I think most sailors feel that way about their boats at some point. Especially during a re-fit."

"I wish it were—a re-fit, I mean. But we're cruising."

Her eyebrows, or perhaps I should say the lines on her forehead, rose. "Where'd you sail from?"

"Juneau."

I watched her take in the boat, looking from bow to stern in one long, critically appraising gaze. Her eyes missed nothing. "In this?"

"Yep. Took almost four weeks." Though the trip had nearly driven me crazy, I found a peculiar pride stirring as I recalled the voyage.

Her expression changed from curiosity to concern. "Well now, that's quite a miracle, isn't it?"

Though the voyage hadn't been easy, I'm not sure I'd have classified it as a miracle exactly. "It doesn't look great, but it floats."

She nodded, her expression clearly unconvinced. Her gaze shifted from the boat to me, and she seemed to look me over with the same exhaustive attention she had just given the boat. A moment went by, and I found myself standing taller, pulling my shoulders back. I didn't understand why, but I hoped that she saw something good in me, something experienced, valuable. Even as I hoped, I wondered. Why, after all I'd been through, would I care about this old woman's opinion? After all, she was old and worn, fraying around the edges too.

But I did care. And I felt disappointment.

In her observant gaze, it seemed to me that she had measured my condition and found it as unsafe as the boat. And in that way, Maggie was absolutely right.

"Well, I'd better deliver this pie," she said, waving it again so that I could hardly miss the scent of apples and cinnamon floating toward me on the warm breeze. "I'll see you later," she promised, pointing directly at my face with her free hand. I watched as she turned away and walked down the dock.

Unlike Timothy, Maggie kept her promises.

❀

I parked in the hospital visitors' lot and reached over to wake Gabby. "Honey, we're here. We're at the hospital."

She yawned and stretched, blinking as she looked around. "Already?"

"It's cold outside, and raining hard. Put on your coat, and we'll go visit Grandma Maggie."

Putting one palm on the side window as if to appraise the weather, she seemed surprised by the temperature of the glass. In Florida the rain never cools glass. "Can I just stay here and wait?"

"No, honey. You have to come inside with me. We won't stay

long." I reached into the back seat for her raincoat. "Grandma is probably sleeping, anyway," I added.

Three years ago, Gabby made it through Timothy's passing with almost no help from me. My shock over his death was so completely overwhelming that I was useless, even to someone I loved as much as I loved Gabby. Now, with Maggie in the hospital, I wasn't exactly sure how to handle the situation.

I figured I'd just take it one day at a time. I opened my car door. "Ready?"

In the ICU, I introduced myself to the swing-shift nurse managing Maggie's care. Swiping his ID badge, he opened the security doors for us and escorted us toward Maggie's bedside. "How is she doing?"

"Not much change," he told me. "She still isn't responding. We aren't seeing any spontaneous motion on her left side. Your being here might be good for her. Maybe she'll react to your voice."

I hoped so. "What does the doctor say?"

"I never see her myself," the nurse said, opening the sliding door to Maggie's glass cubicle. "She comes by in the morning. Right now, we're just waiting for Maggie to regain consciousness. Then, if she gains enough stamina, she'll need rehab. Unfortunately, she's a long way from moving to a rehab center."

As I dropped my purse in a corner of the room, the nurse moved toward the machinery at the head of Maggie's bed. He thumped the IV line with a thumb and finger. "By the way," he said. "There's a note on the chart asking you to call Brentwood Gardens once you arrive. I have the phone number, if you need it."

"I have it, thanks."

I pulled a chair up to the bed and helped Gabby to stand beside Maggie. Holding one arm around my daughter, I could hardly believe the change in Maggie. The old Maggie, the one I'd last visited just after Timothy died, bore no resemblance to the shriveled woman propped onto her side amid a nest of pillows. Above her head, monitors traced the evidence of her life. A bag dripped fluid into one arm. But Maggie, the woman who had so fiercely loved me, was not present.

"Maggie," I said, taking her hand. "I'm here. It's me, Brandy. We came all the way from Florida to see you." She did not respond.

To my surprise, Gabby bent forward, placing her palm on Maggie's forehead. With the softest touch, my daughter smoothed Maggie's hair away from her face. "Grandma Maggie," she said. "Wake up so we can kiss you."

Over the years, I've heard that the unconscious patient is very aware of the people and events going on around them. I've heard that they hear and understand every word. I don't know if these rumors are true. But on the evening of our first visit with Maggie, I desperately hoped that they were.

As Gabby petted her grandmother, I stood beside the bedside, telling Maggie all about our trip, about Eve and our plans for Field Day. And then, when Gabby lost interest and began poking through the closets and drawers of Maggie's room, I whispered my gratitude into the spirit of the woman I loved more than my own mother.

"Live," I told her. "I still need you."

Gabby and I stayed at a Best Western not far from the hospital. After a breakfast where Gabby ate three full-sized blueberry muffins—I didn't have the heart to stop her—we decided to pay a visit to the hot tub. We were soaking and playing when it occurred to me that Maggie might need some personal items from her apartment. Surely, after she woke, Maggie would want her own things—a robe, slippers, her own hairbrush. I remembered the bare closets I'd seen in Maggie's room as Gabby poked around. Her own things had not yet found their way to the hospital.

I decided that we could drive up to Duncan, to Maggie's place, after a morning trip to the hospital. This would give Gabby something to do, and perhaps take my mind off of Maggie's condition.

My daughter the fish was trying, at that very moment, to stand on her hands at the bottom of the hot tub. I reached out and snagged her foot, which brought her blubbering to the surface. "Let's go up and get dressed," I told Gabby. "After we see Grandma Maggie, we'll drive over to her apartment."

Three hours later, we pointed the rental car north on Highway 1 toward Duncan. While Gabby read her Daddy Book out loud, I let the slapping windshield wipers ease me into a trance of my own. I found it entirely surreal, heading back to the place of my youth. With every mile that passed, the terrain itself had the power to send me back in time.

The last time I'd come to see Maggie, I'd gone to visit her in the nursing home, taking Gabby, her namesake, with me. At Brentwood Gardens, her retirement village, I'd made arrangements to take Maggie out to lunch. After that, I'd planned to drive her back to Genoa Bay, back to the house she'd shared with her husband of more than fifty years. It was what she wanted, the only reason she'd agreed to go out to lunch at all. Though she'd been mentally alert at the time, Maggie was failing physically. The outing left her very, very tired.

It had been a long trip, a difficult adventure. She, slow moving, and largely confined to a wheelchair, struggled in and out of the car, the restaurant, the bathroom and back to the car. As sharp-witted and quick-tongued as ever, Maggie was absolutely frustrated by the limits of her body.

Still, she had been full of advice about mothering. "I know you love her, dear," she'd said about the bundle of energy in the car seat behind her. "How could you do anything else? But don't spoil her. That is for grandparents."

At the time, I was still in the throes of grief, struggling with guilt about Timothy's death, living with a constant barrage of "If only…" or "Why didn't I…?"

If only I'd convinced Timothy to leave the Navy, he wouldn't have been flying a jet on the day of his death.

Though I'd never told Maggie as much, even in her failing health, she guessed it. "Flying is what he loved," she said, reaching over to pat my knee. "You could never have changed that. He would have resented you. Treasure the time you had together. Be grateful for it. The Lord has plans for the rest of your life, my dear. Don't let regret take away today's joy."

I still remember her freckled skin, paper thin as it stretched over the swollen joints of her fingers. Though cataracts clouded both eyes, she still looked at me—no, through me—as if she could read the writing on my soul.

It struck me as funny that she knew so much about us— Timothy and I—things I'd never told her, never admitted to anyone.

She knew, or guessed perhaps, that I'd gotten into the habit of picking a fight with Timothy on the night before he left for extended periods. Whether it was a training exercise, or Carrier Qualification, or deployment, fighting was my way of making those separations less painful, my way of avoiding the fear I felt about his dropping a fighter onto the pitching deck of a moving aircraft carrier. I think Timothy knew exactly what I was doing. Sometimes, while I railed, he smiled.

Once, years before Timothy died, I called Maggie for her birthday. She did not wish to discuss her birth. Instead, Maggie advised me to stop starting fights with Timothy. "You don't want your anger to be the last thing he remembers. The last thing you remember." I did stop the arguments, though I never told Maggie as much; at least this gave me some comfort. In taking Maggie's advice, I never regretted Timothy's last departure from our home.

Like so many pieces of Maggie's advice, I tried to live up to it. Tried to give Timothy the room to love his work as much as he loved me. After all, Maggie knew Timothy well. She'd known him almost as long as I had.

I brought him home to Maggie just after I graduated from college, and she had taken to him as quickly as she had taken to me. Loving people came easily to Maggie, and she loved him with the fierce love of a maternal grandmother, though she was not related to either of us. In spite of her strong words, I knew that Maggie worried about Timothy as much as I did. Though she hated his job, she loved the jet jockey.

On our last visit together, when we arrived at Genoa Bay, I managed to get her from the car into the wheelchair and to push it up to the garden of the old house. That was the only time she cried while we were together. Though she had considered renting the house, it had not yet happened. Since she had moved to Brentwood, her precious garden had been left to itself. I think it hurt her, as badly as a broken bone, to see her beloved garden in such disrepair. She could not stay long.

"Take me back," she said, wiping her face with a man's extra-large handkerchief. "I want to go back."

She said nothing on the way home, falling asleep eventually, her head draped back onto the headrest of the rental car. Only her occasional snoring broke the silence.

After I tucked Maggie into the recliner in her room, wrapping her legs in a favorite lap blanket, I left her retirement home in tears. Though I had not said so, I worried that it might it be the last time I would see her alive.

Three

W HEN GABBY AND I ARRIVED at Brentwood Gardens, I was surprised by how little it had changed since I saw it last. Though Maggie and I had chosen the place together, I admit that from the very beginning, the idea of her living there worried me. I didn't like the place.

I don't think I could have liked having Maggie anywhere but the old house that had been our home.

As I opened the lobby doors, I smelled again the misplaced odor of cleaning fluids, and recognized the same silk-flower, worn décor I remembered from my last visit. The same elderly people shuffled along behind wheeled walkers. These are the lucky ones, I told myself as I waited for the receptionist. The ones who managed to live alone in their tiny rooms, to feed and dress and care for themselves.

Not long ago, Maggie had been this lucky.

In Nannette Brown's office, I listened to Gabby as she read out loud. She had picked up the latest issue of *People Magazine*, and I paid scant attention until she launched into a story about a Hollywood star too busy partying to care for her own children. The star had lost custody, and I took the magazine away from Gabby.

It's not always such an asset to read ahead of your grade level. Gabby's next choice: *Sports Illustrated*.

The door opened, and Nannette Brown came into the tiny waiting area. "I'm sorry to keep you," she apologized. "One of our residents needed some special transportation arrangements." She offered her hand, introducing herself. "I don't believe I've met you before."

"No, not yet. I'm Brandy Beauchamp," I said. "My grandmother is Maggie Blackburn." It still surprises me that I can say this with a straight face, as if we share the same blood.

"Ah, yes," she said, distress suddenly filling her features. "We were so sorry to hear about Maggie's medical condition. How is she?"

How could I explain that nothing stronger than cobwebs held Maggie suspended between heaven and earth. God and I seemed to be having a tug-of-war over Maggie; I refused to let go. "She's not conscious yet," I said.

Folding her hands, Nannette made clucking noises that sounded insincere at best. "So, Gabby and I," I put one arm around my daughter's shoulder, "have come by to pick up some of her personal things. She'll need them when she begins rehab."

"Why, of course. That's very thoughtful of you."

"I don't have a key to her apartment."

"Not a problem," she said. "You are listed as next-of-kin, are you not?" I nodded. "Well, then, of course we have a pass key. I can let you inside."

As we headed for Maggie's room, I did my best to defer Nannette's small talk to Gabby, who handles such things with remarkable ease. Eventually, the director unlocked Maggie's room, leading us inside. "I'll have to stay with you while you gather her things," Nannette explained. "And then, of course, you'll need to sign an inventory form. I'm sure you understand."

Unfortunately, I did. Back when I'd helped Maggie research residential facilities, I'd heard all the horror stories. Mostly, when stealing occurred, it was the staff doing the pilfering. "No problem," I said.

I did not know what to expect in Maggie's apartment. I had not been told how the staff had been alerted to Maggie's illness. But from conditions inside, I could have written the record myself. Maggie's dirty breakfast dishes lay on the counter, exactly as she had left them. Her bed was unmade, though her pajamas and dressing-gown were lying across the end of her bed.

Maggie was such a creature of habit that I knew with certainty that the stroke must have occurred after she finished dressing, somewhere between eating breakfast and making her bed. In the space of about fifteen minutes, her life—as she had known it—had been permanently altered. Would it ever be the same again?

A buzzing sound came from Nannette's waistband. She looked

down at her pager, sighing. "Ah, of course. It never fails." She stepped over to Maggie's telephone and dialed. "This is Nannette," she said.

I began gathering items from Maggie's dresser. She would need underclothes, clean pajamas, and perhaps socks, I reasoned, pulling open the top drawer. If Maggie required therapy, and of course she would, they would want her to wear shoes and socks, wouldn't they? I removed a few things from the dresser and laid them out on the bed. In her bathroom, I gathered her toothbrush, moisturizer, eyebrow pencil and lipstick. When it came to make-up, Maggie took the bare bones approach. I'd just found her deodorant when Nannette appeared in the doorway.

"I've been paged," she said, looking slightly harried. "I'm going to have to leave you here. You don't mind?"

"Of course not. Shall I stop by your office on my way out?"

"If you would," she smiled. "Again, I'm so sorry."

Gabby closed the door behind Nannette and came into the bathroom. "Can I turn on the television?"

"I'm almost finished, honey."

"But Mom," her voice rose. "You've already been so long."

How quickly seven-year-old enthusiasm fades. "Alright, but only for a minute."

Gabby used the remote to turn on the television, and I waited until she'd settled on a cartoon before I returned to Maggie's bedroom, intent on finishing my packing. Where was I? Oh yes, the shoes.

I pushed open her closet door, and smiled.

This was not Maggie's closet. Here someone, undoubtedly a housekeeper, had lined Maggie's shoes in a neat little row. Above them, her clothes were organized—shirts together, pants separately, dresses in-between—all by color. This was not the random chaos that Maggie preferred in her closets, and I had to laugh thinking about how she would react to this attempt at organizing her life.

I'd hate to be Maggie's housekeeper.

There were no walking shoes on the floor with the others. This perplexed me. Though Maggie was not strong, she made a great business of taking a daily constitutional around the main floor of her building. With every phone call, I heard about the things she'd seen, the people she'd spoken to while on her daily walk. Though the walk was very short Maggie dressed as if she were training for a marathon. Where were her shoes?

I began to look through the shelves. Here, I found various shoeboxes carrying all kinds of personal items. In one, Maggie had a collection of new birthday cards hidden under a yearly calendar. Opening another shoebox, my nose was assaulted by the ammonia chemical smell of home permanents. Inside, I found a set of permanent wave rollers, along with waving tissues, a rat-tail comb, and a long roll of cotton. Unlike most of her friends, I had managed to avoid becoming the recipient of this very beauty treatment. On stormy winter days, I already sported an auburn afro.

Still unable to find her shoes, I wondered if perhaps Maggie had put them away. Perhaps she'd stopped her daily walk and not told me about it. I pulled a chair from the kitchen nook and set it in front of her closet. On the highest shelf, I found a pair of burgundy heels. In the next shoebox, I found silver sandals.

The guilt I felt when I saw them nearly knocked me off the chair.

Maggie had worn these to a New Year's Eve party the year I'd graduated from High School. Dressed in her party best, she had come downstairs in a silver Lurex™ sweater and an off-white pleated skirt. On her feet she wore those silly plastic sandals. I'd barely looked up from the television to say goodbye. Maggie planted herself between the television and the couch and leaned over to tell me she loved me—her face just inches from mine.

Unable, at seventeen, to admit that I loved her too, I'd misdirected my attention to the shoes. "So, do you wear those things because of the bunion?"

I put the boxes back in place, and began to look around the apartment. I checked under the bed, in the bathroom, under the little sit-down counter in the kitchen. Maggie's white leather walking shoes were nowhere to be found. I looked under the skirt of the loveseat and beneath her swivel rocker.

"What are you looking for?" Gabby asked from her corner of the couch, her eyes never leaving the television set.

"I can't find Grandma's walking shoes." I sat down beside her. "Have you seen them?"

"Not in her closet?"

"I looked there." I sat back, defeated. My cell phone began to ring, and I held one finger toward my daughter. "Just a minute." I didn't recognize the number blinking at me from the screen. "Hello?"

"Hello, Mrs. Beauchamp?"

"Yes."

"This is Sigrid Olsen, from Victoria General Hospital."

"Yes?"

"The ICU staff here at the hospital has asked me to call and let you know that there has been a change in Maggie Blackburn's condition."

"Yes?"

"You should probably come to the hospital immediately."

❀

The next three days passed in a hurricane of arrangements and plans. With the help of Maggie's pastor, himself an elderly gentleman, I managed to pull together a memorial service, held in the tiny chapel of Valley Bible Church. The seniors group prepared food and hosted a small reception after the service.

In the midst of all the decisions and legal documents and plans, I tried to keep up with my work schedule. Thankfully, design work can be done from nearly anywhere. Each night, after I tucked Gabby in bed, I spent several hours on my laptop, trying to finish work assignments. During the day, wherever we could, I spent quiet moments alone with Gabby. We took time to walk in the park, to visit a playground near the hotel, and once, when we were up in Duncan, we walked around the lake trail.

Between the long hours and unending decision-making, I felt myself begin to unravel around the edges, something like an over-used bath towel. But even this edginess, I believed, was more about fatigue than grief. Even in the midst of planning her memorial, I don't think I realized that Maggie was actually gone. Intellectually I knew it, of course. But Maggie had not been a part of my daily life for so long, I didn't yet feel her absence. That would come later.

I think part of me believed that losing Timothy had given me some supernatural strength—when it came to death—that would enable me to plan funerals with the same kind of dispassionate efficiency with which a professional wedding planner arranged a client's nuptials. After all, I was used to it, wasn't I?

And so, when the day of the service arrived, and I found myself missing Maggie with such a profound ache that breathing itself became painful, I was taken by complete surprise. It began when I got out of my car at the church. As Gabby and I walked through the cold clouds of an impotent spring day, it hit me. In an instant, in the crack of a baseball bat, I realized that I had never been at the old church without Maggie.

She had introduced me to church. She had nurtured and coddled and pushed me into my faith. It was only because of Maggie that I had any faith at all.

And from that moment, the memories of Maggie rolled, one after another, through my brain for the length of the entire afternoon. As I looked over the pictures decorating the platform. As the pastor spoke. As her friends, themselves fighting grief, expressed with eloquence and loyalty their memories about my beloved Maggie.

Before the pastor finished the eulogy, I missed Eve. She would have known how to go get through this afternoon. She would have a handkerchief in her purse. She would shield me from strangers, escort me from service to reception, and keep an eye on Gabby.

But Eve had not come.

That afternoon, I learned things about Maggie that I had not known. Unable, as a teenager, to focus on anything outside the circle of self, I'd never asked about her husband. Didn't know when he died. Where she'd grown up, or gone to school. When she'd purchased the house at Genoa Bay. I didn't know that she had volunteered at the Mental Health Center, or at Shiloh Farms. In fact, in all my conversations with Maggie, even after I moved away, she'd never even mentioned the farm.

The group that day consisted of people from all over the community. Most I had never met. In the sea of wrinkled faces that greeted me during the reception, I recognized a few old friends. One of my high school teachers had played bridge with Maggie. One of my friends' parents had been in the garden club with her. Another had managed the yearly plant exchange, which so delighted Maggie. Most of my own friends had left Genoa Bay. Not one attended the funeral.

❀

While Gabby played in the nursery with the only other child who attended that afternoon, I endured crushing hugs and endless introductions. So much of the congregation had changed since I left Genoa Bay. I knew that as I foundered in the surf of emotions, I would remember almost none of these people. Embarrassed at my own inability to remember names and faces, part of me hoped that after the service I wouldn't run into them again.

Though the room was air conditioned, I felt unbearably hot. Grief had finally hit, lucky for me, in the most public of places. I glanced toward the clock, wondering how soon Gabby and I could head back to the hotel. Just when I thought I could bear no more, another person reached for my hand.

"I'm so sorry for your loss," a male voice said. Surprised, I realized that this was not the sandpaper voice of an older man. I examined more closely the man still holding my right hand. "Maggie was a great woman," he continued, smiling. "She made the best strawberry-rhubarb pie on the planet."

He continued to hold my hand in both of his, even after he finished speaking. And, as awkward as this felt—holding hands with a stranger—I noticed that his fingers were thick, his hands both dry and deeply calloused.

"I'm sorry," I began. "I don't..." I could not place this face. He was quite young, not yet forty, with the chaffed red nose and cheeks of someone who spent most of his time outdoors. He wore a dark, full beard, frosted with streaks of premature gray. His blue eyes, surrounded by deep laugh lines, exactly matched the denim shirt beneath his navy jacket.

"I'm Cliff," he said, as if this explained everything. "Cliff Lowry."

"Thank you for coming, Cliff," I said, still slightly confused. He smiled and nodded, releasing my hand as he stepped back. The poor guy seemed nearly as uncomfortable as I, not quite sure how to continue the conversation, and not quite graceful enough to let go.

He gave the air of someone who wished to disappear into the crowd. Instead, he unbuttoned his jacket and slipped both hands into his pants' pockets. "If there is ever anything I can do to help you, you know, move stuff or anything. I'm available."

Cliff Lowry was a stocky man, definitely not slim, but not quite fat. He was broad shouldered, sturdy. Solid. That was the word for him. Though he wasn't huge, Cliff seemed like the kind of guy who could take a hit from a 300-pound linebacker and never yield. His bulk might be handy to have around some day. Looking at him, at his obvious discomfort in this environment, I felt a stirring of pity.

Smiling, I thanked him for his kindness. "And how did you know Maggie?"

Four

ON FRIDAY MORNING, the day after the service, I took my cell phone into the parking lot of the hotel and called my boss. "Look, Daniel, I'm stuck here in B.C. I can't come home until I make certain that someone will look after Maggie's affairs. I need to contact her attorney and see that he closes her estate. There's her apartment, the house. All of it."

"Surely there's someone else."

"I'm the executor. Maggie asked me years ago."

"But she's not even a real relative. You said so before you left."

"She was more real than any of my relatives." I felt my shoulders and neck tighten. I don't know why, but I'd convinced myself that Daniel wouldn't argue. That he would just go along with my plans. "Her brother lives in Toronto. He's too old to do it, and he lives too far away. It's the least I can do for Maggie. The last thing."

"That's not the point. I understand you're in a tough spot. But so are we. We can't afford to have you out of the office this long. We'll be starting staff vacations soon. I've got to have you here, where you can plan, communicate, work with the team."

"I understand. But right now, it's just not possible." Rubbing my neck with one hand, I paced the distance across the patio to the front entry. "I guess you can fire me, if you have to," I said, hoping he wouldn't. "I just don't have any choice. There isn't anyone else."

"Look Brandy, I've really bent over backwards to make this work with you. I took you on part time, right after Timothy died. I've let you be home when Gabby got off the school bus. I've given you every school holiday and vacation. But you've got to be fair about it. I don't know how long we can cover for you. I hired you as a graphic artist. I need a graphic artist. Here, in Pensacola."

"I get it, Daniel." I said, still massaging my shoulder. It didn't take much to anticipate where this conversation might end. "I do. I appreciate all that you've done for me. I'll try to get through this as quickly as I can. Gabby needs to get back to school. I need to be at work. I promise. I'll finish up here as fast as I can. Two more weeks, max."

"I can do two weeks. No more."

"Thanks, Daniel."

"Keep me posted," he said, and hung up.

❀

After breakfast, I drove Gabby out to the house at Genoa Bay. I hadn't been there since the last time I'd visited Maggie. If I had to dispose of her belongings, I'd have to start with the house. The renters had long since left, and the old place had been so long empty, I dreaded what I might find.

By the time we arrived in Duncan, the morning sun peeked from behind broken clouds and a strong breeze made the spring sunshine feel like an impostor. It was cold, brutally cold. At least the rain had stopped.

The roads from the city to the bay are winding and slow, with almost no shoulder. They are frequented by both island deer and human residents, neither one much apt to watch for oncoming traffic. Though I should have focused on the drive, I couldn't. My mind wandered, calculating and recalculating my financial status.

The Death Benefit from Timothy's fatal accident had paid for his funeral services. I'd used a large chunk of it to pay off our car, pay down and refinance our house at a lower interest rate, and install a security system. I'd resisted the urge to redecorate, to splurge on big-ticket items. I'd assumed that Timothy's life insurance, a government-issued policy, would more than help us get on with our lives. It was a fortune I'd counted on. Money that Timothy had wanted me to have.

If anything happened to him, he'd said, he wanted me to be a full-time parent for Gabby. "It's enough for her to lose a father. But if you go back to work, she'll lose both of us." Back then, I'd assumed that things were taken care of.

How little I knew.

It didn't matter how I worked the numbers. I needed my job. While my salary didn't cover everything, it kept us afloat while I battled the United States Government over Timothy's benefits—a battle I had to win. I had no choice. The cost of the fight had begun to eat away at what little savings I had.

I put thoughts of missing wills and legal battles out of my mind. It didn't comfort me that the United States armed forces managed to misplace dozens of wills every year. Knowing that other widows fought the same battle gave me no strength to get through my own troubles.

Besides, I had more important, more urgent things to worry about. What would happen if Daniel fired me? Could I find another job? Would I have to take a full-time position? Would anyone else be as understanding?

❀

"Look at the rocks," Gabby said, pointing out the car window.

"The mountains here are made of sandstone," I said, grateful for the distraction. "The rocks break off and roll down the hill." I glanced over at my daughter, her nose so close to the window that condensation obscured her view.

She wiped the window with her palm and looked at me. "Will they fall on us?"

"No, honey. We're safe."

"But they're huge! They'd crush the car."

She had me there. These were not just boulders, the kind you dig out of the yard before you plant a lawn. The rocks on this part of the island are the size of a detached two-car garage.

"Look closer, Gabby. Most of them already have trees growing out of them. Maple trees. Fir trees. They've been sitting there for a long, long time. Nothing has fallen recently. You don't have to worry." I slowed our car to take a particularly difficult curve. As I pulled through the corner, a mother deer galloped across the highway. I slowed, knowing her babies were likely just behind her. "Look, see the momma deer?"

Gabby, who loves all things animal, cried out in delight. "Stop! Take a picture!"

"I can't stop, honey. It's too dangerous on the highway." I glanced into the rearview. "Besides, there are plenty of them at the house. We can take pictures there."

"I want to show the kids at school." In Florida, show and tell often revolves around pictures of alligators found in conduits and drainage basins. Sometimes Gabby's friends snap pictures of armored lizards found on porches or in garages.

Gabby's delight in the deer reminded me of my first encounter with the house at Genoa Bay. It happened the day after I met Maggie.

When Captain Bill Cherring steered the *Odyssea* into the tiny marina, he'd planned to stay only two days, acquiring fresh supplies before heading south for Victoria. But a storm we'd encountered in our passage from Alaska forced us to change plans. We had repairs to finish, lines to replace. As the most experienced among his crew— which should have alarmed me greatly—this job fell to me. Thus, I'd come to meet Maggie.

But on the day I met Maggie I had not yet finished my assignment. What did I really know about lines and sails? Our captain, a wiry-haired man in his mid fifties, spent our entire first day in port, deep in the engine-room fighting with the diesel engine. Not only had our lines fouled in our short passage, but the inboard engine had failed as well. At one point, Bill steered us through heavy waves with the assistance of a fifteen-horsepower kicker.

Bill told the crew—two other men and myself—that the engine needed nothing more than new plugs. By dinnertime, he managed to replace the plugs and sit down, still covered with grease, to a meal of fresh crab caught in the north end of the bay. In spite of Bill's promises, when I slid into my bunk that night, the engine still did not run.

Frankly, I was glad. I didn't want to leave the bay quite yet; I had too many of my own worries. The engine's failure was only the most recent reminder that the *Odyssea* was no more seaworthy than an inflatable kayak. And though I hated my life in Alaska, I didn't hate life itself—at least not enough to lose it on the passage to Hawaii.

At the same time, I'd never encountered anyone quite like

Maggie, and I continued to think about her long after she'd taken her pie and headed down the dock. I'd wondered about her when the crew returned from town. I'd pictured her and her pie as I put groceries away in the ship's pantry. Though certain I would never see her again, I couldn't quite get her out of my mind. I fell asleep thinking about her, and woke the next morning with a vivid picture of her wild hair dancing in my imagination.

I dressed quietly, and slipped from my bunk in the forward stateroom. Taking care not to wake my fellow crewmen, I moved toward the stern of the boat still carrying my shoes. I intended to inquire at the marina office—quietly, of course—about the potential for summer work.

I tiptoed through the galley, wishing I could snag something to eat on my way off the boat. But the tiny counters were bare, and as was his habit every night before turning in, Captain Cherring had locked the cabinets and refrigerator with padlocks. Though part of my official duties lay in the galley, he had never given me a key to these locks. I wondered, as I climbed the ladder to the cockpit, what kind of captain was afraid to feed his own crew?

By the time I stepped onto the dock, the morning sun had already warmed the air, and a light breeze was blowing from the north. The tide was out and the smell of salt made my nose tingle. As I sat down to slip on my tennis shoes, I watched a mother duck lead her babies through the puddle of bay that flowed under the dock ramp. I remember thinking, as she hustled her babies along, how natural it was for some mothers to care for their young. Why did humans have so much trouble?

When I reached the marina office, a shiny five-gallon coffee pot gurgled with fresh brew and several boaters stood nearby waiting to fill their mugs. Already the Harbormaster's wall-mounted radio squawked with incoming vessel traffic and I tried to blend into the crowd as he barked instructions to his crew via walkie-talkies.

At sixteen, I didn't have much confidence in my ability to get a job. But in spite of my obvious lack of judgment—I had signed on as crew to a junker, after all—my position with Captain Cherring had given my self-assurance a small boost. I had to find work. I knew with certainty that I should never leave the harbor on that old crate. If I cared about my life, I would never again let myself lose sight of land.

I watched the Harbormaster from my hiding place in the cracker and cookie aisle, wondering if he managed the marina, or simply served some higher authority. Should I ask for his boss? And what if he asked about my past, or for proof of identification? Worse yet, what if he recognized me as part of the *Odyssea*'s crew and reported my inquiry to Captain Cherring? Afraid to have this crowd of yachties listen in while I begged for a job, I wandered over to a bookshelf and pretended to look through a Sunshine Coast Burgee book.

Eventually, after the convivial group of men took their coffee and left, the radio fell silent. Still nervous, I convinced myself that my opportunity had arrived. Just as I came around the end cap, the bell over the door rang and a cheerful female voice called out, "Morning, Alan." I turned my back to the counter and found myself gazing at a display of fish lures, lines and hooks.

"Morning, Maggie," Alan answered. "You're late."

I ducked back behind a row of cereal boxes and peeked over the shelves. On this visit, Maggie wore a dark canvas jacket, and a straw hat pulled low over her forehead. "I have a bunch of guests up at the house this morning. Couldn't get away. Haven't even showered."

"The early birds have already come and gone."

"Ah well, I've done the best I can. Selling rolls here doesn't make enough money to worry about."

"You don't charge enough," Allen said, dismissing her. "How many?"

"People?"

"Rolls."

"The usual."

"Maggie, you're as reliable as the sunrise." The Harbormaster turned away from the counter and lifted a large plastic tray from behind the cash register. Setting it on the counter, he removed the clear lid and put down a fresh sheet of wax paper. "There you go," he said. Even from behind the bookshelves, the smell of freshly baked cinnamon rolls made my stomach rumble, and hunger shouted for my attention.

"As beautiful as ever," I heard him comment.

"Oh, don't flatter me," Maggie said. I peeked around the display to watch. Using giant tongs, the strange old woman moved rolls onto the tray. "Just go ahead and take one, Alan. You know that's what you want."

The old guy used two hands to lift a single giant roll. The confection looked to be about six inches across and dripped with thick white icing. Even from across the room, I recognized the look of anticipation on his face. He'd eaten one of these before. And it must have been pure pleasure.

My mouth watered.

While he ogled over the pastry, Maggie finished loading the tray and replaced the hinged plastic cover. Then, after wiping her hands on the sides of her jacket, she pulled a small green book and a pen from one of the pockets. "Initial there, please," she pointed.

"Maggie, it's been the same number every day for ten years. You bring twenty-four rolls, I sell twenty-three. I don't know why you insist on having me sign this silly book." He licked his fingers before accepting the pen.

"Because it keeps us both honest, Alan," she said, sliding the book back in her pocket. "I'll see you tomorrow."

"Tomorrow," the Harbormaster said, in frosting-muddled syllables.

As Maggie turned from the counter, I ducked again, waiting for the bell over the door to announce her departure. I hoped that my chance with the Harbormaster had finally arrived, and I didn't know how much longer I could be away from the boat before someone noticed. I was about to peek at the counter when a voice behind me spoke.

❀

"Mom, how far to the house?" My daughter's voice startled me.

I had no idea where we were. How long had I been lost in the past? I glanced around the car, noticed the entrance to Sprague's Farm, and said, "We're almost there."

"I miss Liz," Gabby said, her words a whisper.

"Me too," I said. "She's pretty cuddly, isn't she?" Cuddling had been my only purpose behind the purchase of our newest family member. I'd gone out to buy her three days after Timothy's memorial service. Somehow, I believed that she would heal the hole he'd left in our hearts. Liz, an eager, bright, and devoted puppy, had done her best.

But Liz was no match for the empty space my husband left behind.

As if by magic, when we climbed the last hill to the house and rounded the narrow corner at the top, we came upon a family of island deer. This time, I had no choice. All three of them posed in the middle of the road. "Mom, look!"

"I told you." Normally, those of us who lived on this street would simply honk and drive on. Like a herd of sheep, the deer casually move out of the way. This time, though, I put the car in park and turned off the engine. Gabby was mesmerized.

And I couldn't help but remember my first look at these same deer, or maybe they were the great-grandparents of this particular group. It happened on the day I'd hidden among the fishing lures in the Genoa Bay marina office. It was Maggie's voice that had startled me.

"Have you had breakfast?" she'd asked.

I jumped so high that I nearly crashed into her. I'd been staring at the counter, waiting for her to leave the little marina store. But she hadn't left; rather, she'd circled around and spoken directly into my left ear. Stunned, I spun around to face her.

"Well, have you?"

I shook my head.

"Then come with me. I've been serving breakfast all morning, and I have enough left over to feed the entire marina." She waved me toward the door, picking up her tray as she passed the startled Harbormaster. "I'd as soon give it to you as throw it out."

I shrugged at him and followed her out the door. On this morning, Maggie wore a printed chiffon scarf to tie down her wide brimmed hat. A pleated skirt, in pale turquoise, clung to her bird legs. She had the same holey tennis shoes on, though this time over long white athletic socks, the tops hidden under the hem of her skirt.

As we stepped off the porch into the cool shade of maple trees, Maggie wrapped her dark jacket around her chest, hugging it close against the morning air. Without a word, Maggie started up the long steep road leading away from the marina.

Because I'd never left the docks before, I had no idea where we were headed. I hung back a few steps, letting Maggie lead the way. Before long my calves began to ache, and I realized that the weeks I'd spent on board the *Odyssea* had already weakened my muscles. My lungs begged for air, and I tried to hide my panting from the older woman ahead of me. Maggie hiked up the hill, setting a brisk pace. My youthful pride demolished, I recognized that she was in good shape—for such an old lady.

Just as the road veered to the right and began to level out, Maggie turned left and started another hill, a driveway this time. I glanced with some longing toward the flat terrain and spotted a family of island deer skipping across the road to graze on the other side. I must have gasped, because the doe paused to look toward me warily. Her twins scampered across the field; but she watched me, statue-like.

I glanced up the hill to where Maggie had turned her back on the driveway and stood watching the deer. "Beautiful, aren't they?" Maggie said, shaking her head. "They come every morning. Nothing I do stops them. Believe me, I've tried. It seems I serve breakfast to everyone—not just the humans." She waved them off and started back up the driveway again.

I trailed behind, disappointed to discover that we faced yet another, steeper drive. Hoping for an excuse to stop, I glanced back over my shoulder. But the deer had gone.

"You have to be still," she said without turning toward me. "They frighten easily."

The narrow driveway to Maggie's place was surrounded—nearly overwhelmed really—by a display of plants and flowers unlike any I'd ever seen before. Blossoms of every color and shape waved in the breezy jungle. Even from the center of the drive, I heard the incessant buzz of insects feasting on flowers. None too soon, the driveway leveled off, making a sharp turn toward the right. There, I spied an ancient white Oldsmobile parked before a broad chain-link gate. Not far away, in a graveled space, I noticed a burgundy SUV and a small import. Somehow, I didn't have to wonder which of these cars belonged to Maggie.

Another fence—it must have been more than six feet—

surrounded the tiny yard of an enormous, but incredibly bizarre, white house. The narrow flagstone path leading to the front porch was lined by masses of bushes and flowers and grasses. Tiny birds, hummers and finches, flitted everywhere.

Opening the smaller gate, Maggie backed it up against a wall of foliage, holding it there as she waited for me. The sight was so strange, and yet so beautiful, so unlike anything I'd ever seen, I couldn't move. From that almost tropical driveway, I gazed, bewildered, at Maggie's peculiar house and the view beyond it for the first time.

Surrounded on three sides by glistening, sparkling water, her home had the most beautiful view I had ever seen. I could hardly take it all in.

"Now," she said, her voice urgent as she waved me into the yard. "Live up to it. I have sheets to wash."

Five

I'D HARDLY PUT THE CAR IN PARK before Gabby unsnapped her seatbelt. "Cool," she said, opening the car door. "A haunted house."

Though I expected Maggie's house to look unkempt, my imagination had not done justice to the reality of what I found at the top of the driveway. Apparently Gabby agreed. I took a deep breath before setting the emergency brake. "It is not haunted," I said. I'd emphasized the "not" and managed to sound perturbed, even to myself.

But Gabby didn't hear me. She jumped out of the car and ran toward the little gate leading to the kitchen door. "It's stuck," she said, fiddling with the latch.

"This house is not haunted," I repeated, determined to convey my absolute certainty on the subject. "Here, let me get that." I reached around Gabby to open the gate. While the latch itself worked, the hinges on the wooden gate had rusted shut. I pushed harder, and with a squeal the hinge gave way, splitting the support post. The gate fell sideways into the yard, leaving exposed cedar as the lone reminder of what had once been. "Great start," I muttered.

Walking toward the house, the bushes snagged our jeans, leaving behind wet denim and bits of old blossoms and seeds clinging to our clothes. "It used to be so beautiful when Maggie kept it," I said, leading Gabby off the path through the grass to the kitchen door.

"She was a gardener?"

"Of the finest variety," I said, stepping onto the porch.

"Do you have a key?"

"Of course. I used to live here, you know."

Gabby nodded. "I knew that," she said.

I smiled, digging in my purse for the old key. "Of course you did," I agreed, opening the front door. "It must be wonderful to know so much, at seven."

Ignoring me, Gabby rushed inside. "Where are the lights?"

I reached for the wall, my fingers instinctively sensing the location of the switch. Of course the power had been turned off, but sunlight slanted through kitchen windows into Maggie's beloved space. The air was filled with the peculiar musty odor of an unoccupied home. My mind thought about the possibility of rodents, and I began to wish I hadn't joined Gabby in watching that Disney movie about a rat-chef.

This wasn't the house as I remembered it, and in the light of what we found inside, Gabby's comment about the house being haunted seemed more appropriate than I liked to think. "What is that smell?" She pinched her nose.

"Nothing. Mold, dust. The place has been closed up for a long time." I turned right, away from the kitchen and toward the front entry. There I opened the drapes in front of Maggie's front door. With Gabby just a few steps behind, I mounted the three steps to the main room. "Wait there, and I'll open the rest of the curtains."

I arrived on the far side of the great room without tripping over any surprises. The drapes opened reluctantly, as if perhaps the runners inside the traverse rod had rusted—not uncommon so near the water. Light flooded the east side of the room, and I looked around, trying to take in the whole space.

All of Maggie's stuff was still there. The lamps, the antique glassware, the antique square piano, the stuffed owl, the clock collection. All of it. And in an instant, I knew there would be more. Much, much more. In that moment, the weight of my assignment hit me square in the gut.

Why on earth had I agreed to execute Maggie's estate? Why didn't I insist that her attorney manage it all? How could anyone close this house, empty it of all this junk, in less than ten years—let alone two weeks? In that sickening moment, I wondered if I suffered from some kind of invincibility complex.

"Mom!" Gabby ran to the center of the great room, pointing at the ceiling. "Oh my gosh. Mom, there's a boat in the living-room!"

I'd expected this. Still, her reaction made me smile. "Well, not a whole boat," I said. "It's the bottom half of a sailboat—forty-four feet, to be exact. It was in the house when Maggie bought it."

"You're kidding. Why would anyone hang a sailboat from the ceiling?"

"That, my sweet thing, is the question of the day."

Gabby's question reminded me of the enormous job I faced. Not only did I have to clean out this sprawling house; but I had to find a buyer. Not just any buyer would do. I needed to find someone crazy enough to buy a house with a sailboat hanging from the ceiling. Someone as crazy as Maggie had been.

❊

Armed with a yellow notepad and a pen I'd brought from the hotel, I planned to survey the condition of the house, trying to get a feel for the enormity of the task in front of me. I remember thinking, as I walked through the great room back to the kitchen, that if things were as bad as I'd envisioned in the rest of the house, perhaps I could simply invite the local fire department to a practice burn.

I had no idea then, how close we would come to doing just that.

Gabby and I began our survey in the kitchen. Having spent so many years in the old house, I knew something of the task I faced. But before I made any concrete plans, I wanted to understand its current conditions. I had no idea if I needed to rent a dumpster, hire a painting crew, replace carpet, or flooring. I wondered if I'd need to hold an estate sale, or request a truck from the local Salvation Army.

In the kitchen, I found cabinet doors open, and deep layers of dirt covering the floor. Rodents left tracks along the baseboards. Maggie's beloved commercial six-burner stove was filthy and covered with grease—a fire hazard in itself. Seeing the house this way brought back waves of fresh grief. Maggie had always loved that stove. When I was young, she'd kept it spotless, even when everything around her was chaos.

As a teenager, when I first came to the house at Genoa Bay, I'd always believed that there were only two kinds of people, slobs and neatknicks—you know the kind, the ones who alphabetize their spice cabinet. But when I met Maggie, I realized that there was also a third category. Maggie was meticulously clean in areas that mattered to her, and remarkably sloppy about things that didn't.

I smiled, remembering my first impressions of the old woman. Her ability to compartmentalize was the only way I could explain her tendency to dress like a bag-lady while at the same time, out-bake Martha Stewart.

Gabby wandered along beside me, opening drawers and touching dishes. "Mom, this is crazy. She has counters everywhere. It's like a maze. And different cabinets," she pointed. "They don't even match."

Yet another reminder of the difficulty in finding a buyer for Maggie's treasure palace. "I know. It's a little crazy, isn't it?" I moved toward the patio doors. "This is the half of the kitchen that Maggie added after she moved here. She never cared that the whole room didn't match. She needed the space to cook for all the people coming to the house."

"But it looks like two separate kitchens jammed together."

"You're right. That's exactly what it is. I never understood it either."

Gabby moved toward a pantry door, reaching out to open it. "Don't," I said, worried about what she might find. "We'll look inside when we clean the place up." I didn't want to frighten her. But I'd already seen enough rodent droppings in the kitchen to fell an entire fighter squadron with Hantavirus. "How about we tour the rest of the house?"

As I expected, the rest of the house was in similar condition. Because of her failing health, Maggie had stopped renting rooms to guests long before neighbors helped her move to the assisted living facility. The condition of the house showed me just how weak, how compromised her life had been before the move—all details she had carefully kept from me.

I found dirty bedding on the floor, and trash in every bathroom. In one guestroom, I found a broken television set, and parts of a stereo system. In another bedroom, a broken toilet stood alone in a corner. In places, the draperies were torn, or removed altogether. Mini-blinds looked as if cats had used them for climbing exercise.

While Maggie had always had cats, she had been meticulous about them. Their litter boxes were always clean, and the house never showed any sign of cat-abuse. In the years I lived with Maggie, I'd never found a single hint of cat hair.

Something had clearly changed in the last years she lived alone.

In every room, with every step, my discouragement grew. The weight of the job seemed insurmountable. It would take far more than two weeks. I needed an army and a fire-hose to clean up this mess. The only glimmer of hope lay in the downstairs apartment I'd shared with Maggie. While it wasn't clean, neither was it a virtual garbage dump.

The apartment sported nothing more frightening than mounds of dust and a labyrinth of cobwebs. This space, at least, could be restored with nothing more expensive than elbow-grease and fresh paint.

"So you and Maggie lived down here?" Gabby said, coming out of Maggie's old room. "Why didn't you stay upstairs in the pretty rooms?"

"Maggie ran a Bed and Breakfast. She rented those rooms— usually for the weekend. By living down here, she let the guests feel as if they had the house to themselves. And, of course, this little apartment gave us privacy too." From the look on her face, I saw that Gabby saw no need for privacy.

"You didn't even eat in the dining-room?"

"Not usually. Sometimes, we used the main floor during the week, when there wasn't anyone staying with us."

"That's crazy. Why have a big old house like this if you can't live in it?"

"I guess you have to think of the house as a hotel. It really doesn't belong to the people who manage it."

Gabby shook her head, completely baffled. I had to agree. Even to me, it didn't make too much sense. "Can I go outside and look around?"

"Sure. Stay in the yard and away from the water, though. Why don't you take a tour of the garden?"

She let herself out through the sliding glass door, and I wandered through the rooms again, letting my memories come alive.

This place had been my salvation, really. Who could tell what might have happened to me without Maggie? I walked through the hallway and entered my old bedroom.

On my first morning with Maggie, I'd followed her inside, stunned silent by the house, its bewildering contents and the woman herself. Fortunately, I didn't have to speak. Maggie sensed my caution, and treated me like she treated the wild birds at her feeders, with respect and slow-motion thoughtfulness.

"Here, have a seat," she said, pointing toward a kitchen stool. She removed her hat and jacket, hanging both on a hook beside the kitchen door.

I sat, sliding my palms under my thighs as Maggie busied herself setting a place for me. She put down a cutwork linen placemat and heavy silverware, followed by real china—the kind so old that the white had mellowed and the glaze had cracked. She poured orange juice in stemware—I thought it might be crystal—and asked if I'd like coffee. "Sure," I said, and then added, "thank you."

The smells of sausage and fresh-baked bread, the clean counters and bright sunlight and the natural, almost careless grace of the old woman sideswiped my emotions, and without any explanation I could think of, I nearly began to cry.

Instead, I coughed.

She did not seem to notice. "So," she began, placing a cinnamon roll on my plate. "How's the trip gone so far?"

That one question, combined with the good food that followed, and the genuine care of the woman in this strange house, somehow combined to pry me open. This, by itself, surprised me. In the next hour and a half—I never once worried about Captain Cherring while I was with Maggie—I told her about everything. I told Maggie about my mother who followed my father from job to job, all the way to Alaska, about growing up in Valdez. I even told her about waiting in the truck outside the bar where my father drank after work. I told Maggie where my name came from—well, almost. "My mother said it was because of the color of my hair. I guess it was red even on the day I was born." I'd never told anyone the real truth about my name, not even Maggie.

While I talked, Maggie loaded my plate with food. As a

teenager, a hungry, hardworking kid, I ate whatever she scooped onto my plate. Without asking questions, she sat across the counter, keeping my juice glass filled, and offering me seconds. While I spoke, she rested her chin on her hands and stared into my face as if I were telling the most inspiring and intriguing of stories. No one had ever listened to me like Maggie did that first morning.

I finished by telling her about our move to Ketchikan, and about my mother's new husband—though I admit that I left out parts of that story. Most of what I told Maggie that morning was true.

"It must have taken something really big for you to leave your family like that," she said.

"Not really," I used the last of a cinnamon roll to swab my plate. "My mom had a new baby, that's all. It was time, you know? I didn't fit in any more."

I could tell by her expression that she suspected there was more. "So, what's next? Where do you go from here?"

"I think I'd like to get a job around here."

Her crayoned eyebrows rose. "What? And not sail to Hawaii with Cherring?"

"I don't think so. I think I've changed my mind." I didn't look up.

"What kind of job?" She took my dishes to the sink and brought back a rag, wiping the counter as she waited for my answer.

"Anything, really. I'm a hard worker. I know boats, some. I could detail powerboats, you know, get them all polished up and ready to sell or whatever. I could work at a marina, helping to dock boats, doing daily maintenance, that kind of thing. I could manage a gas dock. Or work in a marina office."

"What do you know about housework?" she'd asked.

❀

The sounds of Big Ben interrupted my thoughts. I'd always hated Maggie's doorbell. Upstairs, I peeked out onto Maggie's front entry to discover an older gentleman standing on the front porch. He wore a long-sleeved white shirt under a lightweight golf jacket. The wind, blowing up from the water, ruffled his graying hair, and after checking his watch, he reached over to ring the bell again. I unlocked the sliding glass door.

"Yes?" I said, peering out through a narrow opening at this stranger. "Can I help you?"

"I'm Walter Doherty, Maggie Blackburn's attorney." He gestured, as though to tip a nonexistent hat, saying, "And you must be Brandy Beauchamp, Maggie's friend."

I opened the door and welcomed the man inside. "The place is a mess, I'm afraid. I was just looking around to see how much I'd have to do in order to get it ready to sell. Of course, you know that Maggie asked me to be her executor."

He glanced around the main floor and seemed to suppress a shudder. "She told me you'd accepted."

I laughed. "At the time, I had no idea what it entailed. I guess I wasn't thinking."

"That's why I've come to see you. I called the hotel, and the desk clerk said you'd driven out to the house."

"I'd offer you a seat, but there really isn't any place," I gestured around the great room. "The house is in very poor condition."

"I understand. I shouldn't take much of your time."

In spite of the dark surroundings and the dismal results of my survey thus far, I felt a bubble of hope rise in my heart. Perhaps Maggie had chosen someone else. Perhaps I wouldn't have to empty and close the house. Perhaps I could head back to Florida and take up my old life.

"I came out here today, because I think there is something you should know."

The man seemed hesitant, and it worried me. Why not just come out with it? "Did Maggie ask someone else to be the executor?"

"In a way," he said. "You see, things have changed since Maggie signed her last will. Last winter, Maggie's brother passed away. He had no living relatives. That triggered the residual clause in her will."

"Residual clause? I don't understand."

"It's simple really. Under the condition that her brother

pass before Maggie, a secondary plan goes into effect. It's called a residual clause. In this case, the clause states that Maggie has chosen you as sole beneficiary of her entire estate."

Six

The photograph is professional; both subjects serious. Her hand grips his shoulder, the fingers arched and digging into the fabric of his uniform. His eyebrows seem tight somehow, his smile carved in duty. I turn the photo over and read the date. June 15, 1941. Below this, Maggie has written in a younger version of her perfect handwriting, "Maggie and Albert Blackburn, Eastern Air Command." I look back at the photo, and realize that this wedding is overshadowed by the fear of an upcoming departure. Looking again at the bride and groom, I believe that her grip on his shoulder is not quite firm enough.

WATCHING MR. DOHERTY'S BRAKE LIGHTS disappear at the base of the driveway, it occurred to me that I had not heard or seen Gabby since watching her head out the sliding glass door. I checked my watch. Doherty's latest bit of news had changed everything about my carefully laid plans, and I needed time to digest it all.

I decided to find Gabby and head out for a hamburger.

She was not in the yard, so I walked the length of the drive around the garden, finally arriving at the tiny beach where Maggie kept her rowboat. I'd expected to find Gabby here, skipping rocks into the bay. Though the rowboat sat exactly where Maggie left it—wood rotting and paint peeling—my daughter was not to be found. I hiked back up the hill and walked north along the steep hill that marked the edge of the lawn.

Perhaps Gabby had found the path to the marina, and had gone down to look at the boats. At the crest of the hill, where a heavy carpet of blackberry vines and ivy fell away to the water, I shielded my eyes from the sun, and scanned the harbor. No sign of Gabby.

I felt my old fears ratchet up and told myself, quite firmly I might add, that she was probably fine. I called her name again and stopped to wait. In the distance I heard the whine of a skill saw floating toward me in the soft morning breeze, followed by the thunk of wood falling on wood. Considering Gabby's unending curiosity, I knew without question that she had chosen to investigate the sound.

I headed around the house and off to the side lawn where an old pathway led to the marina; but the path was gone, completely covered by the wild growth of vines. I called Gabby's name and went back out to the driveway and down the road to the marina. At the marina store, I stuck my head inside and called Gabby's name. The place seemed empty. I started toward the docks. I tried to reassure myself as I walked. She was probably fine. Nothing had happened to my intrepid daughter.

But no matter how I reassured myself, my steps quickened and my heart accelerated as if I were running a sprint.

At the top of the ramp, I called for her again, louder this time. Because there were so few boats in the harbor, I had no trouble seeing down the length of each finger dock leading away from the ramp. Gabby seemed to have completely disappeared. Where had she gone? Where had the sound come from?

I listened. When I heard the saw again, I jogged down the ramp, following the sound south toward the end of the harbor. There a short line of two-story houseboats lined the walkway. Each of these tiny floating homes sported some unique reflection of its owner. One had what looked to be a hundred-year-old arched door and a porch surrounded with antique glass floats, fishing nets and ship's wheels. Another house had been painted to reflect the bright colors and trim of the Victorian era. One had strings of glass beads hanging in place of a screen door. None of these houses seemed occupied.

Once again, I heard the saw, and in the quiet that followed, voices and the sound of a hammer. I walked along the houseboats until I came to a secondary dock and turned toward the voices. One of these was certainly Gabby's. I called her name.

"Over here, Mom." Air exploded from my chest. I did not know I'd been holding my breath.

The pier made yet another turn. Around this corner, I found Gabby standing beside a man in a flannel shirt, his back to me, bent over a long piece of wooden handrail. Sunlight glimmered from a skill saw—a portable electric, circular saw—resting on the dock. The smell of fresh cedar floated along on the breeze. The man with Gabby was cutting lengths of cedar railing.

I found myself torn between great relief and reasonable anger. "Gabby, what are you doing here? I told you to stay away from the water!" Gabby was about to get the lecture on stranger-danger twice before dinner, and twice more before bed.

"Sorry, Mom," she said, looking up a length of wood she was adding to a carefully laid stack. "I was just helping Cliff."

The man in flannel stood up, turning toward me in surprise. He lifted his safety glasses, squinting in the sunlight. Recognizing me, he smiled and gave a little wave. "You're Maggie's friend," he said, as I approached. "Cliff Lowry. I didn't realize that Gabby belonged to you." He shifted a hammer to his left hand, and offered me his right. "Good to see you again."

I shook reluctantly, still perturbed with Gabby. I tipped my head toward my daughter, saying, "I told her to stay near the house."

"She's no trouble. It's good to have company once in a while. You're over at the house, eh? Maggie's house?"

"Yes, just for a look-see." I hesitated, not sure how much I should tell this stranger. Today, Cliff Lowry looked very different than he had at Maggie's service. His flannel shirt was open at the collar, revealing a worn white T-shirt and a tuft of dark curly chest hair. He had on paint-stained work jeans, steel-toed boots, and a carpenter's belt. "You live here?"

"I manage the marina." He pointed toward the office building. "But yes, actually, I do live here."

"We're rebuilding the porch, Mom." Gabby pointed to the work in progress.

"This is your place?"

"I'm helping a friend," he said, smiling. "My place is over on the end. Things are pretty quiet here in the spring."

From the looks of the marina, I'd have said the place was deceased, not just quiet. But I kept my thoughts to myself. After all, small talk isn't my big strength. "Well, I guess we should be going." I reached out to place a protective arm around Gabby's shoulders.

"Ah, Mom. Let me stay and help Cliff. You have all that stuff you need to do over at Grandma Maggie's."

Great. Tell the guy everything, Gabby.

"Maggie was your mother?"

Did this guy have no manners? I glanced down at Gabby. "Yes," I said. "Well, sort of." I refused to launch into my family history for a stranger. I hardly understood it myself.

Cliff glanced toward me and then spoke directly to Gabby. "Don't tell me your mom is going to try and clean up that mess."

Gabby nodded, her smile widening. "Mom's the executor." She'd pronounced it like I was going to kill someone.

"You are?" He put both hands on his hips and threw his head back, laughing. His was a loud, full-throated, all-the-way-to-his-toes, bellowing guffaw. In spite of my irritation, part of me wanted to join in. "Oh boy, do you have your work cut out for you. That place? All that junk? I'd suggest you burn it down." He took off his baseball hat, and ran a single hand through his curly hair, still chuckling.

"Thanks for the suggestion," I said, frowning as I reached for Gabby's hand, dragging her toward me.

For a moment, he seemed surprised that I was leaving so abruptly. Then, he recognized his error. "Wait, I'm sorry," he said. "I shouldn't have said it that way."

I'd already started back toward our car. Cliff put down his hammer and stepped off the porch. "Really, I'm sorry."

"No, don't be. I'm not offended." Actually, I was steaming. Who was this guy to make those kinds of comments about Maggie's home? I picked up my pace, forcing Gabby to jog along beside me. "We really have to be on our way. We were just going to head out for some lunch."

"I'll walk you to your car," he said.

"No, really. Don't bother."

"Maybe I could take you out to lunch," he offered. "I could make up for being such an insensitive clod."

Like lunch could make up for mocking Maggie. "That's not necessary. Really. I understand."

Suddenly his hand reached out and took hold of my free arm, turning me to face him. I did not resist, though part of me wanted to slap the guy. Who did he think he was, this marina handyman? I heard myself heave an enormous sigh.

He held out both hands. "I want to explain. Please. I'm not saying anything about Maggie, really. It's just that the house is so, well"—he hesitated, shrugging, obviously at a loss for words—"eclectic."

His word choice made me laugh, in spite of myself. "You're saying I couldn't sell it if my life depended on it."

"The house? Maybe," he said. "But the junk inside? Honestly? No way." He looked up at the house, holding court above the marina. Gesturing toward the house, he said, still chuckling, "You'll have to dump everything inside. Gut the place. Especially the sailboat. But it's a great spot, up there on the hill over the bay. You won't have any trouble finding someone who wants to own that."

"Actually, I do," I said.

He looked stunned, confused. "I'm sorry, what?"

"I own it all." And with that, I dragged Gabby up the dock to the rental car.

❁

The condition of the will changed my plans yet again. A new thought, a crazy idea, a developing vision of a new life began to pester me somewhere in the back of my mind. Bothered by the appearance of these thoughts, I did what any red-blooded indecisive would do. I flew home to Florida. The house wouldn't go anywhere while I thought about it.

Four days after returning, with Gabby tucked happily into her own bed, I poured sweet tea over ice into tall glasses. "Mint?"

"No thanks," Eve answered, reaching for her glass. She sipped and then smiled. "Hmm, that's good. It was hot enough to boil water on the sidewalk today." I loved listening to Eve. Her deep Southern accent, rare in the population of Pensacola—the Navy brings in folks from all over the country— always charmed me. No matter what Eve said, it came off sounding sophisticated and lady-like.

"Let's sit inside the screen porch," I said, sliding open the glass door. Liz, our ever-faithful canine companion, slipped out ahead of me, immediately sprawling out on cool tile. "The temperature is finally dropping." I sat down, easing my chair to face the fireflies' evening dance. Satisfied, I put my feet on an ottoman.

Eve chose a bamboo club chair and sat, folding her long legs underneath her. "So, tell me all about your trip," she said. "You didn't call again after the attorney contacted you. I don't know what happened after that."

"The whole thing was a complete surprise, starting with Maggie. She'd been doing well, considering her age. But I guess a stroke is something you can't predict."

"At least you got to see her."

"Yes. Well, in a way. I don't know. She never did wake up." I put my glass down on the table between us, sighing. "At least she's at peace now. I know that. Thanks again for keeping Liz."

She smiled. "The kids loved it. Saves us from getting our own dog."

In the relative cool of a spring evening, we watched a group of sandhill cranes meander through the schoolyard beyond our chain-link fence. Stepping gingerly in the long, damp grass, they stopped only occasionally, posing on one leg. Then, using long cone-shaped bills, they foraged for insects.

We sipped our tea in the comfortable silence of friendship, Eve resting her head on the chair's back cushion, eyes closed. "So, Maggie left everything to you?"

"It looks that way."

"You met with her attorney, I mean after you saw him at the house?"

"Just before we flew home."

"What does that mean?"

"What does what mean?"

"You have to get rid of everything? Sell it all before you get anything out of the will?" She opened her eyes and looked directly at me. "Pardon my ingratitude, honey. But that seems like earning money to me. It's no gift, that's for darn sure." Eve had already endured long descriptions of the mess I'd found at Maggie's house.

"You'd have to spend weeks in Canada to get that done. No one needs a gift like that."

"Actually, when I became the sole benefactor, the job of executor went to her attorney."

"Attorneys do that?"

"Not very often, I don't think. But this guy was a friend of Maggie's, from way back. A guy from her church. I guess she trusted him."

"So, you're off the hook." She sipped her tea. "That was a close one. He'll empty the house, or pay to have someone do it, and you'll get all the money when it sells. How much do you think you'll net from the estate?"

Eve wasn't a gold digger, exactly. But she'd never endured any real hardship. Her parents put her through college. She married a Navy pilot right after graduation. As far as I knew, she'd never even planned a career.

She didn't understand the struggles I faced.

Though I loved Eve, her attitude irritated me. Perhaps it wasn't her exactly, but something else, something inside me. Perhaps it was the fact that an idea had begun to blossom in my heart, one that I had not yet dared to admit, even to myself.

I considered sharing my thoughts with Eve, wrestling with worry that she would say out loud what I myself feared. That it wouldn't work. That it was crazy. That this dream wandering around in the back of my mind was nuts.

"I don't know how much, exactly. Maggie wasn't rich. The house isn't worth anything really. The land is, though. From her house, you can see the whole harbor to the north. Looking south, you can see all the way into the inlet and across to Cowichan." I paused. "I brought pictures. You want to see?"

Eve ignored my offer. "It couldn't come at a better time. How long have you been fighting with the Navy over Timothy?"

"Since the day he died, actually."

"If I hadn't watched it myself, I wouldn't believe it." She shook her head, her blond bob falling into place like a shampoo commercial. "You know, those folks who want free government healthcare should keep this kind of stuff in mind. If the Navy can't even manage to keep track of one pilot's life insurance papers, surely we can't trust them to keep a nation's worth of medical records."

I'd heard this tirade before. In fact, I'd written it. None of the squadron wives could believe that Timothy's will had been lost—simply misplaced—though every one of us had gone through endless bureaucratic frustrations in the course of our husbands' military careers. Why the surprise?

"I'm doing fine without the life insurance," I said, though I was lying through my teeth. Every month I balanced my finances on the end of a pin, praying in utter desperation that the brakes on the van would last another ten thousand miles, and that Gabby's teeth would come in perfectly straight all on their own.

I didn't tell Eve the whole truth anymore. She'd grown tired of the truth, choosing instead to believe what she wanted, that I was fine. That we were fine. That everything would work out in the end.

In the years since Timothy died, I chose to keep my prayer life to myself. While I prayed for God to provide—groceries, a new mattress, insurance money—my friends prayed that I would meet someone new. Someone to replace Timothy. No matter how much I struggled, I couldn't stand any more sympathetic lectures about how "God would take care of everything," even from my closest friends.

"Fine or not, the Navy should pay the insurance to you. You're his wife, for heaven's sake. Gabby was born in a Navy hospital. You have the records to prove that. Why wouldn't the insurance go to you and to his daughter? Surely that's enough to prove the beneficiary records are out of date."

"I have an attorney working on it. By contesting the will, the payment has been effectively suspended."

"But three years?"

"I know," I said wearily. "A long time."

"Why don't Timothy's parents just take the money and give it to you?"

The million-dollar question.

At the beginning, right after Timothy's death, our regular mailman had delivered what seemed like hundreds of letters regarding the fight over benefits; at first, I filled a red expandable file with these legal records. Eventually the file overflowed into a cardboard box.

Then, whether out of grief or exhaustion, I don't know, I stopped opening the mail. If the United States Navy had something to tell me, I decided they'd better do it in person. I couldn't face another sheaf of legalese reminding me that everything I hoped for had vanished in the fiery crash of an F-18.

Eventually, I came to the conclusion that my husband had been wrong. The United States government would not take care of me in the case of a tragic accident. They didn't care what happened to Gabby or to me. In fact their only motive, it seemed, was to prove that the will they had on file—though it was ten years old, and neglected both the wife and child of a US Naval officer—was the only will ever signed and submitted by Captain Timothy Beauchamp.

It took me almost two years to make this momentous decision, as I am rather slow in coming to conclusions. After Timothy died, I realized that I do not tolerate change. And in those days, decisions no more significant than choosing a brand of margarine baffled me; on a bad day, I'd been known to bring home both regular and low fat, along with a pound of whipped butter. Only the size of my side-by-side keeps this indecisiveness in check.

But I digress.

I began delivering these letters instead to my lawyer, a skinny man who occupies an office behind the Dairy Dell on Magnolia. I chose him on the same day our daughter Maggie started morning kindergarten. Something about escorting her into her new classroom, her tiny hand clinging to mine as the tears rolled down her cheeks, made me realize how much she needed me to be fully present in her world.

"Not today, Mommy," she pleaded. "Please. I promise. I'll start school tomorrow."

I recognized myself in Gabby's words. Like my daughter, I'd been promising myself the same thing for two years. She hesitated out of fear. I had quit living because of grief.

Not today, I'd plead, staring at the woman in my bathroom mirror. Tomorrow. I'll start my life again tomorrow. But I hadn't; instead, I'd curled up on the living-room couch and waited for another envelope from the Department of the Navy.

Not long ago, I came to a startling realization. Actually, God showed me, as he is irritatingly faithful to do. The truth was that I didn't really want Timothy's life insurance benefits. Instead, I hoped that one of these official tomes would correct the notification of death I'd gotten from the squadron commander and his handy sidekick, the chaplain.

'Sorry,' this new letter would explain. 'Our mistake. Your husband isn't dead, just misplaced. We found him in a squadron in western Turkey. We'll be sending him home tomorrow.'

On Maggie's first day of kindergarten, I finally realized the letter I hoped for would never come. I stopped waiting for it. And I stopped opening the other letters. I stopped caring what form, what signature, what documentation they needed for their records. Instead I let Simon Briggs of Green, Meredith and Briggs, Inc. worry about the United States Navy.

And I chose to live again. Well, sort of.

"Anyway, with the funds from the estate, you'll have a cushion," Eve went on. "You might even be able to quit your job. That's what you've wanted all along, isn't it? That's what Timothy wanted. Right?"

I nodded, and half-listened as Eve went on about another of the squadron wives who had finished a degree only to decide she really wanted to stay at home.

Truthfully, I wasn't sure what I wanted. Gabby and I rarely went out any more, at least not with other people. Sometime toward the end of the year that Timothy died, I began shunning the few real friends I'd made in Pensacola—though I would never have admitted it. The funny thing about hiding from people is that—unlike a good game of hide and seek—the people you hide from eventually stop looking for you.

In hindsight, this surprised me. Because of Timothy's death, I realize that the ones who hide are the ones who most need finding.

Shouldn't real friends understand this?

At the time, I was relieved. Immediately after Timothy died, the consolation of other squadron wives felt right, comforting. I soaked it up, like a roll of paper towels tossed in a swimming pool. But as time passed, their words felt empty. It seemed that they had begun to want something from me. Something I could not manage.

It was as if my allotted grieving time had run out; they wanted me to re-enter real life. For me, this was impossible. Timothy's death had banned me from the only life I knew. I was no longer a military wife. No longer the wife of a pilot. The parties and social schedules, gossip and news shared exclusively among military officers' families now excluded me.

And somehow, their hollow kindnesses told me they wanted me to get on with my life. I believed that behind it all, they wanted to get on with theirs. It was as if they wanted me to be well, so that they could set me adrift on the sea of humanity, while they cruised off on the good ship *Pilot Wives*.

It didn't matter, really, that they left me behind. It took all my energy to care for Gabby, who was too young to realize what all the fuss was about. Until this day, this evening with Eve, I had not yet discovered the energy to forge a life of my own.

I lived in Pensacola, not because I'd chosen to live there. It was just the last place I'd shared with Timothy. Part of me felt like a purse left behind at a restaurant. Waiting. Waiting for something to happen. For someone to come and claim me.

Waiting to go home again.

Seven

O_N THE FOLLOWING S_{ATURDAY}, my experience with God's voice, with Liz and the back of our van, came full circle.

Late in the morning, after I'd finished the laundry and managed to clean both bathrooms, I opened the refrigerator and poured myself a glass of sweet tea. Though I'd never fully adopted a Southern identity, I could drink sweet tea, wear a full-brimmed straw hat, and fry chicken with the best of my native counterparts. It didn't matter that I didn't really belong. I'd been left here, transplanted from the far North and plopped down in Florida to fend for myself. Though I didn't blame Timothy, I couldn't quite forgive him for leaving me here either, a stranger in a strange land.

I'd promised Gabby that we would head to the mall in search of new tennis shoes, which she seems to destroy with the reliability of a smart bomb. In the past four months, Gabby had grown into quite the bicycle enthusiast. However, she never learned to use the coaster brakes on her bike. Instead, Maggie stops her tiny bike by dragging the toes of her tennis shoes behind her. Even her patent-leather dress shoes were scraped beyond recognition. I'd given up trying to stop this annoying habit, deciding instead to include new shoes in my quarterly budget.

Though I had faith she would learn to use coaster brakes, the cost of shoes was disconcerting. I called Gabby from the screen porch. "Honey, you need to come in now. Time for Josiah and James to head home."

The children groaned on cue, and Josiah, a chubby seven-year-old, took one last trip down the slide. Landing on his well-padded behind, he struggled to stand, brushing off his pants. "See ya, Gabby," he said, waving as he trudged across our yard.

James continued to pump, pushing his swing higher and higher into the air. "James," I warned, my voice in threat mode.

"I'm coming!" He let go of the swing and at the same time gave a mighty heave. His body, as athletic as his brother's was plump, scribed a perfect arc as he flew from the swing seat and landed upright in the bark. I shook my head and closed the screen door. That boy's mother should have to sign a release before he enters our yard.

In the kitchen, I set out a glass of juice and stood at the sink, cutting an apple for Gabby. As she opened the door and stepped inside, I spoke without looking up. "Wash your hands."

Obediently, she padded across the family room, the patter of Liz's paws following her every move, and turned on the water in the powder bathroom. By the time she came back to the kitchen, I had the apple waiting.

We finished our snacks, put Liz in her crate and headed out. Without too much trouble, at a shopping mall not far from our home, Gabby and I bought pink tennis shoes and a pair of black patent Mary-Janes. Though I went through the motions, I was distracted, and couldn't quite get my mind to stay with her in the present. Part of me kept going back to the house at Genoa Bay.

I was still thinking about the inheritance, and the choices I faced, when I ordered Gabby's lunch at the food court inside the mall. Every thought of the estate brought back fresh memories of Maggie, and of all the kindnesses I'd experienced in that big old house. How was a person supposed to sell their past to strangers?

I picked up straws and envelopes from the condiment bar, joining Gabby at a tiny table beneath a plastic palm tree. "Mom, aren't you eating?"

"Not hungry," I assured her, seeing no reason to explain penny pinching to a child. She'd suffered enough.

"You forgot napkins," my daughter complained.

Without a word, I went over to the nearest restaurant bar and returned with an envelope of pickle relish, setting it beside her plate. Gabby wrinkled her nose in disgust, her skin creasing into tiny pink lines over heavily freckled cheeks. "Mom, I said 'napkins'," she protested.

With a shake of her head, she sighed, put down her hot dog, and wiped her lips with the back of her pudgy hand. Giving me an *I don't know what I'm going to do with you* look, she slipped off her chair, saying, "I'll just have to do it myself."

Gabby, though still a child, often loses her patience with me. Somehow, she has managed to compress decades of wisdom into her first seven years. Frankly, I have worried more than a little about how this relationship between us would play out over the years. At seven, she already had her father's even temper, his practicality and his simple, non-emotional approach to problems.

Her chiding brought me out of my daydream, and I watched her start off across the food court toward the condiment bar, where she stood on her tiptoes and removed several napkins from the dispenser.

In the years since Timothy left us, she has often comforted me in my grief, suggested solutions to common problems and reminded me of items I'd forgotten—exactly like the napkins in the food court. Somehow, in those short years, my seven-year-old had her life under better control than I ever would. Before she returned to our table, I'd torn open the pouch of pickle relish and eaten the contents.

Part of me felt a little angry. Life shouldn't work out this way. No seven-year-old should be more practical than her mother. For that matter, no little girl should have to grow up without her daddy.

This, I knew from experience.

And these days, no matter where I was, my mind was still in Genoa Bay. Though work went on as usual, and Gabby demanded my attention, I couldn't focus. Every time I closed my eyes, I saw the old house on the hill over the bay.

Just then, my cell phone rang. Absently, and still thinking about the house and its contents, I flipped open the phone and answered.

"Hello, Mrs. Beauchamp. This is Walter Doherty." I pictured the gentlemanly lawyer, as I'd first met him on Maggie's porch. It surprised me to hear from him on a Saturday morning. "Yes, of course. How are you?"

"I'm fine, Mrs. Beauchamp."

"Please, call me Brandy."

"I'm fine, Brandy. I called this morning, as I said I would. Have you been thinking about the things we discussed?"

If he only knew. I'd gone back and forth, over and over. Sell or… "Of course, Mr. Doherty."

"And have you come to a decision?"

I glanced over at my daughter, happily eating her hot dog. "Mr. Doherty, I've thought of almost nothing else. I just don't know what to do about it all."

"I realize that the estate is a surprise to you. I understand your shock. And of course, there is the grief of losing Maggie. We all feel that. However, I think we should move forward rather quickly. If you want to sell, and I think that is your best decision, it would be foolish not to do so during the summer. Houses don't sell here after Labor Day. The weather and the rain—well, no one wants to think of living on the coast in the winter. It can be quite miserable."

"I understand."

"I think the house would sell best as a second home, or perhaps to an investor, or a developer might be interested. To that end, it would fetch the best price now, during the early summer season. If I list it quickly, an investor would have an opportunity to begin the permitting process before the weather deteriorates."

"And you need my decision soon."

"Immediately, if you want to sell before summer's end. Of course there are taxes due. Maggie put property taxes on hold. And insurance. And there is the liability," he paused and sighed. "A house left empty is asking for trouble. If something untoward happened on the property, you, as the owner would be liable. The economy has slowed down lately. And the housing market isn't doing as well as it might. I just don't think you can afford to wait on this."

Gabby, distracted by a baby in a nearby high chair, put her hot dog down on the napkin. I pointed to it, urging her to finish. "I'm sorry, Mr. Doherty. I've been trying to figure this out. I just can't give you an answer right now."

❈

Gabby and I planned to head back to our car via the south footbridge on the fourth level of the mall. Using the center escalator, we headed up, level by level, toward the fourth floor. Just as we were about to step on to the third-floor escalator, I glimpsed the bright blond of Eve's hair, turning into Mango, one of our old favorite dress stores.

Remembering the fun we'd shared in that store, I decided to catch Eve and say hello.

"Honey, wait," I said, tugging Gabby's hand as I backed away from the steps. "I think I just saw Eve. Want to go see what she's up to?" I pointed toward the store.

Gabby shrugged. "Guess so."

We crossed the mall quickly, dodging customers as we headed for the store entrance. I stepped inside, scanning the racks. Eve is never difficult to find. Her hair is platinum, and her height commands attention in every venue. "I don't see her," I said, surprised at my own disappointment.

"There she is," Gabby pointed toward the back of the store. "At the cash lady."

"You're right," I said. "Good eyes."

We trudged through the elegant store, dragging our bags past a security guard, through a section of overflowing sales racks, and around white couches where several husbands waited. Eve turned toward us just as we reached the cash register. In one hand, she held a long dress bag. Seeing us, she looked startled. "Oh, Brandy," she glanced around the store. "I'm so surprised to see you here."

"I saw you from the escalator. We just came to say hi."

"Oh, sure. Hi." She folded the dress bag, tossing it over her forearm like a waiter with a kitchen towel.

"So, what'd you buy?"

"Just a dress." She frowned, as if to convince me it was a gardening apron.

"Just a dress?" I laughed. "From here?"

Gabby tugged on my sleeve. "Can I look at the shoes?" A display of evening shoes sparkled on mirrored shelves behind us. My daughter had clearly inherited my appreciation for all shoe-related things.

I nodded. "Don't touch, though."

I turned back to my friend. Something about her seemed off. Impatient. Perturbed. I couldn't understand it, not from Eve. "So, show me," I encouraged her. In all the years we'd been friends, Eve had never missed an opportunity to share a find. Part of me envied the way she could wear all the latest fashions, or for that matter, any fashion. Eve took full advantage of it. Nothing pleased Eve more than beautiful fabric, or a striking design.

Of course, she would look stunning in a grocery bag. But her perfect taste in clothes flawlessly complemented her nearly perfect body. If anything would soften her up, surely sharing her latest purchase would simmer her pot.

Instead of opening up, she shrugged. "Really, it's nothing."

"Eve O'Reilly, don't you blow me off," I said, becoming more than a little perturbed myself. "I don't know what's going on here. But you don't have to hide a new purchase from me. I love that you look great in beautiful clothes."

Her eyes softened, and she caught her breath. "It's not that. No. It's not that I think you're jealous." She rolled her eyes, and muttered an expletive. "Oh, alright. Here you are." She unzipped the garment bag and pulled the plastic back.

A brilliant turquoise evening gown, of what I guessed was silk chiffon, hung from a padded hanger. A delicately beaded bodice ended in a high halter. Below this, soft chiffon fell to the floor in a perfect gather. It was, perhaps, the most beautiful gown I'd ever seen in person. "Oh my goodness, Eve. It's beautiful." I reached up to touch the beaded fabric. "It must look stunning on you."

"I do like it." She smiled, caressing the silk.

"What's the event?"

Misery crossed Eve's features, and in that instant I knew—though she said nothing—that this was the question she had hoped to avoid. "The Anniversary Ball," she whispered. "Matt and I are chairing the fundraising committee."

I knew Eve well enough to know that it pained her to admit this much. With these words, Eve had broken her own cardinal rule, established on the day I was notified about Timothy's death. Never, under any circumstances, would Eve ever again mention the events happening at Naval Air Station Pensacola. For the most part, she'd managed to keep her self-imposed rule.

This event, in particular, must have required extraordinary restraint. In the years since Timothy and I moved to Pensacola, the Anniversary Ball had been the One Big Event we'd all looked forward to as couples. Over the years, Eve and I had schemed and saved, scouring magazines and stores in search of the Perfect Gown for the perfect charity event. We'd changed our hairstyles, searched for shoes, even gone to thrift shops to find the necessary accessories. Of course, our husbands laughed at us.

Why not? How hard is it to dress a Navy pilot in formal wear? We took their dress whites to the cleaners.

"Oh Brandy, I'm sorry," she said, scooping me into her arms for a long hug. "I never meant to keep a secret," she whispered. "It's just that I didn't want to hurt you. I didn't want you to miss Timothy."

"I understand," I said, patting her back. In Eve's mind, all airbase news would only remind me of Timothy's death. And thoughts of Timothy would make me sad. And Eve wanted, more than anything, to keep me from being sad. "Don't think another thing about it," I said. "I wish you'd just accept that I want to know about your life. Don't hide it anymore, please?"

She stepped away from me, nodding, and I noticed that her eyes were moist. Her perfect eyeliner was not so perfect anymore. No matter how much I tried to explain, Eve didn't believe me. I needed the contact, the reminders of the life I'd once enjoyed. I didn't want her protection, just her love.

And, Eve—who had never experienced grief—would never understand that when Timothy died, sorrow had moved in to stay.

❀

Somehow, Eve and I managed to squirm our way through the next few moments. I tried desperately to convince her that I wanted to be part of her life. "Really, Eve. It doesn't hurt that you all keep on living. The base doesn't close, just because Timothy's plane went down. I know that. I understand," I said. We hugged, shared another awkward goodbye, and I led Gabby up the escalator to our car.

In the parking lot, I put my parking ticket into the machine and the giant restraining arm lifted, allowing us to exit. As we pulled out of the garage, Gabby asked, "Mommy, can we have ice-cream?"

"Why not?" I said, changing lanes to head for the nearest drive-through. I might not be Bill Gates, or Donald Trump, but I could afford ice-cream. At the order window, I asked for two medium chocolate-dipped cones.

When I handed one to Gabby, her eyes betrayed her utter surprise. Only then did I realize what I'd done. Gabby would never finish the treat—not in a million years.

I turned back toward the drive-up window. "Could we have a paper bag?" Thinking again of Gabby, and the morning heat, I said to the teenager behind the glass, "Make that two."

The teen looked perplexed.

"To stash the leftovers."

She smiled and handed me two paper bags, one already tucked inside the other. Living in Florida requires that ice-cream be eaten with the speed of a hungry lion facing fresh kill. With my own tower of goodness dripping onto my lap, I pulled forward and eased out of the parking lot. Traffic was thick now, and with Gabby fully occupied, I found my mind going over and over my interaction with Eve.

Why did our conversation bother me so much? In the three years I'd been a widow, I'd always encouraged Eve to tell me the latest news, of pregnancies, promotions, social events, and gossip. Something in her resisted. No matter how hard I tried, she kept all news of life on the base out of our exchanges. The logical part of my brain realized that the lives of our friends would continue uninterrupted. And, after all, I wanted them to move on, didn't I? Or did I?

Did part of me want everyone else's life to stop, just because I'd lost Timothy?

If not, why did I have this strange pain in my heart? Why did it hurt to hear about something as simple as a stunning evening gown and a fundraising committee?

I've discovered, in the course of my life, that these moments, these surprising moments of pain, usually hide some deeper secret, some meaningful moment of self-recognition. On my own, I rarely distinguish truth from the discomfort. But when I invite God into the mess, I sometimes find the answer. Just as I began to talk to him about it, Gabby dumped the last half of her ice-cream cone onto the carpet.

"Mom," she wailed, "I dropped it!" Children seem compelled to state the obvious.

"I know, honey. We're almost home."

"But I wanted it."

I looked down at the carpet, where the cone—following all of Murphy's Laws—had landed face down in Liz's dog hair. In thirty seconds, it had already begun to melt into a puddle of white. "No, sweetie. That one's a gonner."

She began to cry. "But I wanted it!" I looked over at her beautiful face, tears rolling down pink cheeks onto lakes of melted ice-cream. Her clothes had fared no better. The cone had bounced off her jeans before hitting the floor, leaving a large wet stain on her lap. Her hands were covered with chocolate. I needed more than carpet cleaner for this mess; I needed a garden hose.

We were only a few blocks from home. "You can finish mine," I said, flipping on the blinker, and managing a one-handed turn onto our street. Out of the busier traffic, I slowed down to hand Gabby my ice-cream cone. Just as I did, I saw something I'd never seen before.

There on the side of the road, just off the sidewalk, stood a sign, blaring at me as if it were written in neon lights. The sign said, "Dead End."

Dead End.

I pulled onto the shoulder and put the car in park. Dead End. The words rang in my head. The truth stuck in my heart the way play-dough sticks to the table of my dining-room. Since Timothy's death, my life had begun to resemble the street we lived on, so much so, that I could no longer separate the two. Dead End.

I had buried my husband, emptied his closet, given away his uniforms. Though I'd put Gabby in school, and gotten a job, I had managed to stay in the same house, drive the same car, hang with the same friends, shop at the same stores. While I continued to raise Gabby, I existed, I moved, I took up space. But I wasn't really going anywhere. I was stuck between life and death—I had chosen to camp in a place squarely between Timothy's death and my own life.

Though I went through the motions of life, I lived in a dead end. Grief Island.

My friends had moved on without me. They were having children, sharing challenges, contributing to the world around them.

And in that moment, I remembered Liz. When our dog had

refused to climb into the back of the car, God had implied that I was just like the dog. I hadn't understood it then; but now I did.

Like Liz, I just kept circling the tailgate, wanting to jump in, take the leap, see what life had for me, but at the same time hesitant to leave what I knew and understood. Something—was it fear, or grief, or some other, unknown force?—kept me circling, indecisive, uncertain.

While I circled, unwilling to let go of my past, I forfeited my present.

I knew in that instant. It was time to make a decision. God had prepared me for this moment, for this question, for this decision. Until the day in the park, I'd felt as though his was a silent, callous response. After all, I was caught in grief. Why didn't he fix me? Why didn't he help me move on? Instead, he'd spoken to me through a stubborn dog fighting with the tailgate of our van. And though most people would see the whole progression as nothing more than coincidence mixed with my own vivid imagination, I knew then exactly what God wanted me to do.

Jump!

Eight

I hold a square cardboard box, flocked in navy blue, small enough to hold a necklace. Removing the lid, I discover inside a silver cross nesting on a cotton mattress. The cross is small, and hangs by a blue ribbon from a bar pin about one inch wide. In the center is the image of a knight on a galloping horse. Around the image are the words, "For Gallantry." On the other side I find a number engraved, and the name, Albert C. Blackburn, 30 November, 1943.

THIS TIME, WHEN I OPENED the door to the old home at Genoa Bay, I was geared up for what lay ahead. Ready to take on the world. Prepared. I took a deep breath and unlocked the kitchen door. Knowing what I was up against had not stilled the anxiety I felt in showing the place to Eve.

"So this is it," she said, coming in the door behind me. "This is what you gave up your life in Florida to pursue."

"Yup," I said. "This is it. Have mercy on me, okay?"

I whistled for Liz, who trotted in behind Eve, and closed the door. "Wait," I said, catching Eve as she started toward the rest of the house. "I'll brighten things up." I hurried into the foyer to catch the lights, then crossed the great room to the draperies and opened them one after another, letting the fading afternoon light into the room. In the distance, Cowichan harbor had already turned raspberry, the color of the sunset reflecting off a faint chop.

Eve moved toward the dining-room window. "I can see why you left Gabby with Timothy's parents," she said, running her index finger over the old antique table. Even in the poor light, her fingers clearly left a trench in the deep dust. She turned toward the windows, sighing. "Well, the view is beautiful, in spite of the house."

For a moment, she stood taking in the harbor, the docks, the boats and the boathouses. She turned back toward the room. I watched as her eyes moved from the stuffed owl on the end table, to the elk head hanging over the square piano. Wrinkling her perfectly patrician nose, my friend made no attempt to cover her disgust. "It's going to take the rest of your life, and an other-worldly fortune to make this livable."

"I hope not. I didn't make that much off the house." In fact, so eager was I to follow God's lead, I'd sold our Pensacola home to the first buyer who made an offer. Adding my savings from the death benefit to the profit from the house, I had a small cushion, actually a very thin cushion, to make my plan work.

"You should have rented the house—not sold it. At least that way you'd have a way out of this mess. When you told me how bad the place looked, I had no idea."

Like I hadn't heard this already. "I don't want a way out," I said. "Really. I've figured out the expenses, I've looked at my funds. I've planned it out. I think I can do this."

Eve's expression betrayed her doubt. Shrugging, she turned toward the fireplace. "What on earth are you going to do with an orange couch?"

"I was thinking of burning it."

"The only logical choice," she said. "What are these?" Somehow, in the shadows, we'd both missed the boxes stacked against the entry walls.

Together, we leaned down to read the labels. "Must be the stuff from Maggie's apartment. I asked Mr. Doherty to have it delivered."

"Oh good," she said. "As if you don't have enough stuff to sort through."

I guess the heat and exhaustion of driving a u-haul across the country and into Canada finally came to a boil. I just couldn't take another one of Eve's sarcastic remarks about the stupidity of my decision. I took a deep breath. "I know you think I'm making a mistake. You've told me, one way or another, every ten miles since we left the Pensacola city limits." I took a rare stab at expressing my real feelings. "But don't you think you can let it go now? This is what I'm supposed to do. I'm sure of it. I'm not going to change my mind now. And I need your support. Can't you give me that much?"

She sighed, blowing blond bangs out of her eyes. Putting one hand on her hip, she said, "Okay, okay. I'll try. I'm just worried, you know? I feel responsible to Timothy. How on earth can you make this place into a Bed and Breakfast? It's a mess. It's at the end of the world. Gabby is right. It looks like a haunted house. Fixing it up is going to kill you, especially if you do it all by yourself. And who can raise a child in a place like this?"

If this was Eve's idea of support, I had real trouble on my hands. "Please, Eve. We've been through this so many times. I know how you feel about it all. Really I do. But somehow, I know that this is where I'm supposed to be. This is what I'm supposed to do. It's time for me to take up my own place in the universe. To really live." I took my friend into my arms, hugging her shoulders with a strength I didn't truly feel. "You want that for me, don't you? To live. To really and truly live?"

When I let go of her, and stepped back, I saw Eve's eyes were full of tears. "Of course I do. I just want you to do it closer to home, that's all," she said. "And Gabby too. I don't know if I can let both of you walk out of my life."

"Florida is your home, Eve. Your family is there. It never was mine. And besides, we aren't walking out. When you love someone like we do, when we've meant as much to each other as we have, moving won't just carve us out of your heart," I said. "Not anymore than death took Timothy out of mine."

She brushed away a tear. "Okay, so what do we do first? Empty the truck or burn down the house?"

I stared.

"Just kidding," she said. "How about we try to find someplace clean enough to sleep? I'm bushed."

❀

Ten days later, I watched as Eve entered the airport security line. True to her promise, she'd managed to help me clean the downstairs apartment, unload our possessions and make space in the kitchen without another disparaging word. I had to give it to her. Eve worked hard. She swept and wiped and scrubbed until the fair skin on her beautiful hands dried to sandpaper.

As I watched her move forward in line, I remembered finding her, just the day before, touring the upstairs rooms. "What are you doing up here?" I asked, catching her in the suite facing the marina.

"Imagining the decorations."

"What do you see?"

"Something soft. Clean. Filmy."

"Taupe?"

"And vanilla crème. Silk dupioni for the bed-skirts."

"I am going to miss you," I'd said, draping an arm around her waist. And I meant it. If Eve lived closer, she'd be covered in paint and sawdust, doing everything possible to make the business a success. Eve loves a challenge, and at that moment, with my arm around my friend, I wondered if part of her were just a bit jealous. I think she, like the dragon slayer she was, might have wanted to take on the project herself.

She waved at me as she approached the security agent, holding her boarding pass toward him for inspection. As he looked it over, she dropped her carry-on and blew me a kiss. "Don't forget," she called over the crowd. "You can always change your mind. I'll come and get you!"

I shook my head, laughing as she slipped off her shoes and went through the metal detector. My last glimpse of her came as she turned the corner and headed toward her gate.

I had no more than put my key in the ignition when it occurred to me for the first time since Timothy's death, just how alone I was. What did I know about building my own business? Making beds in a Bed and Breakfast hardly constitutes expertise. The whole thing had been Maggie's idea, her dream. Could I ever really make it my own?

Feeling the heavy responsibility of my decision, and the utter absence of visible support, doubt crept into the car and set up housekeeping in my heart. I cried all the way back to Duncan. In an effort to distract myself, I called Eve's husband, assuring him that she'd gotten on the plane without incident.

From the house, I called Gabby. "So, how're things in Tennessee?"

"I rode a horse today," she said. The joy in her voice made me smile.

"Did Grandpa ride with you?"

"And Uncle Todd."

"Where did you go?"

"We went for a picnic. Grandma made peanut-butter-and-jelly sandwiches for everybody. And ginger snips."

"Snaps. You mean ginger snaps." I don't bake much for my daughter. *Oh shoot,* I thought, *don't people who run inns have to learn to bake?*

"No. Grandpa called them snips." Without a breath she continued. "I miss you, Mom. How long till I come back? I miss swim team."

If stubbornness were an Olympic Sport, I had a gold medal winner on my hands. Surely this trait came straight from her father. "Gabby, you know that you're coming to Canada. In ten days, you're going to fly all the way to Vancouver. And when you get here, I'll be waiting for you."

The silence on the other end of the telephone lasted far too long. "Gabby, are you still there? Can you hear me?"

"I'll go get Grandma."

Speaking to Timothy's mother always makes me anxious. So, for the next five minutes or so, I chewed my fingernails while she complained about the foolishness of our moving so far away. "Why, Canada is in another country," she said, in her Tennessee drawl.

As if I had missed that detail.

I pulled out my index finger and bit my tongue. Literally. "It's not like we've moved to the Horn of Africa, Mom."

"If you must do something this adventurous, why can't you do it closer to home?"

"You mean closer to your home."

"I mean you don't have to take Gabby so far away from us. With her daddy gone, she needs us."

"You can visit. I'll have lots of room."

"You don't have to retaliate, Brandy. It isn't our fault that

Timothy wanted us to have his life insurance money. We didn't ask for it."

"I know you didn't," I said, offering this small concession. Of course Timothy didn't want his parents to have his money. I knew, because he told me when he did it. Timothy had filed papers to correct that decision immediately after Gabby's birth. Those papers, filed in Hawaii, had somehow disappeared. Strangely enough, Timothy's parents didn't really want the money either. They didn't need it. Timothy's family was made of money. "It's a mistake. The government's mistake," I said, for the fiftieth time.

Just as my resentment threatened to boil over, Doreen said, "You and Gabby would be so happy here on the ranch. Gabby is happy here now. We've lost Timothy forever. Why can't you give us that much?"

Every conversation with Doreen eventually came back to this: If I would stop the legal action against Timothy's will, Timothy's parents would transfer the money directly to us. All of it. The problem was that the life insurance money would come to me with a price: That Gabby and I move to Tennessee to live with them.

I'd been promised nearly everything, our own house—on the property, of course. Private schools for Gabby. Household help. Horses for Gabby. They would see to everything, they assured me. I would never have another worry again. It had been tempting, especially when the drifting tide of grief had threatened to wash me out to sea. But I'd come to my senses, unwilling to trade my emotional independence for financial freedom. Maybe it was the wrong decision, but it was the one I'd made. The one I stuck with.

I changed the subject. "Eve and I got quite a bit done on the house. We finished cleaning the kitchen and most of the apartment. The house is really beautiful. I think she'll love it."

"You don't have to move to Canada. Haven't Chuck and I been hurt enough?" Even a Southern accent didn't cover the snarky tone in my mother-in-law's voice.

"I'm not moving to hurt you, Doreen. This move isn't about money. It's about me. About my life. I have to make a clean start. Timothy is gone. Moving to Tennessee won't bring him back."

"Running won't make it hurt any less, my dear."

Sometimes, even Doreen made sense.

Hanging up, I decided that I needed a project, a big one, to shake the doubt demon that seemed so firmly attached to my right shoulder. I wandered down to the old basement apartment and looked around. Eve and I had cleaned Maggie's room, putting fresh sheets on her old antique double bed. I'd given this comfortable old bed to Eve, while I occupied the pull-out couch in the sitting-room. She'd stripped the sheets before she left, piling the pillows and blankets on the center of the bed.

Though we'd cleaned the galley kitchen downstairs, we hadn't even begun to attack the spare bedroom, nor had we even opened Maggie's office. The spare bedroom, which faced east, was filled with boxes, completely covering the floor and stacked over both twin beds. It was so filled with junk that I could not even fully open the door.

That room had been mine, when I first came to live with Maggie. And I remember being so taken by the view, on my first night there, that I hated to go to bed. Instead, I'd pulled a swivel rocker to the window and watched the harbor until I lost consciousness under an old quilt, exhausted by a long and bewildering day.

On my first night in the old house, I think I was afraid that sleeping would prove my marvelous luck was not luck at all. Part of me worried that by sleeping, I would wake in my bunk on board the ill-fated vessel *Odyssea*, headed to certain doom on the Pacific.

Part of me wanted to relive the day, thinking about the crazy lady who had chosen to hire me as summer help, giving me room and board, without knowing a single fully true thing about me. The cynical part of me wondered about her sanity. Had I jumped from the proverbial frying pan into the fire?

I remember sitting in that chair, thinking about Maggie as she stomped down the docks to confront Captain Cherring. I'd run to keep up, wanting to hear every word, yet afraid of what they might say. I couldn't forget his face, red, blustering, but never quite able to catch up with Maggie's rapid-fire accusations and threats. She had half a mind, she told him, to call the Mounties.

By the time she finished, Cherring was more than happy

to leave me in her capable hands and sail away short one slightly underage crewmember.

I shook my head, remembering. My daughter would love the room as much as I had—though perhaps not for the same reasons.

Looking in, I considered attacking the mess and getting it ready for Gabby. It would take days of sorting, cleaning, and painting—days, I realized, that would slow my progress in turning the house into a business. I had so much to do in the next year, the garden, the guestrooms, some remodeling in the kitchen and dining area.

And as I stood there thinking, it occurred to me that the room faced east. Intense summer sun would shine into that particular window, beginning at dawn every day. Not a problem in winter. But in the summer, that same sunshine—even peering around blackout shades—would wake my high-energy daughter at about 3 a.m.

I might not be the world's best mother, but I was smarter than that.

The apartment had only one other room, the one Maggie used as her office. Built into the hill, the office had only one window, a long narrow frame placed high on the north wall. Covered with stained glass, the light through this window was muted, softened by the glass's blues and grays. Without the stimulation of a brilliant dawn, this room better suited Gabby.

I tried the office door, which was locked, and then remembered that when Maggie moved to Brentwood Gardens, she had insisted on installing a deadbolt. I think Maggie always secretly believed she would return to live in the old house. That her trip to the independent living apartment was only temporary—a small blip in her life as an innkeeper. She told me quite clearly, "Even the neighbors can't be trusted. They'll ransack my personal papers. I don't want them starting up a business as competitors."

I ran upstairs for the key, my mind whirling with a startling realization. Why hadn't I thought of this before? When I lived with her, Maggie kept all of her business records inside this room. All of her contacts, her guest records, her suppliers, receipts, all of it—even her favorite recipes—would be inside. How many times had I come into this room to say goodnight, only to find Maggie poring over the latest collection of cooking magazines discarded from the city library?

If everything were still there, then at least some of the very help I desperately needed would be right here. Right here in the old house. Smiling, I unlocked the door. These treasures would change everything. It would be almost as if Maggie were here to give me advice. Old Maggie, still my mentor.

I found the office as I remembered it. An antique dust-covered oak desk, so large that I had to wonder how it had been moved through the doorway, sat squarely in the center of the room. Behind it stood a matching banker's chair, a metal four-drawer file and a library table—heavily scarred. Against the other wall, a mahogany bookshelf overflowed with books two volumes deep. On top of the bookshelf, stacks of papers and pamphlets still stood, and yes, there it was! On top of it all was Maggie's favorite oak recipe box, its cover held slightly open by the warp of water-damaged wood.

In this room, even after all these years, I detected the faint, but clearly unmistakable scent of Maggie, not of perfume really, but of soap and hand lotion. Even with dangling cobwebs and thick dust, Maggie filled the room.

The sense of her, her nearly palpable presence, wiped away every thought of Gabby. Intent on looking through her file drawers, I was anxious to see how much help Maggie had actually left behind. I moved to the desk, pulling out the oak chair. It did not move. I stepped around to investigate.

At my feet, I discovered a large dress box, roughly two feet by three feet, made of heavy gold cardboard. In the upper left corner, I recognized in black script, the logo for one of Maggie's favorite Victoria stores.

Perplexed, I lifted the box onto the desk, brushing dust off of its surface and wiping my hands on my jeans. I'd been with Maggie just before she closed the house, visiting one last time before she'd moved to Brentwood Gardens. When we locked this room, this box had not been here. I was quite sure of that.

Where had it come from? Who left it here for me?

I reached out and switched on Maggie's desk lamp. Leaning down, I examined the surface of the box. There, in the center, I found written in Maggie's elderly cursive the words, "For Brandy."

My hands shook slightly as I opened the box. It felt surreal, and at the same time exciting, to find this box, especially after making the decision to move, to re-open Maggie's house, to make a go of the old inn. Did she know or did she simply suspect that I might try? If she meant for me to find the box, why had it been left here? Why hadn't she given the box to her attorney, perhaps with an explanation or a personal note?

I had no more than removed the cover when the smells of mildewed paper, photographic chemicals and dust wafted up to greet me. The box was filled haphazardly with yellowed newspaper clippings, photographs—some of them portraits, some snapshots, a few recognizable as old Polaroids—as well as handwritten notes, and postcards. A few stained envelopes appeared to hold letters. A sheaf of faded pink envelopes, all exactly the same shape, had been bundled together in slim satin ribbon. This indeed was a discovery worthy of my attention.

I sat down behind the desk to read.

Nine

ON A BEAUTIFUL AFTERNOON in late June, I met Gabby at the Vancouver Airport. She ran to me, squealing, and jumped into my arms with the enthusiasm of a soldier returning from war. The airline attendant escorting her laughed. "You must be the mom," she said, still smiling. "Goodbye, Gabby."

"So, how was the flight, monkey girl?"

"Boring," Gabby said, squeezing my neck until bright spots began to dazzle my vision. Unwilling to disengage herself, she resisted as I tried to put her down. I shifted her body onto my hip. "Can we have something to eat?"

"Good idea. The next ferry isn't for a while, anyway."

By the time we crossed the straits and drove north toward the house, Gabby's tale of horses and picnics, of pond adventures and ATVs had wound down. With one hand absently scratching an adoring Liz, who had wedged herself in the space between our seats, Gabby began to ask questions about the house, which I answered with as much honesty as I could, considering how very little I knew about our plans.

"When will people come to stay with us?"

"The house won't be finished this season. But by next summer, a whole year from now, we should be ready for guests."

"Is it still haunted?"

Apparently, Gabby had been more impressed by the house than I realized. "It is not haunted," I said, hoping that thought would be banished by the cleaning we'd done. "It isn't quite as messy as when you last saw it. Eve and I cleaned for almost two weeks. And I've been scouring ever since she left. At least the part where you and I will live is clean. The rest of it still needs a lot of work."

"Do I have my own room?"

This, at least, I could assure her. "Yes. You have a beautiful room, with stained-glass windows."

"What is stained glass?"

Okay, maybe she wasn't that impressed. I launched into a description of the window over her bed, describing the glass herons and soft sea colors with as much dramatic flamboyance as a beginning copywriter. "I painted the walls, and bought a new bedspread, with a dust ruffle to match. And on the pillows, I left a surprise."

She nodded, her face solemn. "We're really going to live here, aren't we?"

The misgiving in my daughter's voice was obvious. "That's the plan, honey," I said. She wasn't completely sold on our new adventure. In fact, I was quite sure that her grandmother had spent most of her time with Gabby trying to convince my daughter that we belonged in Tennessee, with her. It wouldn't be a hard job to convince Gabby, with all the horses and toys at Doreen's house.

Gabby just needed a little reassurance. "Maggie's house is wonderful. You'll love the bay, and the boats, and the marina. And when it's all cleaned up, and more beautiful than ever, you'll be so happy that we moved."

"What if I don't make any friends?"

"You will. You already know Cliff." Where had that come from?

"What if nobody likes me?"

"How could anyone not like you?"

"When does school start?"

"In September, just like home."

She turned from the window and looked at me, her eyes distressed. "What will I do till then?"

If only she knew. "We have lots to do, getting the place cleaned up. The yard is a mess, and Maggie's garden needs work. We have to strip wallpaper, paint and decorate the guest rooms. I plan to renovate the kitchen and build a new dining area. We'll be busy all summer long."

"Mom?"

I glanced over at her, frowning. "Yes, honey?"

"Grandma Maggie left the house to you, didn't she?"

"Yes. You know that." While we packed away our Florida lives, I'd gone over the concept of an inheritance with her.

"Then why do you keep calling it Maggie's house?"

She had me there.

At Maggie's place—my place, actually—(would I ever get used to that idea?) I parked the car and carried Gabby's suitcase around to the outside entrance of the apartment, on the lower level of the house.

Standing on the kitchen porch, Gabby asked, "Where are you going? Why are you using that door?"

"This is our door. Our very own private door. No one will use it but you and I."

"We can't use the one by the car?"

"Of course we can. This one is—well, it's private."

"What if it's raining?"

"Come inside, Gabby. I think it's time for a bath and a bedtime story."

Though I have only one child, I've learned that we moms put coats on kids when we feel cold, feed them when we feel hungry, and, as in this case, we send them to bed when we feel like we can't drag ourselves through another step.

❀

Maggie Blackburn, my beloved Maggie, was a collector, and the contents of her various accumulations filled the old house to overflowing. On every table, in every corner, covering the mantle and the hearth, on shelves along the great room, on bookcases, Maggie had displayed every conceivable variety of junk. My first order of business was to rid myself of as many of these dust-catchers as I could. While I might save a few for display, my vision of the finished inn was entirely different than the home Maggie created.

The description of the strange items in Maggie's house would fill a book unto itself. Most of it, I felt fairly certain, was junk, nothing more. But other pieces, other collectables, I wondered about. Having no antique experience of my own, I decided that I would have to trust the expertise of others. And so, on the morning after Gabby arrived, I woke early and made a list of phone numbers for the nearest antique dealers. As my daughter ate cereal, and later played fetch with Liz, I sat in a porch chair and called these experts.

The dealers from the Duncan area could hardly contain themselves, knowing Maggie as they did. One after another, I made appointments for them to visit the house and go over the items I intended to sell. I asked each of them to bring cash and arrive prepared to remove the items immediately. By noon, I had filled the following Wednesday afternoon and Thursday morning with visits from these dealers. Then, as soon as I hung up, I had the gnawing feeling that I might have made a mistake.

"Gabby, how about we head to the library this afternoon?"

At the regional library in Duncan, I began an Internet search, looking for the current value of the kinds of pieces Maggie had collected. It wasn't easy. Without experience, I couldn't even name most of the items. So, with the reference librarian's help, and several books, I gave myself the beginning of an antiques education.

What I learned is, I know nothing about antiques. Furthermore, after pages of pictures and descriptions and details, I discovered that I wasn't even really interested. Still, I applied for a library card, and checked out a stack of books and magazines.

Just what I needed—more homework.

By the time we walked out the front of the library, all I wanted to do was get rid of the junk I'd inherited—whether or not I got fair market value for it. As the automatic doors opened, I was pawing through my purse looking for my car keys. Finding them, I nearly stumbled into a man entering the library.

"Oh, I'm sorry," I said, holding my keys in the air. "I wasn't paying attention."

"No problem," the man answered, and then, "wait, you're the lady who's living at Maggie's house, aren't you? Brandy, isn't it?"

I looked more closely. Without his baseball hat, I hadn't recognized Cliff. His thick hair curled in dark waves across his head. He wore neat jeans, a North Face fleece, and leather boat shoes. On either side of him, two boys—perhaps ten, or eleven—each with the same curly hair, fair skin and blue eyes, waited politely. One clutched a skateboard under his elbow. Still embarrassed, I stammered. "Oh, yes,

Cliff. Nice to see you. I didn't recognize you."

I certainly hadn't recognized the shift from handyman to handsome.

"Hey Gabby," he said, bending to shake my daughter's hand. "These are my boys. This is Justin, and this is James." He draped a gentle arm around each boy's shoulder. "Boys, this is Gabby." He gestured toward me. "And this is Mrs. Beauchamp," he said.

The boys nodded, each stepping closer to his father's side. As if on cue, Gabby moved toward my leg, still hugging her pile of reading books. She ventured, "Are you guys twins?"

"You got it," Cliff said. "Bookends."

Gabby spoke to the one on the left. "How old are you?"

The boy stood up a little taller. "Ten," he said.

Cliff spoke. "The kids are spending the summer with me," he said, smiling at me. "We're headed in to find some good books." He rolled his eyes. "Their mom gave us a summer reading assignment." He looked at me. "Got any suggestions?"

"For boys? I have no idea. Maybe the librarian can help." I couldn't help feeling a little bewildered by this man. I'd assumed that Cliff was married, though I don't know why exactly. Maybe it was his homey, bearded face. Or perhaps it was his full-figured waistline—the figure of a man getting home-cooked meals. Whatever I imagined, it wasn't this—a single man sharing custody of twins.

He shrugged. "I hope so. Things have changed since I was a kid. What are you guys doing here on such a beautiful day?"

I held up my bag full of books, hoping to cover my wandering imagination. "Research. I'm trying to figure out what to do with some of Maggie's junk."

He nodded, understanding on his face. "She sure collected it, didn't she?"

"I'm having antique dealers over to look. Then on Saturday, I'm going to do a garage sale with whatever is left over."

"You don't have a garage."

"I know. I guess I should call it a yard sale."

He smiled. "No way. Call it an estate sale. You'll have more traffic."

"Thanks for the tip."

"If you need help getting things set up, just stop by the marina office. The boys need something to do, and they'd be glad to give you a hand." The bookend boys shot their father a reproachful look.

"I might. Thanks."

❧

By Thursday evening, the various dealers had made a serious dent in the junk from the great room. They'd taken Wedgewood, Jasperware, a Victorian hair-weaving under domed glass, several moth-eaten tapestries, an ermine stole (complete with tails), dozens of bowls and vases and glassware, including an entire collection of Blue Bubble Depression glass. I'd managed to sell several side tables, three lamps, and five ornately carved wood frames containing oil portraits of heaven-only-knows-who.

They'd taken nearly half of Maggie's teapot collection—the best half, I might add—an assemblage occupying twenty-eight cubicles on the back side of a false wall between the great room and the kitchen. I was so happy to see them go that Gabby and I helped them wrap their treasures in bubble-wrap and pack them into boxes.

I was thrilled to eliminate two additional rocking chairs, and one of the ugliest antique velvet chairs I have ever seen. The clouds of dust they emitted, as they were lifted into the trucks of their new owners, completely embarrassed me. But not enough to reduce their price. Unashamed, I let the dealers choke on the dust and hand over the cash. When the last of the trucks drove down the driveway, I'd collected six thousand dollars towards my renovation plans, and I was feeling pretty good about myself. At least until I went back into the living-room, where it seemed exactly as full as it had when I got up that morning. I sank into a chair with the beginning of a terrible headache.

With an ad already placed in the local newspaper, our estate sale would go on, rain or shine. Fortunately for us, the weather looked as if it might cooperate. After dinner, Gabby and I put Liz on a leash and went out to put up street signs. When we finished, we headed down to the marina to look for Cliff.

We found him on the main dock, using a power screwdriver to

replace boards in an older section of dock. "Hey, good to see you," he said, standing up. He hiked up his tool-belt and tipped his baseball cap. "How'd your appointments go? Did you get rid of everything?"

"They took a lot, but they didn't take it all."

"I figured you'd be stuck with most of it."

I nodded. "I have an ad in the paper for a Saturday estate sale—thanks for the tip, by the way—and I'm going to let people walk through the house to look at the big furniture. But I'm going to need some help putting things out on the driveway. Do you think the boys would like to help?"

"I wouldn't use the term, 'like'," he said, smiling.

"I'd be happy to pay them."

"Now money, they'd like. I'm pretty sure of that."

"Great. Do you want to send them over, say, around noon?"

"Sounds good. Why don't you ask them yourself?" He gestured toward the parking lot. "Hey," he said, "how would you two like some ice-cream?"

"Ice-cream?" Gabby tugged on my jacket sleeve. "We'd really like that, wouldn't we, Mom?"

"The boys and I were going to have an ice-cream cone as soon as I finished replacing these boards. If you join us, you can hire yourself a couple of eager helpers, and give them your own instructions."

I wasn't sure about this arrangement. I certainly never intended to spend time with Cliff and his boys. But I needed the help getting things ready for my estate sale, and Gabby hadn't been with another child since she'd come to Genoa Bay. "Well, I suppose an ice-cream cone wouldn't hurt anyone," I said. "Thanks."

We watched as Cliff placed the last few screws and put his tools away. "The boys are in the marina office," he said. "We can meet them there." Gabby squeezed my hand as we followed Cliff down the dock.

❀

On Saturday morning, I got up early and went upstairs to start a pot of coffee. Startled by a noise outside, I glanced out the kitchen window toward the driveway. There, just beyond the tall chain-fence, stood a small crowd of spectators, apparently eager to get our sale underway. One of them, an older man with a long pony-tail, waved at me.

I dodged the window. What were they doing here? I was still in my pajamas.

I ran downstairs and woke Gabby. "You'd better get up. It looks like our sale is starting whether we're ready or not."

She stumbled out of bed, falling into a pair of sweatpants and a sweatshirt. Together, staying out of sight of the windows, we ate cold cereal. By the time we came out on the porch, the crowd had doubled in size. They cheered as we moved toward the gate. Cheered, if you can believe it. You'd think we were an after-Christmas sale.

Gabby looked toward me, fear in her eyes. "It'll be alright," I told her. "They're just excited about our stuff."

I looked toward the marina and noticed that at this early hour, every single parking place had been taken—probably by the people already standing outside my gate. Cliff would love that. So would the boat owners at the marina.

As I pulled back the gate, people flowed into the yard like ants, yammering and poring over the items laid out on tables and blankets in the yard. They wandered through the house, in groups of two or three, up and down the stairs, through the great room, the media room and the dining-room.

I felt invaded. Before long, I began to wish that I'd asked someone, an adult preferably, to help me with the sale. By myself, I couldn't keep an eye on both the driveway and the strangers wandering through my house. Once, running out of change, I'd gone back into the kitchen to find someone emerging from our downstairs apartment.

I must have looked startled, because the woman stammered, as she edged out of the kitchen, "Oh, sorry. I just needed to use a bathroom."

"There is one off the entry," I pointed.

"It was busy. And so were the ones upstairs," she added.

By nine, I'd sold the dressing-tables from two of the guest rooms, one set of twin beds, two armoires and what must have been hundreds of pieces from the tables outside. The twins showed up about a half hour later asking for Gabby, and I gave them each a ten-dollar bill and begged them to go watch the people inside the house. "Make sure they stay upstairs," I said. "And don't let them steal anything."

On Friday night, I'd put out a lawn chair, expecting a relaxed Saturday, with time to meet and chat with my new neighbors. What I got was more like claim staking during the gold rush. I took cash, answered questions—where I could—and tried to appear as calm as possible while people plucked through the junk like vultures descending on road-kill.

The little box I'd chosen for a cash box soon bulged. People seemed to gloat as they walked away with their treasures, and more than once, I saw a look of absolute triumph as they dickered for lower prices, and won.

Though I had met a couple of my neighbors, and others had welcomed me to Genoa Bay, I was completely worn out by eleven in the morning. There was no relaxing to be done. I never sat down.

At one, the kids asked to go to the marina for sandwiches. The crowd had died down, and I agreed, hoping for a moment in my unused lawn chair.

"Excuse me," a male voice called from behind a long table.

I looked toward the voice, spotting an older gentleman in a golf shirt and dress slacks. His hands were behind his back, his attention focused on me, rather than the items on the table. "Yes," I said. "May I help you?"

"My name is Herbert Karras," he said, offering his hand.

"It's nice to meet you, Mr. Karras," I said, taking his hand. It surprised me to have a customer begin with such a formal introduction.

He pointed toward an area of grass away from other people. "Do you have a minute to talk?"

Puzzled, I nodded. "A moment, I suppose." Tall and very thin, Herbert Karras had a square chin that made his mouth look hard, his lips an unflinching line. Bushy eyebrows overshadowed his eyes and I noticed that his ears were far too long for his face, like those of an old woman after a lifetime of heavy earrings. The lines above his eyes were deeply carved, as if in clay, and I found myself wondering if Herbert spent all his time frowning.

"I understand that you've inherited this property from Margaret Blackburn."

"That's correct."

"How did you know Maggie?"

I felt myself bristle. It seemed an incredibly personal question, one I did not feel the need to answer. "Do I know you?" I countered.

"I don't believe you would. I own the marina below the house," he said.

Of course, Karras had come to complain the traffic. "I'm sorry about all the cars this morning. I had no idea they would park in your lot. It should be over soon."

He waved my concern away. "I don't care about the cars," he said. "I'm here to make an offer on the house," he pointed. "I want to buy the property."

Ten

The black-and-white Polaroid is water spotted, with a heavily worn fold line across the upper corner. In the picture, a dark-haired woman holds a child, an infant really, her hands around the baby's waist as the child stands on wobbly legs. The baby is a girl. I know this by the ribbon—I imagine it being pink—which holds a tiny curl at the very top of her head. The woman looks at the child, and I know, from her expression, that she adores this infant. This baby holds the woman in her tiny fisted hands. I turn the photo over. It is not labeled.

EXHAUSTED AND GLAD to be rid of strangers, I closed the gate at six. The warm afternoon sun had disappeared behind the hills, casting long shadows over the yard. A chill spread through the air, brought on by a breeze spreading over the bay. Light clouds feathered the late afternoon sky, and it seemed clear that the weather was about to change. It felt like rain.

Needing to move the remaining stuff under cover, I called for the kids. They didn't answer.

I wandered through the garden, around to the water, and then crossed over to where I could see the marina docks. From my vantage point, the place looked deserted, the parking lot empty. Neither Gabby nor her new friends were anywhere to be found. Part of me wanted to go looking for her. But another, more practical side realized that the only danger in Genoa Bay was the water itself, and Gabby swam better than most fish. Frustrated that she'd disappeared without asking permission, I began moving all the junk inside by myself.

Somewhere in the history of Maggie's house (which was called

Pickering Place), a previous owner had added a room onto the main floor, separated from the great room by a small arch. With red tile floors and wall-length windows, the space had clearly begun life as a sunroom, the northwest equivalent of a screen porch. By the time I moved in, Maggie had already put in an overstuffed couch and an enormous television, and designated it as an out-of-the-way place for sports-dependent husbands to get their fix while on a romantic getaway with their wives. She called it the media room.

I intended to dismantle the electronic monster as soon as possible and return the room to its original purpose.

I opened the sliding doors and began hauling junk in from the yard, filling every corner of the sunroom with precarious stacks of glassware and cookie jars, bowls, draperies, linens and doilies. The more I moved, the more I understood that a year's worth of garage sales would never empty the huge house of all the clutter Maggie left behind. Part of me resented Maggie for collecting it at all.

I'd been at it a while, working up a sweat as I carried boxes inside, when I heard Gabby call my name. I went outside and spotted her coming up the driveway, holding hands with Cliff, as the twins trailed behind, dragging their feet in the gravel. "Hey Mom," Gabby called again. "We brought dinner!"

Cliff held a white paper bag aloft, his face a picture of triumph. I don't think he would have been more proud of a twenty-five-pound King Salmon. "It's barbeque. I hope you like ribs!"

It occurred to me that I hadn't stopped to eat all afternoon. Just the mention of food set my stomach in motion. I was starving. "Oh thank you! That sounds great!" I pointed to the kitchen door. "Gabby, why don't you and the boys put out plates and napkins. I'll pour tea."

"Do you mind if we skip the tea?" Cliff asked, his face sheepish. "Water, or juice. Maybe coffee?"

"Sorry. Where I come from, we serve ice-cold sweet tea. Where did you find barbeque?"

"I took the kids into town for take-out. We figured you'd be exhausted." He laughed as he handed me one of the bags. "I don't think I've seen this much traffic out here for as long as I've lived in Genoa Bay. You'd think you were giving stuff away."

"I should have. Maybe more of it would be gone," I said, opening the front gate. "There were a lot of people here, that's for sure. I think they knew, or at least they'd heard about Maggie's junk. Some of them seemed to be looking for something specific—like they knew exactly what they were hoping to find." I shook my head, leading the way into the kitchen. "It was a little weird, actually. They were all over the house, upstairs, in every bedroom, even down in the apartment." At the counter, Cliff began unloading the bags, while the kids put out paper plates. "I was so glad the boys were here to keep an eye on things. I hope you don't mind that I hired them."

"Not a problem," he said, laying Styrofoam containers out in a neat line and dropping a pile of hand-wipes at the end. "The kids had quite the tales to tell."

Gabby gave placemats to one of the boys, and handed a stack of forks to the other. I caught her carrying a juice pitcher to the table. "Here, honey, let me pour." She frowned and handed me the container. I turned to Cliff, "I know I sold a lot of stuff, but there's so much left. Next week I'm going to have a Salvation Army truck come. And I've ordered a dumpster for the junk. Still, what am I going to do with it all?"

Cliff looked up. "Have you thought about what you want to have when you're finished?"

"What do you mean?"

"I mean, do you have a plan? A vision? Do you know what the rooms will look like? Which bedroom sets will be where? That kind of thing?"

I shrugged. "Really? I just need to get rid of the clutter. Maggie had so much junk everywhere that I can't even begin to think. Once I narrow it all down, I think it'll start to sort itself out. I'm a designer, after all. Usually paper is my palette, but I think I'll know more where I'm going when I can actually see the walls." I gestured toward the great room and frowned. "The one thing I really wanted to dump didn't sell."

"What was that?"

"The stuffed owl," I said. "I think maybe I asked too much for it."

Cliff threw back his head and laughed.

❊

After dinner, the five of us cleaned up the mess and headed back out to the lawn. Though I had spent years in British Columbia, the evening chill startled me. After a long sunny June day, the temperature plummets as the sun goes down. Maybe I'd lived in Florida too long, but I shivered as we carried things inside. "Where do you want these tables?" Cliff asked. "The media room is jammed."

"How about the great room?"

"You got it." He picked up an end table and put it up over his head as he trudged across the lawn. "You might want to go after those napkins. They've blown into the bushes."

While we were inside, the late afternoon breeze had escalated and the leaves of the alder trees clattered with every gust. I gathered up a group of linen dinner napkins, which hadn't sold, and finished bringing the rest of the things inside. With the yard cleared, I followed the boys into the house. "How about a fire in the fireplace?"

The boys cheered. Gabby, my Florida baby, who knew nothing of fires and fireplaces, said, "Really? A fire? Like camping? Can we roast marshmallows?"

"Why not?"

The old fireplace, made of smooth, round river rock, filled the south end of the great room. With a firebox big enough for a square dance, and a hearth as big as most couches, it wasn't easy to lay a fire that did not smoke out the entire room. Through much practice, I'd developed the right techniques.

I opened the screen and the damper, and began laying a fire, starting with old newspapers. Just as I began to build the kindling into a log cabin, Cliff volunteered in that half-tease I now recognized, "I don't think you'll get a fire going with that technique."

"You forget, my friend, I've been building fires in this firebox since I was a kid. I have this procedure perfected."

He laughed. "I should have known better than to critique an expert."

I reached up to the mantel, and found the old wooden matchbox exactly where Maggie had always kept it. Inside, a few of Maggie's special long-handled matches remained. I made a mental note to purchase more. Touching the paper, the fire caught and blazed. "This wood has been drying for about ten years now. Should make a great fire." I knelt before the hearth for a moment, mesmerized by the flames. The sound of wind playing in the chimney reminded me of old times, warm and safe.

Gabby called from the kitchen, "Where are the marshmallows, Mom?"

"Excuse me," I said to Cliff. "She isn't used to finding things here yet."

In the kitchen, I was struck by an almost overwhelming memory, as if I'd been returned to the kitchen in a time machine. Opening the pantry door, I'd become my old self, my younger self. I found the roasting sticks, the same ones Maggie had bought when I was in high school. They hung from the same nail she'd pounded into the pantry wall. More than once, with the living-room full of friends, or my church group, or even a homework buddy, I'd come to find the sticks exactly this way. I'd carried them back to the great room in one hand, a bag of marshmallows in the other. While we'd roasted and laughed and gossiped, Maggie had concocted the most magnificent hot chocolate on the planet. Her secret was cinnamon.

When I was a kid, everyone wanted to be where Maggie was. Though she was an eccentric, she listened with an intensity that made everyone feel important. It was the way she talked to me that first morning in her house. She never talked down to anyone, never told anyone what to do. She gave advice—what adult doesn't, after all— but she treated teenagers with an unusual, almost reverent tenderness. To Maggie, every kid I brought home was as fragile and precious as a hummingbird egg. She wasn't about to drop any of them.

Maggie was the reason I'd made it through those years. On my own, I was a runaway, a kid with an alcoholic mother, and a deadbeat father. I didn't even like myself, and I certainly didn't expect anyone else to like me. But because of Maggie, I was Cinderella. People put up with me in order to spend time with Maggie.

I shook off the memory, and handed the skewers to Gabby.

While Cliff helped the kids get marshmallows on their sticks, I dragged chairs over to the fireplace. "I'm glad you have at least two seats left after today," he said, sinking into a chair. "This is nice. Thanks for inviting us."

"Thank you for dinner. It was a great idea."

"Food is always a great idea."

I laughed. Cliff lived his philosophy. Stout, but not fat, Cliff's round face betrayed his love of food. "I have to agree with you there," I said. "I love to eat it—food, I mean. I'm just not too confident about cooking it."

"That could be scary. Isn't that what the *breakfast* part of 'Bed and Breakfast' is all about? I mean, as an innkeeper, aren't you supposed to be a cook too?"

"I can cook—well, a little anyway. I like cooking." Cliff was looking at me like I'd lost a screw. I shrugged. "It's just that I haven't cooked for other people much. I'm a little nervous about it." Actually, I was nervous about most every part of my new venture. In fact, ever since Herbert what's-his-name made an offer on the house, I'd been entertaining misgivings of every kind. Doubt had begun tapping across my mind like *Riverdance*.

Maybe this latest offer was God's way of telling me to get out. Take the money and run. Maybe this trip to Genoa Bay was just an adventure, a side trip. Not the main event. I'd have to ask God about it, again. Did he ever tire of me not getting his instructions quite right?

"I had an interesting encounter today," I said.

"I'll bet you had a lot of interesting encounters."

I thought about the woman using our private bathroom, the two women fighting over a linen tablecloth, the man who managed to break a vase just before he paid for it. "You're right," I agreed. "It was nuts out there. But I'm thinking about one in particular. Someone you might know. Herbert Karras."

"He was here?"

"Toward the end of the day."

"What did he want?" Cliff's voice had taken on a new tone. I wasn't sure if I heard suspicion or distrust. But whatever it was, it wasn't good.

"You know something about Mr. Karras," I challenged.

"What I think about him doesn't count," Cliff hedged. "He's my boss. I do what he asks me to do. I don't have to like him. I just try to keep the peace."

"But it isn't easy."

"How did this turn into an inquisition about my relationship with Karras? You were going to tell me your story."

"I'm sorry," I said, and smiled. "I thought I sensed something ominous. Forget it. He made an offer on the house, that's all. He wants to buy it." I'd expected my news to startle Cliff. But somehow, looking at him, I realized that he'd expected as much. "You're not surprised, are you?"

"Not really. He's a businessman. Businessmen always have plans, you know?" Cliff leaned forward, touching James on his shoulder. "Don't set them on fire, son. You'll end up dropping a fireball in your lap. Hold it further from the flame." He reached out and took the skewer, moving the end into the glowing coals at the base of the fire. Satisfied, he gave the handle to his son and turned to me. "I just didn't think Karras would talk to you this soon."

"Cliff, why does he want the house? It's a wreck. A mess. Who would want it? I don't even know why I want it."

In his expression, I watched Cliff wrestle with his answer. He sat back in the chair, one ankle crossed over his knee. He puzzled his moustache as he thought for a moment. "I don't know how much to tell you. I mean, it's what you'd call a pipedream, really. Nothing concrete. But he's been talking about a development here."

"A development?"

"Yeah. Upgrading the marina. Adding a hotel or condo of some kind. Maybe a time-share. Swimming pools. Stores. Yacht sales. Boating supplies. The whole works."

"Here?" I couldn't quite get my mind around the idea. While I knew of developments like Cliff described, most of them in the Gulf Islands, Genoa Bay seemed like the least likely location for this kind of proposal. "Why here?"

"I really shouldn't be talking about it," he said. "He's my boss, you know. I guess the only thing I should say is this: Be careful."

"Careful? He wants my house."

"It's not like he can just take it away from you. He offered you real money, didn't he?"

"But why here? I still don't get it. We're miles from town. There are maybe, I don't know, seven or eight landowners to deal with. He can't possibly expect to buy out everyone on the peninsula, can he? Who has that kind of money?"

"He thinks Duncan has grown enough to support this kind of development. And of course, for the most part, the bay is protected from winter weather. They're running out of space in the Victoria yacht basin. The harbor at Sydney is completely full. That means mega-yachts could be part of the deal. Sixty footers, all the way to a hundred feet or so. Selling to Karras could bring you a lot of money."

"What makes you think I need money?"

He held both hands up, palms toward me. "Sorry. I didn't mean that, exactly. It's just that view property is rare. He's motivated. You ought to come out really well."

"You think I should sell?"

"I didn't say that." He looked at me, frowning. "Besides, you just told me that you had doubts."

"About cooking, not about being here." I shook my head. Men make such crazy connections. "If I sell to Karras, what am I supposed to do? Head back to Florida with my tail between my legs?"

❀

After Cliff and the boys headed home, I took Gabby downstairs and put her in the bathtub. Though I should know better, I let her talk me into adding bubbles, and as she played with bath toys, I leaned against the wall, completely exhausted.

The wind, which had kicked up outside, made a moaning sound as it whipped around the deck above the apartment patio. The drone nearly lulled me to sleep.

I couldn't believe how much a single garage sale had wiped me out. I ached from head to toe, and wished I could sleep for a week. Of course I'd been working non-stop ever since Eve and I had arrived. Still, after nearly four weeks, I hadn't even begun to change the inside of the house. More than that, both the garden and the grounds still needed extensive work. There was so much to do. And after four weeks, I wasn't even ready yet to begin.

In my fatigue I began to wonder if I'd made a huge mistake.

"Mom, are we going to stay here?" Gabby asked, pouring water from one plastic container into another. I will never understand how my seven-year-old comes so close to reading my mind.

"I think so, honey. That's the plan, anyway." I would never tell Gabby, but I couldn't shake the feeling that the offer for the house had changed things. It was like I'd been given an out. A pass. A get-out-of-jail card. And, after a day like we'd been through, getting out of jail sounded pretty darned good.

"How long 'till school starts?"

"About two months."

She rested her chin on the side of the tub, and looked directly into my eyes. "I don't know if I can make it," she said.

I laughed. "Make it?"

"I don't have anyone to play with."

"What about the boys?"

"They're boys."

"Can't argue with you there. What's wrong with that?"

"They play boy stuff."

"Like?"

"War, and climbing trees."

"What would you like to do?"

"I want to go back to swim club." I was pretty sure that Duncan didn't have the kind of swim program we had at the Navy Base.

"What if I could help you find something else to do?"

She sighed. "I want to swim."

"I understand, Gabby," I said, heaving myself off the bathroom floor to reach for a towel. "I'll look into it. Let's get dried off and ready for bed." I held the towel out for her, and Gabby climbed out of the tub, covered in bubbles. I wrapped her in the towel and held her for a moment. She was tired too; she made no effort to resist the hug I needed.

I tucked Gabby under the covers, and immediately slid into the old antique bed in Maggie's room. Picking up a novel, I read for a moment, though the words blurred on the page. I must have read the same paragraph three or four times before I gave up and turned out the light. I was asleep before I pulled the quilt over my shoulders.

When I heard it, the sound exploded out of a dream. A tremendous crash. I sat up to the sound of wood splitting, of glass breaking, and the walls of Pickering Place shuddered with the impact. As I sat trembling, bewildered and frightened, I thought only of the forty-foot sailboat, hanging from the ceiling in the great room. And I wondered what it would look like sitting on the floor.

Eleven

This photograph is more recent, though undated. I know this because Maggie wears her famous Clairol hair color, the same color I remember when I came to live with her. Her hair is styled, though, in the way she wore it during the time between my college graduation and Gabby's birth. She sits high on a garden tractor seat, smiling broadly. Beside her, leaning on a rear fender, a mechanic in dark overalls dangles a wrench in one hand. The figure on the other side of the tractor startles me. With the unmistakable facial features of Downs Syndrome, he smiles at the camera while polishing the engine cover with both hands.

GABBY BURST INTO MY ROOM screaming, and jumped onto the bed; scrambling across the mattress, she wrapped both arms around my neck. "Mom, what happened?"

I pulled her under the covers and held her for a moment, reassuring her. "It's okay, honey. I'm here."

"What was that noise?"

"I'm not sure. I think maybe a tree fell on the house." I reached over her to the bedside lamp and discovered that we'd lost power. In the few hours since we'd gone to bed the storm outside had intensified. The wind howling through fir trees took on a deeper and more frightening tone.

"It was so loud," she said. Though still trembling, Gabby had calmed some.

"I know. It really scared me too." I pulled the coverlet off the bed and wrapped myself; I'd gone to bed in a T-shirt. "You stay here a minute. I'm going to go see what happened."

"Don't leave me!"

"Alright, honey." I took a deep breath, trying to think. If Gabby wouldn't stay in my bed alone, I couldn't let her walk barefoot over broken glass while we inspected the damage. I went over to the closet and slipped into athletic shoes. "I'll carry you, okay?" She climbed onto my hip and I wrapped the coverlet around us both, thinking how hard it must be to be a gorilla.

Seven-year-olds were clearly meant to walk on their own two feet.

Intending first to find a flashlight, I carried Gabby toward the little apartment kitchen, but long before we crossed the sitting-room, I realized what had happened to the house. While still in the dark hallway, I felt cold air blowing in through the shattered glass door.

Stopping at the edge of the sitting-room, I stared. In the shifting moonlight, among pebbles of glass, shards of splintered wood, and broken furniture was the remnant of the giant fir tree that once graced the southwest corner of the property. I didn't need a flashlight to realize that the tree had done extensive damage to the apartment.

"Well, honey. There's your culprit. We had a tree fall on the house."

"A tree? Is this a hurricane?"

Even in disaster, Gabby makes me laugh. "No, not a hurricane, sweetie. It's just an old-fashioned windstorm."

She shivered, and I gave her a hug. "Here, let me put you in this chair while I get a flashlight." She nodded, apparently calmed by having identified the source of the terrifying noise. I wrapped her in the blanket and went to the kitchen. Certain that Maggie always kept a flashlight handy, I dug through the kitchen drawers. When I couldn't find one, I lit a candle and shoved it down into an antique candleholder.

"Mom. Are you coming back?"

"I'm here," I said, holding the candle with one hand, shielding the flame from gusts with the other. "I can't find a flashlight. We'll have to put that on our grocery list." Gabby had curled up in the corner chair, her head peeking out from the blanket. Shivering in the cold, I held the flame toward the destruction, picking my way toward the tree. Rain, which had begun some time after dark, had already begun to soak the furniture.

It's times like these—well, actually, it happens anytime things go wrong—that I feel the most anger toward Timothy. My thoughts begin with irritation and proceed in a definite downward spiral, beginning with, *Timothy, if you had only landed that stupid plane of yours, I wouldn't be here...*

Though this anger rarely solves my problems, sometimes I think that it makes me strong enough to tackle things I would otherwise avoid. "We're going to have to dry this stuff out," I said, putting the candle down on the table near Gabby. "Watch this for me."

Dragging the couch out from under the tree and away from the broken window, I moved it into the hallway, where I was certain it would remain dry. Even as I worked, I wondered what else had been hit when the tree came down. From the angle of the trunk, it might have damaged part of the kitchen. Undoubtedly, it had destroyed most of the deck on the north side of the house. Inevitably, I would discover limbs sticking through the window in what had been my old bedroom. Thank the Lord that I put Gabby in the old office!

Had the tree fallen during the day, I would have found a saw and begun taking off branches immediately. Then I would board up the broken windows. But at night, in the middle of the storm, I couldn't see well enough to accomplish much.

Instead, I retrieved some of Maggie's old blankets from the linen closet. Using the same hammer I'd used to hang pictures in Gabby's bedroom, I nailed blankets over the windows. It wouldn't keep out the cold air, but it would stop the rain from blowing inside. It might be enough to get us through the rest of the night.

When I finally turned around to check on Gabby, she was fast asleep. I picked up the candle and went upstairs to survey the rest of the house.

The tree had done more damage to the main floor than it had to our apartment. The lower trunk had taken out the corner of the kitchen, tearing off the eaves and punching a hole through the sheetrock. Bare studs decorated a corner of the kitchen. Errant branches had broken two of my kitchen windows. And, just as I suspected, the entire deck had been brought down. Standing in the great room, confused and discouraged, I peered out an unbroken window at the tangled mess of splintered wood. I'd hardly begun and already I'd been dealt a setback that would cost me in every way.

I had insurance, of course; or at least I believed so. But no insurance completely covers the cost of repairs. I'd planned to do renovations to the house, but I'd hoped to begin those during the winter, when harsh weather drove us inside. By then, I'd planned to have the grounds in good shape, the garden reestablished, the outside siding painted.

But a single tree had taken what few plans I had, and cast them aside. I leaned my forehead against the cold glass and prayed. "Lord, are you sure *this* was your plan?"

❀

By six in the morning, the storm had cleared, leaving us with broken clouds and a light, though chilling breeze. I had cold cereal, and because of the power outage, skipped my morning coffee. Then, dressed in an old sweatshirt and jeans, I snuck outside. I found a rusting handsaw in the shed and attacked the branches of the fir tree. Not long after I began, I heard a surprised call from the front yard. "What on earth happened here?"

I stopped sawing and brushed sticky hair off my forehead. *Why do people ask such stupid questions?*, I wondered. I pulled the saw from the tree, parted the branches and slipped out, walking around the front of the house. Cliff stood in my front yard with his hands on his hips. In a voice dripping with sarcasm, I said, "I thought I'd cut up some firewood."

"Well, last night's fire was nice and all. But you don't have to go this far."

I rolled my eyes. "What are you doing up this early?"

"I came to see if everything was alright with you two."

I pointed at the tree with my thumb. "Coulda been worse."

"Not by much," he said. "That was quite the windstorm wasn't it? Are you and Gabby okay?"

"Yeah. It scared us, big time. But we're fine."

"We didn't even hear it come down," he said, shaking his head as he examined the enormous wall of roots hanging in the air above my yard. Cliff walked around the side of the house, his attention on the eaves and the deck and the damage to our apartment. "You're going to cover this up? By yourself?"

"Have to," I said. "I thought I'd go into town and buy some plywood, as soon as I get tree parts out of the way."

"I have some boards down at the marina. You can have as many as you need until you start repairs."

Part of me bristled. The guy was nice, and he was my neighbor after all, but did I really want him this involved in my life? Where was all this kindness and consideration coming from? And what did he expect in return? This guy seemed to show up with the regularity of a stray dog.

It made me think of Maggie and our first meal together. Of all people, I should know; you only feed the dogs you want to keep.

"I can help screw the boards in place. They're pretty heavy."

I sighed. Okay, independence is nice. It's healthy. But too much independence is just plain stupid. "That would be great," I said, smiling for the first time that day.

"What about the tree?"

"I don't know. It's down. It's not going to do any more damage. I have time to think about it."

"I have a chainsaw."

I pictured Gabby with her arms around a stray dog. "You shouldn't—I mean—you don't have to. I can have someone come buck it up for us. Then I can split it for firewood."

"Nonsense. After the boys wake up, I'll be back with the chainsaw and we'll get you all buttoned up. We'll be done before you know it."

A stray dog, maybe. But a handy dog, at that.

❁

Two hours later, Cliff, wearing safety goggles and heavy leather gloves, had his chainsaw screaming as he removed the rest of the branches. In a flannel shirt and down jacket, he looked every bit the part of logger. Later, he cut the tree into twenty-inch fireplace pieces. With their dad attacking the tree, the boys and I dragged huge fir branches down to the beach, where I hoped to burn the waste. On top of so much work, every cell in my body screamed, and I could feel the beginning of a nasty headache. Only hours after getting out of bed, my clothes were filthy, covered in pitch, and I was sweaty, stinky, and my hair had blossomed into a crown of frizz.

The noise of the chainsaw woke Gabby, who came out through the front door, still in her nightgown and bare feet. In one hand, she dragged her favorite blanket, trailing the opposite corner across the lawn. She found me resting on a rock, where I'd pulled off my gloves in order to survey my blisters. I was comparing mine with the boys' when Gabby screamed into my right ear. "Mom!"

I jumped. "Gabby, you don't have to shout."

The chainsaw revved up. "I want some breakfast!"

"Okay," I said, glad for the interruption. "It'll have to be cereal. The power is still out."

"The lights are on inside. That means the electricity is back," she said, with a kind of confidence I find unsettling in a child her age. "I think you should make waffles." Her eyes lit up and she clapped her hands. "Let's invite Cliff and the boys. They probably like waffles."

So much for cold cereal.

When the chainsaw slowed, Gabby ran over to Cliff. "Can you eat with us? We're having waffles."

He put down the saw, and looked toward me. "I don't know. What does your mom think about that?"

"She's gonna cook."

He looked at his watch. "I was thinking about getting to church," he said.

"Please come," Gabby said. "If you don't come, I won't get waffles."

Cliff laughed. "Well, now that you put it that way, I wouldn't think of letting you down." He pulled off his gloves and slapped them on his jeans. Sawdust fell to the ground like glitter.

Inside, Gabby supervised the waffle machine while I browned sausages on the stove. I dropped eggs into the grease and let them bubble while I started a new pot of coffee. All the while, the chainsaw screamed and the boys continued dragging the trimmings down to the beach. "The light is green," she said, reaching for the handle.

"No, honey. I'll get it." I lifted the lid and used a fork to remove the waffle. "Why don't you call the boys?"

She nodded, climbed down off her chair and walked over to the hole in the kitchen wall. There, she cupped her mouth with her hands, and yelled into the space between the exposed studs. "Breakfast is ready!"

I had to laugh. "Now, why don't you go outside and do it again—like a lady this time, please?" She shrugged and headed for the front door.

Cliff and the boys ate like starving peasants, and I was glad Gabby thought to cook for them. It hadn't occurred to me that they might have come without eating first. "Really, you guys. I don't know how to thank you for all the work you're doing out there."

"You could pay us," one of the boys—I still couldn't tell them apart—chirped.

His brother jabbed him with his elbow. "Shut up, stupid."

Cliff laughed, and deep dimples graced both sides of his face. The laugh lines around his eyes deepened. "You gotta admit. They know the value of a dollar!"

"He's right," I said to Cliff. "If you won't take money, at least I can pay the boys."

"Forget it," Cliff said. "It's going to cost you plenty to fix the house. We're happy to donate a little time. I'd have done it for Maggie. After all, that's what neighbors do."

"Well, I'm not Maggie. But thank you, again." I put my chin on my hand, my elbow on the table. In spite of the coffee, I think I might have climbed right back into bed and slept for a week. With a tummy full of warm food and a short night behind me, I must have nodded off, because the next thing I heard was Gabby saying, "M-o-o-o-o-o-m," in that perturbed whine that only children can produce.

"Hmm? I'm sorry." I felt my face grow warm. "I guess I wasn't listening."

Cliff waved the air. "I was just asking," he said. "You do have insurance?"

"I think so. Maggie had homeowner's insurance. And since the will hasn't gone through the courts yet, that ought to cover the windstorm. Once I do probate, or whatever you call it here in Canada, I'll have to buy coverage myself." I took a deep breath, letting it out slowly. "I planned to do some inside renovations this coming winter. But now that the house has been partially demolished, I think God may have rearranged my strategy. I just hope I can afford the new plan."

"Well," Cliff reached for a link sausage, and took a bite. "Whatever coverage you have will probably include a deductible. It isn't going to be cheap to replace the deck. The roof needs major repair—especially with the truss damage—and those windows aren't a standard size." He pointed to the broken kitchen windows. "I have an idea that will save you some money."

"Really?" I had a terrible feeling that this might involve a stray dog.

"Yeah. I volunteer over at Shiloh Farms." He took a sip of coffee and then leaned forward to add milk. He stirred, slowly, as if there was nothing more to say.

Farms? Still confused, my fuzzy, sleep-deprived brain reached for a connection. "What do farms have to do with house repair?"

"Oh, yeah. I forgot. You don't know about the farm." He laughed. "It's a long story," he said. "But they have a carpentry school over there. Students from all over the island. Some are kids. Some are adults. Some of the men have even done some time in prison. They aren't fast; the students learn as they go. But they're good. They're dependable. They do what they promise, and if you use them, you'll be doing them some good at the same time. You should give them a call."

"But prison? I don't want ex-cons working at the house!"

Though I liked to think of myself as progressive, forgiving, what about Gabby? Didn't I have an obligation to her? How safe was it to have men I didn't know running around the place? My face must have betrayed my anxiety. Cliff patted my hand. "Relax," he said. "They're good people. They have a great supervisor, and lots of mentors from the community. I could give Peter a call for you."

"Mentors?"

"Yeah. Folks come in and spend time teaching. Some of them show these guys how to bid for jobs. The mentors show how the material works in the real world. Without the volunteers, the school wouldn't exist."

"I don't know." And then it occurred to me. My stray dog was one of the carpentry mentors. Great. Just great.

"And," Cliff said, "I've been thinking about something else. You know, since you won't have this place up and running before next summer, I've been thinking about a way that you could make some money in the meantime."

It startled me that Cliff had been doing that much thinking about my business. We hardly knew each other. What had I done to deserve this much problem solving on his part? "You've been thinking about my finances? What do you know about my finances?"

"Well, I confess, only a bit. But you are worried about the house. And with the renovations including so much rebuilding. Well, actually, I have an idea that might help us both."

"Really?" I reached for my coffee cup. This was going to be good.

Cliff poured more syrup over his waffle, and began cutting it into tiny squares, apparently unaware of my irritation. "You know, we don't have a restaurant over at the marina. Most places do. Nothing big, mind you, but someplace for the boaters to grab a meal, or have dinner out. And I was thinking, since you're going to do breakfast for your own guests eventually, maybe you should go ahead and get started now."

"Now?" I put down my cup. "I'm not ready now. The house is a wreck. The kitchen isn't the way I want it."

"But you could still do a buffet breakfast. I could advertise for you down at the docks. All you'd need is a kitchen that works, and a great room that's clean enough to receive guests. You could do that right now. You'd make money, and I'd keep the boat owners happy. It's different than any other marina in the area. Original, you know?"

"You're nuts. Everything needs painting. The floors need refinishing. The front entry needs a rebuild. I couldn't do it for months."

"But the boating season is about to start. In three weeks, I'll have reservations two weeks deep. And these boaters might end up being your biggest source of referrals. You could serve a breakfast up here, dazzle them with your culinary expertise, give them a brochure for the Bed and Breakfast, and make a little money to keep your remodel going strong."

The idea was both attractive and frightening. Because of the storm, I'd already been forced to rethink my plans for the entire year. And now this. Could I do it? Should I do it? Would the energy of doing a daily meal for guests take away from the energy I needed to get the house ready for business? I felt my mouth flapping like a fish as I tried to think of some intelligent response.

He laughed. "I can see that I've stumped you. You don't have to agree right now. I was just thinking that it would be an asset to both of us. Boaters talk." Cliff shook his head, "Boy, do they talk. If someone here has a great experience in July, everyone in the Gulf Islands will know about it before August. A great breakfast in this weird old house would draw boaters to the marina. It may seem gimmicky, but you'd be surprised. It might boost business for both of us." He wiped his moustache with his napkin. "They say cross-marketing is the way to go these days."

Before I could respond, the doorbell rang, and the five of us looked one at another, wondering who might be expecting company. "Who would that be on a Sunday morning?"

Cliff shrugged. "The power company?"

"Maybe." I scooted my chair back and excused myself.

In the entry hall, I fought with the strings controlling the draperies—Maggie had drapes covering the sliding glass door she'd installed in the entryway. The doors didn't fit the house, or the entryway, and I never understood why she'd put them there. But then most of Maggie's choices perplexed me. I planned to replace the stupid slider as soon as possible. When I finally pulled back the curtain and looked up, I couldn't have been more surprised.

Twelve

"Good morning, Mrs. Beauchamp. I'm glad to see you again." Herbert Karras held his hand toward me.

Perplexed, I shook it, even as I wondered why we were shaking hands like old friends. Between exhaustion and stress, I couldn't quite conceal my bewilderment. "What on earth brings you here this morning?"

"I came by to check on the marina. After last night's storm, I was worried. They told me Cliff is up here, helping you."

Karras said these last words with a tone of heavy accusation, and I couldn't help feeling a little defensive. "He's helping us cut up a tree."

He turned toward the yard, his gaze taking in the enormous root-ball of the old fir, a vertical monument in the front lawn. Much of Maggie's handiwork, flower bushes and vines, still attached to the soil, hung off the tree like something in a fun house. His eyes followed the trunk, hanging high above the garden, all the way to the house's damaged gutters. Satisfied, he stepped away from the front doors, and made an obvious show of looking at the roof, shaking his head. "Looks like you were lucky. That tree might have come right through the kitchen."

"It sounded like it did," I said, remembering the paralyzing fear of the previous night. "But you're right. It could have been much, much worse. Turned out pretty manageable."

"Don't be too certain. You'll have to replace the entire north deck. And rebuild most of the trusses over the kitchen. That will really cost you. There'll be windows to replace, and siding and then painting, of course." For a long moment, he looked at me as if to size me up. "Are you sure you're up to that?"

I shrugged. "Looks like I have to be."

"My offer still stands. I'd be willing to buy the house. Today. As is." His gesture took in the tree and the roof and the deck. "You can walk away from this mess, and I'll still pay exactly what I offered you yesterday."

This guy was getting to be about as welcome as a pimple on prom night. I sighed, wondering how I could make myself any clearer. "Mr. Karras, I appreciate your checking on us. Really. It's very neighborly of you." I backed into the doorway.

"My offer is more than generous." He pulled out a business card. "Here is the name and phone number of a local realtor. If you check into it, you'll discover that I'm being exceptionally magnanimous."

I shook my head, refusing the card. "Thanks. But I'm not interested in selling. I've decided we're going to make our home here." Determined not to say anything I might regret, I smiled at him. "Now, since it's Cliff you're looking for, I'll go and get him for you."

He reached out to stop me from shutting the sliding door. "You know, you might not always feel so firmly about staying. Things happen. People get discouraged. They don't have the success they hoped for." With his other hand, he produced another card from his jacket pocket. Did the guy have a degree in pushiness? "Here's my cell number. When you change your mind, you can give me a call."

I frowned at him, unwilling to take either card. *When*, he'd said, like he knew with certainty that I would eventually give up. This guy just wouldn't quit. I turned toward the kitchen. "I'll just go get Cliff," I said, pointing at the kitchen. Inside, just out of sight, I slumped against the wall, trying to get a hold of my emotions.

What was it about that man that made me so crazy? He had an almost miraculous way of making me feel stupid, young, and incapable all at the same time. Why on earth couldn't he take no for an answer? Why did he think one little windstorm would change my mind about selling the house?

With so much work to be done, a new deck was nothing. An extra day or two. A couple of thousand dollars. No big deal. No sweat.

But there was something more here, something almost, well, sinister. What had he meant, saying, *things happen* and *people get discouraged*? Was he trying to frighten me? Were those words some kind of threat? I shook my head, trying to clear my thoughts.

I was tired; after all, I'd just fallen asleep at the breakfast table. I must have misunderstood. I'd had a short night, and it was proving to be a very long morning. While Cliff talked with Karras, I began washing dishes. Gabby brought her plate from the table. "Who's at the door?"

"No one important," I said. "Just someone to see Cliff."

❀

By the end of the day, we'd managed to cover the broken windows with plywood and close up my poor broken house. When exhaustion forced us to quit, Cliff and the boys refused dinner and dragged their weary feet back down the driveway toward the marina. I felt badly for them all, certain that Cliff had worked much harder and longer than he'd planned.

Poor guy had only come to check on us, and in the end had missed church and given away an entire day. He'd been patient with the kids—who'd lost interest after breakfast. He'd cut and sawed and drilled and lifted and sealed up the house until I felt fairly confident that not a single raindrop would find its way inside.

Cliff Lowry was an exceptionally handy stray dog, indeed.

Early Monday morning I left a message with Maggie's attorney about the storm damage. No matter how much coverage I had, I needed to get repairs underway. Part of me wanted to stay home and worry figures with an adding machine. I could feel the anxiety in the acid churning in my stomach. But worrying wouldn't cover my expenses. No matter what happened, I had to prepare myself with realistic renovation plans and sharp-as-a-knife bids for repair and remodeling.

By the time Gabby got up, I had lined up appointments with two companies for bids on replacement windows. I'd figured out how to rent a splitter for the wood we'd cut and moved. After a breakfast of hot oatmeal, I loaded my daughter into the van and, armed with a map, headed out to meet the head carpenter at the Shiloh Farms.

Nothing Cliff described prepared me for what awaited me there.

Leaving the highway, I started up a long gravel driveway through acres of neatly trimmed fruit trees, and net-covered vegetable gardens. Apparently the deer from Maggie's yard tormented this virtual Eden as well. Everywhere I looked, plants overflowed in neat rows of verdant green, and patchwork quilts of brilliant flowers. Gravel pathways connected various gardens, benches and small grassy meadows.

A separate area featured a piazza of sorts, neatly and securely fenced, with smooth sidewalks connecting whimsical wooden benches. Throughout the area, someone had built waist-high garden plots where dozens of elderly sunhat-wearing gardeners worked.

"Mom," Gabby said, pointing. "Look at all the grandmas!"

"You're right."

"I've never seen so many old people."

Right again. Some pushed wheelbarrows along narrow paths. Others watered using hand-held sprinklers. In another plot, several weeded rows of vegetables. These gardeners chatted as they worked, sharing the intimacy of the soil.

On the other side of the drive, men harvested what appeared to be spinach into small canvas bags. In this Eden, each had his place, his job. Over all this industry a peaceful cloud of purpose seemed to hover.

I got my first look at the old school building just as I rounded the driveway's last turn. I knew the old building had become the heart of the farm—Cliff explained that. But the schoolhouse was larger than I expected—a massive, three-story, white-clapboard building punctuated by a wide front porch. Steep wooden steps led to double front doors. The façade was lined with three rows of identical windows, tall and narrow and undecorated.

From its style, I guessed that the building harkened from the early twentieth century. Most of the details looked original, heavily worn, but tenderly cared-for. Fresh paint graced every surface, and the windows shone in the morning sunshine.

As I sat in the car, looking up at the building, it was easy to imagine hordes of school children running up the stairs at the sound of the morning bell, and I pictured nuns in dark habits, escorting children to their classes. "Well, Gabby, are you ready to see what we can find out?"

"Sure," she agreed, unbuckling her seat belt.

Just inside the front door, two offices faced the hall. At an oversized oak desk I introduced myself to a small white-haired woman in jeans and sweatshirt. "Ah, yes. Peter told me you were coming," she said. "I'm Charlene. Here, I'll walk you over to the shop." She picked up the phone, dialed a number and spoke quietly. Returning her attention back to us, she said, "There now. Let me get a coat."

She spoke to Gabby. "So, you're new to the island."

"Sorta."

"You've been here a while?"

"A whole week."

"What do you think so far?"

"It's pretty boring," she said. "We've only had a windstorm. Not even a hurricane."

As it turned out, Peter Delaney knew Maggie's place well. "Everyone around here knows that old house. My father used to laugh about the boat in the living-room. They tore the whole end of the house off to put that thing inside. It was the talk of the town for months, I hear."

"I have no doubt." I'd learned, nearly fifteen years earlier, during my own stay in Duncan, that no one kept secrets in this small town.

"It's not the kind of decoration most folks put in their living-room." He laughed. "Why don't we go into the shop? Would you like coffee?"

Peter had to be well over six feet tall, lean and suntanned. He was clean-shaven, though he sported curly brown hair hanging from a ponytail under his faded blue baseball cap. He wore a blue Vancouver Canucks sweatshirt, baggy denim jeans and steel-toed work boots. Gabby and I followed him to a corner desk where he offered me coffee in a Styrofoam cup. "I'd offer you a seat, but I only have one," he said. "Seems silly, doesn't it? The old school house is full of student chairs. Every time I think to bring one back, something distracts me." Inside the long building, I smelled the scent of freshly cut wood. Bright florescent fixtures illuminated workstations placed around the room's perimeter. I recognized a table saw and a drill press, a miter saw and even a router. But other tools, I'd never seen before. Simple baseboard cupboards lined long walls. Behind each station, pegboards held neat rows of hand tools. The cement floor was spotless; clearly in this environment everything had its place.

"I don't mind," I said, putting my purse on his desk. "I only came to talk to you about the work I need done at the house. I know you'll have to come by and look it over. I'll want a written bid, of course. But, what I really want to know—what I'm not sure about—can your students do this sort of project?"

He smiled. "I'd be very interested in bidding this one," he said. "From what you said on the phone, it would be a great experience for our kids." He reached for a three-ring binder. "I know it can be frightening to trust your project to students. So, I've gathered these pictures to show prospective clients some of the projects we've finished so far," he said, opening the binder, and turning the pages to reveal scores of photographs.

"You can see that we've handled all kinds of situations—simple remodels, additions, even finish work. We can build cabinets, and custom closet systems. We can do framing, sheet rock and installation of all the cabinetry. We aren't certified for electrical installation or plumbing, so you'll have to bid that separately. But I think you'll find that we're highly competitive compared to other contractors."

He let me turn the pages at my own pace, sipping coffee as I scanned the pictures. "It's my job to find projects that give the students the widest opportunity for skill building. It isn't easy. Our jobs have to be big enough to keep a whole group busy."

In the album I found scores of before and after pictures. The students had taken out walls, changed and hung windows, built new cabinets for kitchens, and constructed decks of all kinds. In fact, from the pictures, it seemed like they could handle just about anything. "You'd have lots of variety at our place."

"Over the phone you mentioned remodeling. What are you wanting to do?"

"I'd planned to wait until winter. But since the storm has forced my hand, I think we might as well do it all at once—provided I can afford it. As a Bed and Breakfast, the owner's apartment is too small for us. Maggie didn't have any children. Over the years, the kitchen has seen some pretty sorry changes. I'd like to restore and reorganize the kitchen, adding the space on the back into the living area for Gabby and I."

"You'll need a draftsman to complete the drawings, and of course, you'll have to get building permits. That can take time."

"I understand." Another cost. Another expense. I felt heat build in the small of my back. How many other unexpected expenses waited for me in the days and months ahead? I shook my head, trying to banish fear, and focus my attention on Peter's voice.

"You said the house is closed up for now, correct?" I nodded. "Well, since you've covered the damage from the weekend storm, you have time to get things in order." Peter took a business card from the top drawer of his desk and printed a name and phone number clearly across the back of the card, handing it to me. "This guy can help you with the drafting."

"You'd trust him with your own project?" What I really wanted to ask was, *Is he cheap?*

"Yep. He's good. Knows what he's doing. In the meantime, I'd like to come out to the house and take a look. That way, I'd be more certain this is something my boys can handle. If you like, we can pencil in the time and save it for you."

Gabby, meanwhile, had wandered over to a window at the corner of the room and climbed up on a chair. "Mom," she said, pointing. "Look! They have horses!"

❀

Peter walked Gabby and *me* to our car and wished us luck with our project. We had just opened the van door when another group of riders came by. I noticed that each horse carried one small child, while as many as three adults walked nearby, spotting the rider.

"Mom, I want to go see the horses," Gabby said.

"I don't know, honey," I said, unwilling to interrupt the students. We had so much to do, and these people were clearly in the middle of something. "They're having lessons, I think."

Peter smiled, patting Gabby's head. "Those are therapeutic horses, Gabby. The kids come here once a week to ride." He looked at his watch. "I think they're nearly done for the morning. If you like, I'll walk you over to the barn and you can meet the teacher. She'd let you pet one of the horses."

Gabby looked up at me, her face shining with hope. I admit it; I'm a sucker for hope. "Okay. We'll go see the horses." Sighing, I shut the car door.

Peter walked us down a dusty path to a weathered barn where he let us through a gate into a small paddock. Across from us, I spotted the last group of riders. After the rider got off the horse, a teenager led the horse inside the barn. The adults gathered around the student, who faced Gabby and *me*. In her face, I recognized the delighted expression of victory.

One of the women, squatting in front of the child, looking at her eye-to-eye, patted her student's shoulder in triumph. Even at this distance, I decided that I liked this woman; I liked her honest smile and the gentle, encouraging hand she held on the child's shoulder.

"Lucia," Peter said, walking toward the group. "I have someone who wants to meet you."

Glancing at Peter, Lucia excused herself. She wore western jeans, riding boots, and a linen blouse, the sleeves rolled up to her elbows. Her dark hair was caught in a French braid ending below her shoulders.

"This is Gabby," Peter said, gesturing toward my daughter. "She tells me that she loves horses. And she would very much like to pet yours." Peter turned to us. "This is Lucia D'Amato. She supervises the therapeutic riding program here. Lucia, this is Brandy Beauchamp, Gabby's mother. She's moved into the old house in Genoa Bay."

Lucia smiled at me with warm brown eyes. Taking off her work gloves, she offered her hand. "Nice to meet you," she said. "And you too, Gabby," she shook Gabby's hand. "So, you like horses, do you?"

"Oh yes," Gabby said, breathless. "My grandparents have horses. I get to ride when I'm at their house," she said. I made a special effort not to roll my eyes.

"Good. Then you should meet Clair. She's dying for some extra attention. Angela is taking off her saddle right now, and I think I have some carrots that would make her morning just plummy. Do you think you could feed her carrots while Angela brushes her?"

"Absolutely," Gabby agreed.

Lucia smiled, glancing at me. "Let's go find her then," Lucia said. We walked into what turned out to be a neatly kept four-stall barn. Three other horses, all of them smaller than average, watched from their stalls.

Angela was just pulling off Clair's blanket when we arrived. Lucia included Clair in the introductions, just as if the old horse were part of her family.

When Gabby finished giving Clair her treats, Lucia complimented her good horse sense. "You certainly know your way around a horse, don't you, Gabby?"

"I told you. I ride with my Grandpa."

Lucia smiled. "Right. You did say that."

"We should be going," I said. "We've kept you from your work."

"I don't want to go," Gabby said. "I like the horses."

I suspected that I'd have trouble getting Gabby away the barn. But before I could respond, Lucia said, "Maybe you'd like to ride with Angela, then? She's going to exercise Old Dan and Blackberry. You might as well help out."

I shook my head. "I don't think so. I don't want Gabby riding by herself."

Lucia laughed. "I'm sorry. Angela is only going to lead the horses around the paddock this afternoon. They don't have students today, but I want them to get some time out of their stalls. They've been inside all weekend. They might as well have Gabby on board." She pointed. "You and I can sit on the fence right there," she pointed, "and watch."

I sighed. As usual, my anxiety had more than taken the driver's seat. It had stolen control of the car and sent it careening down a canyon road without brakes. "I guess that would be fine," I admitted.

While Gabby and Angela finished putting Clair away, Lucia and I climbed up on the paddock fence to sit in the sun. "So, is this your first visit to the farm?"

"Yes. We'd never even heard of it, not until a tree fell on the house this weekend. My neighbor told me to come over and get a bid on repairs."

"We haven't been here all that long. Only the locals know about us. Who's your neighbor?"

"Cliff Lowry."

"Hmm. I don't think I know him. But I just hang out with the horses. Are you interested in therapeutic riding?"

"I don't know anything about it. What do you do?"

"We give disabled children the chance to ride. Riding works their core muscles, and gives them stimulation they would never get in a classroom."

"And it works?"

"I've seen autistic children begin to talk through a riding program. You bet it works." She grinned at Angela, who led a gray horse into the ring. Gabby waved at me from on top of the horse.

As we talked, I realized that we had more in common than I'd have guessed. Lucia had both a daughter and a son; Sienna, a ballet student in a Duncan studio, was two years older than Gabby. Matthew, her ten-year-old, loved computer games. Rick, Lucia's husband, worked for the provincial government as a civil engineer. The family attended a small church not far from the farm.

In a funny way, Lucia reminded me of Eve. Not that they looked alike. Lucia was as dark as Eve was blond. While Eve was tall and statuesque, Lucia was short and lean, but firm. Very firm. Thinking about it, I wondered if it were loneliness that made the connection between the two. What I missed so much, even in my short time on the Island, was a good friend. I made a mental note to call Eve and tell her about the storm.

We talked about Shiloh Farms. "It all started in 1858, when the Sisters of St. Ann came to British Columbia and started schools and hospitals all over the Province. They kept the school going for nearly one hundred years, serving indigenous students as a day school, and later as a boarding school.

"It was a Catholic school and eventually served as a convent." She pointed to the big school building behind us. "They built that in 1928. It's old but it's solid. We're renovating it, adding insulation, new wiring, that kind of thing. We're doing it one room at a time, as we raise the funds. It's slow going."

"It looks like it could be a national historical site. Do you have that sort of thing in Canada?"

"We do. But the board has chosen not to go that route. It really limits what you can do with the property."

At that moment Angela came into the riding ring leading Gabby on an old saggy-backed chestnut horse. Gabby waved as she passed us, grinning with the pride of a derby winner. We waved back.

"What about the gardens?" I asked. "What on earth do you do with all that produce?"

Lucia laughed. "You're thinking about zucchini, aren't you?" she teased. "Like that joke that says you know you have no friends when you have to buy zucchini in the store, right?"

She settled herself on the fence, throwing her braid back over her shoulder. "We sell the produce—all of it, actually. We have a fresh produce service that provides all of the vegetables and herbs for dozens of restaurants in the area—all the way to Victoria. And we go to the farmers' markets here in Duncan and in other communities on the Island. We sell it in our own market up the hill. Did you see that yet? It's further up the driveway." Again she pointed. "You can buy produce and herbs—both fresh and dried—and things baked in our kitchen program. We even have T-shirts," she said, giggling.

"My mind is spinning," and it was. I was thinking about the baking and cooking I had yet to do for guests. Might the old farm supply our place as well? I wanted to know more. "You have a kitchen program?"

She nodded. "You'd have to stay all day if I told you all the things we're into."

"Who does the gardening?"

"The Segue men."

"Segue?"

"Guys who live on campus. They're here to bridge the gap. Some of them are coming off drugs, or off the streets. Some have emotional issues. Some are just out of prison. But they live here on campus and they garden as part of their rehab and recovery."

I shook my head, still struggling with the vast number of the programs that went on in this amazing place. "Back to the kitchen program. What's that?"

"It's for individuals who need ways to live independently. We serve lunch here every day, for everyone on campus—volunteers, workers, visitors—anyone who is hungry. A paid staff member leads the lunch crew. She runs a training program for disabled individuals.

Some of them have Down's Syndrome, others have had head injuries, or strokes. But they all contribute to the kitchen team. Some of them go on to jobs in the community. It's pretty amazing actually."

"I'm way beyond amazed. How long have you all been here?"

"The building and grounds have been here forever. The Sisters have only recently given the property to the foundation. The programs? Well, they've been growing a little every year."

"That explains why I hadn't heard about them when I lived on the Island."

"The farm was here. But the whole project was just a dream in those days."

"Amazing."

"Well, then," Lucia said, sliding off the fence. "Why don't we shock you even more completely? You and Gabby should join us for lunch. I think they're baking lasagna today. And, I smelled lemon bars when I came in. Those are worth a trip here from anywhere."

"What about your students?"

"I'm finished for the morning. Besides, I'm not the therapist. I'm just in charge of the horses. And I'm hungry. How 'bout it?"

I looked down at this friendly woman, one hand on the fence, the other stretched out to help me down, and I wondered if God had just given me a new gift. I'd missed Eve nearly every day since I'd taken her to the airport. Though we'd written emails and phoned often, my loneliness had grown into an ache that accompanied me wherever I went. And in the weeks since Eve left, I hadn't had a moment to myself to connect with the community. It didn't take long to reach a decision.

"Gabby," I called across the riding ring, just as my daughter climbed down into Angela's arms. "I think we're going to have lunch here today."

Thirteen

The title across the top of the yellowed paper read, "Certificate of Live Birth." Excited, I scanned the form, eager to gather the secrets there. I believed that Maggie had never had children. Born at St. Paul's Hospital, Vancouver, British Columbia, on March 3, 1948, the infant's name is Mary Ellen Blackburn. Mother, Margaret Ellen Blackburn. Father, Albert Blackburn. The certificate, filled out in sprawling cursive and signed by the attending physician, gives no other information. No height or weight. The ink has faded over the years, and I wonder, looking at the paper, did Mary Ellen's memory fade as well? And then it occurred to me, is the child, now a woman, still alive?

THAT LUNCH WARMED more than my stomach. Lucia introduced me to many of the staff and volunteers at Shiloh Farms. To my surprise, these strangers greeted me like a long-lost friend. Most knew Maggie's house, and all were excited that I'd chosen to open it again as a Bed and Breakfast. Though the big old room—with its bare wood floors and tall ceiling—seemed cold and institutional when Lucia and I sat down, the people who shared that meal with us formed an enthusiastic community, more than willing to include this Florida transplant.

Our hour in the old dining-room had given Gabby a gift as well. She had been the happy recipient of much love and attention; our time there proved to be a great diversion from the struggles and chores at the old house.

The work being done by the staff at Shiloh Farms intrigued me, and I appreciated their commitment to care for the least in the world, the unwanted, the lost, the misfits. Leaving the farm, I remembered what a misfit I was myself in the old days, and if it weren't for Maggie, I'd be as lost as many of the folks at the farm. And as I drove home, toward Genoa Bay, I felt more certain than ever. If it were possible, I would have the carpentry school complete the work on the old house. Lost in these thoughts, Gabby's voice surprised me.

"Mom," Gabby said, her voice quivering, "I hate it here."

Well, drop a rock on the roof of the car. Where did that come from?

Apparently the attention at lunch hadn't meant as much to Gabby as I thought. "You don't hate it. You haven't even been here for two weeks."

"I don't have any friends. No kids live near us. I can't even ride my bike."

Gabby, like most kids, uses the shotgun approach to complain. I've learned that it's best not to get caught up in her lists. When it came to loneliness, I knew that Gabby meant girls, not kids in general, so I avoided the temptation to point out how much fun she'd shared with Cliff's boys. "It's summer vacation. Be patient, honey. When school starts, you'll have lots of new friends."

"I won't either. Everyone here already has friends. I know it."

"You'll have new friends from church."

"We don't go to church."

She had me there. "You will. We only missed church because we had a tree fall on the house. We couldn't leave until we had the house closed up."

"There's nothing to do here."

"Of course there is. We have lots to do." I realized that Gabby had me caught in the lists. So much for wisdom.

"Only work. The only thing to do at the new house is work." I looked over at my daughter to discover tears rolling down her face. In all of her seven long years, Gabby had never been the tantrum type, and frankly her tears worked a far greater magic without screaming and kicking. When I reached over to pat her knee, she snatched my hand and held it in her own. Tears dripped on the back of my knuckles and rolled down my fingers.

We drove on in silence, my heart squeezed by her pain. I'd

known moving would be hard for Gabby; still, this raw expression of misery hurt. No mother sets out to injure her own children. Until this moment, I'd always believed that kids were resilient. Now I was beginning to have doubts. I hoped that this emotion, this loneliness would pass.

And then I remembered. I'd hoped the same thing for myself when Timothy died.

In truth, restoring the house and opening a business was my adventure. It wasn't fair that I'd forced Gabby to leave the comforts of place and people in order for me to follow what I hoped, what I believed was God's leading.

Once again, I began to doubt my listening ability. Maybe these experiences I'd had with the voice of God were nothing more than imagination, or indigestion, or both. Would God ask me to do anything that caused Gabby such intense pain? Today, with her salty tears rolling off the back of my hand, I wasn't sure any more.

"Gabby," I said, glancing over at her. "What if you and I look for something that you can do this summer? Maybe there's a class around here, or a kids' group. We can find something, I'm sure of it. You're not the only bored kid on Vancouver Island."

She looked at me, her face a mixture of sadness and hope. "What kind of class?"

I didn't want to disappoint her, so I hedged. "We can ask around. There has to be something going on here. We'll get some ideas and I'll let you choose."

"I'd like to ride horses at Shiloh Farms."

"It was fun, wasn't it?"

She looked up at me, her face a practiced picture of sadness. I wonder if she knows how easy it is to work me. "It's the only fun I've had here," she said.

I frowned. "Gabby, I'm sorry, but you can't be part of that riding group. It's for disabled children. It's part of their therapy."

Her face, wrinkled in disgust, reminded me of Maggie. "I want to ride horses with Angela," she said, crossing both arms across her chest.

Thinking back to the horse barn, I remembered that Lucia's

daughter took ballet lessons at some studio in town. "What about dance lessons?"

"What?"

"Lucia's daughter takes ballet lessons. Maybe you'd like to try ballet?"

"I don't know," she said. "It sounds kind of sissy."

"You *are* a girl, you know. Lots of girls like sissy things."

"I don't want to do some stupid dance class."

Her lower lip began to quiver. "I hate it here."

"No you don't. Give it a chance. We'll think of something."

"What about swimming lessons?"

"I could look into it. I'm not sure where they do that here."

"There was a pool at home," she said. "It was big, and there were kids and I miss my lessons there."

"I know. But that was a Naval Air Station. It was a training pool." With my daughter now 3,000 miles away, she sounded as if she loved the base pool. Kids! That pool was kept cool—refrigerated, actually—to help sailors prepare for action at sea. Every day after lessons, Gabby complained, teeth chattering until I could hardly understand her, about the stupid freezing base pool. Now, when the pool was unavailable, she missed it.

Slumping further in her seat, Gabby dropped her chin on her hand, her elbow on the armrest, staring out the side window. "I want to swim."

"You and I can swim in the bay, you know. Or in the lake. We don't need a pool."

"I miss the swim team."

To be honest, Gabby was never on a swim team. But in the half hour after her lessons, the swim team showed up in the locker-room. Though mostly ignored by the teens, Gabby and her friends liked to pretend that they were team members. "How about this," I suggested. "I'll call about lessons as soon as we get home." I reached over and tugged at her ponytail. "I promise, honey. By this time next summer, you'll feel like you've lived here all your life. The first few months are hard for everyone, even me. After that, it's a piece of cake."

How little I knew.

❀

In the weeks after our trip to Shiloh Farms, our troubles seemed to multiply like the hordes of rabbits that regularly ate their way through Maggie's garden.

The three roofing companies who inspected the house and bid the project suggested, because of its condition, that I replace the entire roof—not just the damaged section. And, because of our location, and the soft-pitched lines of the house, they suggested using metal. Right, and why don't I put diamond-studded counters in the kitchen?

Yes, the attorney informed me, the house was insured against storm damage. But, to save money, Maggie had chosen a much larger deductible than most. Only the actual damage caused by the storm would be covered. If I chose to replace the roof at this time, the additional cost must be paid from my own pocket.

In the space of a few days, one slightly damaged corner turned into a major outlay of funds.

In short, by the time I considered both the deductibles and the additional cost of roof replacement, I found myself significantly squeezed for money. Maggie had left the house and all her worldly goods to me. I assume she meant the inheritance to be a good thing. A gift. A bequest that would enhance our lives.

The problem, of course, was that Maggie had no worldly goods other than the house. The cost of renovations and repair would use every dime of the funds Timothy had left us, as well as most of the money I'd made from the sale of our home in Florida. It seemed that I'd reached a point of no return.

It was time to leap, and never look back.

Under these conditions, the cost of renovations and repairs might never be returned in the sale of the house—unless I could sell it as a well-established and successful business. As a private home, Maggie's house was worth no more than the land underneath it.

As yet, we hadn't made a single dime on our investment.

The pressure of finances began to build; until just two weeks after the storm, it became clear that I had to do something to bring in some money. Now.

I began to seriously consider Cliff's suggestion that I serve a daily breakfast buffet to the guests at the marina. After all, as a Bed and Breakfast, serving a daily meal would eventually become a routine part of our existence. Starting sooner, rather than later, wouldn't make any real difference to me. In fact, starting sooner might be the only effective way to bring in the money I needed to finish renovations.

Once again, as I considered my options, I felt a wave of grief wash over me. Having been married for more than ten years, I would never forget how much security I gained from my partnership with Timothy. In every decision, big or small, I had depended on Timothy's input. While I didn't always follow his suggestions—in fact, he would probably say that I rarely did—I always valued his opinions. His input provided an endless source of creative ideas. The depth of wisdom he'd gained in his short life was a treasure to me.

This was the hardest part of being left alone. Considering decisions without him.

I did pray about these financial concerns. After all, if God led me to Genoa Bay, I figured that my finances were now his problem too. I asked. I waited. And most of the time, I didn't hear much of anything. Sometimes, following God can be completely exasperating.

I needed money. Serving a buffet seemed a likely answer.

This decision represented a big shift in my thinking. I'd hoped to have a full year to help Gabby and *me* settle into our new home. I wanted the old inn to feel familiar, safe, before I introduced strangers to my transplanted and already shell-shocked daughter. This change of plans unsettled me; but there seemed to be no other options.

While the draftsmen worked on plans and permits, I began to strategize. If I were careful, separating the space with vinyl or a temporary wall, I could continue to use the kitchen, even during construction. It occurred to me that if I served breakfast Wednesday through Sunday, ending by ten on the weekdays, construction crews could begin work, pounding and sawing and drilling, after my guests left. That plan gave construction crews full access to the house on Mondays and Tuesdays.

However, before I began, I would need to redecorate both the great room, and the landscaping leading from the marina to the house. Thinking back to a business and marketing class I'd been forced to take in college, I began to consider my options. I had to establish a budget, develop a menu, plan a brochure, and figure out how much to charge for such a service. Of this list, the only thing I could confidently complete was the brochure. I was a graphics design major, after all.

Of course, I needed a business license, and perhaps a restaurant license as well. Then, I'd need whatever permits were required for the development of the property. I began by researching provincial and city agencies via the web. The rules and regulations and application forms felt as overwhelming and difficult as swimming in Karo syrup.

Undaunted, I woke early every morning and worked at the task. I looked at the ads of other Bed and Breakfasts, comparing their menus and those of established local restaurants. I noted the cost of groceries, fresh produce, and other expendables. I began to consider how many guests I could serve each morning. Feeling like a four-year-old trying to design a space shuttle, I tried to estimate the costs of serving a quality meal, adding in what felt like an appropriate profit.

My mind swirled with options and decisions, and as often as not, I felt completely alone in the task. I made frequent appointments to talk with local regulators, completed various applications and drove back and forth to the various municipal and government agencies.

While I waited on the applications, I chose to get the great room ready for guests.

On a rainy Friday morning, Gabby and I went into Duncan with a supply list. Armed with fabric samples and photographs cut from magazines, Gabby and I started at the local paint store. I compared color samples while Gabby sat at a children's corner filled with books and toys.

"May I help you?"

A middle-aged man decked out in a green apron and rimless glasses stood behind me. I smiled. "Yes. I'd like that. I'm trying to match this color." I handed him a fabric swatch, and pointed to the color behind one of the flowers. "I want a pale seafoam, just exactly that hue. But I can't seem to find it on your sample chart."

"That's no problem," he said, smiling. "I have a color matching system. I can create it perfectly." He held the fabric at arm's length. "Is this your couch?"

"No, side chairs. But I have four of them. And I want the whole room to exude a soft, calming effect. I think this blue-green will be perfect for a house by the water." In spite of all my thinking and planning, I felt a sudden wave of doubt. "But now, I'm not so sure. What do you think?"

He laughed. "I'm no decorator. I just mix paint." He looked at the pictures in my hands. "May I?" I gave him my collection and he spent an admirable amount of time gazing at the photos. "Well, they're certainly beautiful. But I'll tell you what—why don't we ask my wife? She's much better at this than I am." He gestured to the other side of the store. "Come with me. She's over in housewares this morning."

I followed him through aisles of paint rollers, wood stains, and plaster repair materials, across the store to where an older woman in a matching apron stood high on a step stool, folding towels for wall display. "Linda," he said, looking up. "Can you take a look at this?" She patted a hand towel into place before climbing down the ladder. Her husband continued, "This young lady is redecorating a place by the water. I told her you have an eye for this sort of thing."

The man winked at me as he handed my pictures to his wife. "I'll leave you two, for now," he said. "When you're ready for paint, let me know."

Somehow, I'd been suckered into asking for advice from a woman I'd never met. Part of me was a little miffed. As a graphic designer, I ought to be able to choose colors and fabrics for a room renovation. Why should I listen to some old lady from a hardware store? Her tacky name-tag read, "Hi, I'm Linda Stevens."

"I love your photos," she said, setting them out over a stack of new bath towels. "Tell me about the house."

We talked about the home, and my desire to create a calm, restful room for my breakfast guests. "I can't do the whole project at once. It's too expensive. But I can afford enough to get started. I can pull things together later." I pointed to my graph-paper floor-plan as I described my plans. "I'll be serving breakfast in this area, so I want to use colors over here that unify the whole space."

She nodded, approving. "I think you're doing a beautiful job. What direction does the room face?"

"East," I said.

"And what do you have covering the windows?"

"Drapes. Horrible, thick, heavy old drapes." I laughed. "I'm going to throw them away. I can't wait."

"What will you replace them with?" She continued to gaze at the graph paper, as if she could see room itself. "Of course, you'll want something over the windows. The eastern sun is very bright, and with a view, you won't want any trees or landscaping in the way."

Window covering. I hadn't thought of that. I looked down at my floor-plan, mentally counting the seven windows on the east side of the house. Two more faced the marina. I felt myself blush. For someone so capable, I'd dropped the proverbial decorating ball. "I don't know what I was thinking. I hadn't even thought of that."

"You'll want to protect your guests from that morning sun; even this far north, without protection, your room will get too hot. But at the same time, you don't want to block their view." She looked at me, frowning. "I assume that's what they've come to see." She laughed. "And you don't want to bake your customers. Believe me, I know. We live over on Genoa Bay. If I don't close my windows in the morning, I can cook breakfast on the window-sills."

Still shocked by my mistake, I didn't notice, at first, that she had declared herself a virtual neighbor. "I didn't budget for window coverings."

"Maybe you can cover it. Let's take a look at some of the products we carry."

Carrying my folder of plans and clippings and across the store, Linda brought out book after book of shades and blinds and shutters. "There is quite a difference in cost between products, so you'll have to choose wisely." By the time we got around to estimating materials and installation, she'd nearly reduced me to tears. At seven hundred dollars a window, I was in big trouble.

"I can see you're a little overwhelmed," she said, kindness in her voice. "Maybe you need time to think about it all." She closed one of the books. "I can write up estimates for the things we've looked at and let you go home with samples."

I sat down on the counter stool and covered my face with my hands. I couldn't even buy paint without running into some new, expected expense.

Linda put her hand on my shoulder, patting gently. "You know, redecorating should be fun, not horrifying. Don't let this overwhelm you, kiddo."

At this point, she must have thought that I was hopelessly emotional. "I'm sorry. It's just that I inherited this stupid house with a sailboat hanging from the ceiling. And it needs so much work. And I have no money, really. And then, in that last storm, a tree fell on the house." I dropped my face onto my arms. "I need to make money, and soon. But I can't. Not yet. The whole thing just keeps getting crazier and crazier; even I don't know what I'm doing here anymore."

She looked at me for a long moment, surprise registering on her face. "Don't tell me," she said, raising one gnarled finger toward me. "I can't believe it. You must be talking about Maggie Blackburn's house."

"You know it?" I asked.

"Don't I!" She put her hand over mine. "We're your next-door neighbors. At least for a while we are," she said. "We just signed papers to sell. As a matter of fact, you might know who is buying our property. He's your neighbor too."

With dread filling my gut—like I'd eaten bricks for breakfast—I knew with absolute certainty exactly who had bought Linda's Genoa Bay home.

Fourteen

A crane sits in front of the old house, which remarkably, is missing its entire west facade. From the arm of the crane dangles the hull of the sailboat, half in and half out of the front entryway. The yard is bare dirt. Nearby, men stand in work clothes, some watching, some leaning on shovels, some holding ropes as they guide the 40-foot hull into the house. I know from their clothes—canvas pants worn high on the torso, with work shirts buttoned all the way to the collar—that the photo is very old, though it carries no date. I'm guessing the boat was moved sometime during the Depression. I count. There are at least eight men involved in the insane process of hanging a sailboat from the ceiling of the great room.

IT WAS STILL RAINING on the day we scheduled to paint. The kids arrived one by one, the first driving himself, others delivered in the cars of parents or friends. By nine-thirty, there were five teenagers in the great room, eager to open paint cans and get color on the wall. While they seemed to know one another, I couldn't quite keep them straight.

Liz seemed to believe that I'd brought the children in for playtime. Unable to keep her out from under feet, I tied the dog to a chair leg in the media room, where she sat whining her displeasure.

The kids seemed ready to work. They came dressed in old jeans and sweatshirts—though I think they hadn't thought about their shoes. The girls had tied up their hair. One of the boys even wore a kerchief over his head.

According to Lucia, who had recommended the members of my painting crew, Liam and Kayla were the oldest. In the spring these two would graduate from the Shiloh Farms Alternative School, and move on, either to technical school, or perhaps join the carpentry school full time. Celeste, another Alternative School student, had just finished her first year. Lucia told me that she had chosen to work with the Elder Garden over the summer, and was happy to pick up some extra money on her days off.

I worried that Seth and Janessa were too young to work well. Moments after they entered the room, I found them juggling paint brushes, and tossing tools across my living-room. "Come on kids," I said. "I'm not insured for skewering one another."

Gabby looked at me from the stairwell, where she sat watching it all, and raised one eyebrow. Even my seven-year-old thought I'd blown it, bringing this crowd of losers into the house. I might have made an error, but at least it was a mistake I could afford, and with so many things I couldn't afford, this one had to work. It had to.

"First things first," I said. "We probably aren't going to get to even open the paint today. We have to clear the room, clean the walls and tape off all the woodwork. At some point, with the furniture out of the way, we're going to rip this carpet out of this part of the room," I pointed. "And then, after we've got the whole thing prepped, we can start painting. I expect that might be tomorrow, at the earliest."

I could see collective dread in their eyes. "Ah, come on. It won't be so bad. There are a lot of us. Now that we're all here, we'll start by moving all this furniture to the north end of the room. We aren't going to be painting in there now, so just pile everything up against the windows." I gestured toward the dining area.

"Wow, you really got hit in that storm, didn't you?" Celeste said, noting the wooden boards over the corner windows. Though I'd had the tree's root-ball removed, I still hadn't replaced the windows. Considering the remodel, I figured I might as well get the whole thing done at once.

"A tree hit the roof," Gabby offered.

Together, the five of them managed to shove and drag couches and chairs, tables and lamps into what would become—once we renovated the kitchen—the new dining area. In the process, they managed to break only one lamp, which was fine by me. I'd never really liked it anyway.

For the rest of the morning, I had them taking down draperies (which we dumped in the front yard), pictures, and electrical plate covers. By the time we broke for lunch, the big old room echoed with boisterous teen voices. Because of the cool, wet weather, I served hot chili and fresh cornbread, with warm brownies for desert.

Lounging against the empty walls, we ate together, and the crew was gradually transformed, in my mind, from strangers into individuals. Mostly I listened in, though not secretly. After all, I was sitting right next to them.

I admit that part of me was curious. What kinds of kids end up in an alternative high school? I mean, if I hadn't left Alaska, if my step-father hadn't visited me on the couch in my mother's apartment, might I have landed in the same place?

They seemed so cooperative. Most of the time, they were friendly, though they clearly kept themselves at a distance. I attributed this to my old age. They were willing to follow my directions and for the most part, they worked as a team. These kids didn't seem like the misfits I envisioned when Lucia made her suggestion.

They were just ordinary kids, from what I could see, though clearly not your National Science Fair types.

After listening for a while, I tried to engage them in conversation. I asked Kayla, a petite teen with mousy brown hair, about her family.

She shrugged. "We live in Duncan, on the west side of the highway."

This, apparently, was all I needed to know. I tried again, asking Celeste what she planned to study after graduation.

Another shrug. "I'm going to look for a job," she said. "I can't afford school."

The silence that followed each of my failed attempts at conversation warned me away. It wasn't like I was trying to be their therapist or anything. I only wanted to be nice—you know, interested. Actually, having survived my own childhood, where mistrust surrounded every adult in my life, I think I wanted to avoid being thrown into the basket with all those other bossy, invasive, and overly nosy old people.

Eventually, I gave up, letting the kids take the lead.

Liam, who in my mind became Soul Patch, because of the

meager hairs he had cultivated below his bottom lip, complained about the cost of keeping a car on the road. "I just had to buy a new set of tires," he said. "Four-wheel drive, man. You replace one tire and you have to do the whole thing."

"At least you've got a car," Celeste said. She was a big girl, tall and thick, with coarse, dark hair caught in a clip at the back of her head. She removed the clip and shook out her hair. "I have to catch a ride, everywhere I go."

At this point, all joined in with a general mumble of appreciation for her problem. I remembered those days, waiting for the freedom of a driver's license. I asked, "So, do your parents mind? I mean, driving you around."

In the awkward pause that followed, I realized I'd said something wrong.

"I live with my Grandma," she said. "My mom split."

"Oh," I said, my mind desperate for some appropriate response. What could I say? *I'm sorry your mom left you. At least you have a grandmother.* Anything I came up with sounded empty, or worse, patronizing. The kids seemed as caught off guard as I was. I wasn't all that different from these kids. I'd had a rough life too. Why couldn't I figure out what to say?

In her innocence, Gabby saved the day. "I'd love to live with my Grams. She lets me eat cookies any time I want. Do you get cookies?" While the kids laughed, I groaned inwardly. In the short time Doreen had Gabby, she'd carefully drilled my daughter on the advantages of living with Grams. Great. Just great.

The kids laughed. "I wish," Celeste said, shaking her head. "My grandma doesn't bake."

Kayla had been fairly quiet up until that moment. She turned to me. "So, Mrs. Beauchamp, why did you buy this house, anyway?"

I smiled. "It's a little unusual, isn't it?"

"Yeah, man," Seth said, pointing to the hull hanging from the ceiling beams overhead. "What kind of person hangs a sailboat in the living-room?"

Kayla elbowed him, hard enough to spill chili from his bowl.

"It *is* kinda weird," Liam said, apparently in an effort to defend his friend.

"It's totally weird," I said. "Actually, I didn't buy the house. I inherited it—from the lady who lived here before me."

"She a relative?" Liam looked at me, interest brightening his eyes. "Your mother or something?"

I saw my chance. "Actually, I'm the one who split from my mother," I said, looking at Celeste. "I ran away from home when I was sixteen and landed here in Genoa Bay on a sailboat. Maggie Blackburn, who owned this house, took me in. I stayed here until I was married. When Maggie died, she left the house to me."

In Celeste's eyes, I saw something change. She identified with my story, though perhaps she did not yet fully trust me. Before I told her about my teen years, I'd been just another adult. Now, I was different, somehow. I wondered how long it would be before I recognized trust in those eyes.

"And you're going to live here?" Liam couldn't quite cover the surprise in his voice. "With the sailboat? You're not going to just sell the place?"

"We're going to run it as a Bed and Breakfast," I said, putting one arm around Gabby. The last time the old house hosted paying guests, these kids were no more than toddlers. No wonder they doubted my ability to bring the inn back to life. "As a business, the sailboat isn't just weird; guests will think it's quaint, maybe even charming, I hope. When Maggie ran the house, people came for the scenery, and the fishing, and sometimes for the boating. We hope they'll keep coming."

The faces of my painting crew reflected serious doubt. "Sure, whatever," Seth said, his voice declaring my insanity as clearly as a printed medical diagnosis. "Do you have any more of these brownies?"

❀

The new wall color matched my hopes exactly. It was the exact hue of sea glass, the color of Japanese floats, a pale blue-green that reminded me of sea and beach. I was pleased. We'd no more than finished when a week of bright sunshine and warming temperatures coaxed me into the yard again.

Gabby played outside while I focused on the gardens facing the marina. In that week, I edged and fertilized the lawn, attacked the weeds that had infiltrated Maggie's upper flower beds and began hacking my way through the ground cover that had completely obliterated the path to the marina.

If guests were to come to the house, this would be the part of the house they saw first. I envisioned a flagstone pathway from the field through the yard and up to new French doors on the porch.

It was tough work and soon I understood why much of North America had classified ivy as an invasive weed. Every morning, before the sun grew hot, I fought the roots with a pick-ax. When I cleared enough ground to walk, I went after the crown with garden shears, widening the path. Between playing with the dog, and reading books in the grass, Gabby helped by dragging the vines to a wheelbarrow.

In spite of gloves, my hands bloomed broad blisters that burst and peeled, leaving me with painful, oozing sores. In the evenings, I covered these wounds with tea bags, and wrapped my hands with gauze. Soon, it seemed, most of my work clothes sported tea-colored stains.

Every morning, I removed the gauze, layered new exam gloves under clean work gloves and started over.

In one corner of the yard, I cleared a new garden bed. Facing what would eventually become the new dining-room, I transplanted a low-growing vine maple, surrounded it with azaleas, and then filled the area toward the house with milkweed and dense clusters of zinnias, verbena and marigold—all removed from their pots by Gabby's capable hands. One by one, I began cleaning and refilling the hummingbird feeders Maggie had collected over the years. I hung these from the strongest arms of the maple tree, from the old hooks on the porch, and from sheep hooks in the south yard.

Between the new bed and the feeders, I hoped that my breakfast guests would have both hummers and butterflies—monarchs, if everything worked out as I hoped—to watch while they enjoyed my sumptuous spread. Okay. To be honest, I thought if the guests didn't like what they ate, maybe the entertainment would save the day.

One morning, while Gabby dawdled inside, I attacked the path with new gusto. In the last four days, I had finished nearly thirty feet of trail, and with every foot I gained, I envisioned another crowd of happy boaters coming to eat breakfast at the crazy house with the boat in the living-room.

I raised the ax above my head, and just as I brought it down, a voice said, "Hey, Brandy." I nearly dropped the ax. It was Cliff. I turned around and saw him fighting his way through the lower reaches of ivy. In the morning sun, he looked a little like a modern-day Meriwether Lewis.

"Oh, you scared me. I get so focused, you know?"

He laughed. "I've been watching. You look a bit like a sociopath. Are you taking out some deep-seated anger on this stuff?"

This must be his idea of a joke. "Not anger, really. But if you can do better," I said, offering the ax, "feel free to show me how."

He held up his hands, fending off the tool. "No thanks. I didn't mean to insult you, really. In fact I came to ask if you and Gabby would join the boys and I on an outing."

"Outing?" This guy never ceased to amaze me. His kindness went so far beyond neighborliness, that I'd begun to question his motives. He turned up with the regularity of the morning sun, and always with some gentle act of generosity. Was it possible, in this modern era, that this kind of gentleman still existed? Or had I run into a first-class fake?

"It's my day off. I have to run into Cowichan to pick up a boat part. And since I'm going out, I thought I'd take the boys to the Butterfly Garden over by Brentwood. After that, a little lunch. And then, a stroll through the Butchart—that is, if the boys haven't already imploded. I wondered if you and Gabby would like to join us."

I hesitated. Already filthy, I had so much left to do. So much yard left to reclaim. And then there was money. Both the Butterfly Garden and the Butchart were expensive, even years ago, when I'd moved away. How much more now?

And then another question slid by, so quickly that I almost didn't recognize it as a conscious thought. Where was all this attention going? Did Cliff Lowry have some ulterior motives for all this kindness? "I don't know," I admitted, shading my eyes from the morning sun. "We're kind of on a budget." I felt badly. Poor Gabby hadn't gotten away from the house in a long time.

"Oh, no. You don't have to pay." He held up a small laminated card. "I have a family pass. Pays for itself, actually. We can bring friends." He put his hands in his pants pockets. "Actually, it would help me if you came. The boys are feeling a little lonely. There aren't many kids out here. Not like their home."

It was a beautiful day; it would be good to get out. Banishing my other concerns, I brightened. "When are you going?"

"Meet us in the parking lot at eleven?"

I considered the offer. Having a day with Cliff might give me a chance to ask some questions about the things I'd heard from Linda Stevens. Maybe Cliff knew more about what Herbert Karras was doing than he'd let on. An outing would be a great opportunity, one I couldn't let pass. "You're on," I said, feeling my spirits instantly lift. Maybe I needed an outing too. "Should I pack a lunch?"

"Nope. I've got it covered."

An hour later, Cliff, dressed in a cotton Hawaiian-print shirt, opened the car door for me. All the kids squeezed into the back seat of an old Ford Focus. The air conditioner didn't work, which forced us to keep the windows down and shout over the roar of road noise. We'd hardly reached the main highway before I began to wonder how much of a break this outing would give anyone.

I already had the beginning of a headache.

We stopped at a marine supply store on the outskirts of Cowichan, and I waited with the kids while Cliff went inside. I had finally figured out which of the twins was Justin and which was James. Though they appeared essentially identical, I discovered that Justin was left-handed, so predominantly so that only a moment of observation betrayed his true identity. While we waited for Cliff, I turned to the back seat.

Gabby, her hair in long, blond pigtails, leaned over, staring into the screen of Justin's electronic toy. Absorbed by the game, Justin completely ignored her. "Don't you talk?" she said, her face just inches from his ears.

He frowned, but did not answer.

"He talks," James said. "Trust me. It's better when he doesn't."

"Why is that?" Gabby asked.

"He's not very nice."

I could see this wasn't progressing in a necessarily helpful way. "What do you like to do, James?"

He ran his finger over the window, tracing imaginary pictures. "I like to ride my bike. And I like soccer—we play on a team at my mom's house. And we're both on the swim team in Duncan," he said. "But I'm the fastest. Way faster than Justin. Way."

Gabby's eyes got big. "A swim team? In Duncan? Mom. Did you hear that?"

Cliff came around the side of the car, unlocked the trunk and placed a package inside. He opened the door and dropped into the driver's seat. "Sorry. That took longer than I thought. They had the part waiting, but the guy who put it away was out for lunch. Nobody knew where he left it."

"James tells us that the boys are on the swim team."

"Monday, Wednesday, and Friday."

"Can anyone join?"

"I think so. As long as they can swim one pool length, unassisted."

"Well now, that's an answer to one young woman's fervent prayer," I said. Cliff looked over at me, confused. "Gabby swam in Florida. She loved it, and really misses the pool."

"She's in luck. Leanne Wilmer has a great program. She has older kids serve as summer coaches. I think the next session starts in a week or so." He backed up, only to wait for a long line of cars clogging the main street.

"Things have sure changed here," I said. "This place used to look like a ghost town, even in the summer."

"Yep. Cowichan has been gentrified some since you moved away. I'm about to show you why."

I couldn't begin to guess what Cliff had up his Hawaiian shirtsleeve. He turned toward town, eventually pulling into a four-stall parking lot in front of what might be an ordinary building. However, from the siding above the front door, a full-sized antique bicycle hung, decorated by loaves of bread. Funky.

"This is it, folks. Come on inside."

The air inside was redolent with the smell of freshly baked bread, and with other scents as well—cinnamon, ginger, and basil.

On one end of the room, a glass wall separated the retail store from a giant flour mill. On the other end, small wooden tables allowed room for customers to enjoy bakery treats. At a nearby counter, giant stainless pots provided self-service coffee. The floor was made of wide, recycled planks. The walls were wood as well, rough and unfinished.

The whole of the space glowed in the soft caramel of rough-cut cedar.

A crowd of customers clustered around the display area, pointing as they marveled at the variety of bread and pastry. Behind the counter, signs, white chalk on black flint, featured organic breads, most made with whole grains, seeds and nuts. The store carried spelt and potato flour products as well, and even featured one entirely gluten-free bread—though I'm not sure how that is even possible.

Cliff waved at one of the women behind the counter. "Hey, Brenda," he called. "Boys, what kind of sandwich do you want?" The twins moved toward the counter, their noses pressed to the glass.

"This is the picnic you mentioned?" I asked.

"You didn't think I was actually going to make anything, did you?" he laughed, as he stepped into the back of the customer line. "No. If you want to survive a date with me, you've got to order up."

A date? Did Cliff think this was a date? I was stupefied. Maybe I'd heard him wrong. Maybe the smell of cinnamon rolls, or fresh bagels had affected my hearing. Stunned, I requested a sandwich and waited silently as Brenda, or whoever she was, prepared our order.

Moments later, we carried a bag of sandwiches and a tray of drinks to a picnic table on a grassy knoll overlooking the harbor. Below us, a boat launch disappeared into bouncing waves. A gravel beach seemed to call for beach combing, and a light breeze cooled the air. I shivered. "Here," Cliff said, slipping out of his fleece. "I'm not cold. Why don't you put this on?"

Oh man. My antenna for weirdness was vibrating like a washing machine on spin cycle. He draped the jacket over my shoulders. Unwilling to look at him, I made a big point of opening the food bags and distributing drinks.

Still anxious about being with this unusual man, I listened while Cliff gave thanks for the food, and the kids argued about which drink belonged where. "You said you were hungry," he said, pointing at my sandwich. "So, eat up already."

Fifteen

In the photograph, Albert and Maggie wear hiking boots, hats and shorts, safari-style. Smiling, they lean against a fence, the happy foreground in a striking alpine vista. Some distance away stands a young woman, arms crossed, her weight balanced on one hip, her chin set, her face a carefully masked tornado of rage. In this picture, I recognize those emotions. They are mine at the same age.

I ATE HALF MY SANDWICH, wrapping the other half and putting it back in the white paper bag. "Can we go explore the beach?" Justin asked his dad.

Cliff responded quickly. "Sure. Just stay within shouting distance, eh? And don't go in the water."

I turned to Cliff, a giggle escaping before I could catch it. "Eh? Did I hear you say 'eh'? When an American says 'eh' they are usually mocking the locals."

Gabby tugged on my sleeve. "Yes, you may," I said, wrapping one arm around her as I kissed her hair. "Ditto for you too. We're going to be out all day, so don't get wet. If you do, you'll be cold. Got it?"

She waved over her head as the three children ran toward the concrete ramp leading to the beach. We watched in silence as they began to explore the pools in the tidal zone.

He laughed. "You can be kind of cruel, you know. I've been living on the island since '98. I guess you just pick up the Canadian accent, eh?" We both laughed at this. He swirled his juice bottle. "You going to finish that sandwich?"

I pushed the bag toward him. "Go ahead."

"Something bothering you? You've been awful quiet this morning."

"I'm tired. I started on that ivy before six."

He nodded, unwrapping my leftovers. "You've put a lot of effort into that old place," he said. I heard caution in his voice and I tensed, waiting for what would certainly follow. "I know it's none of my business," he began—which is the way most nosy and opinionated people begin—"but are you sure you know what you're doing? I mean, it's not just the money. You're putting your heart and soul into this project. What happens if it doesn't work?"

Avoiding his gaze, I put my chin on my hand and stared out at the kids. Gabby was turning over rocks and looking for tiny crabs, screaming as they scampered out of the sun. "It will," I said. "Work, I mean."

"But how do you know? How many years will it be before you start to turn a profit? And how long can you keep pouring money into it while you wait?"

I looked at him, surprised by the intensity of his voice. "I'm new at this. I'll give you that. But I'm not stupid. I have a budget, and a plan. I'm good at marketing. And what is this anyway? Last time we talked, you were encouraging me to serve breakfast to the marina guests. What's changed?"

Cliff looked down at his sandwich, suddenly mesmerized by ham and cheese. "No. That's not it," he said, fooling with the sandwich wrapping.

"Then what is it, exactly?"

"I don't know. I guess I'm worried."

"I'm not yours to worry about."

"We're friends, aren't we? I can worry about my friends."

He still hadn't looked me in the eye. So, I reached out and touched his hand and smiled when he looked up. "Yes. We're friends," I said. "You've been great to us. I wouldn't be as far along as I am without your help and advice."

This seemed more direct attention than Cliff could bear. He looked down to the beach and shouted to one of the boys, who had made a game of jumping across the spaces between driftwood, "James! Be careful. That wood could tumble!"

"Cliff, since we're friends, I need to ask you something. It's something that's been bothering me for a couple of weeks."

He glanced at me, his attention focused on the boys. "What is it?"

"When I went into town to buy paint, I ran into one of the neighbors. Linda Stevens. She works at the hardware store in old town. Do you know her?"

"Sure," he admitted. "She owns the Spanish house on the corner across from your place."

I nodded; I knew the place. Most Genoa Bay residents had chosen a Northwest look for their homes, daylight basements, wood siding, a cedar roof. Linda's home had pale stucco siding, complete with a tile roof, and arches between the posts on her porch. Saltillo tiles covered the patio behind the house. Hers was the yard where Maggie and I had first seen the deer family. "Has she lived there long?"

"She and Ken moved here after their kids left home," he said. Cliff put his elbows on the picnic table and cupped his chin in his hands. Fingering his beard, he considered. "I'd say they've been there about seven years."

"She was pretty excited that I was a neighbor. She had lots to tell me. But some of it was upsetting. I need to ask if you know anything about it."

"What did she say?"

I took a deep breath. Though I wasn't really confronting Cliff, my body didn't seem to know the difference. My heart hammered in my ears as I spit it out, "She said that Herbert Karras made an offer on their house. It's contingent on a bunch of hoop-jumping, of course." I waited, watching Cliff's face for any sign of surprise. There was none. "You knew that," I said.

"There have been rumors."

"What else have you heard?"

He sighed, put down his hands and, as if he were polishing his story, began rubbing the nail of his right thumb with his left. "I think he's made offers on every house in the Bay. I know that he's approached all the homeowners above the marina."

"Why? The development thing? Are people really willing to sell? What are his plans?"

"Wait. One question at a time."

I took a deep breath, and then forced myself to swallow—as if by these actions I could break up the sense of doom that seemed to crowd my consciousness like the fog over the bay. Was this why Cliff tried to warn me off the business? How much did he know? And more importantly, how much would he be willing to tell me? "So spill it."

"Brandy, he's my boss. I work for him."

"So, you have your loyalties."

"Not at all. I'm just saying that he doesn't exactly consider me his confidant."

"But you know something. You weren't surprised by the offer on their house."

"I hear things. Nothing with any detail, really. He keeps an office at the marina. Sometimes, he talks on the phone. Sometimes, people come to see him there. That's all. I do my job, and I let him do his."

"But why? Why is he buying up everything?"

He hesitated. "I don't think it's a big secret, really. I told you the night we roasted marshmallows at your place. He's planning a development."

"For what?"

"I'm only getting the information as I pick it up. It seems he wants to build a big, fancy marina, with condos, a hotel, the whole fishing village thing. He wants swimming pools and guest cottages, and tennis courts, and he wants to expand the marina facilities."

I must have looked stunned. I tried to speak but no sound came out. I knew that he wanted to develop his property, but I couldn't wrap my mind around an idea this big. I'd categorized his plans as expansion. The concept Cliff described was light-years from the tiny marina we knew. For a few moments, I let my imagination run with it, ticking off the changes that such a plan would force. A bigger road. The destruction of old growth forest. Dredging the bay. A building site that large would demand the complete reconfiguration of the peninsula where the old house stood. And what about zoning? What would that kind of development do to the ecology of the bay? Would anyone consider the loss of habitat?

"How long has this plan been cooking?"

"Actually, I don't know."

"How many owners have agreed to sell?"

"I don't know that either."

"You're a library of information."

"I told you. I only work for him."

"What about money? Where is the money for all of this development coming from? I mean, you have to be talking millions and millions of dollars!"

"Probably many times that much."

"Does he talk to you about that? The money involved?"

"Not at all."

I began to worry about all the things I didn't know. "I told him I wouldn't sell."

"I know."

"You said he didn't talk to you about it."

"You told me," he said. "On the day it happened. Remember?"

I didn't remember. "What happens if I'm the last house left? Can he force me to sell? Like ~~imminent~~ *eminent* domain? Do you have that in Canada?"

"Not for a private development. I don't think so."

"This is like one of those nightmares, where some little old lady ends up in a tiny house completely surrounded by ninety-story apartment buildings."

This time, Cliff touched me, a gentle squeeze on my shoulder. "You aren't an old lady," he said. "And we aren't talking ninety-story condos."

An old friend roared in my gut. I recognized it by the jagged knife wound left in my stomach lining. Fear. "I'm not going to quit, you know. I'm not going to give up before I even start."

"I know that. You're not a quitter. I just think you should be careful," he said. "That's all. Be wary. This is business. And Karras has been doing business longer than you've been alive. Bigger business than you're used to. I don't know anything specific. I just hear things. He's nothing to mess with, you know? I'm just asking you to be careful, okay?"

❀

The day was too beautiful, and I chose to tuck Cliff's warning away; I could always worry later. With bright sunshine and warm temperatures, all the world looked to be on summer vacation. As we put on our seatbelts in Cowichan, Cliff looked into his rear-view mirror and said to the kids, "They have the best ice-cream in the world at the Butchart. But, if you want, we can go see the butterflies first."

"Ice-cream first," James said, nearly coming off the back seat.

"Ice-cream it is," Cliff agreed, sneaking a wink at me.

The Butchart Gardens occupy more than fifty acres of ground just outside of Victoria, Canada on the southeast end of Vancouver Island. Through most of the summer, the Gardens teem with visitors from all over the globe. I hadn't been back since my college days, when I used to go with Maggie. She loved her annual summer visit, where she told me she found new inspiration for her own garden.

Frankly, I didn't understand Maggie's enthusiasm. Her garden was a wildly informal mish-mash of color and texture. Behind the house in Genoa Bay, Maggie kept no ground bare, no tidy rows, no uniform splashes of broad color. In Maggie's garden, you found statues of the seven dwarfs, a garden elf, and even a three-foot toad. Unlike keepers of formal gardens, Maggie hid lettuce plants among her dahlias, and corn behind her azaleas. She displayed hand-made signs for her garden visitors, both human and animal.

The Butchart Gardens are exactly the opposite.

Everything about the Butchart is measured. Exact. Formal. Each color plays off the others in carefully designed patterns. The flowerbeds are weedless. The lawn is immaculate, perfectly edged, completely level, without weed or crab grass. The roses are perfectly pruned and consistently fertilized. The fountains are formal, with angels and nymphs springing out of granite and marble. There are no clear-cutting rabbits at the Butchart. Designed by professionals and maintained by a staff of hundreds, the Butchart is impressive, but it is not personal.

Being there made me miss Maggie. As we walked the cement paths, I remembered vividly how she praised the work of the gardeners there. While Maggie gardened in her own unique style, she never lost her enthusiasm and respect for those who chose to do it differently.

Hordes of tourists, each sporting some variety of camera, crowded the sidewalks. Cliff and I followed a group of enthusiastic teenagers, shooting pictures with their cell phones, through the gardens. Our own children ran ahead of us, ignoring our instructions to stay nearby. Cliff seemed oblivious to the kids' energy. Instead, he joined the tourists, taking photographs of every bloom, every basket, and every vista—from the Sunken Garden, through the Italian Garden to the Piazza.

Before long though, the heat and sunshine wore us out and we gave up. Leading the kids to the visitor area, we bought soft ice-cream in hand-made waffle cones. "This is so good," I said. "Must be the full-fat variety."

Cliff agreed. "Not your normal watery fat-free stuff. Hey, look. They're starting a show," he said, pointing to the Welcome Plaza. "Kids, you want to go see a show?"

While pirates and damsels sang their way around portable sets, the kids sat on the concrete, clapping and laughing and clearly enjoying the show. Cliff and I chose a bench at the back of the crowd, eating slowly and enjoying the sunshine. "It's so beautiful here," I said.

"I know. I try to capture it in photographs. It helps to look at them in the dead of winter. Almost like a promise that winter won't last forever."

"We should all keep some kind of reminder like that."

"I know. Up here, winter lasts a long, long time. Sometimes, we don't have spring until after July 1st. After Florida, you might be a little overwhelmed by the rain."

"I wasn't thinking about the weather."

"What then?"

"About other dark places. Like grief. Or loss. Or change. Those things can seem to last forever too. It would help if we could keep a picture of better times somewhere. Maybe we'd remember that even dark emotions don't last forever."

"It doesn't, you know," he said, looking at me. "Last forever."

I sighed. "That's what they say."

"But you don't believe it."

"I wish I did."

When the show ended, we took the kids to the restroom, washed their hands and headed for the car. I was tired, happy to call it a day. But James and Justin were not about to give up a trip to the Butterfly Farm.

"What is a Butterfly Farm anyway?" Gabby asked.

"I've never taken her to one," I explained.

"It's a tent, sort of. And inside, the place is crawling with butterflies," James piped up. "They're everywhere, crawling all over you. You have to be careful, or you'll squish 'em."

I glanced back, and recognized horror in Gabby's expression. "Honey, you won't squish one."

Cliff must have seen it in the rearview mirror, because he laughed and said, "The farm buys butterfly chrysalises from all over the world. They let the cases develop into butterflies that hatch right where we can see them." He looked at me, apparently hoping that I could help.

I shrugged. I'd never been to a butterfly garden either.

He went on. "They show species we don't have here, butterflies you'll never see for the rest of your life. You won't believe the colors and sizes. They're beautiful and very gentle."

"Besides," Justin said, looking up from his electronic game, "nobody really squishes them. You can feed them, though."

Gabby visibly relaxed. "I knew they didn't squish them," she said, with a bravado I knew was completely false.

After we bought tickets, we went through an exhibit designed to teach the children about the life-cycle of the butterfly. We observed a large collection of chrysalises and saw live larvae.

"Those are dead," Gabby said with certainty.

"Nope, honey," Cliff said. "They look dead, but they aren't. Even though we can't see it, there's a butterfly growing inside that case. Someday, when it's ready, the butterfly will chew its way out of the case and fly away."

She looked doubtful.

"I know," James said, eager to explain. I could imagine this little guy in a classroom, nearly jumping out of his seat as he raised his hand. His voice held that same tone of triumph. "Sometimes, when God is at work, you can't see it. But that doesn't mean that nothing is happening."

Justin added, "Like when the whales go from our place to Hawaii every year to give birth. Nobody knows how they know to do that. But God planned it that way. And then one day, every single summer, the whales just show up, right back here."

Gabby put one hand on the display window and brought her face very near. I could tell by her silence and concentration that she was mesmerized by this idea—that something very important was happening inside these lifeless shells.

It made me think, as I bent down to her level and looked inside. Was something happening inside me? Something I could not yet see, or feel? Some new kind of life, about to be born? I put one hand on Gabby's shoulder and squeezed. She looked up at me, smiling.

I hoped so. Dear God, please let something be changing.

The butterfly enclosure amplified the heat of our summer day. With high humidity and matching temperatures, I felt as if I'd truly been transported to a rainforest. The plants and flowers were lush, fragrant and exotic.

There were parrots and other tropical birds flying inside the enclosure. I was surprised by the sounds of these birds, and the beating of their wings. I don't know what I expected, really, but certainly not such an extravagant display of life. Everywhere I looked there was movement.

The softest of these was the gently fanning wings of butterflies. They were everywhere, hundreds, if not thousands of them. Of course we saw those we recognized, the soft fall colors of Monarchs, and Painted Ladies. But there were others—many, many of them we had never seen. They featured brilliant and surprising colors, deep blue, soft periwinkle, bright orange and soft white. Some flapped against the walls of the enclosure. Others hid among the foliage. And I had to admit that James was right. A few foolishly rested on the concrete pathways where eager children ran unaware.

Eventually, I'm certain, some were squished.

Cliff bought nectar cups for the children and they eagerly approached the resting insects, hoping to score the honor of being first to feed a butterfly. Unfortunately, more butterflies flew away than responded.

"Be patient," Cliff advised. "Let them come to you."

But patience is not a child's strongest virtue. I took Gabby's hand, and led her to a bench in the sunshine. "Here," I said, pointing to the seat. "Hold the cup in your lap and sit very, very still. Let's see if someone comes to us."

We sat. Though Gabby is hardly hyperactive, sitting quietly was a strain. I saw it in her face, in her eyes as they followed every movement around her. I held one hand on her leg, a reminder of her intent to stay still.

And sure enough, a butterfly, turquoise with black edges along its wings, landed on the edge of her nectar cup. Gabby's hand trembled slightly, whether from excitement or exhaustion, I did not know, and I prayed the butterfly would not fly away.

As we watched, the insect walked carefully around the edge of the cup, apparently doing an insect version of a security check, and then, miracle of miracles, it drank.

At that moment, as he so often does, God spoke to me.

"Most children are like butterflies," he said. "You must make them safe, and let them come to you."

And I knew, without a doubt, that he had spoken about the kids from Shiloh Farms.

Sixteen

Maggie's pumpkin scones

2¼ cup flour
½ cup brown sugar
1 tbsp. baking powder
¼ tsp. salt
2 tsp. pumpkin pie spice
1 tbsp. cinnamon
½ cup butter
1 egg
½ cup canned pumpkin
⅓ cup milk.

Sift dry ingredients together. Mix wet ingredients in separate bowl. Cut butter into dry ingredients; add wet ingredients. Roll into thick 10-inch circle. Cut into 8 wedges. Bake at 425 for 12–15 minutes.

ON THE MORNING AFTER OUR TRIP to the Butterfly Garden, I woke long before Gabby, ate a quick bite and sat down at my computer. Opening the page I'd begun for our brochure, I placed our newly designed logo on the cover. After long hours of indecision, I'd finally settled on a new name for the old Pickering Place. I had decided to honor the woman who had taken me in so many years ago by calling the old inn Maggie's Place.

When I was satisfied with the outside cover, I thought about the rest of the design. I'd been choosy about colors and fonts and copy; but what I needed at this point were more photos, lots and lots of them.

In my old job, we used a professional photographer for all of our media designs. But at this point, I couldn't cover those costs. To make matters more difficult, the house itself was not yet finished. My photos could not betray this important point. Who would pay top dollar to come to a partially renovated inn for breakfast?

I decided that I would have to stage images that put the inn in her best light. I'd already begun taking these photographs, putting the focus on God's handiwork rather than the house. I took photos of the bay from the back porch and of the new garden bed, with the water sparkling behind it in the afternoon light. I took shots of the back of the house—white siding reflecting the pink of a new dawn. I'd even taken macros of flowers in Maggie's wildly out-of-control garden.

At some point, I'd have to get busy on the garden.

As I drank my morning coffee, I pored over these pictures, editing them electronically to bring out the best of the images. One by one, I placed them in the brochure. But after an hour of work, I knew something was still missing.

I leaned back in my chair, thinking about it as I sipped my coffee. I heard the toilet flush downstairs, and realized that my productive morning was about to come to an end. Gabby was up, and would soon want breakfast.

That was it! I had no photos of food!

If I wanted to entice visitors, I needed to include bright images of the delicious foods they might anticipate here at the inn. I had to take pictures that would make the reader salivate, foods waiting in the morning sunshine for eager breakfast eaters.

"Mom," Gabby said, climbing the kitchen stairs, still in her pajamas. "I'm hungry."

"I know you are, sweetie," I said, opening my arms to her. "You slept a very long time." After a long hug, I kissed her cheek. "How would you like to be my sous-chef for the morning?"

"What's that?"

"It's the chef's assistant in a big restaurant kitchen. I need to take more pictures. So, while we're fixing your breakfast, we can stage some plates, put them out in the sunshine on the buffet, and take pictures. Sound like fun?"

She pulled back, looking at me with sleepy eyes, as she tried to follow my reasoning. "Will I ever get to eat breakfast?"

"Sure, as soon as we take pictures."

She shrugged. "Okay then. What are you going to cook?"

It occurred to me then, that I wasn't really prepared for this overly spontaneous little mother–daughter project. I didn't even have a menu. I couldn't just photograph anything. As usual, I'd come to this plan from the wrong end.

"You know, now that I think about it, why don't we have some cold cereal and talk about it."

"Okay," she agreed. "As long as we eat first."

As Gabby ate breakfast, I rummaged through my own meager recipe box. I didn't need to cook an entire breakfast, just a few items that would make colorful, appetizing photos for the brochure. The idea, I reminded myself, was to entice the customer, not to document our entire menu.

"So, what are we making?" Gabby said, still chewing as a ribbon of milk trailed down her chin.

"I don't know," I said, stumped. "I'm not much of a recipe collector. When I was a kid, Maggie had an entire book full of recipes." The words were hardly out of my mouth before I remembered the box I'd found in her office. "Wait," I said. "I've got an idea. I'm going to run downstairs."

I'd moved the old dress box from Gabby's bedroom into the spare bedroom. On quiet nights, after Gabby went to bed, I spent hours inspecting the contents, wondering about the Maggie I didn't know. The young Maggie. The wife. The mother. The volunteer. The box formed a puzzle of sorts, each saved treasure reflecting a piece of Maggie's life. A revelation of the woman I'd come to love.

I opened the bedroom door and looked inside, quickly spotting the box, stashed behind the door, on the very top of a pile of unmarked moving boxes. I pulled it off the stack, opened it and dug through the loose pieces to the bottom. Yes.

Maggie had left her most treasured recipe book in a place I would surely find it.

"I'm going to start with some pumpkin scones," I said, coming back into the kitchen. I held the book up in triumph as I sat down. "I have Maggie's recipes. Scones will be colorful on her green serving-plate. It would make a lovely picture."

Gabby slipped off her chair, leaving her dish on the breakfast table, and came around the table, trying to look over my arms to the pages of Maggie's book, her chin still wet with milk. "What should I do?"

"Start by picking up your cereal bowl," I said, pinching her nose. "Then, go put on some play clothes. And, when you come back, wash your hands." She frowned; I kissed her forehead, took her by the shoulders and turned her toward the stairs. "Every great sous-chef remembers to wash her hands," I said.

"I'll be right back. Don't start without me."

The phone rang, and as I reached for the handset, I heard her little slippers shuffling across the kitchen floor.

"This is Betty, from Small Business Licensing, North Cowichan district. May I speak with Brandy Beauchamp?"

"Yes," I said, a bit too eager. "I'm so happy to hear from you. How is the permit process coming?"

"I just called to let you know that we need one more item, and then it looks as if everything is complete."

"What did I forget?" Bureaucracy is not my strongest suit.

"I need the floor-plan for the food serving area."

"But I included that."

"It's not with your paperwork. I'm looking at your request for a building permit, and your parking information, and your Food Safe license. But I'm missing the floor-plan. I absolutely must have it for the fire commissioner's approval."

"Would you like me to drop off another copy?"

"I'm afraid you'll have to."

"Not a problem. My daughter has a swimming lesson this afternoon. I could drop it by around two?"

"That would be a big help."

"How long until the process is finished?"

"I'm not supposed to promise anything, really. We don't want you to get your expectations up. Normally, the process can take as little as two days. Inns take longer. Except for the fire commissioner, all of your approvals are complete. I'd guess, if you get it to me this afternoon, by the day after tomorrow, you could pick up your license."

"Wonderful! That's so great."

"But that isn't a promise, mind you."

"Of course not. I'll drop by this afternoon."

The idea of a having a license by the end of the week drove me back into the kitchen, the photographs all that much more important. I began setting out the ingredients for scones, measuring the flour and sugar into a large ceramic bowl, cutting the butter in by hand.

"Mom, you're supposed to wait for me," Gabby said, coming back in a pair of turquoise shorts and a yellow top. I made a note to myself; remember to work on Gabby's style choices.

"I am waiting. I need you to climb up in the pantry and bring me the cinnamon and the baking powder."

She dragged a chair across the floor, opened the pantry door, and placed the chair in front of the shelves. Pointing with one pudgy hand, she scanned the labels, sounding out the contents as she searched for her quarry. Remarkably, Gabby had just returned to the counter with the correct ingredients when the doorbell rang.

"Can you get the door, honey?" I said, measuring baking powder. "Mommy needs to get these scones in the oven so we can photograph them before swimming lessons."

She ran to the front door, and I heard her slip the lock and slide open the glass door. Expecting her to return with Cliff's boys, I was surprised to hear the exchange at the front door continue at some length.

I sighed, put down my measuring spoon and headed for the front door, wiping my hands on a kitchen towel. "May I help you?" I said, to the middle-aged woman standing on my front porch.

"I'm Pam Fleming, from next door," she said, pointing to a Queen Anne style home, just over her shoulder. "I came to talk to you about your property."

"My property? Is there a problem?"

"No. I don't think so," she said, smiling. "I mean, not really. I've been talking to Mr. Karras."

I felt myself stiffen, standing a little straighter as anxiety tightened my shoulder muscles. I felt my eyebrows rise. "Yes. I've met him."

She smiled, relieved. "He told me he'd spoken to you."

Instead of a more polite response, I heard myself blurt, "What about it?"

I had not introduced myself, nor had I issued this new neighbor an invitation to coffee, which I would have, under more normal circumstances. But these were not normal circumstances. Everywhere I turned, Mr. Karras and his fancy plans for the development seemed to have turned people into mush.

Apparently Pam expected the normal niceties as well. She hesitated. "Well, he mentioned that he'd approached you about selling your home. I wanted to talk about it with you." She paused, and glanced inside, apparently expecting an invitation.

"He did," I said. "I'm not selling."

"That's unfortunate," she said, her smile now tight upon her face. "He's telling everyone on the hill that it's only a matter of time. That you'll sell. And, he's offering all of us a better price if you're included in the deal. My husband thought it would be a good idea to speak with you directly. So, I…"

"How much better?" I asked, interrupting her. "The price. How much better?"

"We don't have to talk about it like this, out here on the porch. If I could come inside…"

"How much better?" I asked again, "If I'm included in your deal, how much more will you get?"

My directness had obviously offended her. She stammered. Looking away, she avoided my gaze. I crossed my arms, staring at her until she caved. "We, ah," she started, hesitating and then looked directly into my eyes. "One hundred thousand over the appraised value—and we get to choose our own appraiser."

❀

Somehow, even as I steamed about the neighborhood conspiracy, Gabby and I managed to make a plate of scones—well, actually only a single recipe. And, I made a small batch of blueberry pancakes. By the time we finished, the sun had risen so high that we had to move the buffet to another corner of the great room, placing it in the sunlight to catch a beautiful close-up.

After a half hour of shooting, we had maybe five shots of the scones and several more of pancakes. Sitting on Maggie's hand-thrown green plate, a dark mahogany sideboard in the background, morning sunshine casting strong shadows, I have to admit the scone shot was beautiful.

Another twenty days of this, and I'd have a real brochure.

I downloaded the file onto my computer while Gabby changed into her swimming suit. Loading her into the car, I gave her two scones, and called them lunch. Then, I called Cliff from my cell phone and told him we were headed down the driveway. He sent the boys up the dock and we met them up in the parking lot of the marina.

I drove out just as Herbert Karras drove in. It was all I could do not to stick out my tongue. Sometimes, the child in me wants out.

❀

At the pool, the boys scurried off to their own dressing-room and I followed Maggie into the girls' locker-room. I helped her put her clothes away, and supervised her quick shower. As we entered the pool area, Gabby's hand in mine, she asked, "Is it okay if I'm a little afraid?"

"Of course," I said. "You wouldn't be human if you weren't a little nervous."

She nodded, forcing a quivery smile.

"You'll be terrific," I said. "Everyone takes time to adjust. But once you get comfortable, you'll love the pool here just like you loved the pool in Florida."

We found her teacher without too much trouble. I sat down in the bleachers to watch for a while before I headed off to the licensing office. Gabby, her little belly hanging out through her pink swimsuit, settled in immediately.

With an hour and a half left before I needed to pick up the kids, I headed back out on the highway, so focused on my mission that I missed the driveway of the North Cowichan district offices. Frustrated, I swung into the next driveway, and toured the lot of a strip mall as I tried to turn around.

Just as I spotted the exit sign, a car pulled out in front of me, forcing me to wait, impatiently tapping my index finger on the steering wheel. I looked around at the shops, hoping to distract myself from my own irritation when I spotted it. An art supply store, with a banner hanging from the front awning. "Art Lessons Here."

In spite of my anxiety about the current time crunch, and the business license, I found myself intrigued. Art lessons? I'd taken art in college; it was required for my degree program. I'd foolishly opted for a drawing class, thinking that the fewer tools I worked with, the less I could mess up. The class nearly killed me. But even then, surrounded by gifted art majors, and completely overwhelmed by my lack of talent, I enjoyed the class, and often thought about it, wishing I could study more.

On impulse, I swung the car into an open parking spot. Inside the art store, I wandered the aisles, looking at the various tools and paints and papers. The old hunger for creativity began to gnaw at my emotions. I missed it. Missed the color and texture and demands of visual media. I thought about the old house, about the many bare walls now painted a lovely pale aqua. Wouldn't they require something to fill the space?

I came around the end aisle and discovered a tiny woman, her hair dyed a deep red-brown; she was explaining the differences between various paints to a young customer. Age-spotted hands and reading glasses hanging from a beaded chain betrayed the saleswoman's real age. In spite of her small size, she wore layers of elegant, flowing linen, her perfectly manicured toes displayed in artful Naot sandals.

When she had finished with her customer, I asked about art classes.

"We start a new watercolor class next week," she said. "You'd be welcome to join us. We meet twice a week in the afternoon."

"But I'd be a beginner," I said. "I've never even really tried it."

"With watercolor, even the professionals consider themselves beginners."

"It's that hard?"

"It's that wonderful," she said, smiling. "Unpredictable. Spontaneous. Delightful. The moment you think you know what's going to happen, you find out how much you have yet to learn. It's the perfect medium," she said, her tiny hands taking in the entire shop.

"I love it more than any other."

"Do you have a business card?"

She led me to the front of the store, picked up a card, and circled the phone number. "You can call me up until the day of class. If you want to join us, I'll be sure to make a place for you."

"Who teaches the class?"

"I do," she said. "You'll love it."

How I wished to love something, anything, again.

Seventeen

In this photograph, Albert holds a heavily decorated sheet cake. Though cut off by the camera, I think the words across the top spell out, "Best of Luck, Albert." In the background, Albert is surrounded by men and women in postal uniforms, and he smiles with the freedom of a prisoner released. Among the others I see Maggie, caught in the midst of applause. She smiles broadly, pride in her expression, love in her eyes.

HEADED HOME FROM SWIM LESSONS, the hope of a new business license and the idea of an art class danced in my head. While the kids yakked about their teachers and classmates, I made plans to upload my business brochure to an online printer. I began to calculate the turnaround time for delivery. Still excited about the new possibilities in my life, I decided to stop and visit with Cliff on the way home.

I admit that this sounded crazy, even to me. In Florida, I would have gone to visit Eve. But here, as yet, I had no Eve. Since I'd moved into the old house, I hadn't had time to make any new female friends—other than Lucia. And as I turned off the highway, I vowed that the time had come to change this. It wouldn't do to encourage stray-dog Cliff.

I left the car in my own driveway and the kids and I took the old path to the marina. Near the water, we found the office locked, which surprised me. The docks, though full of boats, were quiet and most of the dockhands seemed to have taken off for the day.

"Where's your dad?" I asked the boys. "Shouldn't he be waiting for you?"

Since we hadn't found Cliff, I'd gone from feeling silly to feeling concerned. I was relieved that I'd decided to stop and visit with Cliff. What if he'd had to run an errand, and I'd left the boys alone?

"Probably at the house," James answered, running ahead of us.

We passed a sign that recommended life jackets for all children on the docks. I noted with some shame, that all three of our children daily ran jacketless down the ramp onto the dock. Not much of an example for a marina manager.

James circled around behind the marina store, and turned up the furthest dock. I hurried behind, anxious to keep up. I'd never been down this side of the marina before, though I'd always wondered what was over this way. I came around a corner just as he stepped onto the tiny front porch of one of the homes attached to the dock. "I didn't know you guys lived in a boathouse," I said.

"It's a floating home," Justin said, correcting me.

"It is, is it?" I pulled my purse up over my shoulder. "I guess I never knew that."

"Mom, don't you know anything?" Gabby, in oversized sunglasses and a beach towel, walked by me swiveling miniature hips.

I heard James throw open the front door, and yell, "Dad! We're home!" Slamming the door behind him, he left Justin, Gabby and I standing on the dock.

I stopped dead, struck by the unique character of Cliff's bayside home. Beautiful, perfectly clear cedar enveloped the tiny house. Beside the front door, a hexagonal window—of perhaps four square feet—framed a stained-glass orca. Two simple Adirondack chairs, on either side of a tiny table, served as the only furniture on the porch. Built-in window-boxes, each spilling over with geraniums, asparagus fern, alyssum and bacopa, surrounded the porch rails.

Sitting behind a simply framed screen door, the front door was an antique unlike any I'd ever seen. With eight raised panels, and nailed leather trim, it was in perfect condition, and I wondered how on earth Cliff managed to care for it in the salt air of Genoa Bay.

The place was spotless; not a brown leaf, nor a misplaced toy distracted from the perfect scene that seemed to have sprung from a movie set. I'd misjudged my stray-dog friend. This tiny garden betrayed a meticulous, attentive gardener, and I felt a little ashamed of my own pride in the subject.

The kids passed me, eager to go inside. They threw open the screen door and slammed into the front room.

Through the open door, I heard Cliff call. "Brandy, come on out back. We're outside."

I hesitated. It seemed rude to traipse through his home, unaccompanied like this. I took a few steps around the side of the house, wondering if I could reach the back without going through his living-room. "Hurry up," he called. "I've got something to show you!"

I took a deep breath and stepped onto the porch, following the sound of laughing children. Inside the front door, I found myself in Cliff's tiny living area. Here vertical cedar paneling framed a warm and inviting space. He had a red-plaid loveseat, and a worn leather recliner sitting on a braided rug. A floor lamp shed a soft glow over the corner behind the recliner, and piles of books covered the table beside it.

To my immediate left, steep stairs led to a rear loft. Beyond the stairs, and beside the living-room, was a sixties-era dining-table, with chrome legs and a laminate top. In the back of the cabin was an L-shaped kitchen, its white Formica counters perfectly clean. A sliding glass door—also left wide open—separated the living area from a rear deck. Through this, I spotted the children outside in the sunshine, their backs to me. They were kneeling on the deck, crowded around something, talking and laughing. I stepped outside.

The back deck was as perfectly kept as the front porch, though much larger—in fact Cliff's deck was larger than his living-room. In one corner stood a square picnic table with four miniature benches. In the other three corners, masses of potted plants bloomed artistically, flourishing with the same care as his front porch. In one of these corners, Cliff had managed to grow a dwarf apple tree in a half-whiskey barrel. And if that weren't surprising enough, the small tree was laden with green apples, short sticks propping overloaded branches.

"Mom. Come look," Gabby called.

I turned back to the children, who were, I noticed, gathered around a small box. I knelt beside them, and watched as Cliff pulled a newborn kitten from the box. Eyes still closed, the little hairball was mostly white with black spots.

At that moment, I saw my own future as clearly as any palm reader; it didn't take a rocket scientist to figure out how three kids would take to a box full of kittens.

❀

After we gave the kids all the appropriate warnings about over-handling the babies, the kids settled onto their knees peering into the box. While they cooed over the newborns, Cliff and I sat down on the benches by his table, he leaning against the rail, and I against the table itself.

"I can't believe you'd do that," I said, pointing to the box. "What were you thinking?" Hardly a gentle reproach, I know. But still, what was I supposed to do when Gabby began begging for a kitten of her very own?

"The mother cat hangs around the marina. She's been here for years. She gave birth yesterday at low tide—right under the porch. If I'd left her where she was, they would have all drowned."

"Oh please. She would have carried the kittens out of danger."

"I didn't know that."

I sighed. "You are such a sucker."

"I like you too." He leaned back, crossed one foot over his knee and chuckled. It irritated me, his laughing at my frustration. Cliff seemed to be able to laugh at just about everything. In fact, because his laugh lines were perhaps three shades lighter than the rest of his skin, I suspected he spent most of his time smiling.

You can't trust a man who smiles that much.

As if to change the subject, he took off his baseball hat and ran his fingers through his hair. His hair was so curly that it fell across his forehead in ringlets. Though his beard showed traces of gray, his hair was inky black—darker than the bay at night. Unaware of my musings, he spoke. "Anyway, you didn't know I had kittens to show off. So what brings you here, to my humble abode?"

I frowned at him, trying to remember my irritation. It wasn't easy. Whenever I found his deep blue eyes focused on my face, without thinking, I found myself blushing. This guy was not my type. With a lumberjack's body, he was a fishing guide, a marina manager, a *Field and Stream* model, not the kind of man I'd ever paid any attention to before. I wasn't about to pay attention now.

"Listen, before you did this unbelievably stupid thing—showing newborn kittens to innocent children—I came to tell you that I'm about to get my business license. The office called this morning. While the kids were swimming, I dropped the floor-plan off for final approval. I should have the license by Monday, maybe Tuesday."

"Good. You'll be able to serve breakfast before the boating season ends."

"I know. I'm excited. If things go well, I should be able to pay for a new roof in cash, even before they finish the remodel."

"That's great. How are you going to advertise?"

"Well, I wanted to ask you about that," I said, leaning forward, my elbows on my knees. "Since it was your idea to invite the boaters to breakfast, I was wondering if I could leave brochures at the marina office. Everyone will see them as they check in. You don't have to promote it. It isn't like you'd have to mention it, or anything."

"Seems like a good idea."

"I'm uploading the brochure to the printer as soon as I get home," I said. "Turnaround could be as little as four days. Do you need to see the brochure first?"

"You're a brochure professional," he said, smiling again. "I'm sure it's perfect."

"It's funny how much more important a project is when it's your own."

He uncrossed his knees and leaned forward. "You're sure you want to do this?"

I frowned at him. "Don't go there."

"I know." He slapped his forehead with his palm. "I don't know what I was thinking. Forgive me, beloved inn keeper?"

"Well," I said, ignoring his attempt at humor. "I should be getting home. Gabby needs dinner, and I haven't even thought about what to make." I stood up.

"Stay here. I'm going to barbeque," he said. "You can join us, you and Gabby."

I shook my head, looking down at my watch. "I've got too

much left to do. I have to call the draftsman, and I need to work on the brochures. I'd like to have it done before the end of the business day."

"Do you ever stop?"

This time it was my turn to laugh. "I haven't even started yet. How can I stop if I haven't even started?"

"Believe me," he said. "You've started."

"Gabby, come on," I said, touching her shoulder. "We've got to get home." As expected, she groaned.

"I want to stay and play with the kittens."

"The kittens need to rest," Cliff said. "And I need to go up to the office and close out the cash register. How about if we walk you ladies home?"

"Can I take a kitten?" There it was. Already.

"Oh no, Gabby," Cliff said, down on one knee beside her. "The kittens are brand new. We can't take them away from their mother now. They would die." He reached up and held her shoulder. "I tell you what. You can come visit the cats anytime you want. Sound good?"

Though her lips still sported a powerful pout, Gabby nodded. "Anytime?"

"Anytime." He stood up. "Boys, do you want to walk Gabby home?"

"Nah," they said, nearly in unison. "We want to stay with the cats."

Out on the dock, I asked Cliff about his home. "I don't know much about floating homes," I said, using the correct term for the very first time. "But yours is beautiful. Have you lived there long?"

"About nine years," he said. "I bought it from an old guy who built it almost fifty years ago. Then, I tore it apart and started over. Regulations are so tight these days; you can't possibly build one from scratch any more. You have to remodel one that's grandfathered in."

"You did all that?" I couldn't believe the workmanship. The house, inside and out, was more like fine furniture—with perfect joins and smooth surfaces—than any construction I'd ever seen. "Even the stained glass?"

"My wife did that," he said.

"I don't understand. You said you were divorced."

"I am. She left me eight years ago and took the boys." We turned the corner onto the main dock just as Gabby started up the ramp to the office. At the top, she stopped at the stainless cleaning box, fascinated by a fisherman gutting his catch.

"You were living here? In Genoa Bay?"

He nodded. "It was my idea, coming up here from the States. I'd had it with the traffic and the pressure of city life. I was as happy as a man could be. But my wife couldn't stand it. She hated it from the day she arrived."

"And you wouldn't reconsider?"

"I thought she'd get used to it, you know, with time."

"But she didn't."

"She found a guy from the city up here on holiday. It only took two weeks; she went back to the States with him." Cliff smiled down at me, and shrugged his shoulders. "They're married now."

Having opened that can of worms, it seemed that I had no words to offer. I said the only thing that came to mind. "I'm sorry."

"You know, she made it easy on me."

"What do you mean?"

"I don't know if I'd have gone back to the city, just to make her happy."

"Sometimes it's a mercy that we don't know," I said, thinking of my own life, and the choices I'd made. How would my life have turned out if I'd made other, wiser choices?

"Maybe," he said, nodding. "I just don't want you to think that I'm some innocent victim here. Maybe I shouldn't have moved in the first place. I get so confused looking back that I can't tell any more. It was selfish to stay; that much I know now. I wasn't blindsided, exactly. I just wasn't listening between the lines. I knew she was unhappy. But would I ever have done the right thing, if I'd figured it out in time?" Cliff walked along the dock, his head down, his hands in his pockets. "I guess I'll never know."

"Is she happy? I mean, you must talk sometimes. You have the boys."

"From what I can tell. They live in Redmond, not three miles from our old place."

I nodded, and we climbed the ramp from the docks in silence.

At the office, I turned to him. "You don't have to walk me up to the house," I said. "It's still light out. I can find my own way."

"It's no problem. I have to pick up today's mail."

"Well, I guess I don't mind company then," I said, as we started through the parking lot toward the hill.

"Thanks a lot." There was no missing the sarcasm in his voice.

"You know what I mean." Knowing Cliff's story made him human somehow, and I knew that our friendship had deepened. At that moment, Gabby dashed by us, waving as she took the path to the house. Headed toward the mailboxes, Cliff and I climbed the road, the same hill where I'd followed Maggie from the office all those long years ago.

It was hot and dusty, and the afternoon sun was shining directly into our faces as we leaned into the hill. I noticed that Cliff had put one hand on the small of my back, pushing me upward ever so gently. Even as we walked I wondered if I should pull away, or step out of reach. I chose to stay put, panting a little as we hiked the steep hill.

When we reached the mailboxes, I turned to him. "Not many people can just walk away from their old lives, and hide up here in the middle of nowhere," I said.

"You should know," he said, as he put his key into the marina box.

The guy was as secretive as a CIA agent. I prodded. "So, how'd you do it? Flip your house for a few million? Make a killing on the stock market? What happened?"

He sifted through his mail, avoiding my gaze. "Actually, I sold a project. That gave me a little extra cash and I decided to change my lifestyle."

Undaunted and more curious than ever, I pushed. "What project?"

"If you must know, Miss Curiosity, it was a book."

"A book? You wrote a book?"

"I did."

"What about?"

"A friend of mine had a father who played a big part in World War II."

"And?"

He stopped shuffling, and looked up. "It was perfect timing. When books about the Greatest Generation were hitting the *New York Times* bestseller list, I had a story that spoke to a lot of those readers."

This guy was going to make me beg for every teensy weensy bit of information I could get. Exasperated, I tucked my own mail under my elbow, hoping to look as if I was camped there, blocking his way back until he told the whole story. "What was it called?"

"*Taking Caen.*" He pronounced the word a list of options. Pros and Cons.

"What?"

He repeated the title. "It's a story about US forces taking a little town in France right after Allied forces landed at Normandy. It was a big story, an important town. Our guys made a lot of sacrifices to do it."

"You really are something, aren't you?"

He looked genuinely perplexed. "What do you mean?"

"I mean, Cliff Lowry, that you're hiding up here like some blue-collar red-neck, with not a skill in the world. But you've written a book. And you do woodwork like an Amish furniture maker. I don't know what to think about you."

"Good," he said, smiling. He turned away, and headed back down the hill waving envelopes over his shoulder. "That's the way I like it, Mrs. Beauchamp. Just exactly the way I like it."

I shook my head, and climbed the rest of the hill to my own driveway. *Inn Keepers* magazine, a new subscription for me, had finally arrived with my mail, and I leafed through the front pages, wondering if it might provide some good recipe ideas.

Not paying attention, I lost my footing in the gravel, slid some and dropped the magazine. I was just standing up when I saw it, scrawled across the front of the inn, black letters on pale siding.

If I'd gone home via the path with Gabby, I would have missed it. Instead, I'd gone up the hill with Cliff, giving me a clear view of the front of our home.

There, in clearly printed letters, I read the words, "Sell your house. Now."

Eighteen

I lift a yellowing newspaper clipping from the box. In Maggie's penmanship, I read "March, 1984" written across the upper corner. A photograph accompanies the article, showing Maggie and Albert, his arm draped softly around her shoulders, standing on the south lawn, the harbor behind them, the garden in all its glory. "Last weekend," the article begins, "Maggie and Albert Blackburn, formerly of Kensington, officially opened their new Bed and Breakfast, named Pickering Place." I look more closely at Maggie, and I notice—even in the grainy surface of the old photo—an expression of deep pride. She is happy about the adventure they have begun.

BY THE TIME THE POLICE LEFT, all of my exultation over a business license had vanished—like a precious electronic file inadvertently deleted from a hard drive. Gone. Empty. Flushed.

I knew I shouldn't let my emotions rule my life. But I couldn't help wonder, how does anyone deal with an unknown enemy? How do you do battle with someone you can't actually see? Even the police seemed resigned to the event.

"I'm sorry, Mrs. Beauchamp. It's not very likely that we'll ever figure out who did this to your house," the responding officer said as he climbed into his cruiser.

I wrapped my arms around my chest, shivering as I thought about someone, some stranger, having this much anger toward me. "I know. I didn't really expect you to."

"We've taken a report. If you need it for your insurance, you can drop by for a copy later this week." He closed the car door and rolled down the window before he continued. "The best thing you can do now is clean it up. Try to forget it. Move on. It's probably just a one-time thing." He started the car and gave a little wave.

As I watched him pull away, I knew he was wrong. This wasn't a one-time thing. The paint was an opening volley. A clear message. Somehow, completely against my will, I'd been pulled into a battle I never knew existed. The question remained:

Should I stay and fight?

As I stood in the driveway, my mind kept returning to that episode with the dog. Had I made it all up, that thing with God's voice? Did he lead his kids into battles? Was this where he wanted me? Or had I imagined it—the outgrowth of my own longing to escape the memories and struggles of my life in Florida?

After all, when it came to escaping, I was an expert. Discouraged, I breathed a prayer. "Lord, are you sure about all of this?"

I whistled for Liz, who after following the police car to the street, had sprawled out on the warm pavement for a late evening nap. "Come on, girl. No time for a nap. We have work to do."

Gabby and I ate hotdogs for dinner, and while she built a fort out of blankets and furniture, I went outside with a pail of hot, soapy water and a stiff brush. Within the first few minutes, I realized that these weapons were useless against the paint permanently adhered to the old wooden siding.

Using a garden hose, and a pressure nozzle, I sprayed the message with water. While the words stayed firm, the paint on the siding began to peel and drip. Clearly, the vandal had left me with only one real choice.

I would have to repaint the front of the house.

In the waning evening light, I sat down on my wet porch, discouraged and feeling sorry for myself. Water soaked through the seat of my jeans. The moon rose and cast eerie shadows across the yard. Liz trotted across the porch and laid her head on my lap.

I scratched the dog between her ears and prayed for wisdom. And as I prayed, I saw, in my mind's eye, Gabby jumping into a swimming pool. I didn't recognize the pool, though she wore her favorite suit, a lavender one-piece, sprinkled with bright-pink tropical flowers. In the picture, which flashed through my vision for no more than a fraction of a second, Gabby jumped from the pool edge, grasped her knees with her hands and landed in the water with a crash.

It was a cannonball, the favorite dive of pool parties over the eons. In my mind's eye, water splashed everywhere, over the sides of the deck, and onto me. The picture was so real, I could almost feel it, cold and startling.

Now the thing is, when God speaks to me, he often uses pictures. And usually, though not always, when he does this, I know almost instantly what the pictures mean. Crazy, isn't it?

God was telling me to jump into my new adventure with absolute abandon, maybe even joy (though I couldn't for the life of me see any real joy in the adventure so far). Don't hold anything back. Don't slink in, like a woman afraid of the water, or unwilling to get wet. Take the plunge, he said.

I knew without a doubt that I had my marching orders. No more self-pity. No more waffling. Go for it. Jump in.

I sat out there in the dark, reviewing the picture, and thinking about the message I'd heard. As I pondered my situation, I knew that I hadn't been guaranteed success. In fact, God had me given nothing more than marching orders. If I obeyed, and lost this battle, it would surely cost me. Was I willing to lose so much?

I heard steps on the gravel pathway. "Hey, you."

I recognized Cliff's voice. "Hey."

He stepped into the moonlight, coming across the yard from the trail. "May I?"

I pointed to the space beside me. "Sure."

"The boys told me."

"They must have seen the police cruiser," I said. "Where are they now?"

"Watching a movie."

"What are you doing here? Gloating?" I put my head in my hands. "After all, you warned me. You told me to be careful."

"That's not fair."

"You're right. I'm tired. And discouraged." I turned to face him. "You know, I didn't plan on this," I said, pointing to the words on the siding behind me. "All I wanted was a fresh start. A place to belong. A place that was really mine, you know? Is that so much to ask?"

He put one arm around my shoulder, and squeezed. I felt

myself stiffen against his touch. "I don't think so," he said. Letting go, he leaned forward, and began polishing his left thumbnail with his other hand, in what had become a familiar gesture. "Really, this is your home now. You should be able to do what you want with it. But the real question is, what do *you* want to do?"

He turned to look at me, and I saw the moonlight sparkle in his blue eyes. "You don't have to fight, you know. Just because Maggie left you the place, you don't have to stay. Maybe the money from the sale of the property is what she wanted for you. A new start. The funds to go where you want to go."

"But she wanted me to run the inn. She left a whole box full of things for me, so that I'd succeed. Recipes, plans, memories." Though I wanted to add my convictions about a calling, I didn't know how to explain it all. How could anyone explain God's leading in their lives? I didn't really understand it myself. I'd rather have Cliff wonder if I was crazy, than explain my visions and remove all doubt.

"Maybe she didn't want you to feel stuck. Maybe she wanted to give you the resources to choose your future. Whether you take the money or the lifestyle is your choice. Selling wouldn't be failure, you know."

I thought about that for a moment, and as I did, the picture of Gabby and the swimming pool came back. Again, I saw the water splashing over everything in the scene. "I know. I could quit. I could walk away. I wouldn't think of that as failure."

"But you won't," he said, his voice soft in the moonlight. "You won't quit."

"I can't," I said. "You wouldn't understand; I know that. But I can't walk away."

❀

The business license and the permit for renovation arrived in my mailbox the very next day, and in spite of the words still clearly printed on my house, I felt my mood rise. I called Peter Delaney at Shiloh Farms and gave him the go-ahead to begin the bidding process based on the drawings his draftsman had created. "I have my last appointment with him today," I said. "If everything is finished, you should have his drawings this afternoon. Tomorrow morning at the latest."

"Great," he said. "That'll be perfect. I should have the figures to you by the end of the week. If you can give me the okay by Monday, I'll call the lumber store and place the order. I'll have them deliver C.O.D." I heard him shuffling pages on his desk. "I should think they'd be able to deliver by middle of the week. Could you manage that?"

"The expense?" I took a deep breath. Next to buying paint, lumber would be my first major outlay of cash. The first of many, many such outlays, I knew. "Sure. I'll have to transfer some funds. But that should be fine. When can your team start?"

"Our class is busy until the end of next week. After that, I have an opening. Would it be okay if we start your place on the Monday after next—provided that you're satisfied with the bids?"

"Okay? It would be completely wonderful."

We talked for a while longer. Peter's patience with my endless questions qualified him for sainthood. Before hanging up, we worked out the various details, scheduling, materials, the payment procedure for change orders—in case we made changes in the specified plans or materials—and of course the payment schedule. "I'm sorry to be such a stickler about it. But as a non-profit, we have such a narrow margin to work with. You pay for materials, and you pay us for labor."

I didn't mention that I was a non-profit myself these days.

He continued. "Have you made arrangements for the roof?"

"I haven't signed a contract yet."

"We're still doing the truss work and O.S.B.?"

"O.S.B.?" I felt like I'd landed on Mars. There was so much about building that I didn't know. Acronyms, regulations, materials.

"Oriented Strand Board. It's a type of exterior plywood. You probably have old plywood underneath the asphalt tiles on your roof. Where the tree came through, I saw some pretty extensive water damage. I think, though I don't know, that the whole surface will need replacing."

"That's what the contractor suggested. He said it would save some money if your team did the prep work."

"I'll have to do the calculations."

"I trust you, Peter," I said, hoping he didn't hear the little tremor of fear in my voice. "After I go over your bid, I'll try to call bright and early Monday morning."

❀

Two days later, on the day of Gabby's next swimming lesson, I met with the draftsman that Peter had recommended. We went over his drawings, page by page, line by line. I asked questions, and he explained his work, taking notes on a yellow pad next to the plans. Though there were small adjustments still to make, all in all, he'd done an excellent job.

Aware of our constraints, both financial and physical, he'd designed a temporary wall between the great room and the construction area. He'd placed a similar wall between the working kitchen and the new addition to the apartment. He'd specified cabinetry using pre-fabricated pieces available at discount builder supplies. He'd been able to find wood flooring which matched the rest of the house using reclaimed materials from a salvage company. The same salvage company had light fixtures to match the rest of the house. He had specified materials as carefully as if my money were his own.

Before I knew it, I was headed home with a car full of busy children, their hair still wet from the pool. While they argued over who had actually won the breaststroke competition, I found my mind thinking of the house. Would it turn out as well as I envisioned? Would the bid be low enough to accomplish all I hoped? And, ever the impatient one, how long would it take me to get it finished?

After dropping the boys off at the marina, I pulled into the driveway. There, underneath the hateful graffiti, was a box, delivered in our absence. "Gabby, they're here," I said, opening my car door. "The brochures. They're here!"

She came around the front of the car, just as I sat down on the porch, opening the box with my car key. "Can I go inside and have a popsicle?"

"Sure," I said. "Put on dry clothes first, please. And eat it outside, would you?" She waved as she flew in through the kitchen door. I'd have bet money that she grabbed the treat on her way downstairs, where she would eat it in her wet swimsuit, in front of the television.

Too excited to care about Gabby's obedience, I removed the packing material to find a thousand copies of my tri-fold brochure gleaming up at me. I picked one out and glanced through the panels. Between my carefully chosen photos, and the well-written copy (even if I do say so myself), Maggie's Place looked like a gracious old inn, clean and proud. If only Maggie—who had never engaged in this kind of advertising—could see these brochures.

With only a tiny voice of doubt, I started down the path to the marina office. Cliff, I suspected, would be holed up in his office, working on paychecks, or schedules, or reservations. If Maggie and Eve couldn't be here to celebrate with me, Cliff would have to do.

The bell, hanging over the door, rang out as I entered the office. "Hey, Arianna," I said to one of the younger members of the docking staff. "Cliff in his office?"

She nodded, pointing with one hand, while still holding the VHF microphone in the other. "Roger that, *Misty Morn*," she said. "Bow in. Starboard tie. Slip number C-two-three."

I smiled my gratitude and headed through the store toward the back of the building where two offices sat side-by-side. At Cliff's office door, which was closed, I knocked politely. "Hang on a minute." I heard his desk chair roll across the wood floor. When the door opened and Cliff recognized me, I swear that he missed a breath. For some reason, the surprise and pleasure on his face tickled me.

No one had looked at me that way in a long, long time.

And then I looked behind him. There, in the center of Cliff's office, with his back to me, stood Herbert Karras. He was looking out the window toward the dock. Believe it or not, I recognized him from the back by his ears. No one—other than Pluto—has ears that long. His body seemed tense, his shoulders high and tight, though his hands were clasped behind his back.

"I'm sorry," I said. "I didn't mean to interrupt."

Cliff reached up to scratch his forehead, clearly confused about how to continue.

At the sound of my voice, Karras turned around, recognized me and frowned. "Listen, Cliff," he said, walking toward the door.

"I've made myself clear. Don't make me say it again."

"I understand, Mr. Karras," Cliff said, opening the door wider. I stepped out of the way. Without another word, Karras strode across the store and out the front entry.

"Wow," I said. "A little tense."

"No kidding. Just another day in paradise."

"Maybe I should come another time," I said, suddenly unsure of myself.

"No. Not at all," he said. "Why don't we go for a walk? I need some air anyway, and you can show me what you came to show me."

"How did you know?"

He pointed to the brochure in my hand. "Just a sec. I need my hat," he said. He swung back to the desk, where his cap sat in the middle of his blotter. He touched my elbow as he passed me. "Now let's get out of here."

Leading me by the front desk, Cliff said to Arianna, "I'm on the radio." And we ducked out the back door toward the docks. "Let's go down to the water," he said.

Down on the dock, Cliff headed as far out into the bay as anyone could, on foot. At the very end, where the afternoon sunshine still puddled bright warm light, he sat down, his feet dangling high above the water. Cliff looked at me and patted the dock beside him.

"Bad day, huh?"

"The worst. Sometimes, I wish I didn't work for that guy."

"You don't have to, do you?"

"Nah. But I'm here now. With the house tied up here I don't want to make him angry. He could tell me to untie it and find another dock."

"That wouldn't be so bad," I said, though something inside of me wilted at the thought of Cliff moving his home.

"It might be—bad, I mean. I don't know if I could even find another location. The regulations on floating houses are so stiff, you just about have to stay where you are. It's not like there are any new developments out there."

Cliff stared off across the bay, his eyes following the deserted shoreline, the soft waves rolling over distant rocks. For a few minutes we sat quietly, listening to the sound of the water lapping against the dock, to the distant thrumming of diesel engines and to voices in the distance.

It was peaceful, sitting here with this man who had become a good friend, and I leaned back on my arms, letting my knees break at the end of the dock, my feet swinging in the air. I'd nearly forgotten my mission when he spoke again. "So, what did you have to show me?"

"Oh. Yeah. The brochures came today. I almost forgot." I sat up and pulled a copy from the pocket of my sweatshirt.

"The cover is great," he said. "Good picture." He shook his head, apparently impressed, then opened and read the brochure, word for word, panel to panel, cover to cover. As he did, I realized I was holding my breath. Why was it so important that he like the work I'd done? "So, what do you think?"

"It's great. You've done a great job. You've got everything here. The history, the feel for the bay, the beauty of the house. You're really good at this layout stuff."

"Thank you, kind sir," I said, feeling a little self-conscious. "I hoped you'd like it. After all, if you're going to display it, I didn't want you to be embarrassed by it."

He took a deep breath and sighed, lying down on the dock as he put his hands behind his head. He stared up at the sky.

"What is it? What's wrong?"

"I can't," he said. "Karras just told me. I can't put your brochure on display. Not at the office. Not on the docks. Not even on my own front porch. Not anywhere."

Nineteen

Cliff's favorite ginger-molasses cookies

> ¾ cup shortening
> 1 cup dark brown sugar
> ¼ cup dark molasses
> 1 egg
> 2¼ cup flour
> 3 tbsp. cinnamon
> 1½ tbsp. ginger powder
> 1 tsp. ground cloves
> ¼ tsp. salt

CREAM SUGAR AND SHORTENING. Blend in egg and molasses. In a separate bowl, stir dry ingredients together. Add to wet ingredients. Roll cookies into ball the size of golf ball. Roll in raw sugar. Bake at 350 degrees, for 9 minutes. Do not over-bake.

I met Lucia at McDonald's the next morning. While the kids played on the big toy, she and I bought over-cooked coffee from the counter help. No amount of creamer could improve the taste of that stuff. But I hadn't come for the coffee.

"What am I gonna do?" I asked, wiping crumbs from the seat before I slid into the booth. "I don't have a plan B. I was going to serve breakfast to boaters."

Lucia removed the lid from her cup and licked it. "I can't believe he won't let you advertise. I mean, what's it going to cost the marina anyway? That Karras is a real jerk."

"I think you're missing the point."

"What point?"

"It isn't about costing them. It's about the fight to buy Maggie's property."

"The fight to buy *your* property."

She had me there. I nodded, agreeing. This was why I'd chosen to talk to Lucia about it all. Eve, I knew, would try to convince me to come back to Florida. "I think so. I think he believes if he can keep me from making money, I'll have to accept his offer. He wants me to sell, plain and simple. I think Karras hopes he can drive me out of business."

"Can he?"

I glared at her. "If I can't make any money, I can't stay."

She frowned. "Driving you out of business is only partly about money, isn't it?"

"Are you kidding? It's all about money."

"Isn't it about quitting? Giving up before you find the answer you're looking for?" She palmed the tabletop as if she were smoothing fresh sheets.

I shook my head. "I don't know. When your bank account hits zero it begins to feel like everything is about money."

She laughed. "I wish I had a Looney for all the times Shiloh Farms has been this desperate. And you know," she poked the table with her index finger, "desperation brings creativity. And creativity brings answers. Answers you wouldn't think of without that kind of pressure. That's good, from where I stand."

"You, my friend, stand safely on the sidelines," I smiled and took a sip of coffee. "Okay, you're right. I'm desperate. So where are these answers you keep talking about?"

"I don't know. But when you look for answers, you can't hold anything back. You have to put everything on the table, so to speak."

Her words reminded me of my mental picture of Gabby jumping into the swimming pool. Okay, God. I get the picture. "So to speak," I repeated the phrase. "How do I do that?"

She opened her purse and brought out a tiny wire-bound notebook. Setting it down on the table, she dug again to find a pen. "It's like this. You start by making a list. Just put down any idea you come up with. No matter how silly. Don't evaluate. Just write," she stopped herself, clicked the pen and looked up at me. "I mean, I'll write, and you talk. We start by making a list of all the options."

"That's step one."

"Step one," she agreed. "So, what can we do from here?"

Her word choice warmed my heart. "You said, 'we'."

"Of course. We're friends. We. Friends routinely get in over their heads together."

I laughed, in spite of myself. It wasn't the kind of hope I was looking for, hanging myself with Lucia. But it was hope, none the less. "I don't have any ideas." I took another sip of coffee and shrugged.

"Okay. I'll start." She began printing on the little page. "You serve breakfast topless."

I couldn't help myself. I laughed until I nearly spit out my coffee.

She pointed the pen at me. "I said, 'Don't evaluate'. You're evaluating."

I giggled. "Okay. I get the game. Let's see. I could take out a home loan. I haven't done that yet."

"You have the Karras offer as proof of the house's value."

"I only have a verbal offer."

"That's not a problem. Just tell him you won't consider anything that isn't written down. When he writes it down, you drive it directly to the bank. Then, after you get your loan, you call him back and say no thanks."

"That seems a little dishonest."

"Evaluating."

"Right. No evaluating," I agreed. "Okay. So a loan."

She wrote it down. "What about the game plan?"

"Game plan?"

"Who says that breakfast eaters only come on boats?"

"Okay. Who else eats breakfast?"

She laughed. "You really are distressed. You should hear yourself."

"I know. Everyone eats breakfast. But how do I reach this large crowd of breakfast eaters and get them to come to Maggie's Place?"

"What if you gave out brochures around town?"

"Would people from town drive all the way out to Genoa for breakfast?"

"You're still evaluating."

"Right. Okay. I get it." I looked around the restaurant, still pondering the question when Gabby's bright-red sweatshirt drew my attention to the kids. For a long moment, I watched them play and then, for some reason, realized that my focus had moved from the play area to the drive-through sign on the street outside. Something about it stuck in my mind. A sign. A sign beside the driveway. "I could put up a big sign in the driveway."

"There you go," she said, writing that down. "Now. What do boaters do once they tie up at a marina?"

"I don't know. They hook up the power. They pay for their moorage—which was why I wanted the brochures in the office." I drummed my fingers on the table.

"And then what? Do they just hole up inside those big ol' yachts all day long? I mean, why be on a boat if you're just going to hide inside all day?"

"No. They get off and go for a walk. They look around the marina. They ogle one another's boats. Sometimes they go into town for provisions, so Cliff drives them in the marina's van. When they get back to the dock, they either eat out, or they cook on board. Groups sometimes do pot lucks."

"And, at Genoa, the ones who go for a walk, they walk right up the hill past your driveway, right?"

"Sure."

"So what if you built a beautiful sign that held the brochures?"

"You mean let them pick up the brochures at my place? Right on the property."

"Why not?" She wrote that down. "And by the way, how close are you to having guest rooms ready?"

"Not even."

"What's left to do?"

I put my chin in my hand, trying to think of all the items left on the list. "I have to have the wood floors downstairs finished. I have to finish the remodel. I have to paint and redecorate upstairs. You wouldn't believe the junk Maggie has up there."

"Maggie had," she corrected. "It's your place now. What kind of redecorating?"

"It all needs paint. The wood trim is in horrible shape. Most of the rooms need the wallpaper stripped. Right now it looks completely Victorian. I want to change all that. The windows need new coverings. I haven't decided what to put up."

"They don't need much. You don't want to cover the view."

"Right, and privacy isn't an issue. The windows look out over the water."

"So, what else?"

"I have to buy bedding, and replace mattresses."

"Furniture?"

"No. Not right away. Maggie had beautiful antique beds. I can leave them for a while. Someday though, I want to go with king-sized beds."

She shook her head. "Not until you start making a profit. If you can stall an expense, do it. Put as much off as you can. In the meantime, you can sell the smaller beds with words like antique, cozy, and comfortable."

"Cozy, as in three adults in a mummy sleeping-bag," I offered.

"Exactly." She had started a new list on a second page, noting all of the decorating chores I had left to complete. "How soon could you have guests if you did everything you need to do? Could you move the date from next summer to this fall?"

Stunned, I stared at her. This hadn't even occurred to me. In my very sequential world, every part of the renovation and redecoration had been carefully mapped out, with the opening of guest rooms coinciding with spring of the following year. There was so much to do, so much to accomplish. "Could I do that?"

"I don't know," she said. "I asked you."

"There's so much. Painting. The garden. Floors. Heating."

"What about hiring kids?"

"The Farm kids?"

"They're all out of school. They need the work."

"But I can't pay much."

"You can pay enough. More than no job at all." She wrote furiously. "If you get a home loan, you'll have plenty of money to keep them going."

"How would I hire them? I don't even know these kids."

"Leave that to me. I know them all."

❀

I drove home thinking about the things Lucia had suggested. As we passed the city limits, I broached the subject of a sitter with Gabby.

"What do you think about having a baby-sitter?"

"You mean go to day care again?"

"No. Not day care. I'm thinking about having someone at the house. Someone you can play with during the day. That way, when I'm working, you won't feel so lonely without me."

"But you'd be right there?"

"Absolutely."

"And I could still do swimming lessons?"

"Just like always."

She turned to look out the window, obviously giving my suggestion serious thought. "I guess it depends on who comes to stay with me. I don't want someone dorky, or boring. And I definitely don't want someone bossy."

"Never bossy," I agreed.

"What would you be doing?"

"I'd be working. Upstairs, or outside, depending on the weather."

"So, if I had a sitter, I wouldn't have to work?"

I looked over at her surprised. "Are you trying to get out of doing your chores?"

"Uh-huh."

"Not a chance," I said, laughing at her. "But, you won't have to paint, or work in the yard. And, you'll always have someone to play with, even when I can't play."

"Okay, then."

"Okay?"

"Yes. I'll take a sitter," she said, with an exasperated sigh. "I can't wait until I'm too old for a sitter. They can be such a nuisance."

At home, I parked the car and headed directly to the telephone. Of all the ideas we'd discussed, the idea that made the most sense to me included getting a small loan on the property. To do it, though, I'd have to act fast—before I lost my nerve. I dialed the marina office and asked for Karras.

He picked up, and I knew from the sounds in the background that he had answered not in the privacy of his office, but in the general store. "Mr. Karras, this is Brandy Beauchamp."

"Yes," he said. "What do you want?" Though he was abrupt, it seemed clear from his tone of voice that he was suspicious as well. He hadn't expected my call.

"I've been thinking about your offer."

"To sell the property?" He didn't even think of the old inn as a house. A business. A home. "I told you," he said, his voice full of blustery confidence, "that you would come to your senses. You should never have tried to make that place into a business."

Some day, I might just have to strangle that guy. But not today, I told myself. I went on. "Well, I've given it a lot of thought."

"Very wise of you," he said.

His tone had changed, from suspicious to superior and proud. I plunged on. "Anyway, I've decided that I can't make any decision without a written offer." Then, remembering his disregard for the business Maggie ran, I added, "And don't forget, Mr. Karras, that you would be buying both a business and a house, not just an empty lot. I would only consider an offer that included the full value of the inn."

"Humph." There was no mistaking the scorn in his voice. "It isn't a business yet, I can assure you. And there is no reason you should expect that kind of value in an offer."

"However," I said, with exaggerated patience, "I don't have to sell. I can choose to open the inn myself. If you want me to take the offer seriously, it must reflect the full value of the house, the property, and the business."

There was silence on the other end of the line. Breathing. And then his voice dropped. I could not mistake the menacing tone that emerged. "And, remember, Mrs. Beauchamp, I don't have to buy," he said. "You never know what might happen in the future. Becoming an inn keeper can be very perilous. There are a great many dangers involved. Whether or not you can make it as an inn keeper is highly speculative." He cleared his throat. "You have no training. No business experience. You're alone. Unprotected. I wouldn't be so confident." He waited, apparently for my response.

I squeezed my teeth so tightly that my jaws ached. Though he had not said anything directly, I felt his threat. Karras meant for me to feel it. He might himself be a source of danger. Though the hand that held the phone trembled, I gave myself stern instructions. I would not fear him. Memorized words from the book of Isaiah rang through my mind. *If you fear God, you need fear nothing else.* I held my breath, unwilling to speak. We were playing chicken on the phone. I would match him in this sword fight, thrust for thrust.

He caved first. "And when is it that you want this written offer?"

"I'm in no hurry," I said. "And, I remind you, that the place still belongs to me. I don't have to sell, no matter how much you offer. However, you realize that I can't give your proposal serious consideration until I have your best and final offer, in writing."

This time he laughed outright. "You don't have to sell, yet," he said, placing great emphasis on the word, "yet." In the background, I heard the sounds of the office, the squawk of the VHF radio. Karras continued, "You never know how things will turn out. It might be that you'll come to me—begging me to take the place."

"Mr. Karras, now you sound over-confident."

He seemed to consider this. "I'll have to consult with an attorney."

"Of course," I agreed. "And in the meantime, I'll begin the process of getting a professional appraisal." I hoped this would warn Karras that I was an informed businesswoman, perhaps triggering a higher, more aggressive offer. "So, until I hear from you again, you have a good day," I said, hanging up before my knees collapsed entirely.

"Mom!" I heard in Gabby's voice that peculiar quality that makes any mother break into a run. From the sound of it, she was outside, in the yard at the back of the house. And even before I got there, she was screaming. "Mom. Hurry. There. Is. Something. Wrong. With. Liz."

As I rounded the corner of the house, I saw Gabby, squatting by Liz, who was down, trembling and shaking in a way I had never seen before. Gabby ran her hand over the dog's neck as tears streamed down her tiny face, her blond hair mingled with Liz's golden fur. I knelt beside them, girl and dog, and put my hand on Liz, speaking quietly. "Good girl," I cooed. "Stay calm, Lizzy, we're here."

She was having a seizure, from what I could guess, and even in the midst of the uncontrolled motion of her legs, she continued to try and get up. I held her down, as I continued talking, encouraging, and praying. "Oh Lord, help her," I said. "Quiet, girl. It's almost over."

Gabby asked over and over, "Is she okay, Mom? Is she going to be okay?"

"I don't know, Gabs. I don't know."

The seizure continued, and though I know it couldn't have lasted much longer than a few minutes at most, I think I aged several years in the process. Just as she started to quiet down, I noticed a trail of vomit leading from the marina path across the lawn to our dog. "Gabby, we're going to make a run to the vet, okay?"

"Now?"

"Yes. Right now." I rearranged myself around Liz, my knees bent in preparation for the lift. The dog seemed stunned and exhausted by her ordeal. Then, scooping her into my arms, I commanded Gabby, "My keys are on the kitchen counter—can you run and get them? Meet me in the driveway."

Still crying, Gabby turned and ran up the back stairs to the porch. The dog was heavy, perhaps eighty-five pounds, and I honestly don't know how I managed to carry her through the yard, but I did. All the while, talking softly and using my baby-talk voice, I begged the dog to stay alive. In the back of my mind, though, I knew we were going to lose her.

Gabby burst through the front door and into the driveway just as I came around the yard. "Open the van door, honey," I said.

She held the key fob toward the door.

I would have liked blankets under the dog, something to comfort her, something to protect the car in case she lost control of her bowels. But I did not have any of these things. "Get in your seat and fasten your belt. We're going into town."

With my cell phone, I tried to call Cliff as I drove out of the driveway. "Pick up. Pick up. Pick up," I begged.

"Mommy," Gabby said, her voice full of tears. "It's happening again."

I glanced behind me. "I know, sweetie. There's nothing we can do."

I hit the "End" button, and tried to call Lucia. She answered on the third ring. "We have an emergency. I need a vet, right now."

"What happened?"

"No time. Just tell me. Where can I take our dog?"

"Rayna Landry is the best. Head into town on Trunk Road. Turn left on Highway 1. There's an emergency clinic where I take our animals, about three-quarters of a mile south. You can't miss it."

"Thanks. Gotta go."

"Wait," she said. "I'll meet you there."

I speed-dialed Eve, and got her voice-mail. "Pray. Something horrible has happened to Liz," I said.

I drove as carefully and quickly as I could, considering the terror I felt, both for Liz and for Gabby. I'd brought Liz home as a puppy. She'd moved with us, loved us, and cheered me when nothing else in the world could lift my grief. I prayed out loud, a repetitive, pleading prayer. "Lord, help us. Help us. Help us."

My daughter had made the transition to Canada, but it hadn't been easy. How would she react to losing her precious companion? I didn't know, and I didn't want to find out. Grief was something I wanted to avoid at all costs. "Help us. Help us. Help us."

And before I knew it, I was crying too, because every loss brought back the pain of losing Timothy.

Somehow, though afternoon traffic was busy, I located the clinic and parked. Before I got around the side of the van, Lucia was there, concern in her dark eyes. She put one hand on my shoulder and said, "It's okay. We're here."

I opened the side door to find Liz quiet again, her eyes closed. She was still breathing, thank the dear Lord.

"Here, let me help you carry her," Lucia said. And together, we bent over the dog, each struggling to carry half of her limp body across the parking lot. Gabby ran ahead to get the door. "What happened?" Lucia whispered over Liz's tail.

I sniffed, unable to wipe my nose. "I think she's been poisoned."

Twenty

The black velvet box is square, the hinge rusty, squeaking as I open it. Inside, I find a lady's watch, the kind that might have rested on the full bosom of a Victorian woman. The one-inch face is mother-of-pearl, with gold numbers. I turn the case over, and find on the back a diamond-encrusted dragonfly with ruby stones on its antennae. The gold chain appears handmade, its fragile links holding on to one another with large intertwining loops. I wonder for whom the watch was purchased, and how Maggie came to possess such beauty.

LUCIA STAYED WITH US at the clinic while we waited. At first, Gabby was inconsolable, crying, clinging, and unable to calm herself enough to receive comfort. The staff brought her juice and cookies, and tried to divert her attention with a DVD.

Eventually, the vet came out to speak with us, her hands deep in the pockets of her scrub jacket. "Hey," she said, squatting in front of Gabby. "I'm Doctor Landry, but you can call me Ray. I hear you're pretty worried about your dog, eh?" Gabby nodded, looking more like a toddler than a child, eyes wide with concern, glassy with tears.

"Well, I want you to know that I'm taking care of her myself. And I'm going to do the very best I can."

Again Gabby nodded. "Can we take her home now?"

Dr. Landry touched her arm, a gentle, reassuring squeeze. "I'm afraid I have to keep her with me for a couple of days. Would you like to see her?"

To my surprise, Gabby hesitated.

Dr. Landry continued. "She's sleeping right now. Just like she does at your house." She gestured toward an assistant. "Martha would be glad to take you back to pet Liz—just for a moment though."

Martha, a young woman about my age—who'd been waiting behind the front desk—came forward, offering her hand to Gabby. Gabby looked at me, and I nodded. Together they went back into the clinic.

Dr. Landry greeted Lucia with a hug, and then introduced herself to me. "I'm Rayna Landry," she said, shaking my hand. "Your dog seems stable now. She's getting fluids and resting. The seizures have stopped. But she's still in bad shape. We'll know more in the next twenty-four hours."

"Will she make it?"

"I can't make any promises. To her credit, Liz's size helped her. A smaller dog would have died before she got back to the house. Do you have any idea what she got into? It would help if we could narrow it down."

I looked at Lucia, mystified. "I haven't any idea. We live near a marina. So, I imagine there are chemicals and things all over the place down there. Solvents. Paints. Diesel supplies."

"Maybe bait for rats?"

"I don't know," I said, shaking my head. "No one has mentioned anything."

"Rayna," Lucia began, "was there food in the dog's stomach?"

"Yes. Her stomach was full." She looked at me. "I pumped it, of course. But it looked like dog food. How long since you last fed Liz?"

"Last night. We feed her every night." Even in my confused state, I understood the implication of Lucia's question. "Does that mean she got into poison that was mixed with food?"

"Maybe," Rayna said. "But before we go jumping to conclusions, remember that dogs are pretty hard to second guess. She might have found food somewhere that was fine, and then gone by a driveway and licked up antifreeze. We just don't know, and unfortunately, dogs never tell.

"I've done some testing. We should have a better idea what happened when the results come back. For now, I was able to empty the stomach and counteract the systemic effects of the poison. Now, it's up to her liver. Hopefully, we'll know more tomorrow." She smiled at us, and asked, "Would you like to see her?"

Lucia and I joined Gabby in the clinic, a bright room with white subway-tile walls and polished floors. We found Liz asleep on a cushioned pad, a bag of fluids dripping into her shoulder. Gabby stood beside her, petting her neck, and whispering love. Liz, apparently oblivious, slept on. "She's been through a lot," Dr. Landry said. "We should probably let her sleep."

❀

Before we left, I made a deposit on Liz's care. As I wrote the check, I felt guilty. Guilty about spending funds on a dog, and guilty about not wanting to take care of Liz. My over-active conscience couldn't win.

I followed Lucia and Gabby out to the parking lot where I put one arm around Lucia's waist and whispered, "I don't know what we'd have done…"

"Nonsense," she interrupted. "We're here. Liz is going to be just fine."

Gabby hugged her too. "Thank you for helping us find Dr. Landry."

"She's the best, isn't she?" Lucia said, smiling as she patted Gabby's back.

Gabby nodded, anxiety still clouding her tiny features. Children shouldn't have to worry, I thought. And Gabby had survived entirely too many agonizing moments in her young life.

"Well, let's go get some dinner," I said, turning to Lucia. "Join us?"

"No. Thanks anyway. I have to get home; Rick is with the kids. I wouldn't want to over-tax the poor man. After about thirty minutes, he sort of self-destructs—like the tape on *Mission Impossible*." She smiled, and gave me a phone signal with her hands. "Call me, when you know more?" I nodded, and she turned toward her car.

I helped Gabby into the van and buckled her belt. Patting her knee, I asked, "Where would you like to go eat?"

"I don't care."

"What do you feel like eating?"

"I'm not really hungry."

I closed the door and went around to the driver's-side door. "You feeling okay?" She nodded, her chin in her hand, her elbow on the door rest. I started the car and turned back onto the highway. "Would you rather just go home? I could make hot dogs, or macaroni and cheese."

She shrugged, and we drove home in silence.

We'd hardly unlocked the front door when the phone rang. Without the niceties, Cliff pounced on me, sounding both worried and irritated. "Where have you been?"

I admit. I bristled. "What do you mean?"

"I've called and called. You didn't pick up."

"I'm sorry," I said, feeling not one bit sorry. "We took Liz to the animal hospital."

"What happened?"

I turned my face into the corner between the cabinet and the wall and lowered my voice. "Poison."

"What?"

"That's what the vet thinks."

"Is she...?"

"For right now, she's fine. She has to stay there, though. Gabby's crushed."

"Where on earth did Liz get into poison?"

I recognized concern in Cliff's voice. The writing on the siding had bothered him; this would only add to his worry. "I'm asking myself the same question," I said, picturing him as he pulled off his hat and combed his thick hands through that curly hair of his. "We don't know. We may never know."

"Can I talk to Gabby?"

That took the air right out of my chest. I hesitated, "I don't know. I'm not sure if that's a good idea, Cliff." I was tired, too tired to explain that I didn't want my daughter falling for the marina guy, getting attached to some stranger, getting her hopes up, viewing Cliff as a daddy figure when he would never be more than a family friend. I didn't want to let Cliff break Gabby's heart.

And I was way too tired to admit that I wasn't about to let

Cliff break my heart either. "You know, I think I'm just going to fix some dinner and have some quiet one-on-one time tonight. I hope you don't mind."

"I understand," he said. He sighed. "I'm just going to say it, Brandy. I'm worried about this whole thing. Would you be careful? Lock the house? Pay attention? Maybe it's just a coincidence. But I'm getting a really bad feel for all of this. Okay?"

I shivered, and took a deep breath. I didn't want any of it to be true. But there was no denying the message written on the front siding. "It's so silly. I mean, it has to be a coincidence. A message, well maybe. But poisoning a dog? All this over a piece of land," I said. "I don't think so. We'll be fine. Really. Fine."

❀

The sound of banging on my kitchen door woke me from a hard sleep. I'd been dreaming, a nightmare I knew very, very well. Though I hadn't experienced it in years, it was back. The same old images, coming at me with the same intensity and emotions. As I came to, I realized that it was already hot, a rare condition so near the bay, even in the summer. Sweat ran down my back and between my legs. I threw back the covers and got out of bed, calling, "I'll be right there."

I dashed water on my face, ran my fingers through my hair and wrapped a short robe over my T-shirt. Running upstairs to the kitchen, I called again. "Coming."

The banging started again just as I reached the kitchen door. I threw open the door in mid-knock. Celeste stood outside, dressed in canvas pants and an oversized T-shirt. She carried gloves in one hand, a hat in the other. Beside her stood another teen, a thinner version of Celeste, in cut-offs and a halter-top. Long bangs completely obscured her eyes. She did not look up.

"Oh," Celeste said, looking at my robe and bare legs. "We must be early."

Shoot.

I'd completely forgotten that Lucia had promised to get help with the yard. The episode with the dog had completely overshadowed any plans that I remembered. "Oh, no," I said, embarrassed, "You're right on time." I wrapped the robe around my chest and retied the belt. Stepping out of the way, I opened the door. "Come on inside. I'm so sorry. I just overslept. Have you had breakfast?"

The girls looked at one another, apparently confused by the crazy condition of their new employer. Celeste spoke, touching the younger girl on the shoulder. "This is my sister, Danielle. She goes by Danny."

"Welcome, Danny," I said. "Gabby, my daughter, is still asleep. We had a rough day yesterday."

Concerned, Celeste asked, "What happened?"

"Our dog got into something. We had to take her to the vet."

"Is she going to be alright?"

"We think so," I said, forcing a smile. "What would you guys like for breakfast?"

Somehow, I managed to get my act together while scrounging up some pancake mix. I dropped blueberries onto the batter before turning them on the grill. Still in my robe, I served breakfast to two girls who ate as if they hadn't been fed in the last two months.

As she wiped up the last of her syrup with a fork full of pancake, Celeste asked, "What are we going to do today? Lucia said something about clearing out your garden." She stopped to shovel the food in her mouth, and continued, "I don't know all that much about gardening. I can work hard. But I'm no gardener."

I laughed. "That makes two of us. Everything I know, I learned from helping Maggie." I looked from Celeste to Danny, who seemed confused. "She's the woman who took me in when I lived here. But she was a good teacher. Most of what we need to do is just clearing out the clutter. The garden has been untouched for years. It's going to take a lot of work."

Danny spoke up, "What do you want me to do while you guys work?"

"Have you done much babysitting?"

She shrugged, "A little. How old is your little girl?"

"She's seven. So, she's going to need a companion more than a babysitter. Mostly, all you need to do is play with her. Keep her safe, away from the water, off the docks, out of the woods. She loves to play-act imaginary stories. School. House. Hospital. Yard games. That sort of thing."

She nodded, shrugging. "I can do that." Then she lifted her plate. "Can I have more pancakes?"

While the girls finished breakfast, I went downstairs to wake and dress Gabby. Still sleepy, she climbed the stairs and sat down with the two girls to eat. We rinsed dishes and dropped them in the washer. The girls wiped the table and put away the condiments. When everyone had finished, I led them all outside.

I'd no more than come around the corner of the house than my heart sank. The garden surrounded the south lawn, filling the enormous space below the house and the water, perhaps a half-acre. I could not see the garden from our apartment, nor from the living space in the main house. Though I'd walked around it—on the driveway leading to the water—I'd somehow managed to avoid really looking at it.

Until that morning.

Then, with Celeste on one side, Gabby and Danny on the other, I found myself confronted by the absolute chaos of the space. As I stared, I wondered what on earth I expected to accomplish. The entire staff of *Sunset Magazine* could not make peace in this space.

The garden overflowed with weeds. This late in the summer, most had already gone to seed and created yet another generation of sprouting confusion. Maggie's white gravel pathways could barely be seen through the heavy mat of dandelions and grass that grew there. Her roses were twiggy and diseased. Maggie's lilies were leafy and overcrowded, with hardly a flower among the lot of them.

The shrubs were misshapen. The fruit trees, their leaves spotted and diseased, were surrounded by a smooshy mush of decomposing rot. Other plants hosted pests; leaves sporting round holes warned of insects everywhere. I saw aphids covering the new growth of fully leafed bushes. Standing there, looking at the sad confusion that had been Maggie's splendor, I could almost hear bugs chewing.

I hardly knew where to start. "I'm glad I'm the babysitter," Danny said. "Gabby, let's go find something to do."

Celeste asked. "You think we can do this? Just you and me?"

She had me. "Well, we can try. Sometimes, a job just seems bigger before you get started."

She turned to me, her face full of concern. "I don't think this is one of those times."

"Let's go get some tools."

We headed to the shed, where Maggie kept her gardening tools, and threw open the double barn doors. Inside, was the Kabota tractor, covered in equal parts rust and dirt, Maggie's beloved tractor. Nothing made her happier than to drive it around the property, hauling compost, or gravel, or firewood. I think Maggie was part pioneer.

As for the rest of the tools, unfortunately most were in the same shape as the garden. Unkempt. Rusty. Bent. Dull. I knew that Maggie would never have intentionally left her tools this way. But over many years the humid, salt air had found its way into the shed and caused every bit as much damage as it had to the house and grounds.

Walking inside, I looked at the carefully hung tools and shook my head. Neglect has a way of damaging nearly everything. I turned over a wheelbarrow, and found the front tire had no air. The bucket was rusted, and when I reached out to spin the wheel, it would not move.

I made a note to spend some time oiling and sharpening Maggie's old tools. I would need to fix the wheelbarrow as well. I picked out a rusty shovel and a three-pronged cultivator, and handed these to Celeste. "Here, could you carry these?"

Then, I went around the back of the shed and located the two plastic buckets Maggie used for weeding. I dropped in clippers, another cultivator, and the familiar handsaw.

And then, I spotted them, hanging from a nail in the rear corner of the garage. The gloves I'd given Maggie on her last birthday before I left for college.

Caramel-colored, deerskin gloves, clean, and oiled, they looked out of place among the rusted tools. Over the years, the moist air had been kinder to the gloves than the rest of the garden implements. The leather was softer now than it was when I'd bought them, and all these years later, they still held the shape of Maggie's hands.

I took them off the hook and slid one on, flexing my fingers and feeling the stretch of the leather. It surprised me that the gloves fit; Maggie was far taller than I. I smiled to myself, thinking I should have bought her bigger gloves. I put the other glove on, and decided then and there. They would be mine.

Shaking away old memories, I headed back toward the garden and found Celeste standing at the edge of the lawn. "Where do you think we should start?"

I laughed. "Maybe we should start with a bulldozer."

She looked at me, surprise on her face, apparently wondering if she'd gone to work for a mad woman. "I'm kidding," I said, patting her on one shoulder. "If Maggie were here, she'd say we should start in one corner and move out from there."

"One corner?"

"Yep. It was the way she taught me to clean my room. Maggie believed that the only way to conquer any impossible task was to start with the smallest possible step and spread out from there. She said getting started is the hardest part."

Celeste looked back over the garden chaos, her expression bewildered. "Which corner?"

"Right here," I said, dropping the weeding bucket. "Let's get started right here."

Twenty One

In this color photo, a young woman stands between Maggie and Albert. No one smiles. She wears her dark hair in a ponytail, bangs short and straight across her forehead. Her expression is as tight as her pants. Behind crossed arms, she wears a cardigan and matching shell. Maggie has one arm around her, though the young woman leans ever so slightly away.

On Friday morning, Danny and Celeste arrived, along with three more of Celeste's schoolmates including Kayla and Liam. As we had done the day before, we began the day in the kitchen with a hearty breakfast. While the kids ate, I tried to keep my mind from calculating the total hourly expense for breakfast with my new garden crew. Whatever it was, I told myself, it was only a small part of the big picture.

By nine-thirty, the truck from the lumber company had backed up the driveway and dropped off a forklift, which they used to methodically unload the truck. By eleven, our small front lawn was buried under palettes of two-by-fours, plywood, composite decking, concrete blocks, post holders and heaven only knows what else. I wrote a check to the truck driver, took my receipt and watched him drive away.

Even though I'd expected the bill, I was surprised by the intensity of the anxiety the raw numbers drove into my heart. With every stroke of my pen, my mind shouted, *No Turning Back! No Turning Back!*

After the truck turned up the hill, I slumped onto the porch steps, weak in the knees from all the money—the last of my checking account—which had now been sunk into the old house. Celeste sat down beside me, her eyes worried. "You okay, Mrs. Beauchamp?"

"I will be. I just need to catch my breath."

"Can I get you some water? I was just going in to fill the jug." She lifted the three-gallon thermos that we kept in the garden.

"That'd be nice."

She stood up, glanced over at the wood and said, "It's only wood, Mrs. Beauchamp. You can't do nothin' without a little investment these days. You'll see. Everything is gonna work out fine." She patted my shoulder and went up the steps to the kitchen.

She's right, I thought. To gather a harvest, you must plant a field. Even the poorest farmer knows that you have to sow in order to reap. I took a deep breath. This must be what it feels like to take your very last kernels of corn, the ones that might feed your children, and bury them in the dirt.

Celeste returned with a tall glass of water, ice included, and handed it to me. Dirty handprints marred the outside of the glass, but the water inside was clear and refreshing. Sitting down beside me, she drank from her own water bottle, and looked out over the lawn, smiling. "At least we don't have to worry about this garden for a while."

"We won't even see this garden for a while," I said.

A rap song began to sound from her rear pocket, and she put down her water to answer the phone. "Yeah," she said. I smiled to myself. Cell phones had become ubiquitous, and it seemed to me that every child, rich or poor, now sported one.

I heard a voice—the urgent tone unmistakable—coming from her telephone. Celeste looked at me, and then focused on the phone. "When?"

The voice grew in volume, speaking faster as well, though I still could not make out the words. Celeste stood up and walked away from me, holding the phone to her ear as she put the palm of her hand over the other. "I can't hear you," she said, nearly shouting. "Say that again?"

Something had gone wrong, and though I hardly knew the girl, I forgot my own anxiety and began to worry for her. Had someone been hurt?

I felt guilty for listening in, for sitting so near as to observe her misery. But I couldn't stand up and walk away either. I watched as she paced back and forth across the end of the house, talking fast and apparently trying to calm whoever was on the other end of her conversation. Then suddenly, exasperated, she slammed the phone shut.

"Mrs. Beauchamp, I gotta go," she said, turning toward me as she slipped the phone back into her pocket.

"Why? What's happened?"

"That was my friend. I just gotta go."

"Is your friend alright?"

"Look, I can't talk to you about this," she said. "I'm sorry but I just can't."

"Celeste, it's ten miles into town. You don't even have a car. How will you get there?"

"I'll walk out to the highway and thumb a lift."

"I can't let you hitchhike. It's too dangerous."

She started toward the driveway, her gait hastening toward a jog. She shouted over her shoulder. "I gotta go, Mrs. Beauchamp. But I promise. I'll be back on Monday."

"Wait!" I ran to catch her. "Just a minute. Let's think. The kids all know what we need to do today," I said, gesturing toward the garden. "How about if I leave stuff for lunch on the counter, and I'll take you into town? The kids can keep working. Gabby is fine with Danny." I put my hands on my hips and waited for her to decide.

"You don't have to," she said. "I can walk."

"Not ten miles." I pointed to the garden. "You tell the girls that we have to go into town. I'll go change my clothes." I pointed my finger at her. "I'll only take a moment. Don't you go anywhere, okay?"

Her sigh was resigned, and I thought I saw the glimmer of tears. "Okay," she whispered.

I kissed Gabby, threw on clean clothes, ran a brush through my hair and washed my face. Taking the stairs two at a time, I came back into the driveway to find Celeste leaning against the van, her arms crossed, her expression tense, worry hardening the edges of her eyes. When she saw me, she looked at her watch and started around the car.

As I backed the van around the driveway, my hand over the passenger seat, a man's fist knocked on the driver's window. Startled, I stomped on the brakes. Poor Celeste's head slammed into the seat back. I rolled down the window.

"Are you Brandy Beauchamp?"

"Yes. Do I know you?"

"I doubt it," he answered. "Mr. Karras asked me to give this to you." With that, he shoved a pile of papers through the window space. Without another word, he turned and started back down the driveway toward a small maroon sedan parked on the street.

"What was that about?" Celeste asked.

"I don't know. I turned the papers over in my hand and discovered an earnest money for the sale of Maggie's Place. In a plain white envelope, attached to the papers with a clip, I found a check for one thousand dollars made out to Mr. Karras' attorney. In the lower corner of the check, I read the words, "earnest money."

✿

For a few long moments, I did not speak, my thoughts rolling over one another like waves on a beach. As I headed into town, my mind whirled with the possibilities.

Karras had given me what I'd asked for, an offer on the house. Though the number was not as big as I'd hoped—apparently he was only interested in making an offer on the value of the land— it was alarmingly good. A genuine opportunity to get out from under the house, to come out with more money than Timothy had left me, and a chance to return to my own country, my own roots. I could give Gabby a normal life in the States. I could start my own business, doing what I do best. Maybe a little marketing business, perhaps design and copywriting. Maybe even a marketing group.

"Mrs. Beauchamp, could you drop me off at the hospital?" Celeste's voice startled me, interrupting my thoughts.

"I thought we were driving into town to help a friend."

"I didn't say that."

"You said a friend called," I said. Though I was confused, I spoke as calmly as I could manage. It was time to get down to the truth. "So, what's really going on?"

She crossed her arms over her chest, and stared ahead at the highway.

"Look, Celeste, you don't have to tell me," I said. "I understand. But sometimes, when you're stressed, it helps to sort out your options with a friend."

"You aren't my friend."

Her words took me by surprise, not because I considered myself to be Celeste's friend, but because I'd used the exact phrase myself once, with Maggie, not long after I'd come to live at the old inn. Smiling, I took the rebuke, choosing not to be offended. "Maybe not yet. But I could be, if you needed one."

She sighed. "The phone call," she said. "It was a neighbor, an old lady who lives in the other side of our duplex."

"The one who called?"

She nodded. Thinking of the lesson I'd learned at the Butterfly Garden, I waited, taking a deep breath and holding it. *Let them come to you.*

She turned in her seat, looking directly at me. "My grandma fell this morning," she said, her voice trembling. "They took her away in an ambulance."

"Ah," I said. "I understand." I turned left onto Maple Bay Road and headed toward town. "Did your neighbor know anything more than that?"

Celeste blinked back tears, and shook her head. "No. Nothing."

"Then, we'll go to the Emergency Room, and you can talk to the nurses there. They'll know what's really going on."

We rode in silence. Sensing her anxiety, I put one hand on her knee and squeezed. "It's going to be alright, Celeste. Really it is."

"How do you know?"

She was right. I didn't know. Who was I to make promises? "Okay. You've got me. I don't really know," I agreed. "When I'm worried about something, it helps me to pray. Can I pray for your Grandma?"

She shrugged and looked away. "If you want."

I did. Out loud. With one hand on her knee, and my eyes wide open, I asked God for wisdom for doctors, healing and comfort for her Grandma, and peace for Celeste. I asked in Jesus' name, said, "Amen." As I turned onto Trunk Road, I asked her to tell me about her Grandmother.

"She's old school. A tribal elder. She still speaks Neqemgelisa, and she's trying to teach us."

"Is that hard for you?"

"No. We just play along while we're at home. It's what we're expected to do. She doesn't want us to have friends. And she tries to keep us from going out."

"How long have you lived with your Grandma?"

"Since I was eight. My dad left when I was in kindergarten. And when my mom went to jail, Grandma brought us to live with her. She's a good old lady."

I turned into the hospital lot and parked as close to the emergency entrance as I could. Celeste got out and I met her at the back of the car. "Really, Mrs. Beauchamp. You don't have to come in."

"I don't have anything I need to do. I'll just walk you inside."

"I can do it myself."

"I know," I said, reaching to put one arm around her shoulder. "Everyone needs a friend once in a while. It's not a sign of weakness."

She looked at me, her face full of doubt, and I wondered how many times she'd been wounded by an adult who made promises they didn't keep. Broken promises. A pain we both shared. I vowed to myself that I would keep any promise I made to Celeste.

Inside a busy Emergency Room, I stood away from the desk while she waited to speak with a receptionist. I kept an eye on her progress, and it seemed to me that the woman behind the counter managed to pay attention to other adults, even the ones who arrived after us. But she ignored Celeste. From my position across the hall, I caught the woman's attention, nodding toward Celeste.

Remarkably, the woman understood. She scowled at me and offered to help my young friend. She made a short phone call, and spoke with Celeste again, this time in quiet tones, pointing toward the reception area chairs. Celeste, still holding tension in her shoulders and face, moved away from the desk. "She says Grandmom is in radiology. I can see her as soon as she's finished."

"What's the problem?"

"They think she may have broken her hip."

"I'm so sorry."

"Me too."

"How old is she?"

Celeste frowned. "I don't really know."

"Is she healthy?"

"Not very. She's old, you know?"

I debated whether or not to continue my questions. I already sounded like an intrusive old woman. "Not healthy?"

"She smokes," Celeste said, shrugging. "And she drinks. A little."

We sat in a full waiting-room, where children played in a toy corner, and a hanging television broadcast the latest angst of daytime soap opera characters. I tried to read a magazine, while Celeste sat hunched forward, her hands in front of her, fingers touching. She did not look up, and made no effort to pass the time. Nurses and doctors, patients and staff came and went and still there was no word on Celeste's grandmother.

An hour after we'd taken our seats, I asked her, "Are you hungry?"

She looked up from her hands. "No. Not really."

"I don't believe you. I'm starving," I said. "We've been working all morning. How can you not be hungry?"

She shrugged.

"Come with me," I said, and took her hand.

Glancing around at the others nearby, she said in hushed tones, "For a nice lady, you can sure be bossy."

"You have no idea. Let's get some lunch."

After informing the receptionist, we headed into the hospital to find the cafeteria. Inside, I handed her a tray and led the way into the food service area. "Now eat up," I said. "I don't want you losing strength in my garden."

We both chose a meat sauce over linguini and I added a salad to my tray. "Get a drink," I said, "and pick a dessert." I pointed to the dessert selection. "I would, but I can't eat that stuff without ballooning into an elephant. It happens after you have children."

She looked at me like I'd sprouted an extra ear. "Okay," she agreed, drawing out the word, the way you might when speaking with the mentally unstable. She chose an éclair, and we headed for the cashier.

Though there were few people in the dining area, I chose a tiny table for two in the furthest corner of the room. I wanted to give Celeste as much privacy as possible. It couldn't be easy for her, handling this kind of stress with a complete stranger at her side. She joined me, drank some of her soda, and propped her chin on her elbow, staring out the window.

"It's good. You should try it," I said, pointing to the linguini. "Much better sauce than I make."

She blinked, clearing tears, and then focused on me. "Why did you run away?"

My turn to blink. "Excuse me?"

"You said you left home. You were young. Why did you run away?"

I smiled. "Because I didn't have a grandma who loved me. We were stuck in Alaska, a million miles from anyone who cared. Because my mom had a lot of problems. And, because I couldn't see any other answers. Looking back, I'm not sure it was a smart decision."

"But you met Maggie."

"I did." I pictured Maggie as I'd seen her on the dock that first day, her wild hair and bright toenails poking out of the holes in her tennis shoes. "I'd be tempted to call that luck," I said, "if I didn't know better. It shouldn't have happened. But it did. Maggie always said that God brought me to her."

Celeste dropped her elbow and looked directly into my eyes. "What about your mom? Why would you leave your mom?"

"I didn't leave her, really. She left me." I took a sip of my ice-water. "She started drinking when I was still a kid. At first, it was just at night, you know. After a long day at work." I shook my head. "It's such a long story. You don't want to hear this."

"I do. I don't get how you could leave your own mother."

I began to understand Celeste's perspective. Having been left, she could not envision anyone who wanted to leave. I took a deep breath. I would share my story, but I was determined to keep the telling as short as I could. "My mom followed my dad to Alaska from Montana. She thought he'd marry her if only he knew she was pregnant. She was wrong.

"After I was born, my mom did everything she could to lure my dad back into a relationship. Every afternoon, we'd follow him to the tavern where he went after work. I remember sitting in the car in the tavern parking lot, waiting with mom while dad drank. Even after years of waiting there, every single afternoon, even when he'd never paid her a moment's attention, she still believed it would happen. Dad would see me, recognize mom and decide to be with us." I shook my head. The whole story sounded foolish even this many years later.

"It never happened. Still, we waited in the stupid parking lot, freezing to death, so that he could see me when he walked to the truck.

"Eventually my dad left Valdez and went to work in a fish-processing company in Dutch Harbor. She left me with a sitter and went to see him. When she came back, she was never the same. I don't know what happened there, exactly. She had a series of boyfriends, and two more babies. She went to work at the tavern where my father used to hang out. When I was twelve, I came home one Saturday and found her passed out on a pile of dirty laundry."

I shook my head, trying to dissolve the memory. "She said she named me Brandy because of the color of my hair. I think it was because Brandy was her favorite afternoon snack. After a while though, she drank anything."

"So you left? Because of the drinking?"

I smiled. "No. Mom was mild-tempered when she drank. She'd just drift off to sleep." I put my hands in my lap, remembering the night that I'd made the decision to get out. "No," I repeated, feeling the awful gut-wrenching horror of the night. I reminded myself that it was only a memory. Gone. Over. "Eventually we moved to Anchorage, with my mom's latest boyfriend. We had this little two-bedroom apartment, and there wasn't a bed for me, so I slept on the couch. One night, her boyfriend came to visit me. And I was gone before the sun came up."

Celeste was silent. An operator, paging over the intercom, broke the spell. "Would Brandy Beauchamp please return to the Emergency Room?"

Twenty Two

CELESTE WAS STILL ARGUING when I unlocked the car doors. "We should stay. Grandmom might need me."

"Honey, Aida's having surgery. You can't help her right now," I handed her my cell phone. "Here. You carry this. The doctor is going to call as soon as she's moved into Recovery. You can take the call, and ask all the questions you need."

"How long do you think it will take?"

"They said one or two hours," I reminded her. Though the doctor had spoken to both of us, Celeste seemed to have missed most of the details.

"Will I get to see her afterwards?"

"Probably not until she moves to her own room. And after that, I don't think she's going to be very clear-headed." Once again, I reached out to pat her knee. "By tomorrow, she'll be back to her old self."

"Where are we going?"

"I thought we'd run some errands."

"Like what?"

"Well, let's start with the animal hospital."

She turned to look at me, frowning.

"As long as we're visiting the sick, we might as well see how Liz is doing."

We dropped by the animal hospital, and went back to see Liz, who greeted us with many licks, much tail thumping and whimpering. Clearly, she wanted to play, but didn't feel well enough. Celeste petted and caressed Liz, as if she were her own dog. According to Rayna, Liz was recovering nicely, and might be able to come home as soon as Saturday. "It was a close one, Brandy," Rayna said. "The lab results look like intentional poisoning. It's not anything I can prove. But you'll want to keep a close eye on her from now on. No more running through the neighborhood loose."

"She's going to be fine?"

"I think so."

With this good news, we returned to the car, where I suggested we drop by Celeste's home to pick up some clothes. "You and Danny can stay with us overnight."

"We don't need to do that."

"I know you don't need to," I said. "But think about your sister. She's young. This could be pretty scary for her. She might do better with people around. We'll clean up an upstairs room and you guys can have your own space."

Celeste looked at me, confused. "You'd let us stay with you? Why?"

I remembered my own surprise at Maggie's kindness and smiled, "Why not? Tell me where I'm going." I pulled out of the parking space, put the car in gear and waited. For some reason, Celeste didn't answer. "So, which way?"

She sighed. "I'm an adult, you know."

"I agree. No discussion." Still, I waited, parked in the middle of the lot, where no car could possibly get around us. A sedan pulled up behind us and honked. I glanced in my rearview and waved politely.

Celeste turned in her seat to look back. "Okay," she said, resigned. "Go out onto the highway and turn left."

Relieved, I obeyed. Turn after turn, Celeste led the way to her home, which I discovered was a run-down duplex in an equally dilapidated area outside of Duncan. Pulling into the driveway, I noticed that the grass in the front yard had long since died of thirst. There were no bushes. No decorations. No cheery welcome home sign on the porch. Strips of peeling paint hung from faded beige siding. A pink sheet covered the front window. Metal blinds, bent and broken, hung in the two bedroom windows. The front door was deeply scarred from the scratches of a pet.

I parked behind an old pickup. "I'll wait here for you," I said. Celeste nodded, climbed out and went to a rock beside the front door. Underneath she extracted a key, and disappeared inside.

My own emotions surprised me. This was where I'd come

from. Broken. Poor. Hopeless. I blinked back tears, remembering the distressed apartment house I'd left behind in Anchorage. What had happened to the people in that apartment? Where were they now? I found myself wondering if my mother ever found happiness.

Another more frightening thought nagged me, one I avoided at all costs. I remembered my two sisters and wondered what had happened to them. Were they still at home? Was my mother still with the boyfriend? Had he visited them in the middle of the night?

Over the last fifteen years, I'd always wondered if I really cared. My own tears gave me my answer.

Waiting, I turned on the radio and listened to the banal conversation of a daytime talk show. Though the voices centered on Canadian topics, the comments and emotions could be extracted word for word from similar American programs. I changed the channel. I had all the conflict I needed, right in the center of my own life.

Eventually Celeste returned with a bulging plastic grocery bag.

"Did you get some things for Danny?"

She nodded, though she did not speak.

I turned back toward town, avoiding the shortcut back to Genoa Bay. Celeste noticed. "More errands?"

"Just one," I said. "I need to pick up a loan application from my bank."

"A loan application?"

"All that lumber costs money," I said, braking to accommodate the afternoon traffic. I looked over my shoulder and switched lanes. "I'm going to take out a loan on the house."

With new paperwork tucked safely in the back seat, I pulled away from the bank and headed for the old house. In spite of my many reassurances, the tension in Celeste did not ease. She held her shoulders high, as though they were connected by some invisible wire to her ears, her facial muscles so tight she seemed brittle, like hand-blown glass. And as we drove, I began to wonder what Celeste was not telling me.

❀

On Saturday, I took Celeste and Danny into town to visit their grandma. Though still in a great deal of pain, she seemed happy to see us, at least as happy as any woman with a broken hip. She was agitated, and seemed stressed by the hospital and her pain, and so I ushered the children away after only a few moments. Gabby was glad to get away from the hospital.

We stopped by at the animal hospital to pick up Liz. Though still weak, and on a restricted diet, Liz was thrilled to go home. I'm not sure who was happier, Gabby or the dog—who did not move her head from my daughter's lap until we turned into our own driveway.

In the afternoon, the girls and I put Liz in her crate in the apartment and hiked the perimeter of the bay, stopping for a picnic lunch on the point across from the house. There, basking in the afternoon sun, we ate turkey sandwiches and apple bars, and talked girl talk. When the wind kicked up, we started back, walking along the tidal zone, hopping from rock to rock until we arrived at the marina.

On Sunday, we attended Hilmer Road Bible Church, Lucia's home church. I was nervous about taking Celeste and Danny along with us. Perhaps Aida, their grandmother, would disapprove. But when I invited them, the girls just shrugged.

Shrugging is, apparently, a teenage language all of its own.

It was our second visit, and this time Gabby headed for Children's Church like an old pro. The girls and I met Lucia in the foyer. "Oh, great necklace," she said, giving my watch chain a tug.

"Something from Maggie," I said. We sat together in the front of the sanctuary, where instead of listening, I chose to chew my worries. After service, we stopped by the hospital for another short visit.

Though it cheered the girls to see their grandmother, I couldn't shake the feeling that something was not quite right. The old woman recognized the girls, grasping their hands in greeting. But she was not alert, and could not carry on a coherent conversation. Two days after surgery, it seemed to me that she ought to be further along.

Not wanting to upset the girls, I said nothing.

Early Monday morning, Peter arrived with a crew of four to begin work on the house. With crowbars ripping away at the sheetrock, and hammers dropping studs from the ceiling, I fixed breakfast for the garden crew and we took our food out on the back deck to enjoy the sunshine and relative quiet.

Just as we sat down, I realized that I'd forgotten pancake syrup. I headed back through the great room to the kitchen, where I was surprised by the unmistakable smell of cigarettes.

I followed the stench into the end of the dining-room, where a young man, perhaps thirty, used both hands to tear sheet rock from the wall. Out of the corner of his mouth dangled an unlit cigarette. His was no ordinary cigarette. Though it was not home rolled, it smelled like one. "Excuse me," I said, over the clamor of tools. "But I'm afraid you can't smoke in the house. You'll have to go outside."

He turned to face me, eyeing me up and down as he reached into his front pocket and retrieved a disposable lighter. He inhaled deeply as he lit the cigarette, and then blew a wide halo of smoke into the air.

"You must not have heard me, with all the hand tools and noise," I said, more insistently this time. I said there will be no smoking inside this house."

Still staring into my eyes, he dropped the cigarette and ground it into the dining-room carpet. I could hardly believe the insolence. What possessed a man to behave that way? Angry, I nearly said something more. But then I looked into his blue eyes, and I saw something I knew better than to challenge. Something dark. Something dangerous. Though Peter trusted these men, I did not. And this one, this Blue Eyes, I would not trust with anything more valuable than a sheet rock nail. I made a decision then and there to speak to Peter about it.

I would definitely keep Gabby away from that man.

The girls and I ate breakfast out in the sunshine, our backs to the peeling siding, as we watched the marina come to life. Boats came and went, and Cliff's crew ran the docks to keep up with the flow of marine traffic.

After breakfast, a delivery truck arrived with a load of mulching compost for the garden. I paid them and directed the driver, who backed up through the big gate, to dump the pile in the middle of the road leading to the water's edge.

Together, the kids and I inspected our progress and laid out the day's plans. Foot by foot, we had begun to reclaim the jungle that had overtaken Maggie's beloved garden. Hundreds of pounds of weeds and leaves and branches now occupied the compost pile at the bottom of the hill. While the kids had made good progress, they left the most serious plant decisions to me. They overlooked anything that needed transplanting or dividing, pruning or shaping in the more urgent effort to remove weeds, cut back wild overgrowth and bring order to the chaotic space.

There was enough cutting, dividing and transplanting left to keep me busy until December.

After I walked the other teenagers through on the day's most urgent chores, I loaded Gabby and the two girls back into the van to make the now familiar trip into town. We dropped my loan application by the bank, where a young loan officer assured me that he would have an answer by early next week. Back in the car, I found myself calculating. Did I have enough money to make it until next week?

We parked in the visitors' lot of the community hospital, and headed for Grandmother Aida's room. She was gone when we arrived, having been taken to physical therapy, the nurse explained.

"Maybe we should come back later?"

"It shouldn't be long," she assured us. "You can wait in her room."

We settled in chairs around the empty bed, and watched silently as a nursing assistant changed her sheets. Just as he rolled up the dirty linen and opened the door to leave, a tall woman walked in. She wore a mismatched black suit. Her dark hair was cut at ear length, and she wore heavy framed glasses far too wide for her face. Coming to a stop at the end of the bed, she adjusted her glasses and looked at her clipboard. "Oh," she said, finally noticing the empty bed. "Aida isn't here?"

"She's off to therapy," I said. "We don't know how long she'll be."

"I see." she looked down at her notes. "And you're family?" she asked, sweeping across the three of us with the end of her ballpoint pen.

The girls nodded. "She's our grandmother," they said, almost in unison.

"Well, that's just as well," she said, turning to me. "I'm the social worker assigned to her case. My name is Karen Motley." She reached for my hand. I gave her my name as we shook hands. "I've been meaning to call, but your name isn't in the chart."

"That's because…"

"It doesn't matter," she said, waving her hand in the air. "These things happen." She looked down at her notes. "It says here that Aida lives alone?"

I looked at Celeste, expecting her to take over this part of the conversation. With the tiniest of movements, she shook her head back and forth, clearly signaling, "No."

No, what? I glanced up at the social worker, still reading the notes in her chart. She had not yet looked up. I raised my eyebrows at Celeste, confused.

"Living alone is dangerous for someone coping with a broken hip," the woman went on, apparently taking our silence for affirmation. "But in this case it's double trouble." She looked up at me and smiled.

"I just need to explain that the doctor has asked me to find a place for Aida to go into treatment. Of course, it isn't easy, finding a place that can manage her physical therapy and her alcoholism at the same time. After many phone calls, I've found an opening at the First Nations Care Center. We're going to transfer her this afternoon."

In the long beat of silence that followed this rather startling announcement, the pieces started falling into place. Aida's agitation. The sedation. The tremors. Her inability to carry on a reasonable conversation. Suddenly even the tension that Celeste carried all weekend long began to make sense. Aida was not just recovering from surgery. She was drying out. Aida didn't drink occasionally. She was a full-blown alcoholic.

"How long will she have to stay?" Celeste asked, suddenly alarmed.

"No one can be certain," Karen said, directing her answer to the girls. "It really depends on how well she does. The doctor has started medication to help with the withdrawal symptoms. But that has slowed her progress with the hip."

"Thank you for all you're doing," I said, getting up to shake her hand. "We appreciate knowing that Aida is going to a safe environment."

"Now, I don't have a phone number here," she said.

Unsure of what was going on with Celeste, I gave the woman my cell number.

"So then, I'll keep in touch, and let you know when we can have her transferred."

"Thank you so much," I said, walking her out into the hall. I watched until she stepped into the elevator, and then returned to the room. I went straight to Celeste, who was still standing. "Okay, so what was that all about?"

Surprised at my tone, she blinked.

"I think it's about time you came clean with me," I said, leaning against Aida's bed. "Why am I lying for you? And, why didn't you tell that woman that you lived with your grandmother?"

"I couldn't."

"Why not?"

"Because she would have called the authorities."

"Why?"

Celeste looked to her sister and back to me. "You don't know much, do you? They aren't going to let us stay there alone while Grandmom goes to treatment. They'll call the authorities. Child Services, or whatever. Then, they'll separate us," she looked at Danny and back to me. "And then, they'll dump us in some home."

"What about family? Surely you have other family that you can stay with."

She shook her head. "Not anyone nearby. If they sent us to be with family, we'd both have to quit school."

"It would only be temporary, a few weeks at most."

"It wouldn't be temporary." She shook her head. "Not temporary."

Why not temporary? I couldn't understand this child. With my head swimming, I took the seat beside her. "I think you need to tell me everything," I said. "The whole truth. Why would Children's Services take you away from your grandmother?"

"Because she isn't well. She hasn't been well for a long time."

"I don't understand. Alcoholism can be treated. Hips heal."

"That's not all."

"There's more?"

I looked at Danny, sitting like an ice sculpture in her seat, her eyes full of tears. She wouldn't return my gaze, focusing instead on the view of the parking lot below Aida's room. It didn't take a lie detector to realize that this, at last, was the beginning of the truth. Grandmother needed Celeste more than Celeste needed Grandmother.

I took Celeste's hand. "How long have you been taking care of Aida?"

She blinked and looked away, shrugging. "A couple of years."

"No one knows?"

"Who could I tell? My mom is in jail. My dad split. The neighbor though, she knows. That's who called when it happened. She looks out for Aida during the day when we're at school."

I took a deep breath and blew it out, slowly. I certainly hadn't counted on this turn of events. "So. What do we do now? You can't stay at the house alone. It isn't safe."

"Why not?" She gestured to her sister. "We've been alone all this time anyway. I take care of Danny. We get to school. We do our homework. We're fine."

"Wait a minute," I said. "How did you get into the Shiloh School anyway? It takes money. Applications. Signatures. How did you pull that off?"

"I did the applications myself. I signed Aida's name. They gave me a scholarship."

"And what about Danny? Where does she go to school?"

"To a junior high near the house. Danny's a real student. Not like me."

I patted her hand, sighing. "Okay. So your grandmother is going to a nursing home where they're going to try to treat her alcoholism. But what are they going to find out when she gets there? What exactly is wrong?"

Danny spoke up, turning from the window to look at me, tears streaming down her cheeks. "Grandmom has trouble with her memory," she said. "She can't remember anything. Sometimes, she doesn't even know where she is."

"But she always knows us," Celeste said.

My cell phone began to ring, and I plucked it from my purse, snapping it open with more frustration than necessary. "Yes," I said.

As is always the case with cell phones, I had to repeat myself. "Hello," I said, louder this time. "This is Brandy Beauchamp."

Through the buzz of electronics, I heard a voice speaking, "Mrs. Beauchamp, this is Don Prater from the bank."

"Oh, yes, Don. What can I do for you? Did I forget something?" I didn't expect to hear from them before Monday.

"No. No, nothing like that," he said.

I still had trouble understanding him through the background noise. Perhaps the hospital had some kind of shielding. I put one finger to my ear and moved over by the window, hoping for better reception.

"... so sorry. Maybe another..."

"Wait. I'm having trouble hearing you," I said, leaning into the windowsill. "Would you repeat that?"

"Yes," he said, and his voice was suddenly clearer, the fuzzy background noise gone. "I said that unfortunately, we won't be able to accommodate your loan request. We're so sorry. Perhaps you could reapply at another time."

Twenty Three

This pack contains envelopes, all of them pink, secured by a purple ribbon tied in a simple knot. At first, I suspect them to be love letters. Perhaps from Albert to Maggie. I smile to myself as I begin to look through the stack, wondering whether or not to read them. I discover, to my surprise, that the letters are unopened, and across the front of each one, is the same hand-lettered message. "Return to sender." They are addressed, in Maggie's handwriting, to Mary Ellen Blackburn.

ON TUESDAY MORNING, I was upstairs turning French toast with a spatula by the time the work crew arrived. As the gardeners began to mingle with the construction crew, I piled plates on the counter and invited everyone to feast.

I may not have a single dime to my name; but no one can call me anything but generous.

After everyone settled into their chores, I left for town. It appeared that only an in-person visit with the agent who carried Maggie's home-owner's insurance would move my payment forward. Though the adjuster had promised me a check for repairs, I'd yet to see a penny of it. The reimbursement wouldn't cover everything, but it would keep my creditors at bay for a little while longer.

I'd tried gently putting the adjuster on fast forward. He didn't respond. Perhaps the agent, who needed my business, could speed up the process.

After I had waited in the two-chair waiting area for nearly twenty minutes, the agent escorted me into his personal sanctuary. While he did not know what had held up my check, he promised to look into the missing payment. After much reassurance, given in the tone of a kindergarten teacher helping a frightened student, he walked me back into the waiting-room and I left feeling little relief.

Among my other chores, I wanted to purchase supplies to strip and paint the upper bedrooms of the big house. Since moving to Canada, I'd learned the wisdom of the old proverb, "Man proposes; but God disposes." The windstorm damage and the arrival of our new, but temporary teenaged guests, had changed most of my well-laid plans. Celeste and Danny needed a clean place to live, at least for a while. And, with the renovation of the apartment, and the replacement of windows and siding, Gabby and I would also need to move upstairs as construction progressed.

All of this added together would force me to finish the upstairs rooms. My next errand involved purchasing supplies.

After the frightening message painted on the side of the house, there was no way that I'd choose to do business where I might run into neighbors again. So, armed with photographs clipped from magazines, I headed to the big box store on the highway. In the paint department, I sought the help of a salesclerk (a woman who normally sold washers and dryers), who loaded my cart with everything I needed to clean up the second-floor bedrooms, including painter's tape, drop-clothes, and chemicals, which she confidently promised would remove century-old wallpaper. In fact, this laundry expert even convinced me to add chemical thinners to my trim paint. "It will flow like cream," she assured me.

Oh, the joys of renovation.

After filling the car with my new painting supplies, I pulled onto the highway. On this beautiful day, I knew that I shouldn't let my anxiety take control of my well-being. This philosophy is, of course, much easier to believe than to live out. After my loan was denied, money worries stuck in my thoughts the same way caramels stick to the teeth. No matter how much I rolled ideas around, turning them over and over, nothing seemed to unstick the mess I'd made for myself.

Even prayer seemed less than effective.

Once again, I struggled with the unfairness of losing Timothy's will. My husband had done everything he knew to ensure that Gabby and I would have enough if the worst should happen. The worst did happen. Would the government ever find his papers? Would the action brought by my attorney ever pay any dividends?

As always, my thoughts circled around to Timothy's parents. And I felt my spine stiffen as I resisted their desire to control my future. Though I loved them, as any daughter-in-law might, I did not want to live under their shadow. I wanted to raise Gabby myself, providing for her as best I could without Timothy.

I wanted to make my own future.

But what future did I have to look forward to?

I couldn't serve breakfast to the boat crowd because I couldn't advertise on the docks. I couldn't start hosting guests because the house wasn't finished. I couldn't finish the house because I didn't have the money.

In the face of these undeniably difficult problems, I had somehow managed to add two teenagers to my household, hire a complete garden crew and begin kitchen renovations on top of storm repairs. Clearly, I was not born to be a businesswoman.

My actions didn't make any sense—even to me.

I was complaining to God about the situation when it occurred to me that it was time to visit Walter Doherty. From the day we'd first met, Maggie's lawyer had promised to help me as much as he could. Though I hadn't seen him often, maybe he'd have an idea about what I should do.

Perhaps he'd tell me to take the only reasonable option. Sell, while you can still get on with your life.

I caught Mr. Doherty as he was walking out of his office, a pile of folders under one elbow, a briefcase in his other hand. "Walk with me, Brandy," he said. "I'm headed to my car, but maybe I can answer your questions on the way."

"I should have called."

"Nonsense. Usually, you'd find me sitting behind my desk hoping for a distraction. Today, I have to visit a client." He checked his watch. "But I have a few minutes." He led me toward the parking area behind the building.

"I'm not expecting you to have all the answers," I said. "But I'm at the end of my rope. I need money to finish the repairs on

Maggie's house. I've applied for a loan, but they turned me down."

Doherty stopped walking and turned to face me. "Turned you down? Who turned you down? For what reason?"

"My bank. And, they didn't really give me a reason. I was on my cell. The reception was bad." I put one hand to my forehead, brushing my hair from my eyes. "I could try again. Another bank, maybe. I own the land, and I even have a written offer from Karras. I thought the offer would encourage a bank to make the loan—knowing that someone else would buy it immediately if I defaulted."

"That shouldn't make any difference. None at all. Most banks would jump at the chance to make a loan on that property. With no other debt involved, it would be a no-brainer." He shook his head. "I never expected it would come to this."

"What? Come to what?"

"Karras. I know he wants your property. He's even spoken to me about it. Asked me to talk you into selling." He frowned. "But to ensure that you don't get a loan. I never thought he would go that far."

"That's silly. It's not possible, is it? Not in this day and age. He couldn't influence the bank, could he?"

"Not officially, of course." Doherty shifted his files to his other arm, freeing his right hand to gesture. "But in the business world, not everything is official. Karras has partners, investors. I'm certain of it. Karras couldn't come up with enough money to do a development like he's planning. I don't know who the investors are exactly, but I have my guesses. So far, I've heard nothing more official than rumors."

"I don't understand. What do his investors have to do with me?"

"Karras has to have outside money coming from somewhere. And those people, whoever they are, are being very careful about staying silent. There's no record of a formal partnership. At least not yet."

"So, these secret partners," I said, still confused, "how are they affecting me?"

"I think they have pull, influence. A phone call here. A contact there. A promise to leave money here, or a threat to move money there. Nothing you can trace, of course. But with that kind of money, they can throw their weight around. Make sure that loan officers won't do business with you."

"You're kidding. It's like *The Godfather*, or something."

He laughed. "Not quite. You won't find a horse's head under your bedsheets. But no matter how the laws read, people still do business the old-fashioned way. Loyalty. Alliances. Handshakes. Vague threats. It all revolves around money—who has it, who doesn't. Who needs it. Who wants more. Nothing in human nature changes, really."

"So, what am I supposed to do? Give up? Sell? Move out?"

"Brandy, what do you want to do?"

Tears filled my eyes, and I blinked, trying desperately to hold them back. "I just want a life of my own. I want to make a home for Gabby and me. And, I want to be able to make a decent living. Maggie gave me that chance, and no matter how hard I try, I just can't seem to make it work."

"Then take it, Brandy. Take the chance."

"How? Where will I find the money to finish what I've started? I don't have much time. They're working on the house now." I put my hands on my hips. "I sound like a whiny kid, I know. I don't even like the way I sound. But I just don't know what else to do. Tell me what to do."

"In the end, Brandy, when everything is finished and the house is livable, can you make it work?" He looked at me, really looked at me, and I sensed in his words both challenge and encouragement, like a father giving a child the strength he needs to run a difficult race.

"It won't be easy, but I think I can."

"Then don't let anything hold you back. Why don't you work up a loan proposal, and bring it to me. If Karras can corral investors, then so can we. How much do you need?"

"I think twenty thousand would take me over the hump."

He waved the number away as if I'd asked for pocket change. "Make an appointment, and we'll talk." And with that, Doherty reached out and wrapped me in his one free arm, hugging me hard. "And don't give up," he said. "Maggie told me I would like you," he said, moving away from me. "She was right."

❀

I was home, unloading stuff from the car when Cliff wandered up the driveway, his hands in his pockets, his baseball cap low over his forehead. On this hot August afternoon, instead of his usual flannel shirt, he wore instead a short-sleeved denim, the marina logo embroidered over the chest pocket. "Can I help you carry this stuff inside?"

"Sure," I said, handing him a box of one-gallon paint cans. "I never refuse help."

"Good." He smiled, though I noticed the smile never quite reached his eyes. "I need something to do."

"What? No big yacht captains to drive into town this afternoon?"

"Not a one."

We loaded ourselves with as much as we could carry and headed up the stairs to the second floor. "Here," I said, dropping a bag of supplies in the front bedroom. "Let's leave everything in here. We'll use this room as storage until all the wallpaper is off."

"I didn't know you were going to start up here."

"I haven't talked to you recently. Things change fast around here. You have to keep up." I laughed, putting my hands on my hips. "In fact, I'm having trouble keeping up myself."

He squatted, lowering the heavy box of paint to the floor. "What do you mean?"

"Well, now I have two semi-temporary guests. I've hired a bunch of kids to restore the garden. The Shiloh Farms crew is working on the wind damage. And, I've decided to redo the north end of the kitchen, as long as we have to repair the siding, and roof joists. And then, of course, there is the new metal roof." I ticked these items off on my fingers. "So you see, if you miss a day at Maggie's Place, you've missed some very serious developments. By the way, where have you been? We've missed you guys."

"I was trying to spend as much time as I could with the boys. I only get six weeks every summer." He walked toward the window, looking out over the water, his arms across his chest. "They left this morning on Harbor Air."

"I'm sorry," I said, feeling genuine sadness. I couldn't say goodbye to Gabby for nine months every year. "I can't imagine what it is to have your kids scream in and out of your life that way. It must just about tear your heart in two every time they leave."

"That's the way it feels. You know, the experts are always worried about how kids survive divorce. And I know it's important. After all, they're just kids. But still, you hope it will be okay, the sharing custody, the going back and forth. But it hurts everyone. Parents too, like driving a knife into your heart, every time they leave."

I stood beside him, putting one hand on his shoulder. "I'm sorry," I said again, wishing I could think of something wise, more sensitive, more comforting. It's at moments like these that my brain fails me. I want to respond, but I end up sounding lame—even to me. "At least you say goodbye knowing that you'll see them again. They'll be back." I was thinking of Timothy, of course.

He looked at me, his eyes shining with unshed tears. "If anyone knows better than that, it should be you. We just assume that we'll see one another again." He gave me a weak smile. "And, someday they won't come back. They'll have jobs. Girlfriends. Cars." He looked back out over the water. "And by then, when they need my influence the most, I'll be up here, living out my dream." He shook his head. "I was pretty stupid. You know?"

"Cliff, everyone makes mistakes. And besides, from what you told me, don't you think there's enough blame to go around?"

"Maybe. But the kids are the ones who pay."

"Looks like you're still paying."

"Maybe," he said again, though he sounded unconvinced. "Let's go get the rest of that stuff down there." He turned from the window and started for the door. "Besides, I came up here to ask you a question."

❀

After we finished dinner, Celeste and I washed dishes while Gabby and Danny cleared the table. In the days since Danny had come into Gabby's life, my little girl had grown up. She now watched Danny's every move, copying her as she picked up the place-mats and shook them out over the sink. Gabby helped put away the salt and pepper, the salad dressing and brought the empty glasses to the sink.

"Can we watch a video?" Gabby asked, as Danny finished wiping the table.

"Sure. Do it in the media room though. I don't want you guys traipsing through the sawdust on the way downstairs."

"Will you make popcorn?"

"Maybe Danny can make it for you. It's in the pantry."

With the popcorn in the microwave, they went off to choose a movie. I turned to Celeste, leaning one hip on the counter. "Can I ask you something?"

"Of course." She lifted a saucepan from the rack and began to dry.

"Would you mind if I slipped out for a little while tonight?"

She shrugged. "Why not? We'll keep an eye on Gabby. Where are you going?"

"Cliff, the marina guy, wants to take me for a boat ride."

"Oh yeah? After dinner?" Her voice betrayed her amusement. She shook her head. "Be sure to take a warm coat, and maybe a blanket."

"I will," I said. "I shouldn't be long."

"No hurry," she said, hanging up her kitchen towel. Now that I think about it, I'm certain that just before she turned away, I caught a mischievous twinkle in her eye.

Heeding Celeste's advice, I carried a heavy knitted throw and a windbreaker down to the docks. I was just about to start down the ramp when I heard Cliff call me from the door of the marina office. "Brandy," he said, "up here!"

I waited while he jogged down the steps and across the lawn. In the hours since I'd last seen him, his expression had lightened. "You're on time!"

"What, women are never on time? Is that what you're saying?"

"No. Not that. I'm always late. I get focused on a task and get lost. It's like when I'm concentrating, my internal clock shuts down."

"Okay. I'm duly warned."

"Come on. We need to get on board."

"What's the hurry?"

"Trust me. It's worth it."

He took my hand and led me down the dock ramp. With high tide nearing slack, the ramp was nearly level, and the still water underneath glistened with the dark, oily shadows of late evening. The air turned cold, and I was glad that Celeste had suggested a blanket.

I followed Cliff down the ramp and around behind it, where a row of dinghies lined the dock in the shallowest area of the bay. At the end, a small ski boat floated on inky water. Cliff jumped in, turned and offered me his hand. "Step on the seat," he said. "It's easier."

"Where do you want me?"

"Take the co-captain's seat," he said pointing. He dove into the tiny cabin at the front of the boat and popped out, moments later, holding an inflatable life vest in one hand, another around his neck. "Here," he said, handing it to me. "Put it on like a coat, and snap the buckle in front." He demonstrated.

I watched as he primed the outboard engine, started it, and cast off from the dock. Before I knew it, we were gliding through the marina past yachts and fishing boats, the little engine putting along quietly, the cool air on my face, the sun low in the western sky.

I remembered the package I'd brought down to the boat. "Here," I said, handing a plastic bag to him. "This afternoon, you looked like you needed cheering up."

He reached for the bag, grinning. "My cookies! Where did you find the recipe? Maggie told me the recipe was a secret, just for me."

"She was a sly one," I said and laughed. "Remember the box I told you about? I found the recipe in there."

He opened the bag and brought out a cookie. "Now if I only had milk."

I pulled a thermos from my bag.

"I think I love you," he said, his voice mocking. "You think of everything."

Bracing the wheel against his leg, he took the thermos with one hand, set his cookie on his knee and began to pour milk into the red cap. "To a woman who knows how to cheer a guy up," he said, lifting the cup into the air.

"Thank you, kind sir. I certainly try."

"Oh, my goodness," Cliff groaned, still chewing. "This is absolute heaven. Molasses cookies and milk. Does anything ever get better than this?" He held the bag toward me.

"Like heaven," I said, taking a cookie. "Tell me how you charmed Maggie into developing a cookie just for you?"

"I told you," Cliff said, bringing the boat around the end of the docks. "I did little things for her. Things she couldn't do any more."

"She told me she had an old friend, a neighbor, helping her."

He laughed. "I'm a neighbor."

"I thought she meant a really old friend. Not some young buck."

"I'm a young buck?"

"You know what I mean. How did you and Maggie get to be friends?"

"Brandy, you lived here. It's a small community."

"Why are you so secretive? Why does everyone here have to keep a secret?" I thought of Celeste and her sister, of my own neighbors, of the investors. This secrecy thing was starting to aggravate me.

"It's not a secret. No big deal. I met Maggie when I took the job at the marina. Back then she was still baking goodies for the boaters here in the summer. When my wife left, of course she heard about it. Everyone within twenty miles heard. She decided that she would be a one-woman antidepressant."

I laughed. This was the Maggie I remembered. "What'd she do?"

"She baked for me, constantly. Cookies. Breads. Pies. Most men lose weight when their wives leave them. I gained twelve pounds. She invited me to church until I thought I was going to go crazy. She actually came down to the dock and brought dinner for me. Sometimes she dragged me up to the house on the pretense of some chore she needed help with. She listened while I talked. She was good medicine, that woman."

"I know. I took the same medicine."

"When I was a young man, I didn't need God. He was for weak people. A crutch. But there I was, a broken man, a guilty man. I'd had this one chance, you know? I had this family, and I'd let it slip through my fingers because I had to live my own life, my own way. I was so depressed, I could hardly manage."

Cliff was speaking as much to himself as he was to me at that point, his mind drifting off as he watched the water in front of the boat. "Maggie saw it. She saw the guilt eating me away at the inside. And she showed me the way to forgiveness." He glanced at me, smiling a little sheepishly. "I'm a little embarrassed about how long it all took to sink in. I mean, I know that God has forgiven me for my part in the whole mess. The thing is, I'm still learning to forgive myself. On days like today, when I have to live the consequences of my own stupidity, well, that's when I have the hardest time forgiving myself."

"I know. Choices," I said, sighing. "We all make choices."

Cliff pulled back on the throttle, slowing the boat down. Then, he pointed up to Maggie's Place. "Have you ever seen your house from the water?"

"Not since I was a kid."

"It's pretty magnificent up there, isn't it?"

I looked up at the old house, at the wide bank of windows facing east, at the wrap-around porch, and the garden—which didn't look so bad from this distance. And I wondered how it could be that a place—nothing more, really, than wood and nails and siding—could evoke so much emotion. The old inn was more than just my home. It was my salvation, my place of belonging, of starting over. It was the first place I'd ever felt love. The place where I began to think of myself as more than an inconvenience. The place where I began to have hope.

As we floated past, I felt a huge lump twist somewhere in my chest. I had to make the place work, somehow. I had to save it. "It's still beautiful," I whispered.

Cliff didn't hear me. He'd already revved the engine and brought the little boat up on plane. For a long time, we bounced across the water, slamming down over waves, and flying up again on the other side. I wrapped my legs in the blanket, tucking the edges under my thighs, pulled my jacket hood over my head and tied it in place.

"There is a reason that old people drive big slow boats," I shouted at Cliff.

"I'm sorry," he yelled back. "A little rough?"

"What is it with men and speed?" I bellowed.

He backed the engine some. "We're late. I'm afraid we'll miss it."

"Miss what? For crying out loud, you'd think we were on our way to catch a plane." Between the boat speed and the evening wind, the brisk air coming over the windshield threatened to shear my face from my skull.

"Not white."

"What?"

"Not quite." He said it slowly, enunciating carefully. My mistake made me laugh out loud. Cliff began a wide turn around the west end of what appeared to be an uninhabited island. This close to land, the boat was protected from the wind, and I was glad for the relief. Good thing Cliff and I were nothing more than friends. With my hair blown to bits, and my eyes squeezed shut against the wind, I had to look like a terror.

"Are we almost there yet?" In spite of the blanket wrapped around my legs, I'd grown cold, and impatient. I couldn't, for the life of me, figure out what would be worth this uncomfortable trip in the evening air.

"You sound like the boys."

"Sorry," I said, without an ounce of repentance. "But are we?"

He didn't answer. Instead, he cut the engine again and we went sputtering in toward the island. Cliff gave the wheel a sharp turn, and we entered a tiny slip of space between giant sandstone cliffs. In this shadowy canal, water swirled away from the bow, breaking on the cliffs in little wavelets. In the quiet of the putting engine, I heard the soft spat of water breaking on the outside of the fiberglass boat. But my eyes were fastened on the cliffs themselves, which rose above us in the colors of hot chocolate, whipped cream and face powder.

In all the years I'd lived here, I'd never seen anything quite like it.

Without speaking, we crept along that passageway, mesmerized by the water and the high walls on either side. I wondered where this tiny opening led, and just as I was about to ask, Cliff spun the wheel, turning us toward the east, as he gave gas to the engine.

We had entered a tiny harbor, lined on the beach side with four anchoring buoys. The buoys were empty, and I scanned the beach, looking for some way to identify our location. "Look," Cliff said softly, touching my shoulder. "This is what we came to see."

I had just turned to face him, wondering what he meant, when I saw it. A full moon rising at that very moment from behind Mt. Baker.

The mountain had turned fiery pink, reflecting the magnificence of the receding sun. In the foreground, at the entrance to the bay, a sailboat, with a single bare pole, floated at anchor, a silhouette against the deepening hues of approaching darkness. At the top of the mast, the anchor light flickered with the motion of the water.

We sat in the boat, watching without words, as the sky turned crimson and light streaks of clouds reflected the brilliant tangerine of the setting sun.

Twenty Four

This picture is quite recent. Maggie's thick figure has slimmed, and her swollen feet pour over the edges of her shoes, like bread dough left too long to rise. Her back is to the camera, and with one hand, she points toward the eaves of the old house. Her gaze is fixed on a man who leans away from the top of an extension ladder high above the lawn. In one hand he holds a long pole, the end made into a homemade torch. With his other hand, his fingers cling to the shutters of an attic window. The flame dances below a large wasps' nest clinging to the eaves of Pickering Place. I look closely at the photo, holding it up to the light. The profile of the man's face is unmistakable, though the beard is darker here, the body slimmer. Cliff is burning wasps for Maggie.

AT HOME I FOUND DANNY and Gabby asleep on the couch. Celeste, who let me in through the front door, put one finger to her lips and whispered, "I was just finishing the movie," she pointed to the children, "then I was going to put them both to bed."

Liz sniffed the knees of my jeans, apparently checking my identification, and then returned to snooze in the exact center of the floor, her huge body forming the canine version of a bearskin rug. She was asleep before I poured myself a glass of sweet tea and sat down in the recliner.

"How was the boat trip?" Celeste asked me.

"It was beautiful. I've never seen a sunset quite like that."

"I didn't mean the view, silly."

I smiled. "You really think you have this all figured out, don't you?"

"I'm no expert," she said, "but I'm not blind. He really likes you."

I felt my own cheeks grow warm. "We've gotten to be good friends. We've been through a lot of the same things."

"Yeah, right," she snorted, smiling. "Friends."

"Shsh—" I said, pointing to the screen. "You'll ruin the end of the movie."

While Celeste watched the last scenes of *Return to Snowy River*, I thought about my evening with Cliff. Clearly, something about the evening had changed my thinking. I couldn't deny that. But the changes made me uneasy. Nearly queasy.

Cliff was kind, no question. He was a good father; I gave him full credit for that. He was a man of deep faith. A loyal friend. He wanted the best for me. This was the reason he tried so hard to talk me out of my decision to renovate and run Maggie's Place. He was trying to protect me from both the present and future struggle the business would bring into our lives.

During our boat ride together, I had learned another secret about Cliff Lowry. He was indebted to Maggie, to her remarkable ability to take in stray dogs and give them health—both spiritual and emotional.

I should know. I had also been one of Maggie's strays. Cliff and I had that much in common. We both understood the power of love, extended in the context of forgiveness and faith.

As I sipped tea, I realized that something else about Cliff's story made me uneasy. Perhaps friendship explained only part of Cliff's kindness toward me. Perhaps Cliff had offered his friendship simply as compensation, his way of repaying Maggie's kindness. But if that were the case, wouldn't he want the old place to succeed? To see it run again as it had in the days when Maggie reigned over the old inn?

Until that night, until we watched the sunset together, until he shared the pain of losing his wife, Cliff had been nothing more than a friend. He reminded me of good old Al, the handy helper for Tim the Tool Man.

Cute, but not handsome. Friendly, but not passionate. Helpful, but not necessary.

A good man, perhaps—but never the leading man.

And what did I care anyway? I hadn't returned to Genoa Bay looking for a leading man. I had come home to start my own life, not to find a soul mate. I shook my head, trying to clear my thoughts. This kind of thinking would get me nowhere, except perhaps into trouble.

Putting a forceful stop to my wandering mind, I got up and carried Gabby downstairs. After putting her to bed, I brushed my teeth and combed my hair. Then, in a favorite old tank top, I opened the window to the bedroom and slid into bed. I spent the first dark hour trying to banish Cliff from my mind.

I spent the rest of the night dreaming of him.

The unmistakable clanking of metal against metal shook me from my sleep. I tried to banish the sound, to reclaim the slippery magic world of sleep. But the clank was layered with voices, men's voices, and sleep would not come.

I turned over, and lying on my back, I stared at the ceiling, thinking through the week, trying to remember if the builders were due. No. No builders today. No kids.

What on earth was happening outside the apartment window?

I climbed out of bed and put on a robe—an old terrycloth robe, worn at the front edge, torn at the hem where I had once caught it in a doorway. Unwilling to be seen by the men whose voices I heard, I climbed the stairs to assess the situation more unobtrusively through the windows of the refurbished dining-room.

The sun shone over the marina pathway, and I squinted against the bright sunlight. I heard the sound again, metal on metal, and looked down into my own yard, where I found, to my utter surprise, a ribbon of fluorescent orange hanging between long spikes of rebar, newly pounded into my own lawn.

Two men, both wearing orange T-shirts and yellow hard hats, leaned over another spike. The heavier of the two pounded it in place while the shorter man tied another length of ribbon. Without another thought about my appearance, I turned from the window and ran to the front door, down the steps and out to the side yard.

"What on earth do you two think you're doing down here?" I said, panting from both anger and exertion. "This is my property."

The taller of the two tipped his hard hat. "I'm sorry, ma'am," he said. "We've been hired to build a fence here."

"In my yard?"

He pointed to another man, standing at the intersection of my driveway and the roadway. This man, wearing jeans and heavy boots, carried a clipboard. As he worked, he peered into some kind of tripod. It certainly looked official. "Actually, ma'am, that man there is a surveyor. And according to the property lines on the deed, your property line goes here, right through the north edge of your lawn."

"What? What deed?"

"To the marina, ma'am."

"Well, I beg to differ. The lawn has marked the edge of my property for years. You can't build a fence here. It will block the view. It will block access. We've used this pathway to the marina for as long as I can remember."

He took a deep breath and exchanged glances with the man still holding the spool of ribbon. "Not anymore, ma'am."

"What about a gate? Are you going to build a gate here?"

"A gate hasn't been included in the plans."

"Who gave you your instructions? I want to talk to him, right now."

Obviously grateful to be off the hook, the man pointed again. "The boss is right over there, ma'am. I'm sure he'd be glad to talk to you."

I followed his arm; this invader had pointed toward the road, where, halfway between the driveway and the marina parking lot, someone was getting out of a white pickup truck. He wore a white shirt and a bright orange vest. I shielded my eyes from the eastern sun. The glasses were unmistakable.

Karras was the man in charge of building this fence.

I re-wrapped the robe and pulled the belt tight. Then, in bare feet, I headed toward the truck. Bad decision. The sharp rocks of my gravel driveway began eating away at the souls of my feet. Within ten steps, I was hobbling like a ninety-year-old woman. Hardly the impression of power and ferocity I meant to convey.

I approached the truck, and stopped in my tracks. "Mr. Karras," I called, crossing my arms over my robe. I hoped this would force him to walk at least part of the way toward me. After all, the man wore boots. "What on earth are you doing here?"

He looked at me, an expression of pleasure coming over his features. My anger pleased him. "Why, Mrs. Beauchamp, we're building a fence."

"You can't do that. You can't block access to the path. It's been there for years."

"The marina is private. The land is mine. I don't have to provide access to you."

"Do you have any idea what that will do to my business?"

"You don't have a business, Mrs. Beauchamp. Not yet," he said, putting his hands on his hips. "And if you want to stop this fence, you'll have to do so in court."

I don't believe I've ever felt as angry as I did in that moment. It was one thing to offer to buy. Another thing to convince my neighbors to gang up on me. But to build a fence? To work at making me fail? "I should have expected this kind of thing from you," I said, my voice trembling with rage. Tears formed in my eyes, and before I made a fool of myself, I turned and stomped back to the house. My feet weren't the only things hurting.

❀

I stewed about my problems all through the rest of Monday morning. I was so angry with Cliff that I gave myself heartburn. He had to have known, all through that romantic boat ride, that Karras was going to build a fence. How did he manage to get through an entire evening without telling me? And why?

Of course I was angry with Karras. But Karras was the enemy. I expected him to do these kinds of things. With Cliff, I felt more than anger, I felt betrayal.

At noon, I called Lucia. "I have an errand I'd like to run today. Do you think you could take Gabby into town for swim lessons?"

"Not a problem."

"Could she stay with you after? I'll put Celeste and Danny to work in the yard. They can make their own dinner. I should be home early in the evening."

"I don't know why not. We're having pizza. Is that okay?"

I smiled. "Gabby will think she's in heaven."

As soon as I got off the phone, I opened the Victoria phone book and looked for the listings of local antique stores. Then, putting the little velvet box into my purse, I took Highway 1 into town, and made my way over to Fort Street. There, high over the bay, I managed to park the van and started down the sidewalk, asking God to direct me to the right store.

If the idea stewing in my mind worked, my money problems might finally be solved. Without a bank loan. Without borrowing from Maggie's attorney.

Fort Street, it seemed, had nothing but antique stores. I passed one after another, one specializing in furniture, another in vintage clothing, another teeming with nothing more than household cast-offs. A thrift store called, surprisingly, Precious Momentos. Eventually, I came to a corner store, where through the front window, I recognized an enormous U-shaped jewelry counter. Each window of the glass case bore locks, and the clerks wore keys around their necks.

This seemed right somehow. I murmured a prayer and went inside, introducing myself to the woman behind the counter. "I wonder if I could speak with the owner?"

The lady, an older woman with elegantly coiffed silver hair, smiled at me. "Mr. Owens isn't in this afternoon. I wonder if I could help you."

I must have looked disappointed. It was a long drive, and I wouldn't have many opportunities to return to town.

Sensing my hesitation, she continued. "I'm Roberta Sutton," she said. "And, I've been here about twenty years, if that helps. I've seen just about everything. Go ahead, see if you can stump me."

I pulled the box from my purse. "A friend of mine left me this piece of jewelry. I have no idea what it is—I mean, I know it's a watch—I just don't know who made it, or how old it is." Just as I lifted the chain, she slid a black velvet pad across the counter.

"Or how much it might be worth," she finished for me, smiling. Roberta placed a pair of reading glasses on her nose. "Ah," she said, looking across at the watch. "May I?"

She stretched it out across the black velvet, straightening the chain, leaving the watch face up. "It's lovely, isn't it?"

"I thought so."

"It just speaks quality. The chain, as you can see," she pointed with perfectly manicured nails, "is hand-made. Each link is hand-wrapped. Eighteen karat gold. Very lovely. And the face, mother-of-pearl, I think, has gold hands and numbers." She turned it over. "Mmm, and look at the dragonfly. So popular in this period."

"When? What period?"

"I'm guessing, of course, but I'd place it in the range of 1890 to 1910."

"Really?"

"It was made in Switzerland, by the Aggasiz company. I'm certain of that. I've seen a number of these—though none this elegant. They made many, many watches of this quality during that era. This one," she said, laying the piece down, "I think may have been made for Tiffany." She turned toward the counter behind her, picked up a magnifying loop and attached the loop to her glasses frame. Bringing the watch up toward her eyes, she examined the case carefully. "Ah yes. For Tiffany. It has the name right here."

"You mean *the* Tiffany Company, in New York City?"

"Absolutely. Of course they made watches for other companies too, companies all over the world. But this one, absolutely for New York's Tiffany and Co."

My heart began to beat faster, and I felt sweat bead up on the tips of my fingers. I couldn't begin to guess how Maggie had come to own something so unusual. But the bigger question was left pounding in my temples. I tried to control the anxiety I felt. I whispered, "How much do you think it might be worth?"

She turned the watch over, examining the diamonds on the dragonfly's back. "Well, these are European cut diamonds for the back and the wings, and these are definitely rubies for the antennae." She opened the back, revealing the enamel work behind the gold cover. "And this is hand-painted enamel. Look at this beautiful setting of a lake with water-lilies." She shook her head, and took off her glasses. They fell to her chest, left dangling from a pearl chain.

"You just don't see pieces this beautiful, in this condition. Remarkable really."

"I wouldn't know," I said. I put one hand over my chest, trying to still the thundering inside. "I only recently discovered it. But really, I need to know. How much is it worth?"

Again she smiled, reaching out to pet the chain as she smoothed the links. "I would be doing a disservice to give you an absolute number. After all, you can only get what any particular buyer is willing to pay. It might be more; it might be less. If I were to buy it from you, here in Victoria, I'd have to allow for a store profit, and for the risk. We rarely sell items of this value. You'd do better at auction, I'd think."

"I'm sorry. I've never done this before. I don't have any idea what you're saying."

"Well, remember, I'm guessing." She put one hand to her mouth, sliding her forefinger along her lips. "But at an auction, I'm guessing it would fetch nearly twenty thousand dollars, Canadian."

I could hardly think as I drove home. What would twenty thousand dollars do toward restoring the old house? Would we be able to open the upstairs rooms? Could we skip the breakfast idea? Could we do both? My phone rang.

I glanced down at the cover. It was Cliff. I hit the silence button. As I fought with the late-afternoon traffic leaving Victoria, the phone rang again.

I picked up. "Yes?" My tone was gruff. I recognized Cliff's voice.

"Brandy. Thanks for answering."

"What do you want?"

"I wanted to talk about the fence."

"You mean the fence that you forgot to mention last night?"

He was quiet for a minute. "I guess I deserve that. I didn't tell you, you're right. I should have. I'm sorry."

I didn't answer.

"Honestly, I didn't know when it would happen. He—Karras—asked me to be in charge of building it. But I couldn't do it. Couldn't do that to you. He threatened to fire me, so I made an excuse."

I blinked back tears. I couldn't honestly tell why I was felt so angry, so betrayed by Cliff's involvement in the fence. Certainly it wasn't his idea. I couldn't blame him for that. Cliff didn't want me to fail; Karras did.

"I tried to talk him out of it. He told me it wasn't my business. I told him that I'd been hired to manage the marina, and I couldn't build the fence and keep the marina going in the middle of the summer. I thought that would buy you time. Honest, Brandy. I didn't think he'd go out and do it himself." He took a breath. "You can fight it."

"Right. I can hire an attorney for three hundred an hour and take Karras to court."

"Please, forgive me."

"Really. There's nothing to forgive," I said. "It's not your fence."

When I got back to Duncan, I picked up Gabby. "Mom, they're having a swim meet, and we get to stay overnight in a hotel!"

I have to admit, I was tired. I didn't listen. "Thanks for this, Lucia," I said, as she walked us to the car. "I have good news, I think. I may even have found the answer to my money problems. At least a temporary answer."

"I'm glad," she said, drying her hands on a dishtowel. "Call me when you have a chance. I want to hear about it."

"Mom," Gabby whined. "You never listen when I'm talking."

While she climbed into the car, I stowed her gym bag in the back seat. "I'm sorry," I said. "You're right. I'm tired. What were you saying?"

"I was saying that I've been picked to swim in our next swim meet. The coach wants me to go with the team."

I slid into my seat, and buckled my belt. How I hate to be the bearer of bad news. "I'm sorry honey," I said. "But there's no way I'm sending you off by yourself."

"It's not by myself, Mom. It's with the team. I finally have friends and you won't let me go with them?"

I wasn't tired enough to miss the fact that I was about to draw fire. As surely as a gunslinger in the old West, Gabby had put her hands over her holster and commanded, "Draw, pardner."

"Maybe when you're older, honey. But not this time. Not alone."

"You can come too."

"I have too much to do. Too much going on this summer to go to a swim meet. Besides you're too young. Maybe next year."

With that, Gabby crossed her arms across her chest, and pouted all the way home.

Twenty Five

I OPEN A LETTER-SIZED ENVELOPE, and discover inside a newspaper clipping, yellowing, the edges smeared, though without a single wrinkle. A bold headline reads, "Police investigate cause of a four car collision on State Highway 2, near Steven's Pass Summit."

Below the article continues: "Two people were killed and several more transported to area hospitals with injuries last Saturday night after a commercial truck jackknifed in the eastbound lanes of Steven's Pass. While the driver of the truck was cited for negligent driving, the ensuing collision and fire may have involved alcohol. Killed were the driver and passenger of a 1970 Karmann Ghia, Ron Leslie, of Wenatchee and Mary Ellen Blackburn, of Duncan, BC. Bill Westfall, the driver of the truck, belonging to Western Transport, of Yakima, was not injured."

I suck in a sharp breath. Maggie had lost her only child.

When Friday afternoon rolled around and the last of Peter's crew drove out of the driveway, I was pretty astounded at the progress they had made. Most of the outside work had been completed, though not yet painted. From the driveway, our house looked like a startling mosaic of new siding, bare plywood, old color and spray paint.

All the new windows had been installed. The roof was ready for its new metal skin, which would arrive on Monday.

Inside, the demolition was finished, and newly framed walls stood watch over the kitchen exactly where I'd always dreamed they should. These skeletons, already drilled for electrical and plumbing, marked the beginning of the transformation of the old house from Maggie's place to mine. The restored kitchen—though smaller— would function more efficiently, having designated work areas for dishwashing, food storage, cooking, baking and serving. No longer would it resemble a laminate countertop maze.

The new dining-room, once it was painted and the floors refinished, would feature a built-in cabinet for guest dishes, glassware, and linens. The new windows gracing the marina end of the house featured wood frames which would eventually match the painted trim in the great room.

In the front of the house, the dreaded sliding glass door was at last gone (and I sang a loud hallelujah for that), replaced by a new door set, salvaged by our draftsman, and a newly tiled entry.

There was so much more that I wanted to do. But for now, this was enough. With these details, Maggie's Place would soon be ready for company. In my humble opinion, this called for a celebration, including, among other things, home-delivery pizza—the perfect end to a hard week of labor. I made the call and went downstairs to Gabby's room, where Danielle and Gabby were listening to music and dressing fashion dolls.

I knocked on Gabby's door and ducked my head inside. "I've ordered pizza," I said. "Dinner should be here in half an hour."

"Right-on!" Gabby pumped both arms in victory, which set the bed to bouncing. "Wow. We never order pizza!"

I frowned at her. "You silly girl." I turned to Danny. "Where's Celeste?"

"Upstairs, I think. She was on the phone."

"Okay. I ordered cookie dough with the pizza. So, I'm putting you two on cookie duty. You'd better go upstairs and preheat the oven."

I closed the bedroom door and started up the stairs through the kitchen, noticing once again how close we were to reconfiguring the apartment stairway. Once that began, there would be no access to the apartment. The three of us would have to spend most of the weekend in the guest bedrooms if we were going to finish painting before we moved upstairs. I made a mental note to make certain I had enough trim paint.

I passed through the great room to the guest stairs and climbed to the first landing. Just as I put my foot on the second half of the stairway, I heard it.

I stopped, listening carefully. The sound seemed to be coming from Celeste's room. She was crying. From behind her closed door, I heard the soft, smothered cry of the truly heartbroken.

I paused on the stairs, wondering if I should intrude. Was she crying for her grandmother? Was she homesick? In my own career as a mother, thus far I'd managed nothing more serious than bandaged knees. Even our move from Florida had been relatively pain free.

When Timothy died, Gabby had missed him, but only for a short time. At first she had asked about him frequently, and then less and less often, until within months, she seemed perfectly content to live in a world with only one parent. Perhaps her response was due to his recurrent absences. As a Navy pilot, Timothy had appeared and disappeared frequently during those early years.

Or, perhaps her response was due to the remarkable ability of this particular four-year-old to suffer loss with strength and dignity. In that way, she made *me* look like a four-year-old. I certainly contributed nothing more than my half-hearted presence to her recovery.

Standing there in the hall, I began to doubt myself again. What did I know about teenagers? Maybe Celeste would be better off if I just went downstairs to wait for the pizza guy. I turned to start back.

Again, the muffled sound of pain wafted down the stairway. I heard the bed creak, and imagined Celeste strewn across the mattress in the posture of the brokenhearted. I pushed forward, climbing the stairs with renewed purpose. I might not be trained, but even the inexperienced can love.

I knocked on the door as gently as I could. The sound of crying ceased immediately, and the bed creaked. "What?"

"It's me," I said. "Can I come in?"

For a moment, she did not answer, and I wondered if I had overstepped my bounds. Then, "Okay." It was barely above a whisper.

I opened the door to find Celeste sitting on the edge of the bed. Her face was streaked with tears, her eyes swollen. I moved to her side. "May I sit down?"

She looked surprised; wiping her face with the palms of both hands, she looked up and nodded.

"I don't mean to intrude. But I heard you crying."

Tears began to leak from her eyes and trail down her face. Again, she nodded.

"It's okay," I said, another of my brilliantly phrased counseling expressions.

Inwardly, I groaned, and put one hand around her shoulder. In that simple gesture, that one touch, Celeste seemed to melt, wrapping my waist with her long arms. She laid her head on my shoulder and the tears gave way to sobbing. This was no controlled Hallmark Channel emotion. These tears came with gut-wrenching noises and lots of fluid, which promptly soaked through my T-shirt. I happened to have a clean tissue in my shorts pocket. I dug it out and handed it to her.

"Want to talk about it?"

Her head, buried deep in my neck, shook vigorously.

"Sometimes it helps to talk."

She gave another rasping cry and sat up to blow her nose. "I'm so stupid."

"Everyone is stupid at some point in time," I said, smiling as I patted her arm. I turned on the bed, sitting with my legs crossed. "Just the other night I was explaining it to Cliff. Over at Heron Island, I said that very thing. 'Everyone is stupid'."

What began as a tiny giggle ended in a grating howl. "Not like this."

"Try me."

"My boyfriend broke up with me." She wiped her face again, this time with the sleeve of her shirt. Her beautiful brown eyes swam in tears.

"Boys do that."

"I can't believe how stupid he is."

"Boys can be." So far, so good. I hadn't messed this up too badly.

"We've been going out for two years." She blew her nose again, and I began to worry about the tissue. Certainly it had reached maximum capacity. "He said he loved me, and that we'd get married as soon as I graduate next spring."

"That's pretty young for such an important decision."

"I thought we'd be together forever," she said, as a new outpouring of tears surged down her lovely dark cheeks. "I thought he meant what he said."

Suddenly, I had a terrifying vision of where this alarming conversation might be headed. This was more than a story of lost love. "Oh, Celeste, no."

She gave in to another bout of weeping.

"Oh, Celeste." I put both arms around her shoulders and pulled her into me. "I'm so sorry." I patted her arm. "I know it hurts. I know."

She dissolved then, her body collapsing into shuddering sobs. "I'm pregnant," she said through racking breaths. "I'm pregnant, and he doesn't want me."

This, I realized, as I held her racking body, vainly patting her shoulders, was a problem that even pizza delivery would not solve.

❀

We spent the weekend working on the upstairs bedrooms.

At Celeste's request, I said nothing about her condition, though I refused to let her handle the chemical wallpaper strippers. I had no intention of allowing her in a room full of fresh paint either. Anything that smelled that potent couldn't be good for the unborn.

She spent Saturday morning on kitchen duty.

Danny and Gabby did not seem to notice Celeste's special treatment, as they took far too much joy in peeling long stretches of paper from the walls. Soon it became a contest to see who might pull the longest strip. I participated, my competitive streak soundly crushed by my more patient and persistent daughter. Danny followed along behind us, patiently scraping tiny bits of yellowed paper from the smooth walls.

With CDs playing on Danny's portable boom box, we worked. Peeling, cleaning, spraying and scraping some more. For all of Saturday, the paint cans stood unopened in the front bedroom.

When we finished washing the newly bare walls of the east bedroom, I opened the windows and let Celeste begin taping the woodwork. She seemed content to work this way, quietly, by herself. And I found myself wondering about what to do in this new situation. What could I do for this young woman who had almost miraculously landed in my lap?

In any ordinary case, I would have helped Celeste to face her family. No matter how angry parents are, I believed that good parents recover from even the most grievous insult, given the right support. Parental love can overcome most difficulties.

But Celeste had no family support, other than an alcoholic grandmother, who also suffered from age-related dementia and a badly broken hip.

What could I bring to this situation? I could hardly manage my own family affairs. I was nearly broke, and about to open a questionable business with almost no training or experience. What should I do?

As I worked, I worried too about the father of her baby. How had this situation changed him? What was my obligation to this young man? Did his rejection of Celeste reflect fear of responsibility, or a true desire to escape the entire situation?

After lunch, Gabby announced that she could no longer tolerate being used as slave labor, though she did not exactly use that term, and I dismissed Gabby and Danielle to play video games in the media room.

Upstairs with Celeste, we opened the windows to a strong breeze from the bay. I put a two-inch brush and a tiny container of paint in Celeste's hands and set her to work trimming the woodwork with the new wall color. Rather than follow her with the roller, I started in the other corner of the room and applied trim paint as I worked toward her.

With the air off the water, I could hardly smell the paint.

I changed the CD to something more soothing, and prayed for inspiration. I am no counselor, but Maggie taught me a thing or two about loving a teenager with problems. I asked questions. I listened. And I avoided commentary as much as I could.

In the process, I discovered that providence had sent me a delightful and charming young guest, loyal to her sister, thankful for her grandmother, and doing her best to create a better future than she had known. Yes, she was confused, misled, and in some ways very angry. But Celeste had remarkable potential.

"Do you have anyone you could talk to about this? Your pregnancy?"

"No."

"What about a doctor?"

"I haven't seen one, if that's what you mean."

"Could there be a mistake?"

"I took two drugstore tests. They were both positive."

"Have you thought about what you want to do?"

"I don't know what to do. My mother got pregnant with me before she was married. I didn't want to do that."

I could hear the approach of another meltdown. "Ah well. We all make plans. Sometimes they don't turn out the way we think they will. So, we have to make new plans. You can do that. We can figure it out."

"I don't have any money. I don't have a job. I wanted to finish school. I wanted to be the first in my family to graduate from high school." Her voice broke.

"You can still graduate, Celeste."

"How?" She turned to me, her brush sweeping through the air as she spoke. "I don't want to have an abortion. I can't do that. But I can't take care of a baby." She sat down on the drop cloth, setting the paint can between her legs.

The mention of Shiloh Farms Alternative High School triggered an idea. "You know, your high school has probably dealt with this situation before. You aren't the first teenager to face an unexpected pregnancy. Maybe you could talk with someone there."

For a moment, Celeste looked surprised, and then she tipped her head. "I could talk to Ms. Loper."

"Is she a counselor?"

"A teacher."

"Well there you are," I said. "The big thing to remember is that you aren't alone. You don't have to face any of this alone. I'll help you find whatever support you need. I promise." I'd no more than said it than I remembered my own vow to keep my promises to Celeste. At the time, I hadn't known what that might cost.

And with that, Celeste got up and walked across the room to wrap me in a hug, the paintbrush still in her hand. "Thank you, Mrs. Beauchamp," she said. "I don't know what I'd do without you."

❁

We attended church again on Sunday, sitting by Lucia in our usual place. After service, we had cold sandwiches and left-over pizza. Then, when the dishes were done, I asked Celeste to watch Gabby so Danielle and I could roll paint onto the walls of the east bedroom. Danielle seemed relieved and excited about her promotion.

Only Gabby was surprised by the change of roles.

"Celeste worked so long yesterday, I think she needs a day off," I explained.

This seemed to satisfy Gabby's curiosity, and Celeste made things easier by adding, "How about we hang out in the kitchen? I'll give you a full make-over."

"With real make up?"

"Fingernail polish and everything."

"Wow," Gabby said. "Mom, can I have my toenails done too?"

I smiled at Gabby. "Sure honey. Just be good to Celeste." Giving Celeste a grin and a thumbs up, I started downstairs to change clothes. I called over my shoulder, "Danny, time to get into your work clothes."

Unfortunately Danny got nearly as much paint on the floor as she did on the wall. First, she tripped over the paint pan, sending a full quart out over the plastic drop cloths. Together we rolled up the plastic and set it in the hall. With a new drop cloth in place, somehow, the roller flew off the handle extension as she moved it from the pan to the wall. The fully loaded tool landed on the uncovered carpet in front of the closet.

Danny was horrified by the mistake. She stood in front of the closet, the errant roller in one hand, her mouth wide open, her eyes threatening tears.

I put down my roller and handed her a bucket. "Go fill this with warm water." She looked startled. "In the tub," I said. "Hurry."

I ran downstairs for the shop vac that Peter left in the new dining area. Then, moments later, as Danielle poured water onto the carpet, I used my bare hands to swish water into the paint. As the color floated to the top of the water, I sucked it up with the vacuum. Over and over we repeated the technique. Rinse. Vacuum. Rinse. Vacuum. Little by little the paint faded.

"I'm so sorry. I don't know how it happened," Danny said.

"Honey, the whole world seems to be in mistake mode," I told her, smiling. "Everyone is doing it."

"But the carpet. I messed it up."

When I'd gotten as much water as I could from the rug, I dropped an old towel over the stain and began blotting. "No problem. We diluted the paint and soaked it all up. You can't even tell where it happened. Should be good as new in the morning."

"I won't do it again," she said. "I promise."

I picked up the towel and wiped my hands, tossing it onto a plastic drop cloth. "I know you won't, honey. It's really fine."

I began rolling paint again, working steadily toward her side of the room. "You know, Danny. The thing with mistakes is that no one ever stops making them. Even if you get over one mistake, you'll always find new ways to mess up." I laughed. "You wouldn't live long enough to hear about all my mistakes."

"I'm so sorry," she said again. The poor girl sounded like a CD stuck on a particular phrase; I wanted to tap her shoulder and make the CD player move on, already. Danny, in her concern, had begun moving slowly, so deliberately as if to be absolutely certain not to spill another drop of paint.

"Honey, listen. I won't kick you out for a mistake. Not for the first one. Not for the second one. Not for the one hundredth mistake. It's okay, really." I bent over my paint pan, adding paint to the roller. When I returned to the wall, I noticed that Danny had stopped moving. I looked up at her, wondering what she had spilled this time.

She stood in the corner of the bedroom facing me, the roller hanging loosely from one hand, her clothes and hair and face covered with paint. Her face was filled with wonder. "You really aren't mad?"

Twenty Six

As the new week dawned, progress on the house continued. The girls and I finished two bedrooms, and moved the old furniture back into place. I loved the fresh clean look of the rooms and had the strongest urge to nest—bringing in new bedding and pillows, chairs and draperies. It took every ounce of my strength to avoid putting all those finishing touches on credit.

I could almost hear Timothy's deep voice saying, "Patience, Brandy. Patience."

I refused to let the girls move in until all trace of old fumes had dissipated. With two upstairs bedrooms left to finish, I hoped to get paint on the walls by the end of the week. Then, if everything went well, both Gabby and I could be out of the way when Peter started work on the new stairwell.

The roof went on in a flurry of banging and hammering amid the startling noise of metal sheets being dropped on the roof as if from a hovering helicopter. I'd never heard such a racket. The house bustled with workers—electricians, plumbers, roofers—and I fed whoever landed in my kitchen, be they stranger or friend.

In a quiet moment, I called Lucia, asking for advice about Celeste. "So far, we haven't officially informed anyone about the girls staying with me. I'm worried that I'll be in trouble when someone figures out that I'm not really a relative."

"Celeste is eighteen, so there isn't a problem there."

"But Danielle is just a kid."

"Right. But she's living with her sister, who is legally an adult. That's really pretty common around here."

"But what do we do about the big problem?"

"You mean the pregnancy?" She paused. "Well, the good thing is that God gave you about seven more months to work on that one. I think you wait. You talk. You listen. You have patience. You let her take all the time she needs to think."

"What about the father? He's just a boy."

"I can't tell you what to do about that. She's already notified him, so I think she's fulfilled her moral obligation. She said that he doesn't want anything to do with the baby. In my experience, it's best to leave it at that." She paused, speaking to a child in the background. "Sorry about that. Sienna wants to know if Gabby is coming to the swim meet?"

I laughed. "Gabby has been asking the same thing every day since her last lesson. Are you driving?"

"No, I'm sending the kids with one of the neighbors. I have a class on Friday. I can't miss it. What about you?"

"Gabby's too young."

"Don't be silly. She's old enough. It's just an exhibition."

"You don't think it's too much pressure?"

"She's been working like a slave out there at that house of yours. Let her be a kid for a while."

I laughed. "Did she tell you that?"

"Of course not."

I turned to look out the kitchen window, eying the lumber still piled in the front yard. It would be good to get away from the house for a while. Celeste and Danny would enjoy the trip. I'd love to sleep somewhere without sawdust in the bedsheets. "Where is the meet? Gabby couldn't remember."

"You didn't hear? It's just over in Vancouver."

"Vancouver?" I thought about the cost of a night in a hotel, and the expense of taking a car to the mainland via ferry. "I don't know," I said, still hesitant. And then I remembered the necklace. Maybe I could squeeze in a visit to the Vancouver auction house. It might be an important piece of my financial puzzle.

"Alright," I said. "We'll go. Do you have a map?"

"You should have all the information in Gabby's swim bag. The only thing you need to do is call the coach and tell her you're in."

❀

I made reservations at an inexpensive, breakfast-included motel not too far from the swim complex, and contacted the auction house in Vancouver. Gabby was ecstatic about swimming in her first meet, and the older girls could hardly wait to get off the island. Danny badgered me until I agreed to stop at a mall on our way back to the ferry terminal. "We never get to real stores," she told me.

Unwilling to leave Liz alone, I wondered who might watch the dog. I was still mad at Cliff, and didn't want to give him any reason to think that I'd forgiven him. On the other hand, I didn't have anyone else to watch Liz. Reluctantly I called and asked him to keep the dog while we were gone. "We'll only be gone one night," I told him.

"Does this mean you forgive me?"

"Oh please. I told you, there's nothing to forgive."

"I'll take that as a yes."

"Whatever floats your boat."

"You're going to try to drive over that early in the morning?"

"I can't afford two nights at a hotel."

"You'll wish you did. You'll be exhausted."

"I know. It's the nature of motherhood."

"Well, don't say I didn't warn you."

Friday night we loaded the car and went to bed early. Gabby was so excited, she could not sleep. After two tries, I let her climb into bed with me. She slept fitfully; I slept hardly at all. Between kicks and wiggles and punches, somewhere Gabby started snoring.

At six-thirty, we drove our car onto the ferry at Sydney. All of us climbed to the observation deck and watched as the big boat plied the calm waters between Vancouver Island and the mainland. "Do you get off the island much?"

Celeste answered, "I don't remember the last time."

Gabby tugged on the hem of my jacket. "Mom, do you think I'll win today?"

"I don't know, sweetie," I said. "I know you'll do your very best. And I know you'll have lots of fun. You'll get to see new things, and meet lots of other swimmers."

Still holding my jacket with one hand, she clutched the railing with the other, her face a collage of concern.

"Don't worry about it, Gabby," Danielle said. "In the Olympics this year, some guy from the United States said that winning takes lots of racing. You shouldn't expect to win the first one."

"I shouldn't?"

I didn't have the heart to put it quite that bluntly. "You shouldn't worry about winning, honey. The big thing is to do your best."

We ate breakfast in the upper dining-room. The girls ate as if they hadn't eaten in years. But Gabby seemed too anxious to eat. She chose milk and a donut and left most of both.

We arrived at the swim complex around nine, and went inside with a crowd of swimmers and spectators. I helped Gabby into her swimsuit and we went out into the holding area together. When her coach presented her with a tiny warm-up jacket, the embroidered team logo on the pocket, I thought Gabby's chest might explode with pride. Even her posture changed as she wore her new jacket.

Gabby was a swim star.

"How long until she races?" I asked the coach.

She looked at her clipboard. "At least a couple of hours."

"Would you mind if I ran an errand?"

"Not at all. She can stay here with me."

"I should only be an hour or so."

Danny volunteered to stay at the pool with Gabby, which I attributed primarily to the large numbers of muscle-bound young men stretching near the edge of the pool. I leaned down to whisper in her ear. "Way too old for you."

She looked up as if to say, "Who, me?"

"Way too old," I said, repeating myself.

❁

Celeste and I drove into town, parked near the auction house and went inside. We met Stuart, an egg-shaped, balding man, in his office, where I showed him the pocket watch. "It is lovely," he breathed. "Just as you said."

I waited as he inspected the watch with a magnifying headset. "It's very unusual, this design. I don't think I've seen one like this before."

"Do you think it would sell?"

"Of course it would sell." He pushed the headset onto his forehead. "I think your estimate of its value is about right. However, I can't predict the selling price. Of course we can start with a minimum bid, if you like."

I didn't know how to ask my next question. "After the sale, um, how do you decide... er, what is the percent that...?"

"Our house takes twenty percent."

I did the math quickly. It seemed like a large chunk to lose. Should I forfeit a percentage, or should I simply take the much smaller offer that Roberta had made? I couldn't decide. "I don't know," I said, hesitating. "When is the next auction?"

"Five weeks from this Saturday. You can let me know later," he said.

"I don't come to the mainland often."

He considered this for a moment. "Well. If you like, you can consign it to us, fill out the paperwork and leave it here. Then, you can take as much time as you need to think about it. You can give us the final go-ahead later, by telephone. Or, you can retrieve it when you are in town."

"You can guarantee its safety?"

"Of course. We're bonded and insured. We keep everything in a locked safe until the date of the auction. We'd be nothing if we weren't secure."

I nodded. "Let's fill out the papers."

I was in the process of signing when my cell phone rang. "Mrs. Beauchamp," Danny said, "the coach asked me to call you. They've rescheduled Gabby's race."

❁

We hurried back to the swimplex through the late-morning traffic. When we arrived, Gabby greeted us with hugs worthy of returning royalty. I'd only been gone sixty-five minutes.

"What time is it?"

"Almost eleven."

"When is the race?"

"Soon," she said. "Ask the coach for me, okay?"

As we sat in the bleachers watching the other races, Gabby held my hand, clutching it so tightly that twice I had to pry her loose to shake out the joints. I tried to wrap an arm around her shoulder, hoping this would comfort her. She grabbed my other hand and held on like I might blow away in a gale-force wind.

"Honey, it's just an exhibition," I said. "Try to relax." As the clock inched forward, Gabby had begun to shiver in anticipation. "Honey, you worry too much. This is just an exhibition. Like practice, only at this pool instead."

"I don't feel very good."

"You're nervous. Happens to me all the time," Celeste said.

I smiled over Gabby at Celeste and whispered my thanks. "See? Even big girls get nervous. I used to dread giving presentations at work. How about if I pray for you?"

She nodded and I bent my face to her ear, praying softly for her nerves. As I said amen, she nodded, looked up at me and gave a brave smile. I was surprised by the pallor of her skin, and the bright pink circles sitting exactly on the apples of her cheeks.

Gabby had managed to worry herself into what looked like illness. I hugged her and whispered encouragement into her ear. "You'll do great, honey," I said. "Your only job today is to finish the race. That's all. Just see what it's like to swim with other swimmers your age. Nothing more."

Once again she nodded, still shivering. I squeezed her shoulders and she leaned into me. I was thinking that perhaps my encouragement had finally broken through when she bent her head and threw up all over my lap.

So much for Gabby's first swim competition.

Using every available towel on the adjacent benches, we survived a flurry of vomiting that lasted entirely too long. By the time Gabby sat up, exhausted, we were sitting alone in the bleachers, all nearby spectators—including Celeste and Danny—having fled to other parts of the building. I couldn't blame them.

I don't have an iron stomach myself.

I rolled up the towels and helped Gabby down out of the bleachers. Her performance had caught the attention of her swim coach, who simply waved me away. Clearly, we weren't staying for the rest of the meet.

I signaled Celeste and Danny and we headed out to the parking lot. "I'm sorry, girls," I said. "Looks like our little adventure has been cut short."

We wrapped the still-shivering Gabby in a car blanket, and put her down on the back seat using her new swim jacket as a pillow. She was asleep before we managed to buckle seatbelts around her body. I touched her forehead and recognized the warm dry feel of an elevated temperature.

"Well, the good news is that she wasn't really nervous," I told the girls. "She's got some kind of bug. We're going to have to head home."

Danny groaned. "I wanted to go to the mall."

Celeste shrugged. "You don't have any money to spend anyway."

"I do too. I've saved everything I've earned from babysitting."

"So grow up a little, and care about the baby, would ya?"

I interceded. "It's okay, girls. We'll get over here again, especially if Gabby decides that swimming is her 'thing.' Besides, I'll have to do something about the necklace eventually."

Danny perked up. "What necklace?"

"Get in the car," I said, heading around to the driver's-side door. "I'll tell you on the way to the ferry terminal."

It seemed to me that all of Vancouver had decided to flee the city, forcing us to wait for space on a ferry. Fortunately, since Gabby had fallen asleep, her stomach seemed to have calmed down.

While we waited our turn, I sent the girls for burgers. Cleaning up after Gabby had deadened my appetite completely.

Just after six, we drove into the driveway. The place was deserted, and frankly, I couldn't see any evidence that anyone had made any progress at the house. Disappointed, I took Gabby's temperature, gave her some Tylenol, some apple juice, and put her to bed in her own room. Then, I went upstairs to fix a snack for dinner.

We settled for canned soup and toasted cheese sandwiches. After cleaning up, the girls and I settled down for a movie in the media room. Celeste went to bed before the movie ended, and Danny headed upstairs about eleven.

Feeling restless, I went downstairs to check on Gabby. Her forehead felt cooler now, and she slept heavily, completely unaware of my coming and going. I began to wonder if she'd been feeling poorly when we left in the morning. It explained her uneaten breakfast and the shivering as she anticipated her race. I closed the door to her room and went upstairs to watch the evening news.

I must have fallen asleep quickly, because even now, I cannot remember a single item covered in that newscast. I remember only the blaring scream of the upstairs fire alarm, and the choking bite of smoke that filled my lungs as I struggled up from the depth of exhausted dreams.

Already coughing, I opened my eyes to find the air dark with smoke and the television still on. I raced from the media room into the great room; panic set my heart slamming, like a basketball on a wood floor. Where was the fire?

I stood still, listening for some sign, looking for light in the darkness. I ran to the stairs, looking up through the stairwell. No flames here. I screamed to the girls. "Fire. Get out. Now!" I had the fleeting thought that I should run upstairs and bang on their doors. But a new and more urgent fear had taken hold of my chest.

Gabby was alone in the apartment downstairs.

Twenty Seven

STILL SCREAMING AT THE GIRLS, I raced to the kitchen. Perhaps I'd left the stove on after dinner, or the some electrical connection in the old house had finally given way to fire. As I moved toward the kitchen the smoke grew darker, more intense, though I could not yet feel the heat. I had no more than stepped onto the bare kitchen floor than I realized that the fire had started somewhere downstairs.

Smoke, dark and bitter, billowed out of the stairwell like smoke from a refuse pile. I started toward the stairs, holding my breath, determined to make it down to where Gabby lay sleeping. I had a fleeting vision of a funeral, a tiny coffin, a wreath of flowers. In that instant, I heard myself scream again, instantly shattering the picture that had formed in my mind. I heard a frightened "No!" echo through the bare walls of the north end of the house as I took the stairs two at a time.

I made it all the way to the landing before the heat and smoke drove me back. Though the stairs had not yet caught fire, I could feel the scorching heat rising from the base of the stairs. I dropped onto my knees, bending forward so that I could see through the space below the smoke.

In that moment I thanked God that I had shut Gabby's door when I put her to bed. Perhaps the smoke had not yet seeped into her room.

From that position, I saw fire dance across the floor directly between the bottom of the stairs and Gabby's bedroom door. Even if I could fight my way down the stairs, I could not reach Gabby that way. I would have to run around the house, and come in from the other side, from the yard, or from the outside door. That way, I would have free access to her room, provided I could get there before the fire did.

I turned and ran back through the kitchen, snatching the portable phone as I passed, and dialing 911 as I ran. In the great room, I took the stairs to the second floor two at a time, still screaming at the top of my lungs. The fire alarm had quit ringing by now, and I threw open Celeste's door as I yelled, "Get up! Now! Fire! Get out of the house!"

For some reason, the telephone did not reach an emergency operator. I pushed the end button and dialed again.

Celeste sat up, instantly awake, her face a mask of understanding and terror. Even on the second floor we could smell smoke, the bitter, acrid smell of melting plastics. Panicked, she screamed for her sister. "Danny!"

"You get Danny," I said, shouting from the doorway. "I'll get Gabby. Have Danny go to the marina for help. You run to the neighbors and call 911."

As she bounded from the bed, I tossed her the phone. "Hurry. There's no time to waste." In an instant, I was back down the stairs.

Outside, the cold night air shocked me as I stumbled down the stairs to the lawn. When I reached our apartment door, I found it securely locked. Why hadn't I thought to bring a key? I ran to the glass door and tried it. Again, locked.

I would have to break in.

Through the glass, I saw flames crawling across the tread and moving steadily up the stairs. At the same time, flames spread across the floor toward Gabby's door. At that moment, all logic left me, and my body entered into some kind of Terminator mode—my only objective was to save Gabby.

I needed to break through the glass door and quickly. I forced myself to turn away from the terrifying scene, desperate for a tool to break in. Something large. Something heavy. I remembered the palette of concrete post blocks waiting in the front yard. Thank God we hadn't finished the deck.

I ran around the corner and ripped open the plastic cover. Grabbing a block, I headed back to the door, using both hands to throw the block into the glass. The heavy concrete hit the glass— and bounced! I swore, loud and angry, and picked up the block to try again. This time, heaving with all my might, a tiny crack formed where block contacted glass. Then, nothing.

Astounded, frustrated, I picked up the concrete again. Just as I was about to heave, the tiny crack in the glass began to grow, and with a sound of a baby's rattle, the glass fractured. Taking off my T-shirt shirt, I wrapped my hand and slammed my fist through the remaining crystals.

The door's outer layer fell to the ground in thousands of tiny pieces. But, the inner layer of the double pane did not give. I dropped the shirt and again hurled the block at the glass. This time, the concrete went through the door, leaving a ten-inch hole. The block landed on the sitting-room carpet. The sudden rush of outside air made the fire leap, and in an instant I knew I had made a horrible mistake.

I forced this thought from my mind, rewrapped my hand, and began pushing glass pieces in through the frame. *Get in! Get in! Get in!* The words pulsed through my mind like the sound of a ticking clock.

In bare feet, I stepped onto the carpet inside, giving not a single thought to the danger of broken glass. From here, I had a straight shot to Gabby's door, the fire still a few feet away. I took a last breath of fresh air and ran to Gabby's room, throwing open the door, and leaping onto the bed. Gabby, still hot with fever, lay coughing in her sleep. "Gabby, wake up!" I said. "Wake up! I've got to get you out of here, honey!"

She did not respond. "Gabby! Wake up! You've got to help me!" She did not stir. I bent down, putting my ear over her mouth. Breathing!

Without another thought, I threw her over my shoulder and headed out of the bedroom. In the time I'd taken to rescue Gabby, the fire had intensified. And, though the sitting-room was not yet fully engulfed, the fire seemed to explode, roaring up the stairway toward the kitchen, and flashing across the ceiling—as if the paint itself had burst into flame. I felt fluid rise in my throat.

I had no other exit.

I pulled Gabby's pajama top up over her head and tucked my face inside. Then, stooping low, I made a blind dash for the exit. Just as I hit the fire, a bright shower of ice-water came out of nowhere.

Gasping with shock, I did not stop. I did not think. I simply ran for the hole in the door and burst through it, clutching Gabby in my arms.

Hysterical now, I kept running, all the way across the porch to the grass, where for the first time I heard myself crying. I was sobbing, wheezing in the fresh air. Tears streamed down my face and I coughed hard, doubling over with the effort to clear my lungs. I had not yet let go of Gabby.

"My God. Brandy!" Cliff shouted over the sound of rushing water. "My God. What were you doing in there?"

I did not answer. Though I looked, I could not see him. In the frame of black, all I saw was the bright orange of flames. Even then, I recognized that the fire was taking away everything I knew.

"Honey. Put her down." I felt his hand on my back.

I could not let go. My muscles refused to release my daughter. Still crying, wheezing, coughing, I dropped onto my knees, unable any more to stand. Cliff tried to pull Gabby away and I held on even more tightly, my arms rigid, fiercely determined.

"You've got to let me have her, Brandy," he said gently. "Let me help. Please, let me help."

A spasm of coughing sent me onto my face in the grass, my arms still clutching my daughter. Cliff knelt and pulled her from me, rolling her onto the grass and uncovering her face.

"She's breathing, Brandy," he said. And even now I remember the wonder in his voice. "She's alive."

❈

I do not know how long it took for the ambulance to arrive. I remember only Gabby's tiny face, peaceful in the flickering light of the fire. I remember Cliff hovering over her, and I remember praying, out loud, in half-wheezed, half-coughed sentences. Sentences that made no sense, I'm quite certain, to anyone but God.

I remember the EMTs putting a clear mask over Gabby's face and gently lifting her onto a stretcher. They wrapped her in a blanket, and tied her down in what seemed a single fluid motion. I followed her, stumbling and crying, as they rolled her through the yard, around the lumber, to the back of the ambulance.

I remember being half-shoved, half-lifted into the same vehicle and dropped onto a bench beside my daughter's stretcher. As the doors closed, I caught one last glimpse of Danny, weeping, as she stood beside Cliff on the driveway.

Inside, one EMT sat beside me, leaning over Gabby as he started an intravenous line. I saw another face. Another floating face.

On that wild ride, I remember that they asked me questions, but I do not know which, if any, I answered. I could not take my eyes from the little mask over Gabby's face, from the tiny cloud of condensation that assured me that Gabby still breathed.

In the Emergency Room, I found myself blinking, blinded by the bright fluorescent lights. I had been given a blanket by someone—I don't know who, or when. Though I was inside, I pulled the dark wool around my shoulders, clutching the edges as I shivered violently. I followed Gabby's stretcher onto the receiving dock, and through the double doors into the emergency area.

Gabby was awake now, her blue eyes bright with fear. Under her mask, she was struggling for air, her chest heaving as she began fighting the hand which held the mask over her face. She began a cycle that repeated itself over and over, even as the medical team fought to save her life. Gabby screamed, then fought, and finally gave in to a round of violent coughing.

Whenever she gave in, it seemed all she could do to get enough air to survive.

I paced beside the stretcher, tears streaming down my face, at once begging her to cooperate, then stopping to hold her down and finally letting go as she folded into her next coughing fit. My own coughing continued intermittently, and the shuddering would not stop.

Trembling in terror, I watched as the nurses came and went, in and out of our little curtained cubicle. Several asked if I needed to see a doctor. One in particular, a young brunette, assured me that Gabby would pull through this. But at that moment no amount of reassurance would calm the horror I felt. I would not let myself cry.

Could not let Gabby see my fear blossom and grow fruit.

The nurse came back—to draw arterial blood gasses, she said. She asked if I would help Gabby cooperate. "This is a particularly painful draw," she said. "I'll put a little anesthetic on the skin. But I can't have her wiggling during the procedure."

We got through it, partly because Gabby could not breathe well enough to fight both of us. She looked at me, her face an expression of horrified betrayal, as if I were the enemy, rather than the woman who had braved a fire to save her life.

When it was over, she cried louder and longer than I had ever heard her cry. The sound of it, wailing punctuated by rasping fits of hacking, broke my heart. Helplessly, I held her hand, still praying, unable even to wipe the tears that pooled around her oxygen mask.

The nurse entered the cubicle. "The fire investigator is here to see you."

"Not now."

"I think you should talk to him." She pulled back the curtain. "We have a little waiting area where you can talk in private. He says it's important."

"I can't leave my daughter." I brushed away tears. "If he wants to talk, he'll have to do it here."

She turned to a cart and pulled tissue from a box. "Here, honey," she said, handing me both the tissue and the box. "Normally, we don't allow it. But I'll see what I can do."

I took the chair beside Gabby's bed, unwilling to let go of her hand, even for a moment. Several minutes later, the nurse escorted an older man into the cubicle.

Mark Richards, in a dark, fine-gauge, V-necked sweater and blue jeans, looked as though he'd just come from dinner at an expensive restaurant rather than the site of a house fire. He wore his fine, silver hair cut short, with a matching mustache, precisely trimmed. His pale blue eyes were attentive, intense. "Mrs. Beauchamp," he began, offering his hand, "I'm so sorry about your daughter."

I ignored his hand. "Me too," I said, still cradling Gabby's free hand in both my own. The curtain opened again, and the nurse delivered a second chair.

Richards thanked her, and pulled the chair close as he sat down. Dropping his hands into his lap, he laced his fingers together, like a priest listening to confession. "Can you tell me what happened?"

"I don't know what happened. I just woke up to a fire."

He looked me over, his piercing gaze beginning at my still bare feet, and ending at my smudged and smoke-covered face. "Where were you when the fire broke out?"

"I fell asleep in the media room." I tried to replay the evening in my mind, but I could come up with no memories other than that of flames, of smoke and of bone-shattering terror. "We'd had a long day in Vancouver. Gabby came down with something there. A bug. Food poisoning. I don't know exactly. When we got home, I put her to bed downstairs—in our apartment. The girls and I ate dinner and watched a movie. After that, they went to bed upstairs." I paused, thinking about Celeste; she'd gone to bed early. It didn't matter, did it, that she'd gone upstairs before Danny?

"What girls? I was told you had only the one."

"I have two teenagers staying with me."

"The ones who went upstairs?"

I nodded. "They've been staying with me since their grandma broke her hip."

He looked perplexed for a moment, and I wondered if this detail had been missed in some previous briefing. "And they—the two teenagers—went upstairs after the movie. When, exactly, did you put your daughter to bed?"

"I didn't look at the clock. As soon as we got home." I paused, thinking about the ferry schedule. "Probably some time after six."

"And she slept?"

"She was out cold. She spent all morning vomiting. She had a fever, and was exhausted. We caught the early ferry to Vancouver."

"Did you go back down to check on her?"

Guilt flooded my thoughts; once again I blinked back tears. Though I had gone to check on her, I chastised myself. I should have stayed downstairs, with Gabby; then I would have been there when the fire broke out. I might have done something. Something more effective than drag her, half dead, from a burning building.

Why did I stay up for the news? "I did," I said, beginning again to cry. "At about ten-thirty. A little before the news came on."

"But you didn't go to bed downstairs? Why not?"

"I can't tell you. I don't know." I blew my nose. "I should have. Maybe this wouldn't have happened." When I brought the tissue away from my face, I saw that it was black with soot and smoke.

"But when you checked on her, everything in the basement was fine. Nothing out of the ordinary?"

"Nothing." I thought about the bare wood stacked and ready for the new stairway. "We were remodeling. I had a crew working inside. There was wood everywhere."

"I see. Did you see anything in the apartment last evening that might have caused a fire? Something out of the ordinary? A heater? An extension cord? A power strip?"

"Nothing that I can think of."

"Then what happened?"

I continued my story. "After the girls went upstairs, I was watching the news. I think I must have fallen asleep, but I don't know when. Because the next thing I knew, I was coughing and the alarm was going off."

"Where is the media room?"

"On the main floor, the south end of the house."

"Go on. What happened next?"

I told him the rest of my story, of finding the fire, getting the girls out and breaking in from the outside.

"You look exhausted. Have you seen a doctor?"

"I don't need a doctor. I'm fine."

"You should get checked out anyway. What about your feet?" He pointed to my bare feet, mud under my toenails, grass still clinging to the skin. Spots of blood marred the linoleum where I sat. I hadn't noticed these details before. As I looked down, I realized that my feet were cold, ice cold. I shivered. "And your hand." He reached out to hold my right hand. "Maybe you should get stitches for this." He touched the knuckle where a cut ran over my index finger.

"Nothing that won't heal," I said, pulling my hand from

his. "It just needs a bandage. When Gabby is feeling better, maybe then."

"What does the doctor say?" He looked at my daughter, and the expression on his face betrayed honest concern. I liked him for that.

"She said that we'll know more when the tests come back."

Twenty Eight

MARK RICHARDS HAD HARDLY LEFT when the curtains opened again, and Cliff slipped in, his face full of concern, the lines at the corners of his eyes creased so deeply that they gave the impression of a frown. "Oh my God, Brandy," he said, opening his arms to me. "What happened?"

I fell into those arms, my dirt-crusted, smoke-smelling body feeling real comfort for the first time since my husband's funeral. My anger had completely vanished. "I don't know," I said. "I have no idea." Under a canvas jacket, his flannel shirt smelled clean and fresh, his arms warm and safe. Before I knew it, I was crying, sobbing actually, and I felt his palm patting my shoulder as he whispered comfort into my hair.

"Where are the girls?"

"With the neighbors."

"Which ones?"

"Ron and Sandy."

"From the A-frame?"

"The very same," he said. "What can I do here? Can you sit down? Have you seen a doctor?"

"I don't need a doctor," I said, my voice rasping and angry. Why did everyone insist that I see a doctor? I stood back, brushing tears from my sooty face. "I'm fine. It's Gabby," I said, unable to finish the sentence. "I can't let anything…"

"Nothing will happen," he said, guiding me to a plastic chair beside the bed. "Here. You sit. Rest." He patted my shoulder and turned his attention to Gabby. Bending over the stretcher, he took Gabby's hand. "Hey princess," he said. "I hear you've had an exciting night." He smiled at her, using his thumb to brush her cheeks. "I'm here with you now. And your mom is here," he said. "And everything is going to work out fine. Do you hear me?" he said. "Your job is to relax and get better. Everything is going to be fine."

From my spot in the corner chair, I noticed that for Cliff, Gabby tried to smile.

Hours later, we moved Gabby to her own room. The nurse on the pediatric floor, sensing that I would not leave my daughter, ordered a cot for me. And as Gabby dozed, Cliff and I waited in the hall while the housekeeping staff set up the extra bed.

I needed to piece together my own strange memories of the night. I wanted to understand what had happened, and why. "Cliff," I began. "How did you get up to the house so quickly? Did Danny come to get you?"

"No. Actually, your dog started barking. I don't even know when, exactly. She was so loud, and so insistent—I knew something was wrong. I got up and went outside. I smelled the fire from my house, must have been the wind. After I called 911, I ran out to help. We have a fire hose on the south dock. I dragged the hose out, and started the pressure. I was halfway up the path when Danielle nearly knocked me over in the dark." He stuck his hands in his pockets. "Thank God the fence isn't finished. We dragged the hose to the house and had a stream of water on the fire long before the fire trucks arrived."

"I felt it. It was like walking under a waterfall in the middle of winter."

He rubbed his thumb under one eye. "I still can't believe you went in there."

"I couldn't wait for the firemen. I had to get her out."

"What were you doing at home? I thought you were going to spend the night in Vancouver."

"Gabby got sick. We came home early." I leaned against the wall, crossing my arms across my chest. "She never even got to swim," I said, my voice breaking.

"How did it start?"

"I don't know." Once again, I explained everything I remembered, finishing, "I woke up to the fire alarm."

"I suppose it could be anything. Faulty wiring. A short in one of the tools. But now? It seems so crazy. The place is almost finished. You've been through so much."

"Thank God you brought the hose."

"We'll see how things looks in the morning, but the fire is out, and I think the house is okay. The firemen got there so fast, I couldn't believe it. They're leaving a crew all night." He touched my hand. "You can start again. The fire may have delayed you, but it won't defeat you."

"I don't know, Cliff." I covered trembling lips with one hand. "After what happened to Gabby, I just don't know. I could never keep going if anything happened… I. Just. Couldn't." I let the tears roll, and once again Cliff held me while I cried.

❁

I did not sleep that night. Instead, I lay on the cot, tight and coiled, peering through the dim light at the rise and fall of Gabby's chest. Because I could not hear her breathe over the whoosh of flowing oxygen, I found that I could not close my eyes. No matter how often I tried, how I chided myself for my lack of faith, I could not turn away from my vigil. I watched. And I prayed.

Though the coughing had subsided, the doctor kept her under a mask for the remainder of the night. He also ordered arterial blood gasses for me, insisting that I consider taking care of myself part of my care for my daughter.

It was the only way I would submit to the test, and he knew it.

Gabby's tests were repeated just before dawn.

Gabby slept through breakfast and through the frequent monitoring of her vital signs. This sleepiness, the nurse assured me, had nothing to do with the fire. "She's been through quite a night, you know," she said. "And, with yesterday's fever, her body has a lot of recovering to do."

Later that morning, Gabby's blood test results came back in the normal range, and the attending physician reluctantly agreed to a noon discharge. "She's had quite a dose of carbon monoxide, though. I want you to see your own pediatrician in a week for a follow-up visit. In the meantime, you'll want to watch for changes in memory, vision, coordination or behavior. Be certain to get help immediately if something changes."

It wasn't until the doctor left the room that I realized that I no longer had a place to live. We had been discharged, but to where?

Exhausted, I paced the hospital room, wondering what I should do. I had no cell phone. No car. No purse. No clean clothes. I smelled horrible, even to me. And even if they had survived the fire, the clothes in my room at Maggie's Place now smelled much worse.

In that hour after the doctor left, the reality of my situation hit home. I called Eve, and told her what had happened. Shocked, she cried as I relayed the story, and begged me to come home as soon as possible.

She still didn't get it. Florida would never be my home.

As much as I hated to, I called Timothy's parents and asked them to pray for Gabby. I expected Doreen to use the fire as another opportunity to tell me how stupid it was to move to Canada.

"We'll be on the next flight out," she said. "You need us. Gabby needs us. We'll be there as soon as we can get out."

I was too surprised to speak. I took a breath. "Thank you. That means so much to me. But, Gabby is going to be fine. I think it would be better if you wait. Let me sort things out first, find a temporary place to live. Then, when I know what's going to happen, I'll call."

"We're here for you, Brandy. Whatever you need. Chuck and I are praying."

When I'd finished making calls, once again, I found myself crying. I went through waves of anger and fear—anger that I'd come so close to losing Gabby, and fear that I might yet lose everything. Back and forth. Fear. Rage. Peace. Anger.

I tried to pray, but words wouldn't come.

A soft knock interrupted my rolling emotions. As the door opened, Linda, my neighbor, the one I'd first met at the hardware store, stuck her head inside. "Good morning, Brandy. May I come in?"

"Of course," I said, feeling foolish. I wiped my dirty nose with the edge of my blanket. I had nothing more than a hospital gown on over my jeans. This stranger had caught me in the midst of a meltdown. I didn't even know this woman, and yet, here she was. I tried to be polite, speaking as though she were a close friend. "How nice of you to stop by."

"How is she today?" Linda moved to the hospital bed, gently placing both hands on the railing. Her eyes swept Gabby's bed, taking in the oxygen mask, and tubes, the intravenous line and the tiny face above white blankets.

"The doctor says we're really lucky. She's breathing easily. The blood gasses are normal. It seems the worst is over. We can go home today."

"That's good," she said, bending over to touch Gabby's hand. "Very good. I was so worried last night. We went over as soon as we heard the sirens. By then, the ambulance had already gone. And Ron and Sandy had already taken your girls."

I smiled. It didn't seem the right time to explain about Danny and Celeste. "It was kind of them," I said. "I haven't even met them, and still they give the girls a place to stay."

"Well, you know, I was talking to my husband this morning, and we decided that we'd like for you—all of you—to come stay with us while you rebuild."

Linda continued, "Our children are grown, and we have a daylight basement overlooking the south bay. Downstairs we have three bedrooms, a galley kitchen and a family room. You should be comfortable there, and you can stay as long as you like."

I must have looked shocked.

"It's no trouble, really," she said, waving off my surprise.

"But you said you were selling the house. Moving away."

"Things change," she said, cryptically. "We'll see about selling." She handed me a piece of paper. At the top, in large letters she had scribbled her home phone number. "I know you'll want to stay here, with your daughter. But as soon as you are ready to come home, call me. I'll have all the beds ready, and some food in the downstairs fridge."

She crossed the room and gave me a hug. Still holding my shoulders, she continued. "Now, are there any foods you really like? I'm headed to the grocery store, and I'd just as soon fill the pantry with things you enjoy."

I could hardly speak. I blinked, feeling at the same time confused and touched. "Gabby loves Oreos," I said.

"Oreos it is," she said, and left the room.

❀

At ten Lucia arrived, carrying two large shopping bags full of clothes. "I don't know if any of this will fit," she said, dropping them onto the cot. "But surely there's something here you can wear."

"How did you know?"

"Cliff Lowery called this morning. He's worried about you," she said, hugging me again. "I think he'd have brought his own clothes for you, but you're not a flannel kind of gal."

Gabby, who had slept through so much that morning, rolled over, and spotting Lucia, proclaimed, "Lucia! You're here." She sat up.

"How are you feeling, Gabby?"

"We had a fire," Gabby said. "And I was inside. It was smoky and coughy. And I was scared. Mom carried me out!"

"Well, now that was quite an adventure, wasn't it?"

"Did you bring me something?"

"I did," she said, tousling Gabby's hair. "I brought you Snug-a-Bunny. It was Sienna's idea. She said that Snug-a-Bunny helped her when she was your age, and that you could keep her for as long as you like." Lucia pulled a fluffy stuffed toy from one of the bags. "And, I brought you some shorts and a T-shirt to wear home from the hospital."

Gabby tucked the bunny under her arm as she reached for the clothes. "These were Sienna's?" Gabby, clearly impressed, touched the fabric with the same reverence as a princess fingering a new silk gown.

"They were indeed," Lucia said, smiling. She turned to me. "I came to take you both home. I heard that you're being discharged, and I thought you might need a friend as much as you need a ride."

The tears started again, and I wondered how long it would be before last night's horror transformed itself into a distant, though unpleasant memory.

Lucia put one arm around my shoulders and squeezed gently. "I understand," she said. "You've been through quite a night." She picked up one of the bags and handed it to me. "You'll find everything you need in there. Underwear. Shampoo. Shorts. My fat ones and my thin ones. Something should fit. A few tops to choose from. I also brought a hairbrush and a dryer. The clothes aren't beautiful, but I'm pretty sure it's all better than what you have on. I threw in a couple of pairs of flip flops. They're probably too small, but we can pick something up on the way home. Now, why don't you get into the shower and wash away all that smoke and soot. You'll feel better immediately. I promise."

She pulled a chair up to the bed and retrieved a small storybook from her purse, handing it to Gabby. "Gabby and I have some reading to do," she said, waving me toward the bathroom.

❄

Clean, but completely exhausted, I spent the drive home trying to rein in my runaway emotions. I knew what awaited us there. I could see it, in my mind's eye. The ruins of the old house, still smoking in the morning sun.

Lucia made an attempt to distract me with the results from yesterday's swim meet. Telling me about one of the children at Shiloh Farms. Giving me the latest scoop on her husband's work-related struggles. None of her reports pulled me from the abyss into which I'd fallen.

"You aren't listening to a word I've said," she chided, her tone only slightly accusing.

"I'm sorry."

"It isn't as bad as you think."

"You don't know that. You haven't even seen it."

"Cliff told me."

"What does he know? He didn't just lose everything."

"You didn't either."

"I did. Everything. I was trying so hard to start over. I've been through so much, and now this." I covered my eyes with one hand, willing the tears to stop.

Lucia looked into the rearview mirror, smiling at Gabby. "Hey

Gabs," she said. "Did you have a good trip to the swim meet? I hear you got your team jacket yesterday."

"Coach Bryan gave it to me."

"Do you like it?"

I understood her point. This was not the time or the place to fall apart. For Gabby's sake I needed to be strong. No matter what faced us, I had to pull it together for Gabby. In a world full of mystery and threats, a place where even bedrooms caught on fire, she deserved a mother she could count on.

When Lucia turned the last corner to the house, I took a deep breath and held it. Here in the bright light of the late morning, I would have to face my demons. My heart beat wildly, and the memories of last night, still so fresh, rose to the surface. I closed my eyes, as if that might stop the video parading through my mind's eye, like an excerpt from a horror movie.

I had not yet opened my eyes when Lucia pulled into our driveway and put the car in park. As she turned off the engine, the trembling began and I could not stop the tears seeping out between closed eyelids. She reached over and squeezed my hand.

"We're here," she whispered.

I could smell the house before I saw it, even through the closed windows of Lucia's car. The scent of wood-smoke mingled with the peculiar odor of burned plastic. I heard Gabby unlatch her seatbelt and climb toward the door. "Gabby, don't go out without Mommy," I said, turning to the back seat and opening my eyes for the first time.

I climbed out of the car and looked up at the house I had so desperately loved. So many emotions rolled through my heart in that moment, that I could hardly feel one before another stomped in to take its place. Gratitude.

The house had been saved—most of it, anyway. As I stood in the front lawn, every part of the structure from the kitchen door south, seemed relatively undisturbed. Except for smoke stains around the windows, the house looked exactly as it had when I'd last seen it.

I looked north toward the marina, taking in the kitchen and the end of the house where our apartment had once been. Horror kicked gratitude out.

The entire front corner of the house, the kitchen, the stairway and the apartment below it remained standing—though now nothing more than a charred skeleton.

Yellow tape fluttered in the morning breeze, a warning repeated over and over along the length of the tape. "DANGER. FIRE LINE. DO NOT CROSS."

The old deck had disappeared entirely—reduced to gray ashes. The new metal roof dripped precariously. The new lumber, stored near the house, had been lost completely.

Gabby, struck silent by the condition of the house, squeezed my hand as we started through the front yard, toward what had once been the front door of the apartment. She covered her nose with her free hand. "It smells, Mommy," she said. "I want to go."

"I know, sweetie."

Gabby, Lucia and I came around to the sliding glass door, now nothing more than an empty aluminum frame, standing alone in a smoky ruin. Again, tears ran freely down my face. Most of everything we'd brought from Florida was gone. The furniture. The books. Our personal belongings. Timothy's beautiful portrait, the one made from his service photo. The Daddy Book. All of it, gone.

I turned away, hiding my tears from Gabby, when Lucia put one arm around my shoulders. Gabby tugged on my shorts and pointed.

"Mrs. Beauchamp." Mark Richards, this morning wearing a hard hat, and a protective yellow jacket, stepped over the door frame and walked toward us. In one hand, he held a digital camera with a large electronic flash. "Good morning," he said, switching the camera to his left hand and reaching out with his right. "How are you feeling this morning?"

I shrugged and looked toward the water. No words could express what I felt.

"I understand," he said. "It's much harder to face in the bright light of day."

"What are you doing here?"

"It's my job to find the cause of the fire."

"When can we go inside?"

"After the investigation is complete."

"How long will that take?"

"It's hard to say. I let the fire tell me what happened. Sometimes, the house reveals everything immediately. Other times, I have to coax it out of the old girl." He gestured toward the apartment. "Already this morning, I've learned some new things. I need to ask you some more questions."

I shook my head, unable to speak. What did it matter, anyway? After so much work, so much investment, it was all gone. I turned away, heading back up the lawn to the front of the house. He called after me, "Mrs. Beauchamp. Don't you want to know? Don't you want to know why?"

In fact, I didn't care.

Twenty Nine

MARK RICHARDS CAUGHT UP with me beside Lucia's car, no longer carrying a camera. Instead he held a tiny yellow notebook and pen. "We really have to talk, Mrs. Beauchamp. It can't wait," he said. "Every delay makes it harder for me to tell what really happened here."

"Gabby," Lucia said, reaching for her hand, "let's go down to the water and play on the tree swing." I frowned at Lucia, and the two headed off across the south lawn toward the beach. A lot of protection Lucia provided.

I sighed. "So what is it? What's so important that you must ask me now, right at this moment?" No matter how I tried to control my emotions, rage lay just under the surface. After so many obstacles, this last disaster seemed too much for any human to survive. I wasn't sure I could keep going.

"You said you were in Vancouver yesterday. Did anyone know you were going away?"

"Yes. I told Cliff."

"The marina manager?"

"Sure. I asked him to take care of our dog."

"The dog whose barking brought him outside."

"That's Liz. She's a golden doodle. She has quite a nose, I guess."

"No one else?"

I stopped to think. "Well, not directly. But anyone might have figured it out. I told you; Gabby was scheduled for a swim meet—her first. The coach knew. Most of the team parents knew."

"Why did you have someone take care of the dog, if you were only going to be gone for one day?"

"We weren't. Most of the team had reservations at a Vancouver hotel. I didn't want to make the whole trip, over and back in one day."

"So Cliff thought you'd be gone overnight."

I didn't like the way these questions were going. I knew Cliff hadn't done anything to the house. "Yes. He was going to watch the dog. After what happened to Liz, I couldn't just leave her at the house."

He frowned. "Something happened?"

"She got into poison. We don't know exactly how. But after a twelve hundred dollar vet bill, I wasn't about to let it happen again."

He made a note in the little book. "Mrs. Beauchamp," he said, squinting in the sunlight, "Did you store ignitable liquids in the basement?"

"Ignitable?"

"I'm sorry. We used to call them flammables. I have a tool—a sniffer—that finds evidence of hydrocarbons. Gas. Accelerants. Fuel. Did you store anything like that in the basement?"

"Of course not. It was our apartment. We lived there. I wouldn't have kept anything dangerous in the living space." I paused, thinking about the remodel and the various tools the crew had been using. "We were going to move to the second floor as soon as they started to remodel the stairway. But maybe you should ask Peter Delaney. He might have had something downstairs. He was leading the remodeling crew."

"Peter Delaney, from Shiloh Farms?"

"Yes. Do you know him?"

"I know of him." Mark shifted slightly. I could see in his expression, his body language, that he was still thinking, sorting, evaluating as he slipped the pen from his writing hand to a position under his other thumb. "I understand the farm works with ex-cons, guys who've done their time. Folks who need a little help to get situated."

"That's what I've been told."

"I'll call Peter." He used the pen to make another note on his pad. "I do have just a couple more questions," he said, looking into my eyes with a gaze so intense that I dared not look away. "What about a gas container? Something plastic, red. Two and a half gallons. Did you own a red plastic container?"

I thought about the shed, about the weed trimmer, the

lawnmower. "Honestly, I couldn't tell you. I have a shed over at the back of the garden. Maggie, the woman who owned the house before me, kept all the garden tools in that shed. There might have been a gas can there. I wouldn't know. I haven't been here all that long, myself."

"Have you checked the shed since the fire?"

"I just got here. You saw me drive up."

He nodded. "Shall we have a look?"

"I told you," I said, the anger boiling just under the surface. I was having trouble keeping it out of my voice. "I wouldn't even know if something was missing."

He held out one hand. "Why don't you lead the way?"

Still shaking my head, I started across the lawn toward the garden. This guy was getting on my nerves. He seemed as anxious to pin the fire on me as he was to figure out what really happened. I was developing a headache, one worthy of a dark bedroom and some serious medication. Maybe the effects of the smoke, or the carbon monoxide, maybe both had finally caught up with me. All I wanted to do was to lie down and crash.

We arrived at the shed and found the combination lock in place, just as I last saw it. I turned the dial and threw open the wide doors, letting sunlight fill the space. "It looks just as I remember it."

He nodded, stepping inside. I watched as he made a short tour of the shed. His manner reminded me of a hunting animal, watchful, observant, noticing every detail. As he walked, he asked, "Do you know where Maggie bought gas for her lawnmower?"

I shook my head. "I never paid any attention."

"Might she have bought gas down at the marina?"

"It seems logical. It's close. She knew everyone down there."

"Did you ever see a red container with the marina name on the bottom?"

"I haven't used any gasoline since we've been here," I said. "Everything outside was a mess." I stopped, remembering. "Wait. That's not true. I mowed and fertilized the south lawn. I guess I did use the mower."

"It started? After so many years?"

"Cliff worked on it. He changed the oil and replaced the gas." I realized what I'd just said. "Cliff didn't do this. I know that." Once again, my body began to tremble and I hugged myself to make it stop.

"Feeling cold?"

"No. Actually, I'm coming down with a headache. I think I need to lie down. I haven't slept in two full nights." I brushed my hand through my hair. "I think it's catching up to me."

"I understand," he said.

I gritted my teeth. I'd had just about enough of this guy's understanding. What I wanted now was peace, and quiet, and a very dark room.

"One more question," he said. "And then I'll leave you alone."

Promises, promises, I thought. "Fine. Shoot."

He stopped in front of me, gazing directly into my eyes. "Is the house insured?"

"Yes."

"Adequately insured?"

"I think so. After the last windstorm, we reevaluated the coverage."

"So, you've recently changed your insurance coverage?" He smiled. "That's good. Your company will need my report to begin the reimbursement. Can you tell me who carries your insurance?"

"Yes," I said, ignoring his obvious cover for the more pointed question. "Maggie, the previous owner, hadn't changed the insurance value in years. My attorney suggested that I adjust my coverage. I'm sure that he'd be happy to answer any of your insurance questions." I gave him the name, spelling it with pointed irritation.

"Thank you. I'll give him a call as well." He wrote down the information. "Now, Mrs. Beauchamp. If you knew that someone had deliberately set fire to your house, who would you suspect?"

"That's easy," I said, shrugging. "Herbert Karras has been after this property from the day I arrived in Genoa Bay. He's behind everything that's happened so far. I don't know how you'll prove it. But he's your man. I'm sure of it."

With that, I turned toward the beach, calling, "Gabby, It's time to go."

❁

In the late afternoon, after a long nap, I sat with Gabby on the edge of the lawn overlooking the bay. We'd moved a lounge chair into the shade, brought out a blanket, and settled down with a book Lucia had brought Gabby. Bright bales of cumulus clouds tumbled in the eastern sky. From this view I knew the Gulf Islands, miles to the east, were in for rain. For some reason, I took pleasure in the oncoming pelting. I'd had enough distress; it was long past time someone else took a turn.

"Mom, turn the page," Gabby said, patting my thigh. "Lenny has to find it."

We were reading *Lenny Lester's Oyster.* "I'm sorry, honey. I was daydreaming." Gabby reached over my arm and turned the page herself.

Loud barking made us both look up. Liz, bounding up the path from the marina, took the lawn in an all-out race. Sprinting across the grass, she pounced, landing with both paws squarely on Gabby's legs. I groaned under the added weight.

"Oh Lizzy," Gabby said. "I've missed you so much." She threw both arms around the dog's neck, and buried her face in fur, Lenny Lester apparently forgotten.

"Hey, you two." Cliff's voice made me jump.

"Thanks for bringing the dog," I said.

"You don't look happy about it."

"I just this minute realized that I hadn't told Linda about the dog."

"You're staying with her, then?"

"Until this is settled," I said, waving a hand at the house. Gabby crawled off my lap, elbowing me in the stomach, putting one leg through the chair frame as she fought to follow her precious dog.

"Here, Princess," Cliff said, snatching her up. He set her down on her own two feet. "You're gonna kill your mom, climbing over her like that."

He turned to me, sitting down on the footrest. The old lines were back in his forehead, a near-frown filling his face. "What do you mean, 'until'? This is just damage. It's fixable. You can start over."

I shook my head. "No. I'm selling."

"But why?"

"Are you kidding me? You can't look at that place and see why I've got to get out? We could've died in there."

"But it was an accident. Things happen. It doesn't mean anything."

"Of course it means something. You don't have any idea what I've been through. I lost my husband. I inherited this disaster of a house thinking I could make my own life, provide for Gabby. And look at us. We've been tagged, our dog's been poisoned, the guy with the property next door has all my neighbors against us—and now this. A fire.

"For crying out loud, Cliff! Even someone who is pathologically stubborn gives up at some point. I'm not destitute. I don't need this grief. I couldn't protect Timothy. This," I pointed again, as my voice broke. "This is so optional. I can protect Gabby. I quit. I give up. I'm going to sell. It's not worth losing my life over."

"I can't make you stay," Cliff said, his voice intense, focused. "But you can't give up because of an accident. That's all it was. I'm sure of it."

"I thought so too. But, I've been thinking. This morning, when I talked to Mark Richards, he asked me if I kept anything ignitable in the basement. And if that wasn't enough, he asked about a red plastic container."

"He found something? In your house, he found something?"

"He doesn't give away information, Cliff. But yes, he asked about a red container. A gas container from the marina, I think. Don't you think that means he found one?"

Cliff scowled and shook his head, clearly confused. "I don't know why the crew would have stored gas in the apartment."

With Gabby and Liz sitting on the lawn beside my chair, I knew this wasn't the place to talk. "You know," I said, pointing at Gabby, "don't you have something else to talk about? We've heard enough about fires."

He nodded, and turned to Gabby. "Hey there, Gabby. Where are Danny and Celeste?"

She looked up. "Mrs. Linda took them to visit their grandmother."

"Are you hungry?"

Gabby nodded, smiling. "I didn't eat at all yesterday. Mom says I'm making up for lost time."

"Why don't you both come down to my place? I'll fix some dinner."

I shook my head. "I don't want you to go to any trouble."

"Not any trouble at all."

"Can we, Mom?" Gabby said, standing up. "I could visit the kittens."

Conspired against, I surrendered, all of the fight burned out of me. "Alright," I told Cliff, getting out of the old chair. "But I warn you. I'm not hungry."

"When you smell my cooking, you'll change your mind. You'll be ravenous."

"Just don't burn anything."

We walked down the old path to Cliff's house, the dog leading the way as if Cliff's floating home had become her new vacation property. As we walked along, I thought of the ivy and wondered what secrets might be hidden there. Had the arsonist gone up this path? Had he escaped this way? Were there clues outside the house, waiting to be found?

Minutes later, I found myself in a chair at Cliff's kitchen table. With Gabby out on the deck petting kittens, we took advantage of the quiet to talk.

"What can I do to help?" I asked, hoping he wouldn't request anything. For some reason, I had no energy. No spunk. I felt as if I could have happily died of old age in that kitchen chair.

"Nothing," he answered, opening the refrigerator door. "I'm not planning anything special. Just simple fare."

"That's fine. I'm sure it's more than I would have managed."

"You need a little pampering after last night."

I nodded. "I don't know if I'll ever be able to close my eyes without seeing those flames again."

"It's over now. You can forget it."

"I don't know how you can say that. Think about what I've been through. I've had it. Life is too short for battles like this."

"You think someone tried to burn down the house."

"And you don't?"

He shook his head; his frown deepened. "It's too soon for that. That's crazy."

"I don't have nine lives, Cliff. I have one. Gabby has one. I can't risk it, staying here to fight for an old half-charred house." I leaned my face on my hands. "What's next? Someone takes out the brakes on the car? An accidental explosion? I feel like I'm caught in a made-for-TV movie. These things don't happen in real life. I want out."

Leaning over the refrigerator drawer, Cliff picked out the makings for a garden salad, dropping items on the counter one after another. He stopped moving and stood up. "What about Celeste and Danny? If you leave here, what will happen to them?"

"I was only filling in. Someone else will take care of them."

"Who? If not you, then who?"

"I don't know. They aren't my responsibility."

"Why not?" Cliff took a seat at the table, all plans for dinner set aside. "Could it be that Celeste and Danny are the reason you came back to Canada? Maybe this isn't about you at all. Maybe this is a fight for those kids."

"What about my kid, Cliff? Who's going to fight for Gabby?"

He began to polish his thumbnail, one thumb rubbing, rubbing, rubbing the other. He stopped and looked up at me. "Let me fight for you."

I shook my head. I must have been exhausted; I hadn't seen that coming. "I don't think so Cliff. You don't even know who I am."

"You've never told me."

"You've never asked."

"So. I'm asking."

I looked at him, at the soft denim of his eyes, at his salt-and-pepper beard, and realized that this man was a gem. A friend. Someone worthy of my deepest trust. I took a deep breath and started. I told Cliff everything. At least everything I knew for sure.

"Thank you," he said, when I had finished. "Thank you for telling me. We're really not very different, are we?"

"We both came to the end of ourselves, and when we did, Maggie was there."

"She was, at that." Again he polished his thumbnail, thinking. "You know, nothing you said changed anything. Now I do know you.

You've told me everything. I still want to be there for you. Let me take over now. Let me fight for you."

I shook my head. "Cliff, you saved our lives last night. But will you always be there to rescue us? What happens next time?"

"There won't be a next time," he said, quietly, firmly.

"There won't be a next time," I answered, just as firmly, "because we're going back to the States."

Thirty

FOR DAYS, I STAYED THAT WAY, wandering through a fog of inaction and passivity. I called the garden crew and told them there would be no more work. I left the composted soil exactly where it had been delivered, squarely in the middle of the driveway. I cancelled all the orders for undelivered materials. I called the North Cowichan building department and told them that because of the fire, I would not complete the renovation, thus canceling our building permit.

I stopped watering the plants we had not yet put in the ground. In the warm dry days of late August, they died quickly. Their dead leaves and brittle soil seemed appropriate somehow. Dreams die. Shouldn't plants?

It would only be a matter of time before Mark Richards officially declared the fire arson. Then, I would salvage what I could from the house, put the property on the market, and wait for a triumphant Karras, or his agent to arrive with a lowball offer.

I would have no bargaining power. But I didn't need power. I just needed to leave Genoa Bay behind. It had been a mistake somehow. I hadn't heard God's voice at all.

During those foggy days, I began to miss Cliff. On the night he cooked dinner for Gabby and I, just before I'd left his house, he'd tried again to change my mind about leaving. I'd gotten angry and said words that I now regretted.

He didn't deserve my harsh words, and I realized that I cared too much about Cliff to have my wrath be the last thing he remembered of me. At the same time, though I would have died before I admitted it to anyone, I longed for him. I longed for his comfort. For his humor. For his tenderness. He wasn't a leading-man type; he was a hometown hero. A gentleman. A friend. And I suspected that he could be more.

Leaving Genoa Bay, I would never know.

Like a sliver setting up an infection, I began to feel worse and worse about my own behavior. I was wrong, and I needed to apologize, sooner rather than later.

Late in the week after the fire, I let Lucia drive Gabby to her swim class, and I walked down to the marina office. It wouldn't be easy, but I had to talk to Cliff.

The same old bell rang as I opened the door to the marina office. A dock hand, one I had not met, manned the radio at the counter. "Is Cliff in his office?"

He shook his head. "You're the lady from the old house."

I nodded. "Is he down on the docks?"

"Not hardly," he said. Something about this boy's tone of voice set off alarms in my mind.

"Do you know when he'll be back?"

"Look lady, I don't know you. I don't think I should tell you anything." His radio started to squawk and he turned down the volume. "I'm not sure he would want anyone to know."

"Know what?" I put on my lion face, the one I used to correct Gabby. If I had any skill at all, it was intimidating children. "Cliff is my friend. I want to know what's happening here. So if there's something you need to tell me, you start. Right now."

Surprised, he took a step back. "Okay. It's not that big of a deal."

"What? What's going on?"

"The police came this morning. Cliff went down to the station in a squad car."

"Why? Why would they take Cliff?" It made no sense. No one could mistake the soft, gentle man I knew for an arsonist.

"Lady, I didn't listen in or anything." This kid—who could be no more than sixteen—looked guilty enough to confess to setting the fire himself.

"You know something."

He shrugged. "I heard something about fingerprints."

Fingerprints. How could anyone be foolish enough to want Cliff's fingerprints? It was like suspecting the Cookie Monster of murder. Sheeze. Morally, Cliff was about as shifty as Bert and Ernie. This fire investigator was so busy listening to the house that he'd completely managed to ignore the obvious. "Okay," I said, turning back to the door. "I didn't hear anything from you."

I walked back to the house, anger surging, pouring adrenaline into my bloodstream like water from a garden hose. Wasn't it enough, all I'd been through? Hadn't I already lost my house, nearly lost my daughter? Now, they were trying to blame Cliff? I wanted to kick something. Hit someone. I wanted to knock the eyeballs out of Herbert Karras.

For the first time since the fire, I wanted to fight back.

But how? What could I do to help this apparently inept investigator find the real man behind the fire? I stormed up the driveway, kicking rocks as I walked.

Something. I had to do something.

I walked around the side of the house, looking again into the cavernous black space that had been the apartment. Part of me wanted to go inside. Maybe I could find something. Something the investigator had missed. I thought about it—and dismissed the idea. I couldn't go in.

My only experience with the law came from television crime shows. And from what I remembered, evidence discovered by anyone other than the official investigator was compromised—wouldn't qualify in a court of law. How would they know I hadn't placed the evidence myself? It would be my word against the arsonist.

I paced the lawn outside the apartment. Back and forth. Over and over, I walked along the edge of the ivy-covered lot between the house and the marina. I walked faster and further, back and forth, wondering what I could do to help Cliff.

At the end of one of these marches, I came to the place where the men from Delaney's work crew took their smoking breaks. Under the shade of a small vine maple, the ground was littered with cigarette butts. I looked at the brittle condition of the dry weeds nearby and thought about the danger of a grass fire. I should talk to Peter about their smoking…

And then I thought of it. What about Blue Eyes?

Other than the incident with the cigarette, ground into my dining-room carpet, I'd never spoken to him. He'd never threatened me. Never gave me legitimate reason to feel afraid. But something about him bothered me. He never quite joined in. Never quite fully relaxed. There was something seething just under the surface in that man. Something powerful. Something dangerous. Could it be?

Out of the birdhouse on the front porch, I picked out a spare house key and let myself into the kitchen. Richards had made it clear that I wasn't to go in—not until I cleared it with him. But this was too important. Too critical.

I grabbed my key ring—blackened with smoke—from the rack in the kitchen, found my purse and headed back out to the car. I could be at Shiloh Farms in less than fifteen minutes. There had to be some way to solve this thing. Some way that didn't involve Cliff. Maybe Peter could shed some light on things.

I drove straight to Shiloh Farms, where I parked beside the carpentry school's pick-up truck. Inside, I found Peter Delaney, sitting at his desk. He was on the phone, and I waited discreetly at one of the workstations while he finished his call.

He waved at me, acknowledging my presence, and then pointed with a helpless expression to his phone. *It'll be a minute*, the gesture said.

I walked the length of the room, observing the various power tools and partially completed projects. I stopped finally, pausing to look out one of the station windows to the lawn. Outside, standing in a small group, were several of the men who had worked at Maggie's Place. Among these, I noticed other men, strangers I'd never seen before. I watched as the group smoked, visiting with one another, tossing jokes back and forth. They laughed easily, sharing the camaraderie of fellow workers and students.

Blue Eyes was there, standing slightly away from the group. On the outside, he seemed to participate. But something about his posture seemed wrong. Awkward. Apart. He drank soda from an aluminum can—a cola can. But he tossed the liquid back in the same way I'd seen men in bars drink straight alcohol. As a kid, I'd spent too much time waiting for my mother in those places.

I was all too familiar with the behavior of drinking men. I'd bet he was drinking that morning. I'd wager my car that there was alcohol in that can.

I watched him follow every swig with a drag from his cigarette.

His shoulders were tense, his eyes watching the other men with the strain of a hunting cat. After Peter hung up the phone, he came to me holding out both arms. I accepted his hug, grateful for his friendship. "Brandy. I can't tell you how sorry I was to hear about the house."

"Not as sorry as I was."

"No. I'll bet. How is Gabby?"

"The pediatrician says she's good. So far, no lingering symptoms."

"That must be a relief." He stood back, taking a half seat on the worktable behind him. "Would you like some coffee? What brings you here?"

I shook my head. "Two things. First, I came to tell you that I've decided not to finish the remodel."

His eyebrows rose. "I'm confused. Have you chosen someone else?"

"Oh no. That's not it. I'm perfectly happy with your work. You guys were great."

"But you're firing us."

"Peter, have you seen the house? Our contract didn't cover that kind of rebuilding."

"We could renegotiate the contract. That's no problem. I haven't seen it yet, but I've heard it's not too bad."

"You mean that Lucia says it's not too bad," I said. "She's wrong. The whole north end is completely gutted. It will have to be rebuilt from the foundation up. All your work is gone. No. I've decided to sell and move back to the US."

Peter seemed surprised. "I guess that's your choice. I'm sorry to hear about it, though." He folded his hands. "You said that there were two things."

"I need to ask you a couple of questions."

"No problem."

"Did you have any reason to have a gas container up at my house? A gas-powered generator? Gas-powered tools?"

"We do use a generator, a gas-powered generator." My disappointment must have been apparent, because he went on quickly. "But not at your place. You already had power, so we just rolled our compressor off the truck and plugged it in. We ran all our tools off your power. I never even took a generator to your place."

"Is your generator gas-powered?"

"Yes."

"What do you store the gas in?"

"I have a twenty-liter, galvanized steel can."

I couldn't help myself. I smiled. The can that Mark Richards found did not belong to the construction crew. And then I realized. If the can really came from the marina, there actually might be fingerprints on it. And they might belong to Cliff. After all, he handled everything at the marina. When the dock staff was short, Cliff could be seen anywhere. He gassed boats, docked the guests, made reservations, manned the radio. He kept the whole show running.

There had to be another explanation. "While you were at the house, did you have any reason to give my house key to the men who worked with you?"

"Look, these are the same questions Richards asked," Peter said. "I'll tell you what I told him. All the guys on our crew used your key at one point or another."

Disappointed, I couldn't be deterred. I'm no private investigator, but I knew I was on the right track. If someone burned down my house, that someone had been sent by Karras. The only problem was, we had to figure out who had been hired to do it; and then we had to prove it. "What about the men who worked with you? Do you trust them?"

Peter nodded. "It's my job to trust them. We make sure that the guys who work for us are clean and sober. They're working hard to make a clean start."

"What about debt?"

"What do you mean?"

"Money. Do any of them have money problems?"

He shook his head, laughing lightly. "Boy, are you clueless."

I didn't like the way he'd said it. "Thanks."

"No, really. In my experience, there isn't an ex-con anywhere in the world who doesn't have money problems. They have wives and kids and no one will hire them. They can't make a living. No one wants to rent to them. They need a car, but can't get credit to buy one. Yes, Brandy. Every ex-con has money problems."

"I thought you only took guys who live on campus."

"That's a different program. The carpentry school students live off campus." He stood up. "I'm sorry I can't help you. Mark Richards was disappointed. He talked to the whole crew, yesterday, and didn't seem to find anything out of the ordinary."

"I guess I shouldn't take up your time, then."

"Not a problem," he said, walking me toward the door. "It's too bad that you and Gabby are leaving Duncan. We'll miss you two. Lucia'll be lost without you."

"I'll miss her too," I said, offering my hand. There were so many people I would miss from Genoa Bay. Cliff's graying beard and soft eyes flashed through my mind. "You've been a good friend too, Peter. When you figure out how much money I still owe you, give me a call. I'll bring over a check. Once the property sells, I should be rolling in money."

"Doesn't seem worth it, does it?"

I shook my head. "Not at all."

Peter walked me to the car, and watched as I buckled my seatbelt. I started the car as he headed back into the building, unable to silence the alarms going off in my head. If Herbert Karras was behind the fire, he hadn't set it himself.

He absolutely had to have someone else do it. Someone from Peter's crew.

They would have had a key to get in, a reason to need the money. And in the case of Blue Eyes, an inherent dislike of me from the very beginning.

I'm not sneaky by nature; I'd never make it as a spy. But I had an idea, one that just might work. Once the door closed behind Peter, I turned off the motor and got out of the car. I slunk low, under the front windows and tiptoed around the end of the building. I had this crazy idea about Blue Eyes—the man with the pop can, the one I'd had the run-in with earlier in the summer.

What if the soda can had fingerprints on it? And what if his prints matched the prints on the gas can left at my house?

I crept slowly along the end of the building, aware of the

laughter and voices in the distance. From here, I could not yet identify individual voices; I had no idea if Blue Eyes was still outside with the group. At the corner, I stopped, waiting and listening. I heard the back door of the building open, and heard Peter's voice call out, "Break's over, guys. Time to come inside."

I waited a beat, and then peeked around the corner. In a group, the guys walked toward the back door, entering single file. Blue Eyes was the last man in line, still swigging from the soda can as he walked. I ducked back, sucked in my breath and took one more glance.

Just as he entered the door, I saw him drop the can into a full-sized garbage can.

Crouching low, I waited there for the sharp snap of the closing door. Certain that they'd all gone inside, I crept along the back of the building, still keeping my head below window level. Bent over in that way, my eyes on the ground, I nearly ran into the garbage can before I saw it. Slowly I leaned over the edge and peered inside.

There, on the top of a large pile of plastic, paper and cardboard was the single can of Coke. Discarded. Okay, I know Canada isn't exactly the United States. But aren't the prints and DNA evidence left on discarded items free for anyone who takes them?

Not wanting to smudge any prints that might be on the can, I looked around, searching for something to pick it up. I found a stick nearby, and slipped one end into the opening of the can, tipping it upside down. With my stick in one hand, I carried my prize to the car. From there, one-handed, I drove straight to the municipality offices of North Cowichan.

❀

Still carrying the pop can on the end of the stick, like a child carries a flag at a parade, I entered the lobby and crossed to the information desk. "I need to see Mark Richards, immediately," I said.

Without comment, the receptionist picked up the telephone and punched in an extension. She spoke, nodded, spoke again. "I'm sorry, Ma'am. He's busy at the moment."

"I know he's busy," I said. "But he's busy with the wrong man. I'm telling you, he needs to see me. And he needs to see me now!" Too late, I realized that my voice had begun to attract the attention of a security officer who walked toward us, looking obviously perturbed.

"Ma'am," he said, in the calm tones one uses with the mentally unstable. "If you'll just take a seat, I'm sure Mr. Richards will come down as soon as he has a free minute."

"You don't understand," I said, trying to calm myself while at the same time trying to appear as a reasonably sane adult. "I have fingerprints here," I shook the stick, which set the pop can to ringing. He looked at my stick and stifled a smile. I lowered my voice, speaking with new intensity. "I am absolutely not crazy, and I'm not kidding. I got this can from the man who burned down my house."

His eyebrows rose.

"I don't want Mr. Richards to arrest the wrong man," I said. "Please just help me take this up to his office."

Sighing, he nodded at the receptionist. "I'll escort the lady upstairs. You call Richards and tell him we're coming."

We went up the stairs to the second floor, where Richards occupied a smallish office at the end of the north hallway. The guard knocked lightly, and Richards answered, nodding at me. He dismissed the guard. "Thanks, Jake. We'll be fine."

Still carrying my prize pop can at the end of the stick, I stepped inside. "Where's Cliff?"

"He's being fingerprinted."

"You're wrong, you know. Even if his prints match, you'd be wrong. Cliff didn't do this. Cliff does everything at the marina. That hardly makes him an arsonist."

"We'll know more soon enough." He pointed to the pop can. "Where did that come from?"

"I picked it out of a garbage can," I answered, handing the stick to him.

He held up both hands, refusing to take it from me. "And what do you expect me to do with it?"

"Test it. It has fingerprints. I know they're there. And they're going to match the ones you found on the gas can in my basement."

He looked completely bewildered. "How do you know this, exactly?"

Embarrassed, I realized that I didn't know any such thing. I shrugged. "Okay. I don't know. But I think they will. I watched one of the guys from the remodeling crew drink out of it. He threw it away, and I brought it here, straight to you. I haven't set it down, haven't let anyone touch it."

"I don't have anything but your word for that."

"I'm not asking you to convict him on the basis of these prints. I'm only asking you to find out if he touched that gas can. If he did, if the prints match, maybe you can connect him to Karras."

"That's all you want."

"That's all."

He shook his head. "You are one nutty woman."

I nodded. "Completely. So humor me." I held out the can. "Please?"

He took the stick. "Alright. But if I dust this can for prints, will you promise me this is the last time you will try to play arson investigator? Believe me, you are not qualified for this kind of work. If someone did burn down your place, you could be putting yourself in danger with this kind of snooping around. Do you promise? No more evidence?"

"I promise."

"Yeah, right," he said, shaking his head, clearly disbelieving my vow. "Right."

Thirty One

In a tiny envelope at the bottom of the box, I find a small note card. Inside, I read, "Dear Maggie, Your letter finally made its way to the treatment center last Friday. I have spent many days wondering what to say. First, I am glad that Brandy has found her way to you. You sound like a kind woman. I am happy to know she is well. I wish I was a better mother to her. But I was young. After the accident, the judge sent me here. I have been sober four weeks. If I stay clean, I may get my other kids back. I am happy that someone has been looking out for Brandy when I could not. Thank you for writing. Please tell Brandy, I love her.

TWO DAYS LATER, I HAD A CALL from Mark Richards. Officially, the fire had been declared arson. He'd taken all the pictures and evidence he needed from the scene. We were free to go into the house and salvage our belongings.

Somewhat sheepishly, he admitted that the prints from my coke can matched those on the gas can, but when the police went to question the suspect, he was gone.

I wondered if Peter told the class that I had come by, if something about my presence had tipped him off. I wondered why God had allowed me to find the prints, and then let him get away.

The very next morning, Gabby and I washed clothes in Linda's laundry room and hung them out on the line to dry. Gabby perched tenuously on the top of a stepstool, holding a bedsheet in place while I stretched out the other end and pinned it.

Slow work, but that's the way it goes when kids help.

"Brandy." I recognized Celeste's voice, and looked over my

shoulder in time to see Celeste and Danny come out onto the porch. Behind them traipsed a short woman with a full head of dark hair. Her black, short-sleeved dress did not disguise her ample frame. Celeste asked, "Can we talk for a minute, Mrs. Beauchamp?"

I don't know why, but I felt my heart turn over in my chest. Had something happened to the girl's grandmother? Had someone figured out our little deception? "Gabby, let's take a break," I said, dropping a handful of clothespins into the laundry basket. Gabby jumped off her stool and went over to hug Celeste.

"Can I watch television?"

"For a while," I agreed. She ducked inside, happy to be released from chores. "So, can I get you ladies anything? I have fresh coffee. Tea?"

"That won't be necessary," the woman said. "Maybe we could just sit down?"

"Sure." I pulled out an old wooden chair, offering it to the stranger. "I'm Brandy Beauchamp," I said, taking a bench across from her. "But you already know that. And you are?"

"I'm Anne," she said, "Anne Schwab. I'm the social worker at the nursing home where Celeste's grandmother is living."

I sat down across from this stranger, perplexed. "How is Aida doing?"

"She's doing better, actually. Her rehab is progressing. She's more clear-headed, now that she's not drinking."

"That's good, isn't it?"

"Yes. It's an improvement."

I leaned over and squeezed Danny's hand. "See? I told you she'd get better."

Celeste blinked and looked down at her hands, folding them in her lap.

"Actually, she is better," Anne said. "But, she's not going to return home. That's why we're here. Last night, the girls told me the truth about who you are. I don't know how it happened, but somewhere along the way, someone assumed that you were a relative. My records indicated that you are Aida Daniels' daughter." She shifted in her seat. "I understand you've allowed the girls to stay with you since Aida broke her hip."

"I had four suites at the old house. The girls were working for me at the time. They were welcome to stay as long as they wanted."

"They tell me there's been a fire."

My heart seemed to skip a beat. Had this woman decided to take the girls and move them to foster care? Was this the very thing that Celeste had dreaded?

"It's true."

"And the house isn't inhabitable."

"Not at the moment."

"So. I guess now that we're aware of the situation, we'll have to make other arrangements."

"Other arrangements?"

"You certainly can't expect us to allow you to care for these two young women when you don't even have a home of your own."

"What arrangements will you make?"

"Well, Celeste is eighteen. Officially, she doesn't need help. Of course, with the pregnancy, she has issues that she'll need to address. But Danielle is too young to live alone. We'll have to find foster care."

"Separate them?" Exactly the circumstances that had frightened Celeste so much in the first place.

"It can't be helped. There is no other way."

Celeste sat up, her expression intense. "There is another way," she said. "If Brandy would take us in, officially I mean, we could stay here." She spread her hands palm up, addressing me. "Yesterday, I realized that we needed to come clean about being here. I was afraid you'd get in trouble if I didn't say something now. So, when we went visit Grandmom, I told Anne about everything. Everything."

I nodded.

"She told me that it's possible to stay with you, if we do it officially."

"Officially?" I looked to Anne.

"Yes," she said. "You'd have to be approved, of course. But we could allow the girls to stay together if they stay with you."

Celeste perked up. "I would work for room and board. I wouldn't be a burden to you. And Danny could keep on babysitting."

"I would," Danny said. "I'd do anything."

"Listen," I said, interrupting them both. "I don't know what I'm going to do." I turned to Anne. "At first, after the fire, I was just going to move back to Florida. You know, sell the property and start over somewhere else. But now, I'm not certain what I want to do." I glanced at the girls, their faces full of hope. "How long can they stay with me while I decide what's next?"

"They've obviously done well here with you. I don't think there's any hurry."

"Can I have a week then?"

❀

The very next morning, because I didn't want Celeste's baby exposed to the contaminants of the fire, I asked Celeste to stay with Gabby while Danny and I dragged our personal things out of the apartment. At last, with the investigation complete, we could really see what might have survived smoke and water damage, and what had to be thrown away.

Fortunately, the fire had been extinguished quickly. Though the sheetrock sagged from water damage, the ceiling of the apartment was structurally well supported. Everything inside was black, and sooty. Much of it was still soaking wet, some of it had already started to mold. Everything we touched gave off an oily sludge, forcing us to wear gloves and masks and clothes we would never wear again.

It was a sunny day, with a cold breeze foreshadowing the coming fall storms. We worked steadily, emptying dressers, and carrying out whatever small items we could manage. I'd had a small dumpster delivered to the driveway, and by noon, we'd filled it nearly half way.

I still hadn't decided what to do. And as the hours passed, my own ambivalence began to make things more difficult. For instance, the mattresses from the beds needed to be thrown away. Full of smoke and water, they could never be cleaned. But why put them in the dumpster if the whole house went to Herbert Karras?

Let him tear down Maggie's Place.

I decided not to drag the mattresses outside. Instead, I determined to focus only on the things I could save.

I'd just dropped an armload of my own clothes, still on hangers, on the east lawn, when Liz suddenly jumped out from under a Blue Beard bush, where she was napping, and ran toward the marina path. She must have seen a squirrel.

"Liz, come back!" I shaded my eyes, following her flight toward the marina, when I recognized Cliff heading in our direction. The dog bounced up, putting both paws on Cliff's chest. He scratched her head, and made doggy love noises.

I shook my head and sat down on the lawn, exhausted and grateful for a visit. I'd have to teach both of them some manners. Danielle brought out a stack of boxes from the spare bedroom. "Sit down, Danny," I said. "Time for a break."

She smiled and began peeling the gloves from her hands.

"Hey, you two," Cliff said, walking toward us. "I have some very good news."

I frowned. "After all we've been through lately, that seems highly unlikely."

"Ah, but I do," he said, bending over to sit down across from us. "I just heard that the police have made an arrest in your fire."

"My fire?"

"Here. This fire." He pointed at the house. "They found the guy you call Blue Eyes. He was hiding in a cabin up near Bear Cove at Port Hardy."

"Oh yeah?"

Cliff's eyes twinkled with anticipation. "Yep. And there's more." My friend looked more like a child on Christmas Eve than a grown man discussing criminal activity.

"Okay. You've got us. What's the news?"

"He apparently told the police everything they needed to know."

"About what?"

"About the fire."

"What do you mean?"

"I don't know what they promised him, but I just found out that the police arrested Herbert Karras at his home early this morning."

Even though this was what I'd suspected all along, it still shocked me—that Karras would be heartless enough to try to burn down our house. He seemed like an ordinary guy—a businessman, not some ruthless killer. What if we'd all died in the fire? What if Gabby… I couldn't finish that thought. "I just don't understand. Why would anyone do that? Why would anyone try to burn down the house with us inside?"

"He didn't. He got Blue Eyes to do it for him. And according to what I heard, Blue Eyes thought you were away for the night. He'd worked at the house during the day, noticed the car was gone, and heard you'd gone to Vancouver for the night. He thought he was burning down an empty house."

"How do you know all this?"

"Are you kidding? I have my sources."

"Oh right. I forgot that you used to be a newspaper man."

He nodded. "I have more." He leaned back on his hands, stretching out his legs, a satisfied look on his face. "Once he realized that you were inside during the fire, he panicked. Started drinking again. Ran from the authorities. I guess he was pretty soused when they found him."

It bothered me that Cliff was having so much fun with this. It was nothing more than a game to him. "Alright. Get it over with."

"Danny, would you excuse us for a minute? I'd like to talk to Brandy alone."

Danny, surprised, looked at me. I nodded. "Why don't you go up to Linda's house and see what's for lunch? I'll be up in a few minutes." She stood up, pulled the scarf off her head, shaking out her hair as she started toward the driveway.

"So, what is it? What is your latest bit of gossip?"

"I know someone who's going to make an offer on the marina."

"Buy it from Karras?"

"Yep. Karras is in trouble. He knows it. For a criminal trial, he's going to need one really good attorney. That will cost a boatload of money. And none of his high-flying financiers are going to stick with an accused arsonist. Even if he gets off, the trial will take a year or two. I'm guessing it will bankrupt him. Selling is the smartest thing he can do now."

I don't know what I'd expected, but this was not it. With Karras broke, fighting criminal charges, he wouldn't be buying Maggie's

Place. And if he didn't buy, what would I do? I'd been so focused on returning to the States, I hadn't even considered what might happen if Karras were actually arrested.

Suddenly my own plans to get out of the mess at Genoa Bay had gone up in smoke as dark and depressing as the smoke from the house. I felt like someone had just hit me over the head with a two-by-four.

"Who? Who is going to buy the Marina?"

"I am," Cliff said. And the smile on his face was like that of a man who had won the Mega Millions Lottery.

EPILOGUE

September 2008

THE WEDDING DAY DAWNED clear and much warmer than we'd expected for late September. After a quick breakfast, I spent the early hours putting the finishing touches on the cake, while Miranda, one of the girls from the Shiloh kitchens, covered crackers with creamed cheese and smoked salmon. Outside, Cliff and Gabby—now eleven—helped place white rented chairs in neat rows across the east lawn.

I'd baked a lemon wedding cake, the groom's favorite, and decorated it with tiny blue bellflowers. "Brandy," Danny said, coming into the kitchen. "What time is the photographer coming?"

"Before ten." I lifted the last cake layer onto its pedestal, holding my breath as I let go. It stayed. I turned to Danny, who was beaming with excitement. She looked beautiful, her skin glowing, her hair piled on top of her head.

"And Eve will have the flowers finished by then?"

"She's in the garage right now."

"Does she need help?"

I smiled. "Danny, I think you're supposed to be helping the bride—not worrying about the flowers. Have you had some breakfast?"

"Grammy, can I have some cake?" Hunter ran into the kitchen and climbed a stool. Celeste's four-year-old, the spitting image of his mother, with dark eyes and thick coarse hair, reached out to touch the cake. I leaned over and gave his nose a pinch. "No, you may not," I said. "Cake is for after the wedding. And you, young man, should be upstairs getting dressed in your wedding clothes."

"Okay," he said reaching for the bowl of frosting.

"Nope," I gave his hand a gentle tap. "Frosting is not for now. You go find your mommy, sweetie."

Hunter is not the type to waste energy on disappointment. He scrambled off the chair and ran toward the great room, flying into Cliff as he went around the corner.

"Whoa, young man. Slow down there," Cliff said, patting him on the back.

"I'm going to find mommy," he said, as if this explained everything.

Danny grabbed an apple. "I'm going to go check on Lucia," she said. "She was setting up the buffet table. Maybe she needs help."

Cliff leaned over the counter, kissing my cheek. "Did you ever think this day would come?"

"Yes," I said, "with absolute certainty." I leaned over the counter and gave Cliff a proper kiss, warm and ripe with gratitude. "Now, help me get these little dolls up here where they belong."

Together, we placed the Precious Moments bride and groom, and carried the finished cake into the great room, where we placed it at the center of a long table. "Here," I said, nodding toward the wall. "Further back. A little more. There." Taking one last look around the room, I wiped my hands on my jeans. "I guess this is it," I said. "Where are Timothy's parents?"

"Outside," he said. "Giving instructions to the pastor."

I laughed. Doreen loved to give instructions to anyone who might listen. Since the fire, she'd managed to give pages of instructions every time she visited Genoa Bay. At least she'd finally accepted our life in the old house. "So, what about you?" I said, patting his beard. "Are you ready? Really ready?"

"I was born ready," he said, kissing me again.

"Cliff, I have something else. Something I think I should show you."

"You've been hiding something?"

"Nothing earth-shattering. But it's important to me..." I reached into my back pocket and pulled out the card my mother had written to Maggie. "Especially today."

I handed the card to him and watched him open it. He read it quickly, looking up when he'd finished. "In the box? How did you save it from the fire?"

I nodded. "I had to show you." I shrugged. "Before the fire, I'd started cleaning out the spare room. I moved the things I wanted to keep into the attic. The fire never got that far."

Though he smiled, he was still clearly confused. "It doesn't change anything. Why show me now?"

"I wanted you to know. The whole truth. Today is such an important day. I wanted you to know everything. It's been bothering me all this time." I pointed at the card. "Maggie found her. My mother. But she never told me." I looked up at Cliff. "Why not? Why didn't Maggie tell me?" My voice broke. "It would have meant so much to know that my mother loved me."

"We'll never know what Maggie was thinking," he said, folding me into his arms. "I think she went looking for your mom because she knew first hand how much it would hurt any mother, not knowing where her child was."

"Like Mary Ellen."

"Exactly."

"But why didn't she tell me my mother had written?"

"Maybe Maggie thought seeing the card would hurt you more. Maybe she thought that without the card, you would always believe that your mother was still looking for you. That she wanted you back."

"Instead of being willing to give me away to a stranger she'd never met. What kind of mother does that?"

"Maggie wasn't really a stranger. She loved you from the day she met you." He stroked my shoulder. "Your mother didn't have the resources to give you the love you needed. My take is that God gave you Maggie—to give you what your mother couldn't."

With my face still against Cliff's chest, I nodded. "No one ever loved me more."

"I'd like to try," he said, kissing my forehead. "Now, will you go get dressed? Enough with the fussing. I'll be waiting for you outside."

❀

When the music started, I turned toward the house. Every guest followed my lead, craning their necks to see the wedding party.

Gabby led the way to the altar at the edge of the lawn. A junior bridesmaid in her first formal gown, she walked down the grass aisle, her head held high, a bright smile lighting her whole face. Behind her, Danny followed, more feminine than I'd ever seen her, in periwinkle satin and beaded sandals.

Just as his aunt reached the makeshift altar, little Hunter started down the aisle, his face focused and serious, his tiny hands gripping the ring pillow with the intensity of a child holding his favorite candy. The music swelled and I stood, turning with the audience toward the bride.

Celeste waited at the back, one arm in Cliff's, her eyes filled with happy tears, as she smiled at her groom. She'd grown so much in four years, finishing school, giving birth, attending a community college. Now, she was taking this step, marrying a man she loved, a man she'd met through her internship in the shipping office at the Port of Victoria. A man as committed to Celeste as he was to God.

As she started up the aisle, I looked at the groom. He too was touched, blinking back tears. Their romance had been difficult, complicated by a child, by old flames and childhood wounds. But they had managed somehow to overcome those things, bringing them both to this joyful day at Maggie's Place.

In the four years since the fire, there had been other teens. Some stayed for days. Others for weeks or months. There had been adults too, people from Shiloh Farms who transitioned to private positions in the community via service at the old inn.

We'd had guests too—lots of them in the past four years. Famous people. Odd people. Lonely people. And I'd begun, finally, to see the house not as the end in itself, but as the means to an end. An end much bigger than anything I'd have ever imagined.

The years had been good, and sitting there in the early afternoon, overlooking the quiet waters of Genoa Bay, I looked forward to many more still to come. God had surely directed me here, to this place, to these wayward children, to this man.

Cliff stepped around the bride and took his place beside me, reaching for my right hand. I held his left in both of mine. How I treasured the calloused skin, the thick fingers, the tender touch of the man I loved. As the pastor began the vows, I turned Cliff's hand over in mine, touching the wedding band that surrounded his thick ring finger. Already, in just these few short years, his hand felt at home in mine. Like we'd always been. It was a good feeling.

He squeezed my hand, and I glanced up just in time to see him wink.